The Mage
Soastan's M

L A Lewins

Copyright

ISBN 978-1-8380462-0-0

Chapter 1

Eagerly, the cloaked rider urged his horse through the night. Although, it had been four days since he'd seen another soul, he knew that his pursuers weren't far behind him. He couldn't stop now, as the consequences would be catastrophic if he did. If he could just make it to the citadel, he would be safe for the time being. With a crash of thunder, a storm opened up above him, the rain falling in heavy sheets obscuring his vision. Squinting, he thought he saw somebody ahead on the road but couldn't be sure. From his right, twin beams of red light slammed into him, tumbling him from his horse. Falling hard onto the ground, the wind was knocked out of him as he tried to reach for his wand.

'Don't,' a voice boomed above him.

The rider looked up to see three wands pointing down at him. One of his assailants jumped down from his horse and walked over to him. 'We've been looking for you, wizard' he said, a cruel smile forming on his lips. 'Get him up and let's get moving'.

***

Since they arrived at the fortress at dawn, the wizard had been incarcerated. He wasn't sure what fate awaited him but knew it wouldn't be pleasant. Footsteps echoed up the stone corridor and stopped abruptly outside the door to his cell. The door creaked open, and in the dim light the wizard saw the outline of a tall, robed man.

'James, at last we meet,' the shadowed man said with a cold hint in his voice. 'You have been meddling in affairs that are not your concern, and for this, you must be punished.'

Raising his wand at James a burst of silver light shot forth, hitting him square in the chest. James' eyes went wide as he fell backwards to the floor. *At least the book is safe,* he thought, as everything around him went dark.

***

The morning sunlight filtered in through the open window. Across the room, Seren awoke and sat up in bed, today was the day. At nineteen, he was a handsome young man with his dark blond hair, green eyes, and lean frame. Stretching, he got up, washed, dressed, and headed downstairs where his mother, Eva, was preparing breakfast in the kitchen.

'Is it here?' Seren asked as he walked in.

'Jansen hasn't been yet, I imagine he'll have a great many letters to deliver today, be patient, Seren. Now, come and have some breakfast, there's a lot of work to be done today.'

Having finished his breakfast, Seren went outside to find his father, Thomas. Thomas Hiptamus was standing by the first of their five long greenhouses.

'Morning, Seren,' his father called as he approached, 'I thought you'd be waiting for Jansen.'

'I wanted to, but mam said there was work to be done.'

His father led Seren to the lake behind the greenhouses. 'The tugweed is ready to be harvested,' Thomas said with an expectant smile.

'Pop, you said once I'd finished school, I'd be able to do some of the cultivating and harvesting in the greenhouses, I've been harvesting the tugweed since I could walk.'

'I know, Son, and you will, but there's a lot to be learnt for those jobs and it'll take time. The tugweed is ready now.'

With a sigh, Seren nodded and headed over to the storehouse to collect the tools and containers he would need. Back at the lake, Seren removed his boots, rolled up his trousers and waded out into the cool water. Although the harvesting of the tugweed wasn't complex, Seren took the utmost care to ensure everything was done correctly. His parents were the owners of the most reputable potion ingredients shop for miles around. Thomas and Eva had opened the shop just after they had been bound. Upon finding that suppliers were less than reliable with the quality of their goods, they'd decided to produce the ingredients themselves on the farm left to them by Thomas' father. They had subsequently become not only the most reputable stockists, but also the largest producers of potion ingredients.

Whilst Seren worked, the time passed quickly, all thoughts of Jansen's arrival went to the back of his mind as he concentrated on the task at hand. Finally, by mid-afternoon, he placed the last lid on the jar, completing the harvest. He stacked the jars on the cart his father had brought out for him and wheeled the fresh tugweed up to the main barn. Exiting the barn, he saw his mother approaching from the other side of the yard. The sunlight reflected off her blonde hair, making it shine. A little plump with rosy cheeks, she was a kindly woman.

'Seren, Jansen arrived a little after lunch, you have a letter, it's on the kitchen table.'

'It's here,' Seren exclaimed and ran off towards the house, as the letter he'd been waiting for would decide how his future would be spent. Still soaking wet from the lake, he rushed into the kitchen.

'Hey,' his father called, brushing his brown hair out of his gleaming, hazel eyes, 'I know you've been waiting for that letter, but don't mess up your mother's clean kitchen.'

'Sorry, Pop.'

Seren turned and made his way up to his room to change. Clean and dry, he returned to the kitchen, poured himself some apple juice and sat down at the table. Picking up the letter, he examined it. On the front was the official stamp of the Magecastle Academy and the impeccable, italic handwriting, which Seren knew had been written by the head wizard of the academy—Serat Johansen. He turned the envelope over in his hands and saw the Magecastle wax seal, which held the envelope closed. The Magecastle Academy of Advanced Magic was the academy all young witches and wizards who were serious about their studies dreamt of attending. It set the standard for excellence for all the academies throughout Soastan. It had been Seren's ambition to study there since his first days at school and he hoped this letter would see his ambition fulfilled. He stared at the letter as if in a trance.

'Well, aren't you going to open it, you can't see through the envelope.' His father smiled.

Upon hearing his father's voice, Seren looked up and saw both his father and mother standing at the end of the table waiting expectantly. Without saying anything, Seren broke the wax seal on the envelope and unfolded the letter. The parchment was of the most exquisite quality and had gold gilding bordering the corners. He read the letter aloud:

Dear Master Hiptamus , Thank you for your request to study at the Magecastle Academy of Advanced Magic. Let me first express my congratulations for your end of school assessments. The quality of your work has been consistent throughout your studies, and your skills within all aspects of your subjects are of the highest standard. It is therefore with the deepest regret that I must inform you that your request to study at the academy cannot be approved. As you will no doubt be aware, there are limited places available each year and on this occasion, you haven't been selected to fill one of these places. I sincerely hope that this decision will not dissuade you from pursuing a career in whichever field you have chosen and wish you all the success for the future. Yours sincerely, Serat Johansen Head Wizard Magecastle Academy

Seren stared at the letter in disbelief as his final assessments had been among the highest in the school. His teachers had assured him that he would be accepted to study at the academy and he couldn't understand why this had happened. His mother came to stand behind him and placed her hand on his shoulder.

'Never mind, dear, there are many things you can do, and you could always send another request next year.'

Seren smiled weakly at his mother, knowing she was trying to make him feel better. But he felt terrible, his dreams lay shattered before him on the parchment. Smiling back at him, she walked over to the counter to start preparing supper. Seren stood up and took the parchment from the table and walked towards the stairs. Just as he was about to go up, his father came over to him.

'Sorry, Son, I know how much you wanted to study at Magecastle, but don't worry these things have a way of working themselves out.'

Seren smiled at his father and climbed the stairs to his room. Closing the door, he threw the parchment onto his desk and flopped onto his bed. He didn't know what to do. He had never wanted anything more in his life than to study at the academy, and now it was the one thing that he would never have.

Falling asleep, Seren dreamt that he was an old man and had just finished his work for the day and was sat alone in a sparse room by the fire. He remembered the day he had been rejected by the Magecastle Academy. At the time, he thought that it was the worst thing that could have ever happened to him, but he had been wrong. Not long after receiving the letter, he had left Shillington and moved to a small village named Halingshire. He'd become an assistant archivist in the small library in the centre of the village. The hours were long and the pay was little. Over the years, he had come to dislike the job and became a bitter old man. He was never bound and in later years found that people avoided him. It had not been a happy life, and he blamed it all on his rejection by the academy. He was awoken from the dream by his father calling him.

'Seren, supper's ready.'

Rolling out of bed, he went downstairs. Sitting at the table, he poured himself some water from the jug as his mother brought the meal to the table. She had made his favourite; honey glazed ham, plenty of roast potatoes and vegetables, and thick gravy. He smiled at her but still felt no better and ate in silence, just listening to his parents talking about the shop. When they had finished, Seren cleared the table, washed, and put away the dishes. Not wanting to stay in tonight, he went to the door and took down his cloak.

'I'm going into town, to the Merryboat, I'll be back later.'

'Enjoy your evening,' his father called back.

Seren left the house and made his way out onto the tree-lined track that led to the south gate of Shillington. It was only a short walk to the south gate, which was open as normal. A short way up south gate road he came to the Merryboat Inn, a large, timber-framed inn that served as a rest stop for many travellers and was one of the better inns in town. There was never any trouble here, and everyone was friendly, but most importantly the beer was the best in town. Inside, Seren saw that his usual space at the bar was free and headed over to order his drink. As the barmaid brought it to him, he thanked her and handed over some coins. Sipping his beer, he thought about the letter. Although he knew he could work on the farm or in the shop for his parents, he had wanted to do more with his life. He had wanted to be a great wizard, a researcher attached to the mages or perhaps an academy, able to develop his own spells and potions for the benefit of others. That chance, however, had passed him by and he would have to find some work soon. But for this evening, he was content just standing at the bar of his favourite inn.

As the evening wore on, Seren chatted to a few people, remaining polite but not getting into deep conversation. Just as he was getting his cloak down from the peg, Horace Merryman approached him.

'Well, Seren, I expect I'll be seeing you in the shop soon, you'll be needing new books for Magecastle.'

Seren sighed, 'Actually, Mr Merryman, I didn't get accepted into the academy, I received the letter earlier this afternoon.'

Horace looked shocked. 'I'm very sorry to hear that, I know how much you wanted to study there. Do you know what you'll do now?'

'No, sir, I hadn't thought about it. I suppose, for the moment, I could help out on the farm but I really don't know beyond that.'

'Well, I was thinking of hiring an assistant in the shop. If you would like the job I would be happy to take you on. Come and see me when you've had a chance to think it over.'

'Thank you, Mr Merryman, I will.' Seren was taken aback by his offer as the bookshop was like a second home to him. He had spent many an afternoon browsing the hundreds of books that filled the shelves.

Leaving the inn, he made his way back down the south gate road, arriving home a short while later to find that his parents had already gone to bed. Making his way up to his room, he sat on the bed and looked out the window at the full, bright moon. He sighed, still disappointed about the academy, but maybe his father was right. Maybe things would work themselves out after all.

Chapter 2

The next morning, Seren awoke feeling a little brighter and decided to go and see Mr Merryman after breakfast. When he went down to the kitchen, his parents were already at the table eating.

'Morning, Seren,' his father said, 'How are you feeling today?'

'Better thank you. I saw Mr Merryman at the inn last night, he's offered me a job in the bookshop, I'm going to go and see him this morning.'

His father smiled, 'Well, there you go, things are looking up already.'

As he wanted to get to the bookshop early, Seren ate his breakfast quickly. Not wanting to keep Mr Merryman waiting, he walked swiftly when he left the house. The bookshop was in the centre of town just past the stone fountain. It was just after the second harvest and wooden stalls heaped with fruits, vegetables, meats and sweetcakes filled the square as Seren picked his way through the crowd of marketgoers. Finally, he arrived at the shop and looked in at the crowd gathered within. There were parents and children buying their first magical texts in preparation for the new term. Some of his former classmates were buying the advanced texts required for the academy, and he felt a pang of jealousy, wishing he could switch places. Not wanting to bump into any of his friends, he walked away and started browsing the market stalls. He stopped at a stall and bought a cup of fresh apple juice from one of the orchard vendors, but kept an eye on the bookshop as he drank, watching people coming and going. After a short time, he saw his classmates exit the shop and walk away from the market square chatting amongst themselves. Returning to the bookshop, Seren found it quieter now. Walking to the counter, he waited while Mr Merryman wrapped up some books for a young child and his mother.

'There you are, young master, I hope they serve you well.'

The boy's mother thanked him, and taking the package, they left the shop.

Seren walked over to the counter. 'Mr Merryman.'

Horace Merryman looked up. He was a short, plump man with greying, brown hair and brown eyes, always pleasant and welcoming, and Seren enjoyed spending time in his shop.

'Seren, how nice to see you again, have you thought about my offer?'

'Yes, I have, sir, and I'd like to accept.'

'Wonderful, dear boy, if you would like you could start tomorrow?'

Seren smiled, 'Thank you, Mr Merryman.'

'Well then, my boy, the shop opens at nine as you know, so if you arrive at half past eight that will give us time to run through everything. And, Seren, please call me Horace.'

'Okay, Mr Merryman, I mean, Horace, I'll see you in the morning.'

Horace waved him goodbye as Seren left the shop feeling happier, despite the disappointment of not being able to continue his studies. He loved spending time at the bookshop and was looking forward to working there. There was still work to be done on the farm, however, and so he began the walk home. Almost at the south gate, he heard someone calling his name.

'Seren, wait for me.'

Turning, he saw Arin Brakespear hurrying towards him.

'Hi, Seren, how have you been? I haven't seen you all summer.'

'Hi, Arin, I'm well thank you. I've been helping my parents on the farm. There's a lot of work to be done this time of year.'

Arin nodded, 'All ready for the academy then?'

Seren sighed, 'I won't be going, I didn't get accepted. I'll be working in Merryman's from tomorrow.'

Arin stared at Seren. 'I'm sorry, Seren, I know how much you wanted to go.'

Seren didn't say any more on the subject as they walked along the road. They had known each other since the first day at school and had become good friends. Whilst at school, it had been discovered that Arin had the gift of sight and had recently decided to pursue a career as a seer. And with his black, wavy hair, hazel eyes and tall but stocky frame, he was already beginning to look the part. He just needed the eccentric robes and slightly bedraggled look and he would be the epitome of a seer.

'Well, Arin, good luck at the academy.' Seren said wistfully as they reached the farm.

'Thank you, Seren, good luck at Merryman's, not that you'll need it with the amount of time you've spent there over the years.'

Seren laughed and waved his friend off before going into the house. His mother was in the kitchen preparing the labels for the tugweed he had jarred yesterday.

'Seren, I'm glad you're back, the mistletoe is ready for collection, how did you get on at Merrymans?' she asked.

'I start tomorrow.'

'Good, now go help your father with the mistletoe.'

Seren left the kitchen and spent the rest of the day collecting mistletoe from the trees in the orchard.

***

The tall, robed figure walked down the dimly lit corridor. He had taken care of the wizard and his brigands should have taken care of his work. He entered the great hall. Seated at the table were a group of red-robed men and women—his brigands.

'Captain,' the robed figure said.

'Yes, sir,' the captain replied, standing.

'What of the wizard's work?'

'We put his house to the flame, all that remains are the ashes.'

'Good, then we can continue unhindered.'

Without another word, the figure turned, making his way back down the corridor until he came to a winding staircase cut into the northern wall and climbed to the top. Crossing the landing, he went through a door set into the wall, coming out onto a flat terrace at the top of the Tanzidant fortress. He drew his cloak around him to guard against the snow. Pointing his wand to the north, he closed his eyes, and a shimmering, translucent beam shot forth and travelled away unseen by all except one.

Chapter 3

Early the next morning, Seren awoke, and wanting to make a good impression, decided to wear his best robes. His parents had had them made especially for the leaving ceremony at school. They were a deep green with purple trim. Unsure if he would need his wand, he tucked it in his robe just in case. He went down to the kitchen where his mother had made him a hearty breakfast of bacon, sausages, and eggs with a thick slice of buttered bread.

'Well, Seren, you look very smart. You will surely make a good impression on Horace,' she said with a smile.

'Where's Pop?' Seren asked between mouthfuls.

'He's already gone into town, some of the stock in the shop was getting low, so he decided to take all the freshly harvested produce in at the same time.'

The clock above the door chimed eight. Not wanting to be late on his first day, Seren quickly finished his meal, said goodbye to his mother and left the house. The air was fresh as the summer was at an end. He drew his cloak around him and quickened his pace. At this time of the morning, the streets were relatively quiet, so he made good progress and arrived outside the shop at eight fifteen. The sign on the door read 'Closed', but he could see that the lanterns were lit. He knocked on the door, and after a short time Horace came into view. Seeing Seren outside, he hurried to the door, took a loop of keys from his belt, and let Seren in.

'Good morning, my boy, bright and early, good good, now come in and let's get started,' Horace said cheerfully.

Stepping inside, the shop was warm and inviting. The walls were lined with shelves from floor to ceiling, all of which were full of magical tomes and texts. It was everything a witch or wizard could ever need. There were large tables throughout the shop all containing yet more books. To the left was a staircase leading to the first floor where the rarer books were kept, as well as the folios. There was also space to sit and read on the first floor, Seren had spent many an afternoon reading upstairs. Towards the back of the shop was the counter, and beyond that, the door to the storeroom.

'Well,' Horace began, 'I know you don't need the tour, by now I imagine you know this shop better than I do.' They both laughed. 'Today, we'll start you off at the counter, I will deal with enquiries, after you are comfortable with that, there will be plenty of other duties to occupy you.'

Seren nodded.

'As you know, the shop is open seven days a week, how would you feel about working five days each week, with the occasional sixth day when needed?'

'That would be fine, Mr Merry... I mean, Horace.'

Horace smiled, 'Good, now in terms of payment, how does ten sovereigns a week sound?'

Seren's eyes widened, 'Sir, that's more than generous. Are you sure you want to pay me that much?'

Horace laughed, 'I know you'll do a good job and I'm more than happy to pay for it. As an added bonus, in the storeroom you'll find the unwanted books, they're the ones that didn't sell, and I have no use for them. So, you may take as many of them as you wish.'

Seren was taken aback by the wizard's generosity and simply said, 'Thank you, Horace.'

Going to the counter, Seren hung his cloak on the hook. He wanted to prove himself today. The clock chimed nine, and with a flick of his wand, Horace changed the sign so that it read 'Open'. It wasn't long before Seren was dealing with the first group of customers.

His first day in the shop proved to be one of the busiest of the year. As the clock chimed six, Seren said goodbye to the last of the customers and closed the door behind them. He looked at the sign, it only had the word 'Open' on it and he wasn't sure how to change it.

Horace came to the door. 'Ah, yes, the sign. All you have to do is point your wand at it, think what you want it to say, and flick the wand upwards. Give it a try.'

Seren did as he had been instructed. He checked the sign, it said 'Closed'.

'Well done, lad' Horace said. 'Now, it's been a good day today and you have proven me correct. I'm glad you accepted my offer.' Horace took a large book from the nearest table and handed it to Seren. 'Here, I would like you to have this. I know you won't be attending the academy, but I'm sure you'll be able to use it.'

Seren looked at the book and read the title, *The Complete Tome of Advanced Magic*. He looked at Horace, 'Thank you, sir, I've wanted this book for a long time.'

Horace smiled, 'You're very welcome, now it's time you were heading home, the night is beginning to draw in.' He handed Seren his cloak, 'I'll see you tomorrow. Goodnight, Seren.'

'Goodnight, sir.' Seren said as he stepped out of the shop and headed for home.

***

Seren had worked at the bookshop for a month and had quickly taken on new responsibilities within the shop. Among these was the large task of cataloguing the books. The system was ingenious. Seren carried a piece of parchment and tapped the book he was checking with his wand. All the details he needed to know would appear on the parchment. Once he was finished, he just tapped the parchment and the details disappeared. Horace had designed it himself. Seren had spent the day cataloguing in between serving customers. He had just finished the last of the tables and all he had to do was move the books that would no longer be on display to the storeroom. He stacked the books and took out his wand. Pointing his wand at the books, he focused on levitating them and watched as they lifted from the table before directing them into the storeroom.

As Seren set the books down and turned to leave something caught his eye. It was an old, leather-bound journal with a silver marker cord. He hadn't seen this book before, and there were none like it on the shelf. He picked it up and turned it over, seeing there were no markings on the cover. He decided to take it, but before he left the storeroom, he selected several more books from the unwanted stock. He had started quite a collection of books, so much so that he was running out of places to store them in his room. He took the books out into the shop and placed them on the counter. Locking the door to the storeroom, he turned and went to the sign on the door and changed it to 'Closed'. It was already dark, and rain clouds were gathering. Collecting his cloak, he pulled it tightly about himself. Gathering the books he had selected, he left the shop, locking the door behind him. Horace was away for the night and had asked Seren to lock up for him. Seren set off at a quick pace, as it was cold, and he wanted to get home quickly, making it just as the rain began to fall. Walking inside he closed the door and hung his cloak up. He was about to open one of the books when his mother called from the kitchen.

'Seren, before you bury yourself in your books, could you go out and get your father, supper is almost ready.'

Seren took the books to his room, placed them on the bed, and changed out of his robes before heading out to find his father. He found him in the third greenhouse tending the deep purple citany bushes.

'Pop, supper is almost ready.'

'Good, I'm famished and finished here for the night, let's go back up to the house.'

They returned to the house to find their supper laid out on the table. After Seren had finished, he went to his room to get the books. Once again, the journal caught his eye and he picked it up and went downstairs to the parlour and sat in an armchair by the fire. As he opened the journal, a piece of parchment fell to the ground. He picked it up and unfolded it. The writing was small and looked as if it had been written in a hurry, as there were smudges of ink on the page. The note read:

To whomsoever finds this journal, keep it safe. I am forced to hide this work as I fear that my pursuers are not far behind me. For he or she who now possesses it should read it well and finish what I have started,

James Berryton.

Intrigued, Seren turned the first page and began to read, tucking the parchment into his pocket for safekeeping.

Chapter 4

The tall figure emerged from the corridor and seated himself at the head of the table within the great hall. His harsh face, black hair, and grey eyes only served to make him look crueller. His name was Archimon, but those who knew him simply called him 'sir'. He looked around at the brigands seated at the table.

'It is time,' Archimon said coldly, 'The scrolls in front of you have your assignments.'

The brigands looked confused as the table was empty. Archimon smiled and waved his hand across the table, and scrolls appeared in front of each of them.

'Ensure that they are carried out to the letter and return your marks to the fortress, unharmed.'

Laurentis opened her scroll, read her assignment, and looked at Archimon, shocked. 'But, sir,' she said timidly, 'How am I supposed to do this?'

Archimon glared at her. 'Well, my dear girl, if you want to keep your place among us, I suggest you find a way.'

Laurentis looked away and thought about her task.

Archimon stood, 'Now, go and make any preparations you deem necessary. I want these tasks accomplished quickly.'

Without another word, Archimon left the great hall. The brigands rose from the table, filing out and leaving Laurentis alone. With a sigh, she stood and returned to her room.

Curled in her armchair, Laurentis read the scroll again, but her task seemed impossible. A knock at the door made her look up, but no one was there when she finally opened it. As she began to close the door, she noticed a book on the floor. Picking up the old grimoire, she closed the door and went back to the armchair. Opening the book, she turned a few pages. It contained many spells and potions, as well as notes on the best way to prepare the ingredients. She came across a potion named dormancy tonic. Although she had never enjoyed making potions, after a quick look over the directions she decided it seemed simple enough and could be useful. Making a note of it, she continued making her way through the pages, working well into the night.

The next morning, Laurentis gathered all the ingredients from the communal store to make the potion from the grimoire. Placing her cauldron into the hearth, she filled it with water. She took a candle from the mantel and touched the flame to the kindling, watching as the fire took hold. While waiting for the water to heat, she took the grimoire down from her shelf and opened it to the page with the dormancy tonic. After checking the ingredients again, she went back to the hearth, where the water was ready. First, she added leaves of citany and tilers root and stirred them until they dissolved, colouring the water a deep shade of purple. Next, she added harpentia, novatice and quince and left them boiling in the cauldron. When the quince had reduced to pulp, she added the final ingredients—hellebore, nightshade, and wolfsbane. These final ingredients gave the potion its potency. She left the potion bubbling over the hearth and took a box of vials from the mantel. Taking five out, she replaced the box. Returning to the cauldron, she checked the potion, finding it was ready. Laurentis strained the last of the quince pulp and poured it into the vials just filling the five she had selected. Corking the vials, she left them to cool. If she had prepared it correctly the potion would turn clear when completely cool. Placing them on the mantel, she walked across the room to her desk. A knock at the door interrupted her. She was surprised to see Archimon standing in the doorway and was even more surprised that he had knocked. Realising that she was staring, she lowered her eyes.

'Please come in, sir.'

Archimon stepped into the room and looked around, seeing the open grimoire and the dirty cauldron still in the hearth and noticing the five vials on the mantel. He turned to face Laurentis, who had closed the door and returned to her desk.

'I see you got the grimoire I left for you and used it already.' He smiled with his usual sneer, 'How goes the preparation for your task?'

'I just have a few things to go over, sir. I don't want to make a mistake.'

'The others have already left, and whilst I admire you for the work you are putting in, this must be done soon. I have entrusted you with a most important task, Laurentis.'

Laurentis blushed, feeling a little embarrassed by his attention and simply said, 'Thank you, sir.'

Noticing her embarrassment, Archimon laughed. 'I shall leave you to your preparations.' Walking to the door, he opened it and turned back to face her, 'Laurentis, I have great plans for you, prove yourself with this task and all will be revealed.'

Without another word, he stepped through the door, closing it behind him, his footsteps disappearing down the corridor. Laurentis sat heavily in the armchair, not knowing what to make of his last statement. Normally, Archimon was always so cold but he had seemed almost friendly. A short time later, she looked over to the mantel. The liquid in the vials had turned clear. It had worked.

Chapter 5

I have begun this journal because I discovered a decrease in my powers. I have been trying to develop a new protection spell, but despite all my efforts I just cannot summon the power I once had to complete the spell. It is not just me either, around town, I hear people talking about problems with potions and spells that they have always used. I decided to turn my attention to this problem. It may just be a natural ebb, but I fear it could be far more sinister.

Having checked through all the literature I possess, I found nothing. There is no mention of a past ebb in power, and so I surmise that this must be the work of a being or beings unknown. However, just to be sure, I will search the archives held within the library. If this sort of thing has happened before, it will be recorded there. I will start my research tomorrow.

For the past six days, I have been examining the archives. All I have found is the occasional mention of people whose power has suffered through illness or injury, but I am in perfect health as are those within the town. I fear that my suspicions are true. This is not a natural event, and I must now concentrate on finding out who or what is behind it.

I have spent my recent days speaking to people in the town, and the closest date I can come up with for the beginning of this event is the last full moon. I suppose it fits as the full moon is a powerful time. But at least I know that it hasn't been going on for long, which gives me hope that it might be reversible. I will pay a visit to Marcus in the morning, he may be able to help me.

This morning, I was with Marcus, the most experienced seer I know. He wasn't able to see the person behind this but did see the northern mountains. I will focus on this range for the time being. However, something is troubling me. In his vision, Marcus said he saw red-robed figures moving through the towns. Although he couldn't tell what they were doing, he sensed the darkness within them. He said that this was a vision of the future, which is why he hadn't been able to find out more about them. As I left, Marcus told me to be careful. I don't know if he had seen something of my future, as he didn't tell me, but I will heed his warning. I am troubled and sense dark days to come. I will rest now as a great weariness has come over me.

Marcus has given me two things to work with—the red-robed figures and the mountain range. For now, I will focus on the mountain range. I am not yet sure what I am looking for, but hopefully, it will become apparent as my search continues.

So far, I have not come across anything that stands out about the mountain range, I will continue my search. Before I do, however, I will send a letter to my friend, Tobias, in the citadel. I cannot leave my success to chance, and if I should fail, someone must continue in my stead. He is the one I trust above all else, and his power exceeds my own. At least, I hope it still does!

I have spent a further three days searching for something about the mountain range and believe I might have found it. In the deepest reaches of the mountains is the Tanzidant

Fortress, it is the only thing that stands out about the mountains, and so must be the key to Marcus' vision.

At the sound of his mother's voice, Seren looked up from his reading.

'Seren, don't stay up all night reading that old book, it's getting late. Your father and I are going up now, goodnight.'

'Goodnight, Mam, don't worry, I won't be up too late. Night, Pop.'

His parents left him alone in the parlour. Seren couldn't believe what he had just read. The beginning read like a story, but as he read on, he knew what the man had written was true. The way he wrote had a sense of urgency that became evident from the way the writing changed as the journal continued. A yawn overtook him, it was getting late, so he decided to go to bed. In his room, Seren carefully placed the book on his desk. Sitting on the bed, he took the folded parchment from his pocket and read it again.

To whomsoever finds this journal, keep it safe. I am forced to hide this work as I fear that my pursuers are not far behind me. For he or she who now possesses it should read it well and finish what I have started,

James Berryton.

The journal had come to him, and he determined to find a way to continue this man's work, whatever it turned out to be. Heeding the note, he took the book from his desk and looked for a suitable hiding place. Crossing to his cupboard, he opened it, tucked the book amongst his clothes, closed the door, and went back to his bed. Curling up under his blanket, he fell asleep, his dreams consumed by red-robed figures and mountain ranges.

***

Awaking the next morning, he immediately thought of the journal. As it was the first of his days off, he would finish reading it and decide where to go from there. He dressed and went downstairs, leaving the journal in the cupboard for the time being. Having slept a little later than normal, he found the kitchen empty when he entered. While he ate breakfast, he continued to think about the journal. He wondered if he should turn it over to the council, but thought, *why hadn't James entrusted it to them?* Deciding he would keep it, Seren tidied away his breakfast plate before heading back up to his room to retrieve the journal. He sat on his bed, opened it, and continued reading.

To be certain that I am correct about the Tanzidant Fortress, I have checked the old maps, They confirmed that there are no other dwellings of any type within the mountains, so I am confident that this place is of great importance. I will make the journey to the fortress but not until I have more information and a plan.

I received a reply from Tobias today. Although he hasn't detected any fluctuation in his power, he tells me there have been rumours of red-robed strangers on the mountain road. It would appear that Marcus' vision is to come true sooner than expected.

I have brewed enough potion for a fortnight. After taking the first draught during last night's full moon, I sent up four returning flares. I will continue to take the potion at the same time each night. Normally, one of these flares would be given a destination, but on this occasion, I simply sent them forth. I sensed that they were being pulled north. How long I will be able to sense them for, and whether they will return, remains to be seen. I can do nothing now but wait.

It has been five days now and the flares have not returned. I have doubled the amount of potion that I take each night as it is becoming increasingly difficult to sense them. However, I do know that they have passed the great plains and seem to be heading towards the mountains. The case for Tanzidant grows stronger.

I have made another batch of the potion, for although it grows increasingly difficult, I can still sense the flares. Whatever has hold of them must be getting stronger, as I am now taking three times the amount of potion to keep my grasp on them.

The flares seem to have stopped. Try as I might, I cannot detect any movement. I wonder if my spell will be strong enough to return them.

I know without a doubt that the flares have been drawn to Tanzidant. I had decided that yesterday would be my last day taking the potion, for I know not what ill effects it could have on me with such prolonged use. However, the flares now seem to be moving again, but heading south. I will continue with the potion.

The flares are returning, albeit slowly. Whatever took them is trying to keep hold of them. It would seem that although my power has diminished, it is stronger than this force and so gives me hope that I may be able to defeat it after all.

Three flares returned last night. I dissipated them quickly as I sensed dark magic within them. I fear in my quest to discover what is going on, I might have alerted the one behind it to my presence. I have raised a protective barrier around the house and immediate area. If attacked, it should give me time to escape. I will write to Tobias again to tell him of these developments and make for the citadel as soon as possible.

Last night, I detected a surge in the barrier. Although I have not finished my research, I was forced to leave and hide in town. I have only brought this journal as it contains everything needed to continue the quest should I fail. I will leave town tonight. The barrier should stand for a time after my departure and might fool them long enough for me to reach the citadel.

I am being pursued. The effects of the potion are still within me and I can sense dark magic. I will make for the town of Shillington.

This will be my final entry. I have arrived in Shillington. It is late, but I have managed to find a room at the Merryboat Inn. Tomorrow, I shall find a place to hide this journal and pray that whoever finds it continues with my work.

Seren looked up, turning a few more pages over, but apart from the formula for a potion and a few maps there were no further entries. None of what he had read had been dated. He needed to find out when this had all occurred, so decided to check at the inn, as they would have a record of when James stayed there. Not wanting to reveal the journal to anyone, Seren copied the formula for the potion onto a scrap of parchment. He would ask his father about it. Tucking it into his pocket, he left his room and went downstairs. As the house was quiet, Seren headed outside to look for his father, finding him down by the lake.

'Hey, Pop, can I ask you something?'

His father looked up, 'Just a moment.' Thomas finished what he was doing. 'Now, what's the problem?'

Taking the parchment from his pocket, Seren offered it to his father. 'Could you tell me about this potion?'

His father read the formula and thought for a moment. 'Well, it's certainly not one I've come across before, and it looks very complex. It's a fairly extensive list of ingredients and looking at the amounts and the way it is brewed it looks quite potent. I would say it's been thought up by someone for their individual need. Where did you find it?'

'Just in one of the books I got from the shop,' he replied, not wanting to give too much away.

His father nodded, 'Well, if that's all, Seren, I must get back to work. This new tugweed won't plant itself.'

Smiling, Seren and left his father to his work, glad that he hadn't been given the task. He walked slowly back to the house thinking about what he'd found out. James had created the potion himself, but for what purpose? He wondered if it was what he had used to sense his flares.

He found his mother in the kitchen preparing lunch. After they had eaten, he helped her to seal and label a fresh crop of dansis seeds that would be going to the shop the next day, which took them the rest of the afternoon.

Following the evening meal, Seren decided to go down to the Merryboat. After saying goodbye to his parents, he set off towards town. Pulling his cloak tightly about himself, he shivered, as winter was just around the corner. Although the weather was turning, the inn was busy as Seren entered. He walked over to the bar and ordered a drink, spotting the owner, Tiberius Lockhorn, at the other end of the bar. He would ask him about James later.

Towards the end of the night, the inn started to empty, so Seren finished his drink and retrieved his cloak before walking to the end of the bar where Tiberius was cleaning up.

'Tiberius,' The man glanced up, 'Is there a man staying here by the name of James Berryton? I found something that belongs to him and wanted to return it.'

Tiberius looked thoughtful, 'I do recall the name. Wait a moment, Seren, and I'll fetch the guest log.' Tiberius crossed the bar and came back with a large book. Opening it, he flicked through the pages until he came to the entry he was looking for. 'Ah, here it is. James Berryton. He arrived late in the evening and only stayed for the one night. He left early the next morning. That was three weeks ago now.'

Seren nodded, thanked him, and turned to leave.

'Oh, wait a moment,' Tiberius said, 'I remember that just before he left, he asked if there was a bookshop nearby. I directed him to Merryman's. Maybe Horace would be able to help you.'

Seren smiled and left the inn. It was too late to go to the shop now, but Seren would be back to work the day after tomorrow and would ask Horace then. Turning down the street, he headed for home.

Chapter 6

Having studied the grimoire in great detail and practicing and perfecting some of the more powerful spells, Laurentis was almost ready to leave and carry out her task. She gathered the vials of dormancy tonic and placed them carefully in her satchel. Tucking her wand into her robes, she took down her heavy travelling cloak and pulled it on. With a last look around her room, she made her way down through the fortress until she came to the stables. She had instructed the stable master to get her horse ready to leave and was pleased to see her ready and waiting when she arrived. The stable master handed her the reins as she mounted the chestnut mare, nudged the horse with her heels and rode off into the night. With the snow falling heavily as she came out onto the road, she pulled the horse to a halt. Gazing back up at the fortress, she saw the lone figure of Archimon on the lower terrace. With one last look, she pulled her hood up and trotted off down the road. From the lower terrace, Archimon watched her ride away until she rounded the bend in the road and went out of sight. It was all happening just the way he had planned. When Laurentis returned he would bring her in on his plans and bind her to him. He had sensed great power within her, it was why he had chosen her. With a last glance at the mountain road he turned and went back inside the fortress.

***

The rest of Seren's time off had passed uneventfully, having spent most of the day helping his parents. He didn't mind, but nevertheless was glad to be back at the shop. It had been busy since they opened, so he hadn't had a chance to speak to Horace about James. As the day wound on, the steady flow of customers began to decrease. It was almost closing time, and the last customer had just left the shop, so Seren seized the opportunity and approached Horace.

'Horace, can I ask you about a book I found in the unwanted stock?'

'Of course, Seren, ask away.'

'I found a journal, an old looking one with a silver marker cord, it belongs to somebody who stayed at the Merryboat and I just wondered how it came to be here.'

'A journal, yes, I remember. I didn't see anyone with it, it just appeared on one of the tables a few weeks ago. I checked through it, but there was nothing of interest in it just a few old spells, so I put it in the unwanted stock. How do you know who it belongs to?'

'I... I found it written on one of the pages. He's no longer in town, so maybe I'll try to track him down when I have some spare time.'

Horace nodded and smiled, 'I think we should close up. I know it's a little early, but I don't think we'll be seeing anyone else today. Why don't you get off home?'

Seren collected his things, said goodbye to Horace and headed for home.

Once there, he went up to his room and took out the journal. He wondered why Horace had said there were only a few old spells in it as the journal that lay before him contained the writings of James Berryton. He examined the journal again. Although he had read about spells that could stop unwanted people reading what had been written, he had never experienced one. It was very complex, practically unbreakable. It could only be overcome if it was in the hands of the one it was meant for, or someone who could be trusted with the information contained within. He wondered why Mr Merryman hadn't been able to see past the spell. Having decided to test it out, when his mother called him down for supper, he took the journal with him. After they had eaten, he opened the journal and left it on the table, before pouring himself some water from the jug and headed for the parlour.

'Seren, you've left your book,' his father called.

Seren turned to see his father pick up the journal and turn a couple of pages.

'What an odd collection of spells. Is this the book you found the potion in?'

'Yes. It belonged to someone who stayed at the inn. I was hoping to find out where he's from and return it to him.'

His father nodded and handed him the journal. 'If you're looking for someone, the best place to start would be the great library up at the academy. They have thousands of records in their archives,' he said as he walked past Seren and left the kitchen.

Seren looked at the journal, which once again held the same entries that he had read before. That confirmed it to him, there was definitely a spell on the journal. He decided he would spend his next days off in the great library. He had a lot of work to do.

Chapter 7

The next five days passed uneventfully with Seren working hard in the shop, his thoughts consumed by the journal and what it had told him. Hopefully, tomorrow he would find some more answers. As the weather drew in, the shop quietened down, and Seren found himself dealing less with customers and more with cataloguing, which he didn't mind, even though he enjoyed his work. He was so absorbed that he was shocked when the clock struck six. Just as he stopped cataloguing and went over to change the sign, Horace came out of the storeroom.

'Six already, my, the days are going quickly of late,' he sighed. 'Well, dear boy, you should be getting home, you don't want to be caught out in this weather.'

'I'd just like to buy a book if I may before I go.'

Horace nodded and Seren went over to one of the shelves and selected a book. He took it over to the counter and gave Horace ten silver coins, which Horace took, handing five back to Seren.

'Call it a discount,' he said with a smile, '*Fortresses Through the Ages,* what's this about then?'

'Just a little light reading,' Seren smiled.

'Light indeed,' Horace laughed.

The book was one of the thickest on the shelves and contained just over a thousand pages. Certainly not everyone's idea of light reading. Horace wrapped it for Seren to protect it from the threatening snow.

'Well, Seren, enjoy your days off, see you soon.'

'Bye, Horace.' Seren shouted back as he left the shop and hurried home.

***

Laurentis was making good time, as she was finally free of the snow that had hindered her through the mountain pass. Now on the mountain road, she would soon near the citadel but couldn't stop there as it had kept its magical protection intact. She wouldn't be able to enter due to the dark magic she wielded, so would ride on through the night until she came to the next town. After her encounter with Archimon, she was especially determined to complete her task before she left. This, she thought, would be the making of her.

***

Taking Horace's advice, Seren didn't linger on his way home, as the first snows were definitely on their way. He entered the kitchen where a steaming mug of malt awaited him, sat at the table with his drink and started looking at the book he had bought.

His mother entered the kitchen, noticing the book. 'My, my, Seren, you are developing some strange interests since working at that shop. Why on earth would you want to know about fortresses of all things?'

Seren looked up, 'It's interesting, Mam. And if the academy doesn't want to educate me, then I'll have to do it myself. Oh, thanks for the malt.'

She smiled and went about preparing their evening meal.

***

That night, Seren didn't sleep well and was up before his parents the next morning. He packed the journal, the fortress book, and some blank parchment into his satchel and headed downstairs. He made his lunch and ate a small breakfast. Just as he was getting ready to leave, his mother came downstairs.

'Seren, you're already up!'

'I'm off to the library, I'll see you later.'

He left the house and walked towards town, kicking piles of fallen leaves as he went. As it was so early, Shillington was quiet with most of the shops not open yet. Passing through the market square, he continued up the north gate road. As he walked through the north gate, he was presented with the sight of Magecastle Academy on top of the hill. An old fortress itself, the name Magecastle coming from the days when it housed the main training garrison for one of the mage's regiments., Although he hadn't been chosen to study there, the library was open to everyone, so Seren made his way up the hill towards the academy. He had been to the library once before, whilst studying for his final assessments at school. It was said that it was the largest and most extensive library in Soastan, and Seren was confident he would find the answers there. If it wasn't in the great library, it wasn't worth knowing, or so they said. Seren arrived at the top of the hill where the road forked. To the right, it continued to the north, heading to the next town. To the left, it led to the imposing iron gates of the academy, Seren took the left fork. Arriving at the gate, he found it closed, and the gatekeeper approached him from the other side.

'Good morning, young sir, you're here early. May I ask what business brings you to the academy?'

'I'd like to use the library, I have some research to do,' Seren replied.

'Very well, please enter and welcome to the academy,' the gatekeeper said kindly as he opened the large gate with a swift flick of his wand.

Stepping inside, Seren looked around the neat but elaborately landscaped grounds with their myriad of trees and bushes placed at regular intervals. Marble statues and stone fountains of different sizes and styles stood all about, and there were areas where in warmer weather you could sit. Built of blue granite blocks, the academy had a round tower at each corner and windows beyond count. He walked through the grounds towards the ornate, grand entrance hall lined with carved reliefs and dominated by the large, wooden staircase that led to the library. He ascended the staircase to the first floor where he was confronted by a large set of carved, wooden double doors. Above the door, etched into the stone in ornate writing was the word 'Library'. He walked towards the doors, and they opened by themselves. For a moment, he stood taking in the sight of books as far as the eye could see. The great library took up the entire eastern wing of the academy. Seren wasn't sure where to start looking. His first aim was to find more information about James Berryton and Tobias. Seren walked through the library until he came to the desk of the head librarian.

'Can I help you?'

'I'm trying to trace someone to return some lost property.'

Handing him a blank piece of parchment, the librarian said, 'You'll want the archives, you'll find them at the end of this tier. Simply write the name of the person or information you wish to find on the parchment, and it will tell you where to find it if we have the records. If you have any problems, please come and see me.'

Seren thanked her and went to find himself a seat. Placing the parchment, the librarian had given him on the desk, he took his own parchment and quill from his satchel and set them down next to it. Picking up his quill, he dipped the nib into the inkpot on the desk and wrote James Berryton. A moment later, more writing appeared on the parchment under the name he had written. It read: *James Berryton, Registry 4372, Section 7B, Alphabetical listing.* Seren made a note of this on his own parchment. After a few moments, the parchment cleared itself. Next, he wrote Tobias, unsurprisingly the parchment showed many names as he didn't possess a family name. He looked at the names at the top of the list:

Tobias Morgan, Registry 6914, Section 21H, Alphabetical listing.

Tobias Alsimus, Registry 0487, Section 9C, Alphabetical listing.

Tobias Helmand, Registry 3598, Section 17A, Alphabetical listing.

Seren wrote the first three down. As the parchment cleared itself again, Seren went in search of the registry files. After a few minutes, he found the first records, continuing his search until he found the corresponding files. He returned to his desk with several large files and opened the one for James first. It held details of his date of birth, his parents, and his education. He discovered that James had attended Magecastle. It detailed his occupation as a mage (retired). The final detail he found was that upon retiring from the mages he had moved to the town of Hallsrock. Seren made a few notes, now he had a starting point for James. He turned his attention to finding Tobias.

The first file was of no help, Tobias Morgan had died over two centuries ago. Seren pushed it aside and picked up the second file. Tobias Alsimus was an alchemist thought to be living in the south of Soastan, although no town was listed. Seren read on for a while but couldn't find anything to link him to James. With a sigh, he pushed the file aside and opened the third. Tobias Helmand had also been a mage and had retired to the Fennbane Citadel. Seren checked the journal, only to find that James hadn't written down the name of the citadel, but nonetheless, it was a link. Tobias wasn't a common name, and there were only two inhabited citadels in Soastan. Seren had a hunch that if he had found the right Tobias, they may have served together in the mages. He used the parchment to search for the mages' archive and a book detailing the primary spells mages were taught when they enlisted.

With parchment in hand, Seren once again left the desk, only to return carrying another large file and a thick book. He went through the mage archive file first, relieved to find that the lists were alphabetical. After a short time, he found James among the entries, noted the details and then searched for Tobias, soon finding the relevant entry. Checking the details against those he had noted for James, he found that they had served in the same regiment for much of their time in the mages. Seren was sure he had found the right person. Feeling pleased with himself, Seren pulled the large tome, *Mage Recruits: A Reference,* in front of him and started turning the pages, hoping to come across something useful. He was so engrossed that he didn't notice the girl walking towards the desk.

'Are you looking for something specific?'

'I'm trying to find out if mages are taught a particular spell, I came across in a book I was reading,' he said, startled.

'Mages use all sorts of spells, but why would you want to know something like that?'

'Just interested is all.' Seren couldn't think of anything else to say.

'Well, if you want to find it quickly, point your wand at the book and focus on what you're trying to find, its basic academy stuff,' she said looking perplexed.

'I'm not from the academy, just here to use the library.'

'Oh, sorry, I had better go. By the way, I'm Tobelle Actimus.'

'Seren. Thanks for the tip.'

'A pleasure,' Tobelle said as she walked away.

Focusing on the concealment spell, Seren pointed his wand at the book. After a few moments, the pages began to turn rapidly until they settled on a page entitled 'Concealment'. Seren began reading. It was a large section, but he soon found what he was looking for and copied the paragraph onto his parchment:

Spells of concealment are commonly used whilst transporting sensitive information. This means that, should the information fall into the hands of an enemy or person(s) it was not intended for, they will see either blank parchment or something of the caster's choosing. As this spell is crucial for confidentiality, each mage is taught the basics and then sent off to develop their own version of the spell. This ensures that it cannot be undone by another. There are only two ways to breach this spell, the first by the caster's own hand, and the second by death. It is normal, however, for a mage to build a final defensive measure into his or her spell—these normally fall into two categories—upon death, the parchment will either erase the message entirely or combust in unquenchable flames, thereby destroying the parchment and the information it contained.

Seren considered this. The fact that the spell on the journal was still active suggested that James was still alive, and he hoped he was safe. A thought bothered him, *how did James know how much power he possessed?* He focused again and pointed his wand at the pages. He read part of the page that had opened but it wasn't what he was looking for, so he decided to try once more, this time focusing on enlistment. He read the page that opened:

Upon enlistment (whether voluntary or conscripted) the witch or wizard is put through various tests to determine their strongest skills and most importantly to measure their power. The results of these tests determine what regiment they are assigned to and at what level.

Seren paused and glanced at the clock. It was past noon and having made good progress that morning decided to take a break. He took his lunch from his satchel and headed out to the grounds to find somewhere quiet to sit in the fresh, afternoon air. Wrapped in his cloak, he sat eating his lunch and thought about all he'd uncovered that morning. He hoped that, after leaving the journal behind, James had managed to keep ahead of his pursuers and made it to the citadel. Seren stared into the trickling water of the fountain, watching as two of the older students rushed across the grounds. He was envious, having only been admitted as a guest. He doubted, even if he applied again next year that he would be admitted to study. With a sigh, he finished the last crust of his bread and made his way back to the library.

Seren spent another hour in the library but was unsure what to look for. James hadn't stated in the journal what he thought was actually happening, only alluding to fluctuating power in individuals. He'd hit a dead end. There was nothing more he could do there without knowing what he was looking for. So, he packed his things away, returned the parchment to the librarian and made for home.

Chapter 8

Seren had spent the rest of the previous day in his room reading the book on fortresses. There was a large section on Tanzidant detailing everything about its construction, its history and some of those who had resided there over the years, but nothing was written about the current occupant. That morning, he sat in the kitchen long after finishing breakfast. He had to tell somebody about the journal, which meant he'd have to go to the wizard council.

Standing in front of the grey, stone council building just off the market square, Seren hesitated, unsure what he would say to the high wizard if he was even permitted to see him. Swallowing his doubt, he started up the steps, making his way into the plain antechamber. The attendant at the desk ushered him to a bench to wait, as the high wizard had appointments to attend to. Four hours later, Seren returned to the desk.

'Excuse me.' The attendant looked at him. 'When will I be able to see the high wizard? It's an important matter and I've been waiting for a long time.'

'Sir, everybody who wishes to see the high wizard has something important to discuss. As you have no appointment you must wait until he is available,' the attendant replied sounding unconcerned.

Sighing, Seren returned to the bench, wondering if he was wasting his time.

***

Three days ago, Laurentis had passed the citadel before stopping in a small, nearby town to rest. She booked into a large inn under a false name, paid, and went straight to the room she had been given. Although her cloak had hidden her red robes, now she'd have to wear something a little less conspicuous, as she couldn't risk being caught and needed to blend in. Pointing her wand at her robes, darkness consumed her thoughts and her robes shimmered, changing from red to black. She smiled, black suited her better than red ever had. She slept lightly that night, but it was enough. The next morning, she left just after dawn. She was close now.

***

After waiting all day, Seren noticed that people were leaving and started to think about going himself.

As he stood and gathered his cloak, the attendant at the desk called, 'Seren Hiptamus, the high wizard can see you now. Thank you for waiting.'

Finally, Seren thought as he walked towards the patterned, wooden door with the brass plaque. When he knocked, the door opened of its own accord and he walked in. The door closed behind him and Seren looked around the chamber as he approached the desk. Shelves filled with old books and papers lined the walls, there wasn't a spare bit of space to be had.

'Well sit down, boy,' the high wizard said. 'Now what is so important that you have waited all day to speak to me?'

'I think something is happening to our magic.'

The high wizard looked perplexed, 'What do you mean?'

'I found a journal that belonged to a wizard called James Berryton. He had written about how he couldn't complete a spell because his power had diminished. He mentioned that others in the town where he lives were having the same problem. I looked him up and found that he used to be a mage, so he knew his power.'

The high wizard rested his chin on tented fingers, 'Where is this journal? I would like to see it.'

Seren hesitated, 'I didn't bring it,' he paused, thinking himself stupid for not bringing the journal with him. 'It has a concealment spell on it.'

'That is convenient. So, you have nothing you can show me?'

'No, sir.' Seren paused again, his face flushed slightly. 'I tried to look into it, but I've hit a dead end. I thought maybe you could help.'

'Well... Seren, is it? I can tell you I haven't noticed any change in my powers, and none of my colleagues have mentioned anything. I can only surmise from what you've told me that this journal, if it exists, is the rambling of an old mage. Now, if you don't mind, I'm very busy.' He gestured for Seren to leave.

'But, sir, he's disappeared.'

The high wizard looked at him. 'Sometimes, these old mages don't want to be found, good day.'

Seren rose and left the high wizard's chamber. He had wasted the entire day and had just been dismissed. He was angry and thought he understood why James hadn't approached the high wizard when he was in Shillington. Leaving the council building, he walked slowly through town until he came to the Merryboat. It was quiet inside, so he made his way to the bar with ease, Tiberius brought his usual mug of beer over to him.

'What's the matter, Seren, you look troubled?'

'I've been sat in the council building all day waiting to speak to the high wizard, and when he finally saw me, he just dismissed what I was saying without so much as thinking about it.'

'Julius has always been a little pompous, he likes to have all the facts in front of him when he's dealing with anything, but don't let it get you down,' he said with a smile. 'Enjoy your drink.'

Seren paid Tiberius for the beer, regretting not taking the journal with him. Maybe the high wizard would have been able to read it. He would try once more, but this time he would take the journal. After finishing his drink, he left the inn for home. He would go to see the high wizard again the first chance he got.

Chapter 9

Laurentis halted her chestnut mare on the brow of the hill, seeing Magecastle Academy on the next crest and beyond that, Shillington. She rode on, passing the academy and down towards the town. Now she was here, she would have to find a way to get close to her mark and observe his movements, but she had to wait until the time was right. If she acted too soon, she would fail. Laurentis rode into town, along the quiet streets in the early evening, knowing she needed to find somewhere to stay where no one would pay any attention to her. The problem was that she was known here. She turned down the east gate road, hoping to find an inn that was busy enough that she wouldn't be noticed. Halfway down the road, she came to the Greenhaven Inn. As it appeared to be busy enough, Laurentis led her horse round to the stable block and found an empty stall. Making sure that nobody else was in the stables, she slid her hood down and changed the colour of her hair from light brown to black with a tap of her wand. Pulling her hood back into place, she walked round to the front of the inn. Pushing through the door, she approached the bar and asked the keep for a room for six nights but hoped that it wouldn't take that long.

From the window of her room, Laurentis could see the council building. Tomorrow, she would search for her mark. Sitting on the bed, she wondered why Archimon had given her this task. He knew that she had grown up here, so, why was he testing her in this way? He had said that he had great plans for her, so, why send her to the place she was most likely to be caught? If somebody recognised her, she may fail. She couldn't fully change her appearance as she didn't know how but hoped the change in hair colour would be enough. Still, she'd have to be careful if she was to succeed. Trying to push those thoughts aside, she lay down to sleep.

The next morning, Laurentis awoke early. The hardest part of her task today would be getting a good look at the council building without raising suspicion. But she would need to work out the best way to observe her mark without being spotted. Walking across the room, she looked into the mirror and saw that her spell was holding. Opening her satchel that lay on the dresser next to the mirror, she took out one of the vials. Although she knew the potion would work, he had to drink it and she didn't know how she would get him to do it. Putting the vial away she closed the satchel.

An hour later, Laurentis walked up the steps into the council building. She approached the desk at the rear of the antechamber and coughed lightly to get the attention of the attendant.

'Can I help you?' he said with an air of self-importance.

Laurentis smiled at him. 'I hope so. I've just taken up residence in town and was hoping to find work within the council.'

'Do you have any previous experience working for a council?'

'Well, no, I've only recently left home. This would be my first appointment.'

'Then I'm afraid we have nothing to offer you. We only take on experienced practitioners,' he said with a slight sneer.

Laurentis nodded and slowly turned, taking in the view of the whole chamber. Scanning the east side of the building, she noted the small brass plaque on the mark's office door. Exiting the building, she walked around the east side. A short way down the street, she found a café with a small front garden. From there, she'd be able to see into the office through the large window, so she took the last available seat.

Laurentis spent almost the whole day sat in the café garden and was glad when she spotted her mark collecting his cloak to leave for the day. Rising, she stretched, blew on her cold hands, and left some coins on the table before making her way back towards the front of the council building. Feigning interest in a market stall, she stopped as she saw him descend the steps. Keeping her distance, she followed him through the winding streets of the northern district. The houses in this part of town were big, some lavishly decorated, *not like my old house,* she thought bitterly. When he entered the largest of the houses on the street, she took note of the location before turning down a side lane and heading back to the inn.

Not wanting to risk being recognised, she ate her evening meal in her room and thought about her task. Now that she knew where he lived, she had two options. She could strike at either his office or his home but had to figure out how to get close to him. Laurentis slept peacefully that night and dreamt of returning triumphant to the fortress.

The next day, Laurentis spent only two hours at the café in the late afternoon. She'd made the decision not to target him at the council building, as there were too many people around and she'd never succeed. It would have to be at his house. A short while before her mark would be leaving, she left the café. Laurentis hurried towards the northern district in order to find a place to observe him before he got home. Hurrying along the streets, she arrived at the house only to find there was nowhere to hide. Seeing a small inn opposite the house, although it wasn't ideal, she decided it would have to do. Inside the inn, Laurentis seated herself at a small table by the window. A barmaid approached her, and she ordered a small meal and a cup of watered wine. Looking out the window, she watched intently, seeing her mark arrive a few minutes later and enter his house. The barmaid bringing her food to the table interrupted her.

'Can I get you anything else?' she asked politely.

'No thank you,' Laurentis replied handing her some coins.

After the barmaid walked away, Laurentis looked back out the window and saw that he had moved into one of the front rooms. She noticed him pouring a drink from a cabinet in the corner and smiled. Now she knew how to get him to take the potion.

Laurentis remained in the inn until closing time and was about to return to the Greenhaven just as the candles in the house were extinguished. She walked towards the house, checking around to make sure nobody was about. Quietly opening the iron gate, she stepped into the neat grounds. Swiftly walking to the window where she had seen him, she peered through the glass and saw that the room was a study. The drinks cabinet sat in the corner containing an array of bottles. Conscious that she might be spotted, she left the window and began walking back to the Greenhaven Inn as the perfect plan formed in her mind. She would lace a bottle of ale with the potion and wait for him to drink it but had to decide on the best way to get it to him. Smiling to herself, she entered her room at the inn. Things were falling into place.

Chapter 10

It had been a week since Seren visited the high wizard, having spent his last two days off helping with the harvest on the farm. He would have to wait another few days before trying again. The shop was steadily quietening down as the winter drew in, and so Horace had begun closing early. Seren had finished cataloguing for the day and was getting ready to close. As he walked back towards the counter after changing the sign, a large, black book on the new editions table caught his eye. Noticing that the only adornment was the mage's crest, he looked at the title, *The Mage's Spell and Potion Guide.* Seren picked the book up and flicked through the first couple of pages. Taking it to the counter, he took out his coin purse and counted out the coins before entering the storeroom to find Horace.

Horace looked up, 'Seren, all done for the day?'

Seren nodded, 'I'd like to buy one of the new editions,' he said handing over the coins.

'Well, dear boy, you'd better be getting home, I don't want your mother scolding me for keeping you out on these cold nights.'

Seren laughed and walked back into the shop, put on his cloak and tucked the book into his satchel.

'Goodnight, Horace, see you in the morning.'

When Seren headed out into the cold, evening air, Horace waved and locked the door behind him. It was relatively early and there were still people browsing the market stalls. Seren began walking towards the south gate road, when a dark, robed witch hurrying in the opposite direction bumped into him, the contents of her satchel falling to the ground.

'I'm so sorry,' she cried, stooping to pick up her things. 'I wasn't looking where I was going.'

'No, it was my fault,' Seren said, bending down to help her.

After picking up one of the vials, and turning it over in his hands, the witch noticed and quickly took it from him, placing it back in her satchel. They stood up, and Seren saw her face for the first time. Seeing his expression, she quickly pulled her hood up.

'Laurentis? Where have you been, you just disappeared.'

Laurentis looked at him, 'Seren, oh, I... I had to get away, things at home became too much.'

'Well, you're back now, I'm sure your parents were pleased to see you.'

'Oh, no, please don't tell anyone you've seen me. I only came back because I heard that people were searching for me, I wanted to ask the high wizard to call off the search. Once I've seen him, I'll be leaving.'

'Just like that, you'll leave again.'

Laurentis nodded firmly, 'There's nothing for me here, Seren.'

Seren sighed, 'If it's what you want, I won't say anything. But I wouldn't hold out much hope with the high wizard, I tried to talk to him last week and he dismissed me like a naughty child.'

'Oh,' she feigned a look of dismay. 'I'll give it a try. Anyway, I have to go.'

'I'm glad you're all right. I hope you have more luck with the high wizard than I did.'

Watching Laurentis walk away, Seren found it strange seeing her again. She had disappeared so suddenly, and nobody knew what had happened. He wondered what had been in the vial and why she'd taken it from him the way she did. He was roused from his thoughts by the first snow of the season gently falling around him. Pulling his cloak tighter around himself, he continued on his way home.

As Laurentis walked away, she could have cursed herself for being so careless. She had been recognised, and worse, he had seen the vials. She wouldn't be surprised if Seren was suspicious, after all, she had simply disappeared and now here she was claiming to be seeking an audience with the high wizard. However, one thing had come out of this unfortunate meeting, she knew how she would get her mark to drink the potion. She would have to act quickly and avoid bumping into Seren again. Hurrying back to the inn, Laurentis spent the night perfecting her plan.

The next morning, Laurentis woke a little later than usual, having worked late into the night going over her plan until she knew it inside and out. She had to act today. After bumping into Seren, she was worried that he'd tell people he had seen her, despite what he said. The sooner she carried out her plan, the sooner she would be away from Shillington.

At slightly past ten in the morning, she looked out the window and saw people going about their business. The market square was busy, so she decided to head out. Laurentis only needed to get the ale so she wouldn't be long, but she knew to be more careful and to avoid people today. Picking up her cloak and satchel, she left her room, went downstairs, and walked over to the bar where the keep was preparing to open for the day.

'Excuse me, sir,' the keep looked up. 'Could you tell me where I might buy an ale called Greenhallows Nectar?'

'Greenhallows, hmm,' the keep said thoughtfully. 'We don't stock it here, too expensive. The best place to try would be Hemdeans down in the market, but if I may ask, why would a young girl like yourself want a drink as expensive as that?'

Laurentis was caught off guard and thought for a second. 'It's a gift for a friend.'

The keep nodded, and Laurentis thanked him and left the inn. She drew her cloak around her and pulled up her hood as she stepped onto the snowy street. Hemdeans was a small shop set into the corner of the square, a large bay window took up most of the frontage, displaying various bottles. A small bell rang as she opened the door and stepped inside. She spent some time searching for the ale but couldn't see it anywhere. She walked over to the counter where a middle-aged man was sitting, reading.

'Excuse me, I'm looking for a bottle of Greenhallows nectar, do you stock it?'

The man looked at her, 'I do keep a couple of bottles, but it's very expensive. Why don't you select something a little more in your price range?' he asked curtly.

Laurentis narrowed her eyes, 'I'm sorry, I didn't make myself clear. It's a gift for a friend, I assure you it is well within my price range.'

The man looked at her with a piercing glare but got up from his chair and went into a room in the back of the shop. He returned shortly with a bottle, which he placed heavily on the counter.

'Fifteen sovereigns.'

Laurentis took out her coin purse and paid the princely sum, then took out a few extra coins and pushed them towards the man.

'If anybody asks who bought this bottle, I would appreciate your discretion, I'm just picking it up for my friend, Seren, he's not very good at choosing gifts.'

The man looked at the coins, 'For a few more, if somebody should come asking questions I'll tell 'em he bought it himself,' he said with a wry smile.

Laurentis smiled slightly and added a few more coins to those already on the counter. Taking the bottle, she placed it in her satchel, and with a final nod at the man, turned and walked out of the shop, leaving him counting the coins. She was about to return to the inn when she had a thought. She would have to leave quickly once she had carried out her plan, so she would need provisions. She also decided to make more of the potion. After all, she hadn't tested it and didn't know how long the effects would last. The last thing she wanted was him waking up before they reached the fortress.

Browsing the market stalls, she bought two loaves of bread, some cured meat, and a wheel of cheese, which would have to last the journey. Once on the move, she wouldn't be able to stop in any towns and she was no hunter. Among the other provisions she bought was a spare waterskin and a large, heavy travelling cloak. All she had left to do was buy the potion ingredients. She did have one problem. The ingredients shop was owned by Seren's parents. Stopping at a nearby stall, she bought a mulled cider, deciding to wait a while and watch the shop to ensure that Seren wasn't in there. She couldn't risk meeting him again. By the time she had finished her drink, she decided it would be safe. Quickly, she crossed the square and entered the shop. Making her way around the shelves, she picked up only what she needed: leaves of citany, tilers root, harpentia, novatice, quince, hellebore, nightshade and wolfsbane. On her way to the counter, she picked up five vials as she hadn't brought any spares. She was relieved to see a young assistant serving behind the counter, and not Seren's parents who would have surely recognised her. Once she had paid for her items, she left the shop and hurried back to the inn. She needed to deliver the bottle before her mark finished for the day and she still had to make another batch of the potion. Another thought occurred to her. She would need another horse as her own couldn't bear both of them. The animal auctions were just outside the northern district and she would pass through there on her way to collect her mark. Arriving at the inn, she entered and made her way up to her room. Stopping only to put away what she had bought, she went back downstairs to the small kitchen at the rear of the inn.

'Excuse me,' she said politely to the cook. 'Do you have a cauldron I could use? I wish to make a brew. I feel as if I'm coming down with something.'

The woman nodded. 'Yes, I have a spare. Bear with me a moment.'

The woman hurried off to a large store cupboard set into the back wall. Soon she came back with a medium sized cauldron. 'Here, you can use this, I hope you feel better,' she said smiling, as she handed the cauldron to Laurentis, who thanked her.

Returning to her room, Laurentis hung the cauldron on the hook in the fireplace. Lighting the fire, she poured water into the cauldron, leaving it to get hot before laying out the ingredients on a small table near the fireplace. When the water was ready, she began making the potion. Once she was at the point where it had to boil down, she turned her attention to the bottle of ale sat on the desk. Carefully, Laurentis uncorked the bottle and poured a small amount of the potion and some of the ale into a cup. She wanted to be sure it wouldn't alter the appearance or smell of the ale. Happy that the ale had remained its proper colour, she smelt it and recoiled. Even if the potion did have a faint scent, the strong smell of the ale masked it. She couldn't taste it, but judging by the strong smell, she doubted it would affect the flavour. She wondered what would possess someone to drink something like this having quickly grown used to the fine wines and juices that Archimon provided inexhaustibly at the fortress. Emptying a little more from the bottle, she poured the contents of the first vial in and took out a second, pouring it all into the ale. Examining the bottle for a moment, the liquid still looked a little low, so she poured some back in from the cup. When she was satisfied that it the amount looked right, she replaced the cork tightly. Checking the potion over the fire, she strained it and poured it into the new vials. She would have to clean the cauldron and leave no trace of the potion. Setting it aside to cool, she went to the desk and picked up the tag she'd bought at one of the stalls, before taking out her quill and ink and writing on the tag:

High Wizard Actimus,

Please accept this gift with my apologies following our meeting last week.

Seren Hiptamus.

Laurentis smiled and tied the tag onto the neck of the bottle. The cauldron was still cooling, so she set about packing her things so she would be ready to leave. She cleaned the cauldron and returned it to the kitchen, thanking the cook once again. Briefly, she returned to her room to collect her cloak and the ale. It was beginning to get dark and the council building would be closing soon. When she left the inn and made her way back to the town square, she noticed people coming out of the council building and hurried over. Walking over to the desk, the attendant looked at her.

'We're about to close for the day, what do you want?'

'I just wanted to leave this for the high wizard,' she said taking the bottle from her cloak and placing it on the desk. 'My friend, Seren Hiptamus, asked me to deliver it as he couldn't get here himself.'

The attendant looked at the bottle. 'Why would he send a bottle of this quality to the high wizard?'

'He told me that their meeting didn't go well. He meant it by way of an apology.'

The attendant considered her for a moment. 'I'll see that the high wizard gets it,' he said, taking the bottle.

She thanked him, turned around and walked out of the building. *Things are now in motion,* she thought to herself as she walked back towards the inn.

Chapter 11

Ever since their impromptu meeting, Seren hadn't stopped thinking about Laurentis. She had disappeared suddenly during the last year of school. Nobody knew what had happened to her. There had been all sorts of rumours about her disappearance, but even with all the searches there had been no trace of her. Laurentis hadn't had many friends at school, and many of the students had either been scared of her or thought her strange. It hadn't surprised him when he heard some of the things they said about her following her disappearance. Seren had wondered whether the school had had anything to do with it but never voiced his opinion, preferring to keep out of it. What he couldn't understand was why she had suddenly reappeared after all this time. She'd said she wanted to ask the high wizard to call off any further searches for her, but the searches had never found anything so how did she know about them? He also wondered about the vials.

When he arrived home last night, he had checked through his books but couldn't find any potions that ran clear, even in the mage book. He wondered whether he should tell someone that he'd seen her, but he had promised not to, and resolved that he would keep an eye out for her and try to speak to her again. If he didn't manage that, he thought he would ask the high wizard when he went to see him again in a few days. Seren was snapped out of his thoughts when he heard Horace calling him.

'You've been daydreaming a lot today, is everything all right?'

'Sorry, Horace, just a few things on my mind, but it'll keep.' Seren went back to his work.

***

Laurentis arrived at the inn and went straight to the bar, and as the keep wasn't around, she spoke to the barmaid.

'I just wanted to let you know I'll be leaving early in the morning, I've concluded my business and want to make an early start home. I was wondering if I could settle up now, so I won't have to wait in the morning?'

'Shouldn't be a problem, I'll just get the guestbook,' the barmaid replied and went to fetch the book. She returned shortly and opened it to the relevant page.

'You booked for six nights, tonight will be the fifth, I will get the coin for the extra night, if you'd just sign here please.'

Laurentis took the quill the barmaid offered and signed the book.

The barmaid handed over the coin owed and said, 'I'll date it for tomorrow as your leaving date, so you can be on your way in the morning.'

'Thank you.'

Returning to her room, Laurentis checked that she had packed everything, not wanting to leave any sign of her stay. Seeing that the new batch of potion had turned clear, she placed them into her satchel and hoped eight vials would be enough. Collecting her things, she checked the room one last time and left the inn via the back door, going directly to the stable block. Her mare was in the stall eating fresh hay and had been well cared for. She saddled her quickly and led her around the inn and out onto the cobbled street. Instead of going directly to the house, she headed up the north gate road towards the animal auctions. A few people wandered up and down the street but paid her no mind.

Tying her horse up at the side of the main auction building, she slipped inside, going immediately to the stables. She walked along the stalls until she came to the sixth. Stopping, she looked inside and saw a jet-black mare. Stepping lightly into the stall, she looked over her. She appeared to be in excellent condition. Laurentis noticed a saddle and reins on a post at the back of the stall, and promptly saddled the horse. As quietly as she could, Laurentis led the mare from the stall and round the side of the building to where her own mare was waiting patiently. Untying her, she led both away from the auction block and through the streets until she came to the small inn that faced the high wizard's house. It was late and the inn was quiet, so she tied the horses to the stand and went inside, taking the table in the window once again. Ordering a drink, she watched the house. She could see the high wizard in his study, and as he was still conscious, he couldn't have opened the bottle yet.

As the evening drew on, Laurentis was becoming disheartened. Maybe he had discovered it was laced, or perhaps it had been the wrong type of ale. Her thoughts were interrupted as the barmaid came over to tell her that the inn was closing. She nodded and got up to leave. Taking one last look at the house, she saw the high wizard look at the tag, open the bottle and pour himself a glass of the laced ale. Laurentis sighed with relief and stepped out of the inn, pretending to adjust the tack on the horses in case anybody saw her loitering.

When the lights of the inn went out, she untied the horses and walked slowly past the house. Looking in the window she saw the high wizard slumped over the desk, the glass half empty. She looked around, seeing the street was in darkness except for the high wizard's study. Quickly, she tethered the horses to the railings and stepped through the gate, going immediately to the door. She tried the latch, but it was locked. Pointing her wand at the latch, she closed her eyes and imagined the door unlocking. Hearing a click, she opened her eyes and tried the door once again. It opened. Rapidly walking inside, she closed the door quietly behind her. Creeping to the door of the study, she extinguished the lamp, plunging the room into darkness and going over to the unconscious high wizard.

Leaning over the wizard she put her arms under his, locking her hands together over his chest and dragged him from the chair. He was heavier than he looked, and it took her some time to drag him out of the house, over to the waiting horses. She let him collapse to the ground and hurried over to her mare, taking the travelling cloak from her pack. Returning to the recumbent form, she fastened the cloak around him and drew her wand, pointing it at the wizard. Slowly, he rose gently from the ground. She had never levitated a person before, and it took considerably more effort than she was expecting, but finally she managed to get him onto the black mare. Putting her wand away, she crossed to her horse and mounted. Reaching over, she pulled the hood up over the wizard's head and took the reins of the black mare. She nudged her horse and rode through the street, turned onto the north gate road and out of town. As soon as she had passed through the gate, she urged the horses on.

When Laurentis could no longer see the academy behind her, she stopped the horses and drew her wand, pointing it at the wizard. His appearance changed in an instant, his grey hair turned brown to match his eyes and lengthened considerably; He seemed to take on a younger look. She undid the spell on herself and her long hair changed back from black to light brown. The journey back to the fortress would take at least a week, and so she wasted no time and urged the horses on once again. After two leagues on the road, Laurentis turned northeast on to a trail that led to the ancient forest. Once within the forest she would pick up the north trail, which would lead her all the way through, emerging three leagues south of the citadel. It would be a longer journey than if she took the road, but it was the safest route. Not many people used the forest trail these days, so the danger that someone would recognise the high wizard was minimal. She would have to pass close to the citadel, which was risky but there was no other route to the mountain pass that would take her back to the fortress. She would aim to pass it during the night when the roads were quiet. As she entered the forest, she cleared her mind. She had to keep her wits about her, there were things in this forest, old things, which was why most people avoided this trail. She drew her wand and nudged the horses into a trot.

Chapter 12

The news of the high wizard's disappearance spread quickly through Shillington. It had been three days and there was still no sign of him. The council hadn't been forthcoming with any information, so nobody really knew what was going on. Seren had been distracted ever since he saw Laurentis. He hadn't seen her again and as much as he tried to push the thought aside, he couldn't help but wonder if she had had something to do with the disappearance. After all, she had said she wanted to see him, but if it really had been her what was her reason? When he left work the day before last, he'd decided that he would pay a visit to the head wizard of the academy. Maybe he could help put his mind at rest, it would only take a glance at the watch list. That morning, Seren left the house early, arriving at the academy as the weak winter sun was still climbing. Stopping at the gate, he waited for the gatekeeper, but no one came. Frustrated and about to leave, he saw Arin walking across the grounds.

'Arin, hey, Arin, over here,' he called, leaning on the gate.

Seeing Seren, and checking nobody was watching him, he quickly crossed over to the gate.

'Seren, what are you doing here?' he asked nervously.

'I need to speak with the head wizard, it's important.'

'Didn't you hear? Since the disappearance of the high wizard they've closed the academy to everyone except the students, and we're not allowed to leave the grounds.'

'I need to see him, Arin., I think I may know who's behind the disappearance,' he said, lowering his voice.

Arin looked at the gate hesitantly, 'We have to be quick then. The gatekeeper will be back any minute.' Taking out his wand, Arin pointed it at the gate and tried to open it but it remained firmly closed.

'Stop, what you're doing right now,' The gatekeeper suddenly yelled, 'And you outside, stay right there, you'll both be going to the head wizard for this.'

Striding over to the gate, the gatekeeper opened it with a flick of his wand. Taking Seren by the arm, he directed him to stand next to Arin, quickly closing the gate behind him. Without a word, the gatekeeper looked at both boys and indicated for them to follow him. In silence, they crossed the grounds and entered the academy. The gatekeeper led them through the entrance hall to the rear staircase, climbing it to the fourth floor. Arriving at a door with "Staff Offices" emblazoned across it, the gatekeeper opened it and they accompanied him to the end of the corridor, where they were ushered into a small reception room.

'Wait here,' the gatekeeper ordered curtly.

When he left the room, heading towards the head wizard's office, Seren glanced at Arin who looked nervous.

'You know I could be cast out for this,' Arin snapped crossly.

'I know. I'll explain to the head wizard that it was my fault, don't worry.'

Waiting in silence, Seren felt guilty, not wanting to get his friend into trouble. He vowed that he would do whatever he could to get him out of it. After a short while, the head wizard, Serat Johansen, entered the room and observed the boys.

'Arin, come with me,' he said sternly.

Standing, Arin began to walk towards the head wizard, gazing back at Seren just as he jumped up and rushed towards them.

'Sir, please. It wasn't Arin's fault, I asked him to let me in so I could speak with you. Don't punish him because of me.'

'Is this true, Arin?'

Arin looked at Seren who nodded. 'Yes, sir, it's true, he asked for my help to see you.'

Serat considered this for a moment, 'Very well, Arin. I will speak with you later, return to your studies.'

Nodding, and with a final glimpse at Seren, Arin left the room.

Serat looked at Seren. 'What is your name?'

'Seren Hiptamus.'

'Well, Seren, you had better come with me.'

With an about turn, Serat headed towards his office with Seren in tow. Opening the door, he ushered Seren in before the door closed itself behind him. Striding over to a large desk near the window, Serat sat down and gestured for Seren to sit. Looking down, Seren walked to the chair, knowing he was in trouble.

'I trust you realise how serious this is. The academy is closed to everybody who isn't studying or teaching.'

Seren tried to speak, but the head wizard held up his hand.

'The fact that you were trying to gain entry by asking a student to help is a very serious matter indeed. I will have to report this to the council, although, I don't imagine they will deal with you until they have dealt with the high wizard's disappearance.'

'But, sir, that's what I wanted to speak to you about.'

Serat looked at him. 'What do you mean?' He asked, curious as to what the boy could possibly know.

'I wanted to ask you if I could look at the watch list, I think I might know who's behind the disappearance. I'm hoping the list will prove me wrong, but I don't think it will.'

'And just who are you looking for on the list?'

'Her name is Laurentis Hapton.'

Serat thought for a moment. 'I don't recognise the name.'

'She didn't attend the academy, she disappeared during our last year at school.'

Rising from his desk, Serat crossed to the first of the large bookcases that lined the opposite wall.

'If she didn't attend the academy, she won't be on our watch list, but we keep the school records from past years,' he remarked, taking a bundle of parchment down from one of the shelves. Crossing back to his desk, he placed the parchment down in front of Seren. 'You realise that under normal circumstances you would not be allowed to see these. After all, they are confidential. But as the investigation by the council seems to be moving rather slowly, I will allow it this once.'

Seren wasted no time and started looking through the parchments. Opening the final one, he began to read the names. Halfway down, his heart dropped, he had found an entry. It read:

Laurentis Hapton, 8

The child was tested along with her classmates at the beginning of her first year. We have found that she possesses great power, but there are indications of a dark presence. She will be observed.

Laurentis has been observed throughout her first four years at the school. She has displayed tendencies leaning towards the darker arts. We can only hope that we can steer her from this path.

The entry ended there. Seren looked at the head wizard and showed him the entry.

'She's on the list.'

Serat read the entry. 'Now, Seren, please tell me everything.'

'At the beginning of the week, I was leaving work when a witch bumped into me. She dropped her satchel and some items fell out. I helped her collect her things and that's when I realised that it was Laurentis, although she had changed her hair colour. She disappeared a year or so ago. When I was helping her, I picked up a vial of clear liquid that wasn't labelled. I don't know what was in it, but she quickly took it from me. She told me that she was there to ask the high wizard to call off the search for her. She asked me not to tell anyone that I'd seen her, and then she left. I didn't see her again.'

'I can understand why you'd be suspicious. After all, it has been quite a time since she disappeared. But just because she is featured on the school's list doesn't mean that she had anything to do with the high wizard's disappearance. I think it unlikely that one as young as Laurentis could subdue and kidnap him. What possible reason could she have? No, I think that if she were here, then she came to do as she said. Some people just don't wish to be found.'

'What about the vials?'

'I couldn't say. Water or a tonic maybe. I understand your reasoning, but I just don't believe she could be capable of such a deed. As there are no further entries about her on the list, I must presume that the teachers succeeded in steering her away from the dark arts. Otherwise, it would have been noted. Now, if that is all, I will have someone escort you from the grounds. Please do not attempt to enter again whilst the academy is closed to outsiders.'

Seren rose from the chair and was met at the door by the gatekeeper who escorted him out. As he followed him, Seren thought about his conversation with the head wizard. Once again, he had been dismissed. He knew he didn't have any real proof about Laurentis, but surely the fact she was on the watch list made her a suspect. His thoughts were interrupted as the gatekeeper opened the gate. Swiftly stepping through, Seren started walking back towards town, hearing the gate slam shut but not looking back. Although he didn't know if the journal and the high wizard's disappearance were connected, one thing he was certain of was that he was on his own. A short while later, he entered the north gate and made his way through town. About to start down the south gate road, he spotted Tobelle over by one of the market stalls. She turned and saw him.

'You! How could you? Where is my father?'

Taken aback, Seren looked at her. 'What do you mean?'

'Don't deny it, you know where he is and the council will get it out of you.'

Glaring at him, she turned and walked away. Seren hadn't previously made the connection that the high wizard, Julius Actimus was Tobelle's father. He didn't understand why she would accuse him of kidnapping her father. Resignedly, he walked back towards the south gate road, *today has been a lousy day.*

The next morning, Seren went back to work. With today being quiet, he was able to leave early. Snow had been falling throughout the day, making his walk home a little longer than usual. Finding the house quiet and dark, he closed the door and hung up his cloak. He walked into the kitchen where his mother and father were sat around the table with two wizards, his mother looking as though she had been crying.

'Seren, these wizards need to speak with you,' she said quietly.

The wizards stood up. 'Seren, please come with us, we need you to answer some questions.'

'Where are we going?'

'To the council building. Now, please come with us.'

Sighing, he walked back into the hall and took down his cloak. When his parents came out from the kitchen, his mother was crying again.

'It's okay, Mam,' Seren said, smiling weakly at her. Slipping his cloak on, he followed the wizards out of the house and back into Shillington.

Chapter 13

Seren didn't know what the time was, or how long he had been sat in the central, windowless room on the topmost floor. Occasionally, he heard footsteps in the corridor, but no one had entered since he had been left there. He wondered what was going on, and more worryingly, what was going to happen to him. The wizards who had brought him there hadn't spoken to him at all, so he was still none the wiser as to what they wanted from him.

Getting up, he paced the room for the fourth time. It was a plain room, no decorations or ornamentation apart from a single door set into the wall. The furniture was just as sparse, a large desk and three chairs sat in the middle of the floor, the only other piece was a small, shabby end table tucked in the far corner. Sitting down again, ready to endure the long wait, the door suddenly opened, and two wizards stepped inside, closing it quickly behind them. Seren hadn't seen these wizards before, they weren't the two who had brought him there. They seated themselves opposite Seren, the younger of the two taking out some parchment and a quill and laying them on the desk. The older wizard looked at his colleague who nodded that he was ready, he looked back at Seren.

'You are Seren Hiptamus are you not?' the older wizard asked.

'Yes, but what's this all about, why am I here?'

'I will be asking the questions, Master Hiptamus,' the wizard said curtly. 'I understand that nobody has informed you as to why you have been brought here.'

'No.'

'You are here in connection with the disappearance of High Wizard Julius Actimus.'

Seren was astonished, how could the council possibly think he was involved in the disappearance? He had only spoken to the high wizard once and hadn't seen him since that meeting.

'If you have nothing to say, then we will begin. And I should warn you not to hold anything back, one way or another we shall learn the truth.'

Seren didn't like that statement, he had read accounts of witches and wizards being questioned by the council over the years whilst at school, some of the methods they used required powerful and dangerous magic, and he didn't want to be the newest addition to their accounts.

'We have reason to believe you are involved with the abduction of the high wizard. We have a statement confirming your purchase of the main evidence.' The wizard gestured to his colleague who took an ale bottle from his satchel and placed it on the desk. 'This bottle was found at the high wizard's house. Its contents have been tested by our alchemist and traces of a strong potion have been found. Whilst he was unable to identify the potion, the ingredients used were traceable. The potion contained leaves of citany, tilers root, harpentia, novatice, quince, hellebore, nightshade and wolfsbane, ingredients that we know you have access to, given your parent's occupation. We are attempting to recreate the potion as we speak. However, it would make it easier on you if you just tell us what it is.'

'I didn't give the high wizard any potion.'

'Really? Our evidence says different. Please read the tag tied to the bottle.'

Seren reached out and drew the bottle closer to him, turning it slightly and lifting the tag, shocked by what he read.

High Wizard Actimus, please accept this gift with my apologies following our meeting last week. Seren Hiptamus.

Seren couldn't believe what he was reading. He hadn't written the tag. It dawned on him that whoever kidnapped Julius Actimus was trying to place the blame on him and it was clearly working. As she was one of the only people he had told about his meeting with the high wizard, his thoughts turned immediately to Laurentis. Although certain she was involved in some way, there wasn't anything he could do about it at the moment. His immediate problem was trying to convince these wizards that he was innocent.

'Do you deny writing this tag?'

'Yes, sir, I do. I didn't buy the bottle, lace it with the potion or write the tag.'

The wizard looked at Seren, 'Are you saying that somebody is trying to place the blame on you?'

'Yes, sir.' Seren didn't mention Laurentis.

'The tag talks about a meeting with the high wizard, please tell us about this meeting.'

Seren explained to the wizard about his meeting with the high wizard two weeks ago. He left out some of the information concerning the journal, not wanting it to be confiscated. All the while Seren was talking, the younger wizard had been writing intently, taking every detail down.

'So, your meeting didn't end well, and you left feeling angry with the high wizard? Is that when you decided to get revenge on him, albeit over something as trivial as a lost journal?'

'No, I told you, I didn't see him again after that.'

'And if, as you profess, someone is trying to place the blame onto you, how did they know about your meeting?'

'After I left the council building, I went to the Merry-boat Inn and spoke to the keep about the meeting. Some-one must have overheard me.'

The wizard nodded, then pushed a piece of parchment and a quill towards him. 'Please copy the label so that we can compare the writing styles.'

Seren looked at the parchment and back at the wizard, he didn't feel comfortable doing this, *what if the tags are switched?*

As if reading his mind, the older wizard declared, 'The bottle and tag have been recorded, if you're worried that your tag will be switched, don't be. The recording prevents any type of tampering.'

Although still wary, Seren felt that he had no choice, so he took the parchment and quill and copied the label word for word. When he had finished, he pushed it towards the wizard who picked it up and examined it.

'I must say, they do look similar, but there is only one way to be certain.'

Taking out his wand, the older wizard pointed it at Seren's parchment.

Seren looked at the wizard who, without looking up, murmured, 'As you can see, the spell has taken the words you wrote and will try to superimpose them onto the tag. If you wrote the original, the words will become part of the tag. If, as you claim, you didn't write it, your words will return to the parchment.'

Seren looked at the blank document in his hand. Surely, if this proved he hadn't written the tag they would let him go. Even though he knew he hadn't written it, Seren began to feel nervous, but the words hadn't yet returned to the parchment. Suddenly, the scrap of paper he had written on looked as if it were glowing. Then, without warning, his words reappeared. He breathed a sigh of relief. The wizard looked at the parchment and then at Seren.

'Well, it seems that you were telling the truth about the tag, but it is not impossible that you had somebody write it for you.'

'Sir, please, the first time I saw this tag was when you asked me to read it,' Seren pleaded, a hint of desperation in his voice.

'Be that as it may, there is still the matter of the witness who said that you purchased the ale. Although some of what you say is evidently the truth, we cannot discount their statement.'

A knock at the door interrupted the wizard. 'Enter' he snapped bluntly.

A small witch entered the room, walked directly to the elder wizard, leant in close and whispered something to him. At the same time, she handed him a vial. He nodded, and she quickly left the room. As the door closed, the wizard placed the vial on the desk in front of Seren.

'Do you recognise the potion in the vial?'

Picking up the bottle, Seren studied it closely. It looked just like the potion that had fallen from Laurentis' satchel.

Still not wanting to tell the council about Laurentis, he looked at the wizard and calmly said, 'No, I've never seen a potion such as this. I didn't know it was possible to create clear potions. It looks just like water.'

'Well, I wouldn't recommend you drink this. I assure you it's not water. Our alchemist has just created this potion from the list of ingredients I told you about earlier. My colleague who brought it to me tells me that it is similar in nature to a sleeping tonic but much stronger. It is likely that a small amount of this draft would render a person unconscious for at least twenty-four hours.' The wizard paused for a moment, 'It has been compared to the traces found in the ale and they are identical. Now, we know how it was done.'

Seren watched the wizard as he sat there looking ponderous, still unsure whether they believed him or not.

'Sir, can I ask where I am supposed to have purchased the ale from?'

The wizard looked a little surprised at the question. 'This particular ale is only available from Hemdeans in the town square.'

'I've never been into the shop, but I have heard that the owner isn't the most honest of people. Was he the one who told you I had bought the ale?'

'I shouldn't tell you this, but as some parts of your story have turned out to be true, on this occasion I will break my own rule. Yes, it was the owner of the shop who told us about you. But why do you ask?'

'If what I have been told about him is true, isn't it possible that he lied to you.'

The wizard looked at Seren, what he didn't tell him was that the owner of Hemdeans had tried to get money out of the council wizards who had questioned him. Maybe it was possible that the boy was telling the truth, and somebody was setting him up to cover their tracks. If this were the case, then they were wasting time with the wrong person whilst the real culprit got away.

'Although he seemed very sure of his story, it is certainly a possibility, and given the evidence that we had, one that we did not consider.' The wizard contemplated for a moment. 'Whilst you are still our main suspect in the investigation, I believe it is necessary to speak with that man again, if pressed he may reveal something further. However, due to the seriousness of the crime, I cannot permit you to leave at this time. You will be held here until I have personally spoken to him.'

'But surely, you can't still believe I'm involved. After all, the test proved that I didn't write the tag and I didn't know anything about the potion,' Seren cried in desperation.

'Young man, I have been patient and listened to you. You will remain here until the witness' statement has been clarified. I will say no more on the matter,' the wizard reprimanded sharply.

The older wizard nodded to his colleague and they both rose from the table and left the room. Remaining seated at the desk, Seren heard the wizards talking as they walked down the corridor but couldn't make out what they were saying. Towards the end, he'd felt confident that he would be released. Now, he was angry. He hadn't done anything wrong, and yet everybody seemed to think he was guilty. At least now he understood why Tobelle had been so furious with him. The council had obviously spoken to her before they came for him. Even if the wizards decided he had been set up, she would be a lot harder to convince.

***

It took the wizards some time to find the owner of Hemdeans. They found him leaving the town by the east gate. Fortunately, they hadn't been far behind him and were successful in apprehending him. Bringing him back to the council building, they immediately began questioning him over his previous statement. The man, Noran Allicor, had appeared shortly after Oliver Hemdean had died, claiming he was his only living relative and had quickly taken possession of the shop. He had seemed pleasant enough at the start, but rumours about his unscrupulous nature had soon surfaced.

'I'll ask you again... did the boy really buy the bottle or are you covering for someone? I suggest you tell me the truth this time as you are testing my patience,' the older wizard said angrily.

As with Seren, his younger colleague sat at the desk taking notes. Unlike Seren's questioning however, he hadn't written very much, Noran wasn't very talkative.

Once again, Noran said the same thing, 'The boy came in and bought the bottle even though I recommended others. He said that he had to have that particular ale as it was a gift.'

The wizard sensed that he wasn't being truthful, he had contradicted what he said in his statement. Details such as the time and date had changed once, then twice, and then back to the original. He was swiftly losing his patience but was determined that he wouldn't stop until he had the truth. Rising from his chair, the older wizard drew his wand, pointing it at Noran, who was immediately pinned to the chair, paralysed.

'What have you done to me? Let me go,' he cried, visibly panicked.

Saying nothing, the wizard raised his hand, his outstretched palm towards the immobilised man. Felling as though he was being stuck by a thousand needles, Noran screamed in pain. Calmly, the wizard looked straight at him, his wand and palm still directed at him.

'I told you to tell me the truth, this is your last chance. Lie to me again and you will wish for death long before I have finished with you.'

Wincing in pain again, beads of sweat poured down Noran's brow. 'Okay, I'll tell you everything, just please don't hurt me anymore,' he pleaded.

The wizard considered this for a moment and slowly lowered his hand, keeping his wand trained on the man and purred, 'Go on.'

Noran contemplated his position, if he told the truth he would be in a lot of trouble, on the other hand, if he tried to keep up his lie he feared that the wizard would indeed carry out his threat.

'The boy didn't buy the bottle, I've never seen him before,' he mumbled weakly.

'Continue.'

'I don't know who she was.'

'What do you mean 'she'?'

'The ale was bought by a girl. I'd never seen her before. When she paid for the bottle, she asked me to say that she hadn't bought it as she was only choosing it for her friend. I told her that, for a few extra coins, I'd say the boy bought it himself. I didn't imagine anybody would ever come and ask me about it, so when your wizards turned up, I told them about the boy.'

The wizard lowered his wand, 'Is there anything else you wish to say?'

Noran slumped in the chair, 'Yes, a lot more.'

Sitting back down, he listened as the man began speaking once again.

***

Alone, Seren sat huddled in the corner of the room. The wizards hadn't returned and the only other person he had seen had been a witch bringing him food. Not knowing how long it had been since he had spoken to the wizards, he was beginning to feel as though he would never get out. Footsteps echoed down the corridor, and as the door opened, the two wizards entered and walked to the desk, the younger wizard gesturing for him to come and sit down. As Seren sat at the desk, he looked at the older wizard, who appeared tired and a little unkempt.

The old wizard began, 'I'm sorry to have detained you for so long, our questioning of Noran Allicor took longer than I would have liked. However, he has admitted that he lied and stated that a girl bought the bottle, and for a price, he agreed to say that you bought it. Following our last meeting, and this new evidence, I no longer consider you a suspect in the high wizard's disappearance. You are free to go, if you will just sign the parchment confirming you agree with our findings.'

The younger wizard offered the document and quill to Seren, who took it and quickly signed. The younger wizard took it back and both wizards countersigned it before rising from the desk.

'My colleague will escort you out. And, Seren, I would appreciate it if you didn't speak to anyone about this. The investigation is still ongoing.'

Nodding his agreement, Seren followed the young wizard out of the room. As he was escorted down through the building, the wizard noticed him watching a man being led out in shackles.

'That's Noran Allicor. After he told us about you, he told us something more. Turns out he poisoned old Oliver Hemdean, and then a few days later made up the story about being his only relative so he could take over the shop. He'll spend the rest of his time in the garrison prison. You never can tell about some people, can you,' the young wizard mused.

Reaching the door, the young wizard winked at him and went back into the building. Drawing his cloak around him, Seran pulled up the hood and stepped outside into the cold, evening air. Without a second thought, he headed for home and the comfort of his bed, unaware that he was being watched as he crossed the square and walked down the south gate road.

Chapter 14

Coming home late and the house in darkness, Seren assumed his parents were asleep. Quietly closing the door, he hung up his cloak, walked into the kitchen and lit the small lamp on the table. He knew he should get some sleep but was ravenous, the food provided by the council hadn't exactly been satisfying. Noticing a pot on the stove he lifted the lid to find the remainder of his mother's beef stew. Whilst he was waited for the stew to warm, Seren sat by glowing embers in the fireplace, stoking them and placing a log into the hearth. Outside the snow was still falling and the walk home had chilled him to the bone. When the fire popped loudly, Seren jumped. Hearing footsteps from upstairs, the next thing he knew his mother came rushing down the stairs and into the kitchen. She stopped dead in her tracks when she saw him and clasped her hands to her face.

'Seren, you're finally home, I was beginning to worry they'd never let you out.'

'They released me a short while ago. I didn't want to wake you.'

His mother smiled, noticing the warming pot on the stove and went over to it to prepare the meal. 'Go and sit down I'll finish this. You must be exhausted.'

Seated at the table, his mother brought him a large bowl of stew and two thick slices of bread. She left the kitchen as he began to eat, returning a few minutes later with his father in tow. Joining him at the table, they made Seren recount everything that had happened over the three days the council had held him. By the time he persuaded them to let him go to bed, he could hardly keep his eyes open.

The next morning, although he hadn't slept much, Seren still planned to go into work. He hoped that Horace would understand and that he'd still have a job. When he entered the kitchen, his mother was already busy preparing breakfast and turned to look at him.

'Surely, you're not going into Merrymans today, you've only just arrived home, you should take a day or two to relax.'

'I have to, Mam, I've already been away for three days. I don't want to lose the job.'

'Horace was very understanding when we went to see him. I'm sure he wouldn't mind if you took a few days to recover. Your father could let him know when he goes into town later today.'

'No, Mam, I'm going in, I just want everything to get back to normal and put this whole thing behind me.'

Looking at him, his mother sighed and went back to preparing the breakfast. As soon as Seren had finished he collected his cloak from the hall and left the house. By the time he reached the town, it was already busy. He picked his way through the crowds until he arrived at Merrymans. In the shop, Horace was serving a customer so Seren stood back and waited patiently. As the customer finished at the counter, he turned and looked at Seren before hurrying from the shop. The gossips in town had obviously been having a field day, they mustn't have heard that he'd been released. Shaking his head, Seren walked over to the counter.

'Horace.'

Horace looked up.

'Where should I start today?'

'Seren, good to see you, I was quite troubled when your parents came to see me and explained what happened.'

'I'm all right, a little tired but eager to put this behind me and get back to normal. So, what would you like me to do?'

Horace shifted his weight awkwardly, his face a little flushed. 'Seren, when I said it was good to see you, I meant it. However, I assume you noticed the reaction of the last customer. You wouldn't believe the number of people who have come in just to ask about you in the last few days. Whilst you have a job here for as long as you wish, I think it would be best if you took some time off until all this blows over,' he said slightly embarrassed.

'But, Mr Merryman, the council cleared me, I didn't have anything to do with the high wizard's disappearance.'

'I understand that, Seren, and I'm pleased for you. But under the circumstances, I think it might be for the best. When all this settles down, your job will be here waiting for you.'

Seren didn't need to hear anymore. 'Very well, Mr Merryman, I understand.' With that, he turned and left the shop.

As Horace watched him go, he felt terrible but as selfish as it may seem, his business had been affected by the idle chatter and he couldn't afford to lose the shop. He hoped this would all be over soon, and above all else, hoped that Seren would forgive him and return once everything was back to normal.

Stepping out of the shop into the cold morning air, Seren walked across the square until he came to the towering statue of the town's founder, a great wizard who had lived many ages ago. He leant against the statue and sighed, nothing seemed to be going his way. In the space of a few short months his world had fallen down around him. First, the rejection from the academy, now, this accusation. He wondered what would happen next. Maybe the dream he had would come true and he would become the bitter old man he'd dreamt of. Venturing over to the malt stand, he bought one of the hot, frothy drinks.

His thoughts were interrupted when a soft voice coldly said, 'They let you go then. If it was me, I would have let you rot for what you've done to my father.'

Seren looked around to see Tobelle standing just behind him.

'They let me go because they don't believe I'm involved. Their star witness changed his statement. Didn't they tell you that?' He said through gritted teeth.

Tobelle looked at him. 'If it wasn't you, then who was it?' she spat.

'I have a theory but seeing as how you've decided it can't be anyone other than me, I don't think I'll share it. Now, if you don't mind, Tobelle, I've had enough accusations thrown at me in the last few days without having to listen to anymore from you.'

Without another word, Seren walked away from the stall, down the south gate road and out of town, making for home. Several pairs of eyes watched him go, and the whispers soon followed. Seren's outburst shocked Tobelle. A pang of guilt washed over her. She didn't want to believe it was him, but there were no other suspects as far as she knew. Watching him go, she wondered what he had meant by a theory. Maybe he knew something she or the council wizards didn't, or maybe, she thought, he was being spiteful after the way she had treated him. Nevertheless, she decided to continue watching him, and making sure to keep a reasonable distance, she followed him.

Seren entered the house, slamming the door behind him.

'Hey,' his mother called, 'Whatever the matter is with you, it's not the door's fault, calm down.'

Not answering, Seren hung up his cloak and walked upstairs to his room, closing the door behind him, not wanting to see or speak to anyone. Having had enough, he flopped onto his bed. He had seen the way people looked at him in town and heard the whispers. Maybe he should just leave, go somewhere where nobody knew him and start again. Staring at the journal on his desk, it was that book that had started it all. If he hadn't found it and tried to convince the high wizard about it, none of this would be happening. He got up and crossed to the desk, picking up the journal then sat on the bed and opened it. Flicking through a few of the pages, he came to the final entry made by James. Something on the next page caught his eye, he was positive that the page had been blank, but now the distinctive handwriting covered it.

When those around look down on you and dismiss all you try to say, when you hear your name whispered and feel their eyes upon you in the street, do not despair. Although few remain, there are those who will believe and help you. Follow your heart and seek them out, and you will know you are amongst friends. Above all, don't give up.

Seren looked up. He couldn't understand how the message had got into the journal, but it seemed that, given what it said, it was meant for him. Gazing out the window, freshly fallen snow covered the land as far as he could see. A harsh winter was ahead, but he knew what he had to do. When he had first found the journal, he'd resolved to continue what James had started. So much had happened since then, but he felt as if he owed it to James to carry on. *After all,* he thought, *now, I have nothing to lose.* He decided that he would spend the next couple of days preparing to leave Shillington and would only take essentials. He knew he might not return, but for the moment that thought was only fleeting.

***

The journey through the forest had taken longer than Laurentis expected. Almost a week had passed since the kidnapping, but she had made it without encountering either man or beast. She was waiting for nightfall before leaving the relative safety that the forest afforded during the day. Tonight, she would pass the citadel and enter the mountain pass. Stooping over a stream, she filled the water skins, tucking hers into her saddlebag. Taking one of the vials, she emptied it into the second skin. So far, the potion had kept the wizard unconscious, and she wanted to keep it that way until she reached the fortress. Laurentis knew she wouldn't be able to subdue him if he awoke during the journey as she didn't have the knowledge or power. Whilst she was waiting, she checked the horses and made sure they were fed and watered. They would be riding hard tonight, and she wanted to be sure that they could take the pace. Satisfied, she ate a heel of stale bread before tipping some of the laced water into the wizard's mouth. As dusk approached, she mounted once again, needing to press on. By the time she neared the citadel, it would be fully dark so it should be safe enough. Urging the horses into a trot, she left the forest behind.

The full dark of night had not long fallen as Laurentis turned onto the road that would take her back to the mountain pass, riding hard. Soon enough, she rounded a sharp bend, and there on the horizon loomed the citadel. The waning moon cast minimal light across the land. *Perfect*, Laurentis thought, *at this rate we will reach the mountain pass before morning.*

Chapter 15

For the last three days, Seren had been gathering provisions and packing and was now finally ready to leave. There was one thing that still stood in his way, however—he hadn't told his parents. He knew they'd try to stop him, but also knew if he left without a word, they would try to find him. The last thing he wanted was to drag them into whatever he was getting himself into. Outside the window, he could see the lamplight in one of the greenhouses where his father was working, despite the snow. Downstairs, he could hear his mother working in the kitchen. Sighing, he laid back on his bed. Several thoughts ran through his head. *His rejection from the academy. His dismissive conversations with both the high wizard of the council and the head wizard of the academy. The disappearance of the high wizard and the subsequent accusation against him. Tobelle and Laurentis.* He dwelled on Laurentis, having no doubt that she was connected to the disappearance, but he didn't understand why. His thoughts turned back to his parents, *I will write them a letter and leave it for them to find after I'm gone.* Seren rose from his bed, seating himself at his desk. Taking a quill and a piece of parchment, he began to write.

Dear Mam and Pop

I have decided to get away from Shillington for a while. After everything that has happened recently, I need some time out to decide what to do from here. I feel that if I stay, I will only become unhappy. I'm sorry that I'm telling you this in a letter, but it's for the best as I know you will try to persuade me to stay. I will return when I feel ready and would ask you not to worry or try to find me. I just need some time.

Love always, Seren

Laying the quill down, Seren read the letter a final time, then folded it. Leaving the letter on his desk, he stood, determined to leave tonight. It was early afternoon, and knowing he would have to wait until after dark, he went down to the kitchen and spent the rest of the day helping his mother to bottle and label the next batch of harvested produce.

***

It had been four days since Laurentis entered the mountain pass. The heavy snow and the horses' slow progress made the going tough, but now Laurentis could see the fortress. Since the gloomy dawn had broken, it had been growing larger on the horizon. She had undone the spell on the high wizard and on her robes, the red now standing out against the brilliant white of the snow. Unbeknown to Laurentis, Archimon had noticed her when she undid the spell and now stood on the lower terrace watching her approach. Watching her making slow progress through the pass, he was eager for her to arrive so he could take possession of the wizard who rode alongside her. Raising his hand towards the path, his palm outstretched, the fallen snow swirled as if a sudden blizzard had taken hold. Down on the road, Laurentis shielded her face from the sudden onslaught of snow. As it cleared, she looked up and saw that the road ahead was clear. Looking towards the fortress, a figure on the lower terrace turned and walked inside. *It must have been Archimon*, she urged the horses forward. A short while later, she entered the stables at the base of the fortress, where Archimon and two brigands were waiting for her. Seeing the high wizard, Archimon clapped his hands together and smiled.

'Take him to the cells,' he ordered the brigands.

The two red-robed wizards walked towards the still unconscious high wizard and pulled him from the horse. Roughly, they both took an arm and dragged him away. Laurentis, without a second look at the wizard, dismounted and handed the reins of the two mares to the stable master who led them away. Archimon stepped towards her.

'Well done,' he said coolly. Placing an arm around her shoulders, he led her through the stables towards the huge, stone doors that led into the fortress. 'Now, let us celebrate. And afterwards, I will reveal my plans to you.'

***

After helping his mother for the afternoon, Seren spent the evening with his parents. Shortly after dark, they retired for the night, leaving Seren alone. Although apprehensive about leaving, he knew he should go tonight. When he was sure that his parents were asleep, he quietly made his way up to his room. From his cupboard, he took the satchel he'd packed that morning. Placing it on his bed, he crossed to the desk and took a crudely drawn map bought from a market stall in town and added it to the satchel. Longingly, he looked at the collection of books scattered around his room but left them where they were. Those he would have liked to take with him were all too bulky and would just weigh him down. The only book that would accompany him was the journal.

Taking the letter from his desk, he picked up the satchel. With a final glance around his room, he closed the door and quietly walked downstairs into the kitchen, placing the letter on the table against the salt pot. Wrapped in his heavy winter cloak, he quietly exited the house through the back door. Crossing the yard to the small, wooden stable block, Seren made his way to the last stall where his grey gelding stood quietly. Patting his neck, he quickly saddled him and led him out of the stall. Taking two small sacks, he filled them with grain and placed them in the saddlebags. Shouldering his satchel, he led the grey around to the front of the house, the snow softening the sound of hooves. Mounting the grey, he took one last look at the house. He had decided earlier he would try to find out what had happened to James, and the best place to start would be his home at Hallsrock. Turning the grey south, he nudged him on and began his journey into the unknown.

***

Since their last encounter, Tobelle had continued to watch Seren, certain that he was involved with her father's disappearance, although now, she wasn't so sure. What he said in their last conversation kept playing on her mind. She'd spent the day watching out for him near his house, but to no avail. Finally giving up, she had begun the walk home when she heard a door being closed. Tobelle stopped and watched from where she stood. After a short while, Seren appeared, leading his horse around to the front of the house. Crouching beside a low wall, Tobelle watched as he turned south and rode away from the house. She wondered what he was up to and decided to follow him, but she'd need a horse. A little way along the road was one of the breeder's smallholdings where she knew there would be horses. Although she didn't like the idea of stealing, if she wanted to follow Seren any farther she'd have to. She ran up the road to the smallholding and silently entered the large, stable block. A few minutes later, she emerged leading a pure white mare. Mounting it, she headed in the direction that Seren had gone, determined to find out exactly what he was doing.

***

The next morning, Thomas Hiptamus was woken by a shriek from the kitchen. Hurrying downstairs, he found Eva crying at the table.

'What is it, dear?'

'Seren's gone,' she said between sobs, pushing the letter towards him.

Thomas took the letter and read it. Sighing, he placed it back on the table.

'He has been very unhappy these past few days, maybe being here just got too much for him.'

'We have to do something, we can't just let him go,' Eva cried.

Thomas put his arm around her. 'I know it's hard, dear, but he's asked us to let him do this. He'll be back once the dust has settled. It might be just what he needs,' he said sadly.

Thomas decided to respect Seren's wishes, not wanting to push his son away in case he never came back. Resolving to wait patiently for Seren's return, he went back to comforting his wife.

Chapter 16

Just past noon, Laurentis lay in bed, having been up into the early hours. The events of last night played through her mind. After arriving at the fortress, Archimon led her to the great hall. As they entered, she saw that all the others had already returned and were seated around the table. Indicating that she should take the seat next to him, Archimon stood at the head of the table.

'I am pleased to say that you have all completed your tasks. Now we can continue unhindered as there is no one left to stand in our way.'

Seating himself, he waved his hand and the table filled with food. They spent the evening eating and drinking. By the time they retired, they were all a little unsteady on their feet. As Laurentis rose to go to her room, Archimon grabbed her arm.

'I'd like you to join me in my suite, I have things to tell you that I don't want heard by others.'

Archimon stood and began walking from the hall, Laurentis following. Situated across one of the upper levels of the fortress, Archimon's suite was grand and decorated with ornately carved furniture. Great tomes and grimoires, old and new alike, lined the walls. Walking through the first of the rooms, Archimon led Laurentis to a small chamber where a fire roared in the fireplace, making shadows dance across the walls. Pointing at a soft couch, he stood at the opposite end while she waited for him to speak. In front of the fireplace he remained silent for a few moments.

'Congratulations on completing your task, you have proved your worth,' pausing, he turned to face her. 'And so, as promised, I will now reveal my plans to you.' Seating himself on the opposite couch, he began. 'You have great power within you, Laurentis. Power that you aren't even aware of, which I will help you unlock. You will become one of the most formidable witches this world has ever known.'

Laurentis looked at him, puzzled.

'I know it might be hard for you to believe, but I promise it's true.' Archimon smiled and crossed to the couch where she was sitting. 'Once I have shown you how to unlock your full power, you will be almost as powerful as I am, then we will be bound together, and no one could oppose us.'

Laurentis was shocked, she had never dreamt this was what he was planning, but it seemed she had no choice in the matter.

'Once united, we shall take over the harvesting of magic. Our power will increase, and eventually, the premise of magic in the south will belong solely to us, bringing all under our control. In time, we can move north and take yet more. We have only Him to usurp.'

Laurentis knew only scant details of the one who was actually in control, but she did know that he was a powerful sorcerer.

'We can't oppose him, he'd destroy us.'

'Alone, we cannot defeat him, but together he could not hope to triumph against our combined power. For now, the harvested magic shall continue to go to him, but very soon, the tides will turn in our favour. By the time he realises what we are doing, it will be too late to stop us.'

Laurentis stared at him in disbelief.

'I understand this might take some time to sink in, but you must not speak of it to the others. Should they find out about our plans, they might betray us. Now, I have detained you long enough, you may take your leave.' Waving his hand over the small, end table, he conjured several books and handed them to her. 'Take these, they will help you understand and begin to unlock your power. Once you have finished them, I will show you the rest.'

Laurentis hastily thanked Archimon and walked towards the door, clutching the books.

'Laurentis,' she turned, 'Remember, not a word to anyone.'

She inclined her head and turned back, leaving the suite, making her way back down to her room.

She'd gone straight to bed but hadn't slept well, which is why she now found herself still abed. Climbing out of bed, she crossed to her desk and sat down, looking at the books she had left there last night. *Could what Archimon said be true?* She was about to start reading when there was a knock at the door.

'Come in,' she called.

'A little too much wine last night? I brought you breakfast, looks like you could do with it.'

Laurentis looked up at the sound of Olivia's voice. She was one of the other brigands and the only other woman in the group.

'Thanks, I couldn't face getting up this morning.'

Olivia smiled and set the food down on a small table near the fireplace.

'Don't let the boss catch you slacking, or you'll be for it,' she said with a grin, 'Catch you later.'

Turning, she walked from the room, the winter sun glinting off her red hair as she left. Laurentis smiled, she liked Olivia. Getting up, she retrieved the food. Placing it on her desk, she opened the first of the books and began to read.

The Trappings of Power.

Power can manifest itself in many forms and at different ages. Some never realise the full extent of their power, whilst others are all too aware of what they possess and have frequently been found to abuse that power in some form. In order to assess potential threats, the law decrees that every child be tested upon entry to school. Any indication of large amounts of power or attraction to dark magic is monitored throughout their time at school and the academies, in the hope of educating students against the use of dark magic. Those with the potential to do good are taught how to open themselves fully to their power, whilst those attracted to the darker aspects of our craft are not schooled in the methods to do this. The following pages detail the correct methods to allow students to realise their powers. There also follows a way to help suppress the knowledge from those with interests in dark magic.

Laurentis wondered, could this be why she didn't know about her power? Perhaps her teachers had tried to suppress it. Archimon could well be right. Turning back to the book, she continued reading.

The rest of the day Laurentis spent reading. By the time she had finished the first book, an extensive pile of notes lay on her desk and she was convinced that her power had been suppressed. She was about to go to the hall for supper when she realised that she hadn't dressed all day. Quickly throwing on a robe, she hurried out of the room. Arriving at the hall, she took her place at the table, which was already laden with food and wine. Archimon hadn't yet arrived, but the others had started anyway. Appearing halfway through supper, Archimon nodded a silent acknowledgment to those at the table, then sat down and ate a light meal. Not once during the meal did he speak to Laurentis, and after a short while, he rose from the table and left the hall. Although Laurentis understood why he hadn't spoken to her, having told her not to speak of their meeting, she still felt rejected. Surrounded by people but unable to talk to anyone, at that moment, she felt completely alone.

'Hey, kiddo, you look troubled,' Olivia said, sitting down next to her. 'This'll take the edge off whatever it is, wanna tell me about it?' she asked, passing Laurentis a cup of wine.

S he would have given anything to have told her what was going on, but Archimon had forbidden it.

'I'm just tired that's all, don't know that this stuff will help,' she said, indicating the wine.

'It'll make you sleep if you drink enough,' Olivia countered.

Smiling, Laurentis lifted the cup and took a drink, spending the remainder of the evening picking at the food and drinking with the others.

The next morning, Laurentis made it to breakfast, albeit with a heavy head. She had drunk too much last night and would pay for it today. After eating a light breakfast, she returned to her room, wanting to find out more about the supposed power she had and how she could access it. She read the first few chapters of the second book, but after a short while her headache finally won over her concentration, and she pushed it away. Taking the notes she had made the day before, she sat on her bed re-reading the section on suppressing power. The book didn't offer a reversal, but she thought that by using the guidelines on how to realise power she might be able to get past any suppression on her. Laying back, Laurentis tried to ignore her worsening headache and relax. Closing her eyes, she cleared her mind as best she could, trying to visualise the power within her just as the notes said to do. As she relaxed, she could feel her headache easing, until finally it had gone.

When Laurentis opened her eyes, she realised she was levitating a few inches above her bed. In that moment of realisation, her relaxed state was disturbed, and she fell back onto the bed. Sitting up, she noticed the light was fading and must have been on her bed for hours. She wondered how she'd managed to levitate. It took great power and skill to master, and few succeeded without the assistance of a wand. Laying back down, she tried to do it again but failed.

No matter how hard she tried, she remained firmly on the bed. With a sigh, she gave up, thinking she must have imagined it. Getting up, she left her room to attend supper.

Once again, when Archimon finally arrived, he ate quickly. Without a word to anyone, he left shortly after without so much as a second glance. Laurentis finished her meal and hurried back to her room. Locking her door so as not to be disturbed, she opened the second book and began reading where she had left off that morning. Reading through the night, by the time the sun crept over the horizon she had completed both the second and third books, and was close to finishing the last one.

Unbeknownst to Laurentis, Archimon was watching her in his seeing stone. He smiled to himself, thinking that this might not take as long as he had initially thought. After watching her until she had completed the fourth book, he decided to take them back later that day, as it would only push her to discover her power faster. With a wave of his hand, the scene in the stone vanished and he walked away, the wicked smile never leaving his face.

Closing the last book, Laurentis added it to the pile, having made masses of notes, which she collected together and placed in the chest at the end of her bed. Realising how tired she was, she lay down and fell asleep almost immediately. Awaking in the afternoon, she found herself levitating once again. As before, she landed on the bed when she realised what she was doing. This time, she definitely hadn't imagined it. Having levitated, she wondered if that meant her powers were beginning to reveal themselves. Turning her attention to the desk, she saw that the books had vanished. Swiftly checking the door, she found it still locked, but that wouldn't stop Archimon. It was most likely that he would have just conjured them to him. When he gave them to her he hadn't mentioned a time limit. Taking her notes from the chest, she started going through them, pleased that she had written so extensively. For several days she repeatedly went through her notes and re-did all the exercises she had found in the books. Archimon had made no attempt to speak with her since their meeting, and she felt herself beginning to resent him. After all, it was he who wanted her to do this.

Two weeks after her conversation with him, she was in her room about to go to bed having spent yet another day going over her notes, when there was a knock at the door. Crossing the room, she opened it to see Archimon standing there, smiling. Not waiting for an invitation, he entered the room.

'I have been watching you these past weeks. You've done well. I can see you're serious about unlocking your power. Now, the hard work will begin. I will teach you things the books cannot.'

Chapter 17

Entering the north gate of Hallsrock, the horseman had been riding hard through the snow and made it to the town just as dusk was beginning to descend. He had set out from his home two weeks earlier and had taken minimal rest stops in order to make the journey quickly. His first priority was to find a suitable inn with vacant rooms and stabling. Tired, he knew that he would be better received after a hot meal and good night's rest. Slowing his horse to a trot, he continued down the road, hoping to find an inn when he noticed a man walking towards him.

'Excuse me, sir, might I trouble you for directions to an inn where I could find lodgings for myself and my mount?'

The man glanced up at him. 'Well, there be only four inns in town, and most be busy, what with the bad weather. Not good fer travelling. Wouldn't catch me out travelling, no, not till the melt,' he croaked.

The rider shifted in his saddle a little impatient.

'I do believe the Mage's Wand still has rooms, tis expensive, though. Yer'll need a heavy purse for that place,' the man said with a chuckle. 'Just head down onto the east road and yer'll find it.'

'Thank you,' the rider replied, nudging his horse forward.

Four stone and timber buildings dominated the corners of the crossroads, but none emitted the welcoming glow of an inn. Turning east, a short distance from the crossroads he found the Mage's Wand. Relieved, he dismounted and stretched his legs. An attendant waiting in the grey, stone porch walked towards him, neatly turned out in black robes and a heavy, winter cloak.

'Can I help you, sir?'

'I wish to take lodgings at the inn, do you have vacancies?'

The man scrutinised him, taking in the dishevelled appearance of the rider.

'We do, sir, for those who can afford our prices,' he said, a hint of distaste in his voice.

'Oh, believe me, I can pay,' the rider said with equal dislike for the man.

The neat man smiled, and taking a small bell from his cloak, he rang it once, replacing it carefully. Moments later two young lads came racing around to the front of the inn, dressed in oversized, winter cloaks and woolly hats.

The neat man looked at the boys, 'Take the horse to the stables, see that he is fed and watered, and ensure that he is groomed and blanketed before leaving the stables,' he ordered one of the boys. Turning to the other, he said, 'Take the gentleman's bags inside and show him to his room.'

The boys set about their tasks with haste, the rider handing the reins of his horse to the first and watching as the bay was led away.

'Follow me, sir,' the second boy said.

Doing as instructed, the rider entered the inn, finding it warm with the tempting smell of roasting meat. As he was led to a large desk in the corner of the entrance hall, a small, dowdy woman stared at him.

'May I help you?'

'I'd like to book a room and stabling for seven nights.'

'You're a wizard, I trust?' she asked in a monotone.

'Yes'

Opening a large, leather bound book, she turned the page. 'You're in luck, we have some rooms available.'

Passing a silver, embossed card to the boy, she intoned, 'The charge will be five sovereigns per night, plus one per night for the stabling fee. What's your name?'

'Tobias Helmand.'

The woman nodded and made a note in the book. 'The boy will show you to your room, enjoy your stay,' she said in the same flat tone.

Tobias followed the boy to the fourth floor where he stopped outside the last door along the corridor and handed the card to the wizard.

'As long as you have your card, just point your wand at the door to open or lock it,' he said, very matter of fact.

Placing Tobias' bags down, the boy tipped his woolly hat and headed off down the corridor and out of sight. Using his wand, Tobias opened the door as instructed and stepped inside, picking up his bags on the way. Closing the door behind him, he removed his cloak, glad to be out of the cold night. Catching sight of himself in the full-length mirror that stood against the wall, he understood why the doorman had acted the way he had. He really did look a state. Finding a basin of cold water in the corner of the room, Tobias washed away the dirt from being on the road before tidying himself up with a change of robes and running a comb through his greying hair. Satisfied that he was now presentable, he made his way downstairs. Seating himself at one of the smaller tables, a little too far from the fire, he waited to be served. After eating a hearty meal of venison stew with thick, sliced bread, he washed it down with a mug of ale before retiring for the night, falling asleep almost immediately.

Late the next morning, Tobias awoke, chiding himself, but had to admit that he felt better for it. After a light breakfast, he set out into town to find James, walking back along the cobbled road until he arrived at the crossroads. Turning north, he followed the road that led up the ridge to James' house. Walking swiftly, he turned a corner and stopped dead in his tracks, as James' house was no longer there. Hurrying over to the site where the house had previously stood, he found nothing but charred timbers, strewn ashes and rubble. He gasped at the destruction. After what James had said in his first letter, Tobias became concerned when he didn't arrive at the citadel following the second letter. Tobias knew something was going on but hadn't expected to find James' house destroyed. Not wanting to raise suspicion, he decided not to linger, perhaps those who had committed this act were still watching the house in case someone came looking for James.

Tobias hurried back to the centre of town and returned to the inn. Once in his room, he slumped in a chair trying to make sense of what he had seen. He rifled through his pack and pulled out the letters, finding the second one, he re-read it. But it simply outlined James' discoveries since his first letter and that he would join Tobias at the citadel. He wondered if James had ever left for the citadel or if those who put his house to the flame had captured him. Being a mage emeritus James should have been able to avoid capture even if his powers had diminished. Tobias was worried. If James had been in trouble, surely, he would have left something behind, something that Tobias could use to track him, but he hadn't sensed anything at the ruined house. There wasn't a trace of James at all. A knock at the door roused him from his thoughts. Answering it, he found one of the boys waiting there.

'Sir, there's someone downstairs to see you, please follow me and I'll take you to him.'

As the only person he knew in Hallsrock was James, his suspicions were raised. Taking his wand, he placed it in the sleeve of his robe for quick access, should the need arise. Until he knew who this person was, he would have to be cautious. The boy led him downstairs and over to the varnished, wooden bar where he left him. Not knowing who had summoned him, he scanned the room before feeling a tap on his shoulder.

'Tobias Helmand? My name is Marcus Lennant, a friend of James. Please come and sit with me, we must talk.'

Marcus ushered Tobias to a small table in the corner of the inn. Taking a seat, Tobias took in the man's appearance, his grey hair and beard were extremely long, and his robes were a deep purple with yellow filigree trim.

'Have you heard from James?'

Tobias regarded him for a moment. 'I received two letters from him nearly four moons ago, but nothing since.'

'May I ask what he wrote?'

'How do I know you're not one of those who razed his house to the ground?'

'You've seen it then.' Marcus paused, 'You're no doubt wondering how I know you're here and why I sought you out. I am a seer. James and I have been friends for many a year. I saw you as one who might be able to help me find him.'

Tobias sighed, 'His last letter said he would join me at the citadel. He never arrived.'

'I feared as much. He came to see me with some troubling news. I cast for him and told him what I saw. I haven't seen or heard from him since and fear he is in great strife. What's more, I am having trouble casting for him.'

'I couldn't sense him at the house either.'

Marcus was quiet for a moment, then said, 'I fear what he told me is true. Magic is being stolen from us. Normally, I can cast for people and find them quickly, but no matter how I go about it, I just can't find him. If I'm losing my powers, it's likely that you are as well, which may explain why you couldn't sense him when you visited his house.'

Tobias had never considered that what James wrote in his letters might befall him.

'Sir, I assure you, my powers are intact, I would have noticed such a change.'

'Be that as it may, my friend, I would advise that you check your power, you might need it soon.' He paused, 'I propose that we try to combine our powers and cast for James upon the next full moon in two days. We might stand a better chance, and if you have the letters you spoke of, bring them. It will help us if we have something that he touched. You'll find my house in the south district. Now, my friend I have things I must attend to. I will see you soon and remember to check your powers.'

Without another word, he stood and left the inn, leaving Tobias sitting alone thinking about what Marcus had said. Although this was their first meeting, he decided to trust him. After all, James obviously had.

Though he hadn't felt any change in his power, Tobias thought he should check. Locking the door to his room, he crossed to the fireplace and set about lighting a small fire. Happy with the fire he retrieved a pouch from his pack and sat on the floor in front of the warming hearth. From the pouch he took out powdered jerecula, mandrake root and gillink. Combining the powders, he threw them into the flames, which turned a deep shade of blue. After a minute, the thick, blue smoke wafted from the fireplace and enveloped him. Inhaling the smoke deeply, it took effect almost immediately, heightening his senses as his mind focused on manifesting his powers. Visualising his power, he saw it as an undulating ball of grey light. When he felt it become static, his mind shifted focus and began to delve into it. After several minutes, the smoke dissipated, and Tobias snapped his eyes open in disbelief. It was true, his power had diminished, not by a great deal, but it was a loss, nonetheless. Magic was being stolen. Tobias became desperately worried. James had discovered something and now he had disappeared. *It has to be connected,* he thought. He hoped that James was still alive. With a sigh, he extinguished the fire and lay down on the bed. The smoke always took its toll and he felt drained and in need of rest.

He hoped that his diminishing power wouldn't lead to a longer recovery, he had to be ready to join Marcus the day after tomorrow. Closing his eyes, he fell into a restless sleep.

***

Early on the morning of the full moon, Tobias arrived at Marcus' house. It had taken him a full day to recover and he still felt a little tired, but if they were to have any chance of finding James, they had to combine their powers and cast for him tonight. Tobias stood in front of the house, taking in the view for a few moments. It hadn't been difficult to find, just like the wizard, it stood out amongst all others. The grounds were jungle-like even in the snow, symbols of the seer's trade adorning the front of the house and metal chimes hanging either side of the door, chinking in the breeze. With a last look around, Tobias trudged up the snowy path, raised his hand to knock, but didn't get the chance as the door opened before him without help from anyone.

'Please come in, Tobias.' Marcus called out.

Stepping over the threshold, the door closed behind him.

'Nice and early I see, good. Now, if you'll just give me a minute to finish here we'll begin. We have much to do.'

Tobias walked farther into the house. It was open plan, just one large room spanning the ground floor with a narrow staircase off to one side. There were all sorts of things spread throughout the house, large, ornate bookshelves crammed with books, crystals and vials. An extensive array of trinkets, weird and wonderful alike caught Tobias' eye, making him smile. He made his way to the large table and sat down to wait for Marcus, stifling a yawn just as Marcus came and sat opposite him.

'Maybe a little too early?' Marcus said with a chuckle.

'Not at all. I did as you said and checked my powers. You were right, I'm losing them, and it's taken me longer to recover than normal.'

Marcus nodded, 'I thought as much. If it's happening to us then it must be happening to everybody. But apart from you, James, and me, nobody seems to have noticed.' He go up from the table and walked over to the range, 'Now, let me get you something to relieve your fatigue.'

'The power must have only been taken in small quantities so that nobody noticed. It would make sense, after all. By the time the majority realise that they are losing power it will be too late to do anything.' Tobias said thoughtfully.

'Indeed, which means that we still have time to act, but I fear without James we have very little to go on, except my past vision. Here, drink this, it will make you feel better,' Marcus said, passing Tobias a cup of something that resembled mud.

Tobias looked down at the cup and then at Marcus who nodded at him.

'My own brew. It's very good stuff. I take a cup every morning as it keeps all manner of ailments at bay. Now, drink up!'

With a slight hesitation, Tobias picked up the cup and drank. Not only did it resemble mud but he was sure that this was what a cup of warm mud would taste like. Placing the cup down on the table, he looked at Marcus.

'Good, isn't it? Would you like the recipe?'

Tobias smiled weakly at him. As much as he never wanted to taste whatever was in the cup again, he didn't want to offend Marcus.

'You mentioned a previous vision,' Tobias remarked, changing the subject, 'What did you see?'

'As hard as I tried, all I could see were the northern mountains and red-robed strangers moving throughout the land.'

'I've heard talk of them at the citadel. People had seen them coming and going through the mountain pass. But from what they were saying, nobody knows anything about them.'

'Maybe, when we perform our casting tonight, we might find out more about them. I feel that they are in some way involved. Now, come, we have much to prepare before tonight, let's begin as we must be ready by dusk.'

The two wizards spent the rest of the day preparing for the casting, stopping only for a light, evening meal. At dusk they made a final check of potions and instruments, beginning the casting as the full moon appeared. Both men knew the night would be long, but if they wanted to find out what had happened to James, they had no choice.

Chapter 18

For four days, Seren had been making slow progress, the deep snow hindering his horse. He had hoped the farther south he went the easier it would be, but so far, the weather hadn't let up. Since leaving Shillington, he'd had an uneasy feeling and made sure his wand was within easy reach at all times, just in case. For the last hour, snow had been falling and it was beginning to get heavy. Seren knew he would have to find shelter and soon, not wanting to be caught outside if the snow continued. Unsure where he was, he pressed on. Cresting a low ridge a few minutes later, he spotted the twinkling of lights in the distance. Sighing with relief, he urged his horse on.

Arriving at the village boundary, he found the gate closed. Dismounting, he landed softly in the snow, which was now almost up to his knees. Leading his horse forward, he knocked on the gate, and heard the sound of bolts being shot back. A moment later, the gate creaked open.

'Who's there?'

'My name is Seren, sir, I've been travelling for several days and wish to find somewhere to rest and take shelter from the snow.'

A man stepped out from behind the gate and looked at Seren. 'Very well, young sir, you may enter. You'll find the inn down the road, opposite the market square, don't get many travellers coming through here, so you should find a room.'

'Thank you, sir,' Seren replied as he led his horse inside the gate.

Hearing the jangle of keys behind him, Seren wondered why they kept a locked and manned gate, most places left theirs open. He pushed the thought to the back of his mind, wanting to find the inn and sleep in a warm bed. The large, timber framed Wood Nymph Inn didn't look much from the outside. Although a little rundown, through the window he could see a roaring fire and plates of hot food being served, which was all Seren needed to see. He led his horse around the side of the building and found an empty stall. After making sure his horse was comfortable and putting some feed in a trough at the back of the stall, Seren collected his bags and walked around to the front of the inn. Stepping inside, he felt the warmth of the fire and smelt the hot food. Smiling contentedly, he walked to the bar, glad to be somewhere warm and dry after four days in the snow. From the other side of the bar, a kindly looking old man approached him.

'Can I help you, young sir?'

'I'd like a room, I've been travelling for days and I'm in need of a rest, also stabling for my horse, the grey in the stall.'

The old man nodded, 'We have plenty of rooms. I'll have one made up for you. You're lucky you arrived when you did, there's a blizzard coming in, so you might be with us for a few days. Now, go and sit down and have something to eat, I'll fetch you when the room is ready.'

Thanking the man, Seren went to find a table. Despite the weather, the inn was busy, but he found a small table near the fire. Settling down for a night at the inn, he ordered his meal and an ale.

***

Tobelle had managed to follow Seren undetected but since it started snowing again, she'd had trouble keeping up with him. The last time she'd caught sight of him, he'd been riding towards a snow-covered ridge, which was where she was now. Checking the ground for hoofprints, she sighed, finding none and fearing she had lost him. With the fresh snowfall, he would be impossible to track. She would have to turn back, but not in this weather. Spotting the lights up ahead, she rode on down to the village, stopping at the closed gate and knocking. She waited until it was opened, a man stepped forward.

'Is there a place in the village where I can stay?' Tobelle enquired.

'My, our little village of Halingshire is getting its number of strangers tonight, you're the second person to arrive seeking shelter. Please come in, you'll find the inn down the road,' the man smiled wearily.

Tobelle nodded at him and rode towards the inn. After stabling her horse, she made her way into the inn, heading straight to the bar and booking a room. At the foot of the stairs, she glanced around the common room of the inn where she spotted Seren sitting near the fire. She hadn't lost him after all. Not wanting to be noticed, she made her way up the stairs to her room. One of the girls who worked at the inn was in the hallway as Tobelle approached.

'It's all ready for you, dear,' the girl said cheerfully.

'Thank you. Can you tell me if anybody else is staying on this floor? I'm tired and don't wish to be disturbed by people coming and going during the night.'

'Just one other person, a lad about your age, but he's down the hall in the last room so he shouldn't bother you,' she said politely. 'Is there anything else I can get for you before I go?'

'A hot meal would be nice, and something warm to drink if it's not too much trouble.'

As the girl nodded and went off to fetch her food, Tobelle walked into the small, but comfortable room. She sat on the bed, pleased to have found Seren after thinking she would have to turn back. Her thoughts turned to how she would pay for her stay at the inn. She had left Shillington with nothing but the clothes she was wearing, a small amount of coin she had in her robes and her wand. There simply hadn't been time to return home to collect more things. There was a knock on the door.

'Come in.'

The girl entered with her meal, setting it down on the table opposite the bed. With a smile at Tobelle, she left the room. Crossing quickly to the table, she found to find a large bowl of steaming hot stew, thick slices of bread and fresh butter, along with a hot malt in a large mug beside it. It didn't take her long to eat the meal, feeling much better as she wiped the last of the thick gravy from the bowl with the bread. Picking up the mug of malt, Tobelle sat back in the chair and relaxed. Thinking about going to bed, she heard footsteps in the corridor. Quietly, she cracked the door open and peered out to see Seren entering his room. She closed the door, happy that she could easily keep her eye on him from there. Having undressed, she climbed into bed, her final thoughts before drifting off to sleep were about her father.

The next morning, Tobelle woke early. As she dressed, she looked out the window to find the snow falling much heavier than the previous night, and realised that she might be staying a while, but then again, Seren would be too. It would be treacherous to try to continue in this weather. She had to be careful as she didn't want to run into Seren, but she needed to find out more. As she sat wondering what to do next, she heard a door closing along the corridor. As she had done last night, she went to the door and watched as Seren walked down the stairs. This was her chance. Taking her wand, she hurried down the corridor. From downstairs, she heard Seren talking to somebody. Checking nobody else was around, Tobelle pointed her wand at the lock and focused on it opening. Nothing happened. Trying the spell again, still nothing. Tobelle knew that some locks wouldn't respond to the spell. Taking her room key from her robe, she tried it but it was too small for the lock. Sighing, she looked at her wand. *Why not?* she thought, and inserted it into the lock, trying to catch the latch.

Finally, she hooked it, lifting it slowly and turning the handle. The door opened. Swiftly, she stepped inside, closing it behind her. She hurried over to the table where Seren's satchel lay and began to look through it. She was disappointed to find only a map and an old journal. Flicking through it, she but found nothing of any use. If he did know anything about her father, it wasn't there. She would have to continue to follow him if she wanted to get to the bottom of this. Getting up to leave the room, she heard footsteps approaching, panicking, as there was nowhere to hide. Drawing her wand, she backed away from the door and waited. She heard a key being placed in the lock, heard it trying to turn but knew it wouldn't. As the door swung open, she held her breath.

'Hold it right there,' Tobelle said quietly. 'Step inside and close the door, you have some explaining to do, Seren.'

Surprised to find her there, Seren did as she asked and moved towards the chair. 'So, you've been following me, I wondered why I felt uneasy. Now I know.'

'Well, you wouldn't tell me what I wanted to know in town that day, so I had no choice but to follow you. So, you'll tell me now, and I mean everything.'

Looking at her and the wand that was pointing at him, he sighed. 'You can lower your wand, I'll tell you what I know, but first you have to believe me. I'm not involved in your father's disappearance.'

Tobelle eyed him for a moment and then lowered her wand.

'I think your father's disappearance is linked with something I found out about, and I might know who's responsible. It started when I found this journal in the bookshop. The entries were written by a retired mage called James. He talks about discovering that his power has decreased. It finishes abruptly, as he was being chased but didn't say who by.'

'I checked that journal and didn't see any such entries,' Tobelle interrupted.

'The journal is protected. Only certain people can read it. I went to see your father because I thought he could help, but he didn't believe me. I was angry with him, but I didn't cause his disappearance. That's partly the reason why I left Shillington. I thought by going to James' house in Hallsrock, I might find out something more.'

'You said you might know who's responsible?'

'Do you know a girl called Laurentis? She lived in Shillington but disappeared last year.'

'I didn't know her, but I heard about her going missing, I was told she was dead.'

'She's not dead, I saw her in town just before your father disappeared. She was acting strange and told me not to tell anyone that I'd seen her, not even her parents. I know it's not definite proof, but I have a feeling she's involved.'

Tobelle considered what Seren had told her. Although, it was sketchy, finally she said, 'Okay, I'll take your word for now, but I'm coming with you.'

'You should go home. I don't know what lies ahead. It could be dangerous.'

'I don't care, Seren, I'm coming with you, and there's nothing you can say or do that will change my mind. I've given you a chance, now give me a chance.'

Seren groaned and thought for a moment, 'Fine, but if you're coming, we have to work together, you have to trust me.'

Tobelle nodded, 'Do you think we'll find him?'

'I don't know what we'll find,' he paused, 'Perhaps when we get to Hallsrock we'll find some answers.' He looked out the window, 'I don't think we'll be on our way anytime soon, it's getting worse out there.'

***

Exhausted, Laurentis fell into bed. She'd spent the past week being tutored by Archimon, and he'd been working her hard. They would work from dawn until well into the night, with little rest to break up the day. Laurentis had made good progress, and with Archimon's help, she had realised the full extent of her powers. Now she had to learn to wield them fully. That night, she slept peacefully and awoke the next morning feeling unusually refreshed. Today, she would rest in preparation for her next lesson. Archimon had told her last night that she would need to gather her strength in order to learn to use her full powers. She stretched out in bed and rolled over, it was nice to be able to lie in, it was a rare luxury. Although it had only been a week, she felt different, and could sense the power coursing through her. The feeling would take some getting used to, but Archimon had assured her, in time, it wouldn't be noticeable. With a great sigh, she heaved herself out of bed and dressed.

Seating herself at the table in the great hall, Laurentis summoned her food with a wave of her hand and began to eat, not bothering to wait for anyone else. Some of the others drifted in looking a little worse for wear, obviously caused by another evening filled with heavy drinking.

Archimon, as was becoming usual, didn't appear, his space at the head of the table remaining empty. After a short while, she finished her food and returned to her room and read for most of the day. As she was leaving Archimon's suite last night, he had given her more books. Some were grimoires written by ancient witches and wizards schooled in dark magic, others were relatively new, written within living memory. Some had been written by Archimon himself. As the winter sun dropped behind the mountain range, Laurentis pushed away the book she had been reading for the last two hours. Lying back on her bed, she contemplated all that was to come. She was nervous about the forthcoming lesson, although she wasn't sure exactly what it would entail, she knew that she would face some difficult trials and a lot of exhausting work. Falling into a light sleep, only to awake in the early hours, she still felt that same nervousness.

A few hours later, as dawn crept over the horizon, tired and apprehensive, Laurentis left her room and made her way to Archimon's suite. Knocking quietly on the door, she waited patiently. Opening the door, Archimon nodded to her as he ushered her inside. As she entered, she noticed a large, dark shape in a side room but couldn't make out the silhouette as it was covered with heavy linen. Seeing her look towards the object, he said nothing, it wasn't time to reveal it to her yet, she wasn't ready. Laurentis made her way into the largest of the rooms and sat on the small couch. From his desk, Archimon took a small item in his hand and placed it on the ornately carved stone podium, just in front of where she sat, and stepped aside. Laurentis looked at it, trying to work out what it was. It was spherical, but not solid, it almost looked like a little round cage, unsure she looked at Archimon.

'That is a hemisphere, it is the smallest example you will find. They are used to contain spells and potions, which is why they are as strong as they are. They must be able to hold the strongest of spells or most potent potions until their release against the intended target. It takes great strength to destroy a hemisphere. Normally, the user will work a destruction spell into it, so that once it has released its contents it will destroy itself. That way, it cannot be traced back. Today, you will try to destroy it. In order to do this, you must focus your power. You may use whatever spell you wish.' Archimon began walking towards the archway, 'I have work to be getting on with. I will return when the hemisphere is destroyed.'

Without another word, he left Laurentis alone with the small hemisphere. Unfortunately, she only knew one basic destruction spell. Thinking back to the books she had read the day before, she knew there were more powerful spells in them but having read so much, it all became somewhat of a blur. Drawing her wand, she pointed it at the hemisphere and tried to focus her mind on destroying her target. A flash of red light flew from her wand and impacted the hemisphere with an explosion of sparks. Laurentis approached the podium and inspected the hemisphere. There was no sign of any damage, it hadn't even moved. Sighing, disheartened, it was as if she hadn't even cast the spell. Backing away from the podium, she tried again.

Unbeknownst to Laurentis, Archimon was observing her from one of the other rooms, using his seeing stone. He smiled at her failed attempt. Placing the stone back into the glass cabinet, he left the suite and made for the great hall where the rest of the brigands were waiting for him. Seating himself at the table he began immediately.

'The time for action is nearing. We are almost ready, but now you must recruit more to our cause. We cannot go north without more willing bodies. You know how to identify those most likely to join us, so go out and find them and do not return empty-handed.'

When Archimon got up from the table and left the hall, the brigands looked at each other and shrugged. Archimon had never mentioned recruiting before, but they went about preparing to leave and carry out their orders, nonetheless.

Laurentis continued trying to destroy the hemisphere for the rest of the day, but to no avail. That night, she fell into bed exhausted and disheartened, doubting she would ever succeed.

Chapter 19

Tobias awoke late the next day. They had finished casting a little before dawn, and whilst they had felt traces of James, they had been unsuccessful in locating him. Desperately worried about his friend, Tobias was disappointed, wanting nothing more than to find him. He felt no closer now than he had done before he met Marcus. Rising from the bed, he dressed and went downstairs to find Marcus in the kitchen.

'Ah, good afternoon, my friend, how are you feeling?'

'Exhausted,' Tobias said, yawning.

Marcus made his way over to a small cauldron bubbling away in the fireplace and removed a cupful of the brew. Returning to the table he placed the cup down in front of Tobias and smiled. Tobias looked down and found the cup filled with the mud-like brew. Silently, he rebuked himself for admitting his tiredness, but as before, he meekly lifted the cup and drank.

'You'll feel better in no time,' Marcus said happily.

Shuddering at the taste, Tobias finished the brew, as Marcus sat down at the table opposite him.

'Well,' Marcus began, 'Whilst we were unsuccessful in locating James, there were faint traces of him to be sensed. This in itself is a good sign, as it tells us that he is still alive, in what condition I can't say, but alive, nonetheless.'

'Can you tie anything from last night with the previous vision you told me about?'

'I fear not, it is possible that there might be a connection. However, from my own experience, I'm inclined to believe if it were related, I would have received the first vision again. I'm sorry Tobias, but I fear we are no further in our search for James than we were last night, I'm unsure where to go from here.'

Both men sat in silence for a short while, contemplating what to do next.

'I think it's time for me to return to the citadel.'

Marcus nodded, 'Alas, there is nothing more that can be done here. I'll continue to cast for James. If I should discover anything, I'll alert you.'

Tobias stood and offered his hand to Marcus who grasped it firmly. They shook, and with a silent nod, Tobias turned to leave. Whilst they had only known one another for a few short days, he trusted the man. Gathering his cloak about him, he approached the door, which opened unaided. Stepping out into the crisp snow, he made his way from the grounds, heading in the direction of the inn.

Back at the inn, he went straight to the front desk, the woman looked up at him, and in her familiar monotone said, 'May I help you, sir?'

'I'd like to settle my bill. I'll be leaving in the morning.'

The woman opened the large, leather bound book and added up silently to herself. 'Twenty-five sovereigns,' she said.

Begrudgingly, Tobias withdrew his coin purse and counted twenty-five sovereigns, a princely sum considering he had spent one night at Marcus' house.

'Leave your card at the desk in the morning,' the woman said.

Tobias nodded and walked away. Making his way upstairs, he entered his room for the last time. The bed gave slightly as he sat down, putting his head in his hands and sighing. He had travelled to Hallsrock to find his friend and was walking away with nothing. He hoped that James might be at the citadel, but in the back of his mind he knew he wouldn't be there when he arrived home. With a final moan, he laid back and fell into a deep sleep.

The next morning, Tobias woke early, wanting to leave as soon as possible. Outside, the snow was still thick on the ground, but none had fallen overnight, so he would be all right to travel. His mount should make it through, but if needs be, he still had the power to cut a path. Packing the last of his things, he checked the room a final time and left. He walked from the inn around to the stable block where his bay was waiting for him. Thanking the stable hand, he passed him a few coins. With a nod, he took the reins from the hand and walked out to the street. The stalls were busy in the market square, despite the snow, although the choice was slim. Once he left Hallsrock, he didn't want to have to stop again until he reached the citadel, so Tobias bought what provisions he could. Stowing his purchases in the saddlebags, he mounted the bay and set off up the north road, pausing at the north gate and looking back.

'Where are you, my friend?' he quietly said to himself. Pulling the hood of his cloak up, he nudged the bay on and headed out into the snow.

***

The snow had trapped Seren and Tobelle in Halingshire for a week and they were growing impatient. After spending time with Seren, Tobelle was beginning to trust him. She believed what he had told her but was eager to be on the road and find her father. Since her mother died, he was all she had. Sitting in the room she was now sharing with Seren, she gazed out the window. The snow had stopped falling but was still thick on the ground. Hearing the door, she turned and smiled as Seren entered.

'I've settled up, we leave tomorrow. I think we've waited long enough.'

'It's still deep.'

'I know, but we can't stay here forever, we have to get to Hallsrock.'

Tobelle hesitated, 'Seren, I want to thank you for helping me out, especially after the way I've treated you. I promise, when we get home, I'll pay back every penny.'

'It's okay, it's only coin, it doesn't matter.'

Tobelle looked away, returning her stare to the window, embarrassed by his kindness after the way she had acted. 'Do you think we'll find anything at Hallsrock?'

'I don't know, but it's the best place to start.'

Tobelle nodded as Seren looked away.

'Come on, we need to stock up on supplies, let's go before the markets close for the day.'

Tobelle picked up her cloak and followed Seren out of the room. It was a short walk to the market, but the snow hampered their progress. The market was quiet, only a few stallholders having braved the weather. Seren and Tobelle picked their way between the cloth and wood stalls, buying what few supplies they could find.

Back at the inn, they sat down at a table near the fire to warm up. Placing their few supplies on the table they looked at each other.

'This won't last us long.'

Tobelle shook her head. One of the serving girls asking if they wanted to order anything interrupted them. Seren ordered two malts and handed over some coins. When the girl returned with the drinks, Tobelle moved their supplies as she placed the mugs down.

'Is that all you got at the market? Not a lot to be going on with,' the girl commented.

'Not a lot of traders were out today, it's the best we could find,' Seren replied, looking down at the meagre pile of food on the table.

'There's always food over at the end of the night, come see me in the kitchen before you leave in the morning and I'll see what I can find for you,' the girl offered kindly.

'Thank you,' Tobelle grinned, 'We will.' The girl left them to their drinks.

As the evening wore on, they ate a light meal and chatted quietly in front of the fire until the clock struck ten and Seren stood.

'Best get to bed if we want to be out early tomorrow.'

Up in the room, Tobelle packed the food into Seren's satchel while Seren hung the blanket up that divided their respective sleeping areas.

'Goodnight, Seren,' Tobelle yawned.

'Night,' Seren replied.

Try as he might, Seren couldn't sleep. Getting to Hallsrock was all he could think about. In a way, he hoped that he could find James, return the journal and go back home, but he knew it wouldn't happen like that. Huffing, he rolled over in a desperate attempt to sleep, but still it eluded him.

All too soon, Seren noticed the dawn light beginning to creep towards Halingshire. Giving up on trying to sleep, he got up to wake Tobelle. Once she was up, he collected his satchel and they left the room. Heading straight down to the kitchen, they found the girl stoking the fire. She glanced at them as they entered.

'Early start? Well, I don't envy you. Now, let's see what I've got.' Making her way into the larder, the girl started taking things from the shelf. Presently, she came back into the kitchen and handed a bag to Seren. 'It's not much, there's a couple of loaves of bread, cheese, some smoked meat and fish. It should keep you going for a few days, at least.'

'Thank you, this will help, let me give you something for it,' Seren said taking out his purse.

'Keep your coin, son.'

Seren paused for a moment before putting the purse away.

'Now, off you go, both of you. No point being up this early if we just stand here chatting.'

With a final thank you, Tobelle and Seren turned and went out the back to the stables where their horses were waiting. Once in the saddle, they gently urged them on, picking their way along the road towards the gate. The gatekeeper watched them as they approached.

'Sure you want to be leaving?'

'We have no choice. We have to get to Hallsrock.' Seren said.

'Snow's still thick, but the going should get easier the farther you travel south.' The gatekeeper advised them as he opened the gate and waved them through. Finally, they were on their way.

Chapter 20

Having spent two days trying to destroy the hemisphere, Laurentis still hadn't succeeded. It was nearing the end of the day, and she was ready to retire for the night. Lowering her wand, the smoke cleared, and she saw once again that the small hemisphere hadn't sustained any damage.

'Why do you taunt me?' Laurentis shouted.

Angry now, more so than she had ever been, she thrust her wand towards the hemisphere, her mind filled with rage, her breathing heavy. She heard a bang. Looking back towards the hemisphere, she saw a crack developing. It spread fast, running around the circumference of the sphere, sounding like breaking glass. To her amazement, the crack spread all the way around, and with a final, shattering sound connected, splitting the hemisphere into two perfect halves. Laurentis was momentarily speechless, having finally succeeded. She sat heavily on the couch and let out a contented breath.

'Congratulations,' Archimon said, stepping out from behind a pillar. 'I knew you would succeed. Through your anger, you managed to tap into all your power and channel it into your spell.'

'So, I have to be angry to use my powers?'

'No. You must simply learn to control your emotions so that they can flow freely at all times. You must believe in yourself, for I am sure that is partly why you were unable to destroy it in previous attempts.'

Laurentis nodded.

'Now, you may finish for the day, tomorrow you should rest. I will send for you when I am ready to begin the next stage of your training.'

Standing, Laurentis left the suite, returning immediately to her room. The fortress was quiet, the others had left yesterday at dawn, although, she wasn't sure why. Entering her room, she closed the door and leant back against it, tired, her whole body aching. Kicking off her boots, she walked over to the glass doors that led onto a small balcony. Opening the doors, she tentatively stepped out, the stone cold against her bare feet, gasping as the wind whipped around her. Although chilly, being out in the fresh air and early evening light was refreshing. She stretched lightly and went back inside, closing the doors tightly behind her before pulling the heavy, velvet drapes. Feeling somewhat better, though ravenous, she made her way to the great hall. Sitting alone at the table, Laurentis summoned her food and ate, returning to her room a short while later. It was early and she wasn't yet ready to sleep. Taking a book from her shelf, she sat in the large armchair in front of the fire and read well into the night. Eventually, tiredness overtook her, and laying the book on the chair, she climbed into bed and fell into a deep, dreamless sleep.

Early the next morning, Archimon ascended the staircase that took him out onto the terrace. The wind whipped furiously around him, but he took no notice. He waited, listening intently. Then he heard it.

'How goes it?'

'My lord, we are making great progress. The wizards have been dealt with and I have given the order to recruit a greater force. I think the time has come to increase the amount of power we are taking from those lesser beings.'

'No, the time is not right, there is still a threat. Turn your attention back to Hallsrock and make sure it is eliminated. I will not tolerate failure, Archimon.'

'Yes, my lord.'

'I do not want to hear from you again until you have dealt with it, now go, there is still much to be done.'

As the voice drifted away on the wind, Archimon was furious. His captain had assured him that they had taken care of the wizard's work. Hurriedly, he descended the staircase and went directly to retrieve his seeing stone. Taking the stone from the cabinet, he placed it on the table and sat in front of it, concentrating intently, touching the stone to awaken it. It flashed a brilliant white.

'Hallsrock,' he said sternly.

Instantly, an image of the town appeared. He set about searching for the perceived threat, determined he wouldn't be undone by this and his plan would succeed.

Chapter 21

Since leaving Halingshire, Seren and Tobelle had been on the road for five days. Even though the snow was melting in places they made slow progress. Cobbled roads were scarce out in the country, so they had followed the cart tracks, a number of which had been churned to thick, cloying mud that sucked at the hooves of their horses. More often than not, they managed only four or five leagues in a day. In places, they had been able to ride alongside the track on the near frozen ground, but as the trees closed in they were forced back into the mud. As they rode, they passed the time quietly chatting. Over the five days, Tobelle had come to see Seren in a different light. Although she didn't say anything to him, she realised he'd had nothing to do with her father's disappearance. He might have his own agenda, but he genuinely seemed to want to help. As dusk began to fall, they rounded a bend in the road and the town of Hallsrock came into view. Halting the horses, they looked at one another and smiled, the prospect of another night spent in the cold had been playing on their minds. With a final, gentle nudge to the horses, they moved off down the road towards the town and hopefully some answers.

***

For many hours, Archimon had been watching the scene within the seeing stone. He had neither eaten nor slept, but still had seen nothing of note. Thinking about the conversation with his lord, Archimon wondered if he had figured out what his real plan was, and this was merely a distraction. Unsure, he kept watching. The town was still, and dusk was quickly approaching. About to put the stone away for the night, he noticed movement at one of the gates. When the scene on the stone re-focused, Archimon watched as two cloaked riders entered the town. There was nothing strange or remarkable about them, except that they had braved the snow to journey to Hallsrock. Settling back into his chair, he decided to watch the two new arrivals for a while longer.

***

There was one other watching over Hallsrock that night. The night after Tobias' departure, Marcus had new visions, this time of two young people coming to town, accompanied by images of his friend, James, and his now ruined house. Whilst the visions made little sense, he kept a vigil at his own seeing stone, awaiting their arrival. This latest vision had a sense of danger attached to it, which disturbed him somewhat. Now, while watching the seeing stone, he was acutely aware of that same feeling once again, as if another darker presence was watching. Marcus sat in front of the stone, resting a cup of the mud-like brew on his knee, tired but determined to stay awake in case they should arrive. His head bobbed as his eyes closed, jolting him awake. Having finished his brew, he was about to get more from the bubbling cauldron when he saw movement at the north gate. Two cloaked figures entered on horseback, their faces hidden by their hoods, but he felt they were the ones he had seen in his vision. Without another thought, he grabbed his travelling cloak and hurried outside to find them.

***

Entering the north gate of Hallsrock, Seren and Tobelle found the streets empty, and the only signs of life were candles illuminating the windows of the timber beamed houses. They made their way down the road, looking for a place to stay. After a short while, they came upon The Slain Dragon, a small inn with a sagging roof and a dark frontage. Not the most inviting of places. Suddenly, the door flew open and a large man fell through it, landing on the road in the slowly thawing snow. Three others followed, brandishing wicked-looking daggers.

'We've told you before, Marlet, not to be coming round here, you ain't welcome. Now get, we don't want to be spending our evening cleaning these 'ere daggers.'

Laughing, the three men walked back inside the inn. The man they had called Marlet picked himself up from the ground and brushed the wet snow away. Looking up, he noticed Seren and Tobelle watching him from their horses.

'What're you two looking at?' he said angrily and walked off up the road in the direction they had just come from.

Tobelle looked at Seren. 'Seren, please, I don't want to stay here, let's find somewhere else.'

Seren nodded and they rode on, turning down the east road until they arrived at the Mage's Wand. Dismounting and handing Tobelle the reins, Seren remarked, 'This looks better. Wait here, while I see if they have any rooms.'

As Seren approached the porch, a man appeared from inside, and after a brief conversation Seren came back.

'They have rooms, but we can't afford to stay here, five sovereigns each a night plus one each for stabling.'

Tobelle sighed as Seren remounted.

'Don't worry, we'll keep looking, there has to be somewhere to stay.'

By the time Marcus arrived at the north gate, there was no sign of the newcomers. He tried to follow the tracks left by the horses, but the snow had turned to slush, leaving little trace of their passage. Walking almost to the crossroads, he heard the sound of hooves coming from the east road and getting nearer. Looking around, he stepped back into a doorway and waited. Moments later, two horses slowly trotted to the middle of the crossroads and stopped. Although he could hear the two riders talking to one another, he couldn't quite make out what they were saying. Wanting to know more about them, he decided to follow them. As the horses moved off towards the west road, Marcus quietly shadowed them at a distance. Hiding in another doorway, he saw them stop outside an inn. When one of the riders dismounted and went inside, he realised they must be looking for a place to stay and crept closer. When he had moved as close as he dare, he stooped beside a small, protruding wall and waited. A short while later, he heard footsteps and then voices.

'Sorry, Tobelle, this one's full. The barkeep told me that the only inn that has vacancies is the expensive one we were at earlier.'

'What are we going to do? We can't stay out here.'

'I don't know. Maybe we could find James' house and stay there.'

Shocked to hear them mention James, Marcus thought back to his vision, *they have to be the ones.* Taking a deep breath, he stood up and stepped out, walking towards them.

'Excuse me, my friends, but I couldn't help overhearing that you're having trouble finding a place to stay.'

They looked around at the approaching man.

'Have you been following us?' Seren asked firmly.

Stopping, he looked at Seren. 'Alas, my boy, I have, but with good intentions. I mean you no harm but I had to be sure you were the ones I saw in my vision. When I heard you mention the name James, I knew it had to be you.'

'Do you know James Berryton? We need to speak to him urgently, it's important,' Tobelle said, the words spilling out quickly and without thinking.

Seren glared at her.

'There will be plenty of time for questions later. Please, come with me, I have rooms you can use, let us hurry and get out of the cold.'

Wary, Seren looked at the man, but they needed somewhere to stay. Nodding to Tobelle, they followed him to his home.

'I don't have any stabling, but it's sheltered around the back, your horses will be all right there.' Taking out his wand, he conjured two horse blankets. 'Here, these will keep them warm,' he said handing them to Seren, who led the horses to the back of the house and began tending them.

'Now, come in, my dear, you must be frozen,' Marcus said, ushering Tobelle into the house.

Stepping inside, it was warm and inviting.

'Please, have a seat and I'll fix you and your friend something to eat.'

'Thank you, sir.'

Marcus smiled and went off to make supper. A short while later, Seren came inside and sat down next to Tobelle.

'Has he said anything?'

'No, just that he would make us some food.'

Seren sat back, although still cautious, it was nice to be warm and dry. It wasn't long before Marcus beckoned them to the table. Seating themselves, he placed a bowl of steaming hot broth in front of each of them and a loaf of crusty bread. As they ate, Marcus spoke.

'My name is Marcus and I'm a seer. Indeed, I do know James, he's a close friend of mine. May I ask why you seek him?'

Between mouthfuls' Seren replied, 'I found something that belongs to him, I wanted to return it.'

Marcus looked at him, 'Something of James', may I see it?' he asked eagerly.

'Well, I'm not sure. I'd rather give it to James himself, it's very important.'

Marcus sighed, 'I'm sorry, my young friend, but that won't be possible. You see, James has disappeared, and try as I might, I can't find him.'

Seren looked first at Tobelle and then back to Marcus. Rising from the table, Seren went to his satchel and retrieved the journal, handing it to Marcus.

'You had better take this then, it might help.'

Turning it over in his hands, Marcus enquired, 'Where did you find this?'

'At the bookshop in Shillington.'

Nodding, Marcus tucked the journal into his robes. 'We'll talk more in the morning. Follow me and I'll show you to your rooms.'

Marcus led them upstairs, and minutes after climbing into bed they had fallen asleep. Settling himself into an armchair in front of the fire, Marcus took out the journal. Opening it to the first page, he began to read.

The next morning, Seren and Tobelle slept late. By the time they went downstairs, Marcus had already been out to the market and was preparing breakfast. He smiled at them as they came down the stairs.

'Good morning. I trust you slept well. Have a seat, breakfast will be ready in just a moment.'

After they had eaten, Marcus cleared everything away and came to sit back at the table.

'I read the journal last night and it troubled me.'

'You could read it too? I thought I must be the only one,' Seren interrupted.

Marcus looked at him for a moment, 'You were able to read all of James' entries? Then this journal was meant to come to you. I'm glad that you're acting upon it.'

'What do you mean, it was meant to come to me?'

'James is a gifted mage and wizard and has placed a charm on the journal so that only certain people can read it. People who could help him, people who would view this in the same way he does. If you were able to read it, it means that you are someone whom James can trust.'

Seren pondered this for a moment. 'I'd like to help but I don't know what to do. That's why we came here.'

'All in good time, dear boy, first there is something that you need to see.'

As they got up to leave, Tobelle asked, 'Marcus, my father, the high wizard, has also disappeared. Seren thinks that it might be connected to what this journal says. Do you think he could be right?'

Marcus considered what she had said. 'It's possible, yes. It's a pity that you didn't arrive a few days ago when Tobias was here. He too was looking for James. You might have even passed him on the road.'

Seren looked up when he heard the name. 'The same Tobias who James talks about in the journal?'

'The very same, he's heading back home to the citadel as we speak.'

Seren could have kicked himself. If only they had left Halingshire earlier, maybe they could have found some answers.

'Come now, let's go,' Marcus said and led them out the door.

Walking through the town, the streets were busy, crowded with people doing their best to avoid slipping on the slushy snow. Picking their way through the crowd, Marcus led them back towards the north gate, then turned and followed a path running along the inside of the wall until they came to a ridge. As they crested the ridge, Seren and Tobelle looked at the destruction before them.

'This is all that remains of James' house. No one knows how it caught fire, all we know is that James is nowhere to be found.'

Seren and Tobelle looked at each other in dismay. They had been hoping to find James, now their chances seemed even bleaker than before.

***

Archimon smirked as he observed the scene unfolding before him. If this was the threat, then it would be easy to extinguish. His plan could go on unhindered. Turning back to the stone, he saw the three figures walking away from the burnt out remains of the wizard's house. He would have his captain deal with these three. But now, it was time to see if Laurentis was ready for the next stage of her training.

Chapter 22

For the third time that night, Seren was out of bed pacing the floor. All that Marcus had told him and the sight of James' ruined house were playing on his mind. Earlier, he had thought about returning home but knew he would feel guilty if he walked away. Sitting on the bed, he put his head in his hands and sighed deeply. Lying back down, he went over everything for what felt like the hundredth time. Seren knew he would have to seek help if he was to go on, he couldn't keep stumbling about from one place to another not knowing what to do. His thoughts turned to Tobelle. Over the short time they had spent together, he had grown to like her but worried for her safety. He knew she'd never agree to go home, as least not until she found her father, but he felt the need to protect her. In the morning, he would ask Marcus to teach him how to defend himself. Pulling the blankets up, he rolled over and tried to fall back to sleep.

The next morning, Seren slept later than he wanted to. Jumping out of bed, he dressed quickly and ran downstairs. Marcus was in the kitchen at the table, but Tobelle was nowhere to be seen.

'Didn't sleep so well last night?' Marcus asked quietly.

Seren shook his head.

'I can understand, yesterday must have been a shock.'

'I thought that once I was here everything would become clear, but I still don't know what to do. I know I should seek out Tobias, but beyond that, I just don't know.'

'Give yourself time, Seren, the answer will come.'

Seren smiled weakly but remained silent for a time. 'Marcus, do you think you could teach me to defend myself?' he asked finally.

'Of course, I'd be happy to, but not just yet. You need to rest. In a few days, I'll teach you.'

Marcus set about making breakfast for Seren, who remained at the table, silent in thought. Looking over at Seren from by the stove, he felt sad that one so young should be burdened by so many troubles. Breaking the silence, he said, 'At the next full moon, we'll hold our festival to welcome the new year and warmer climes that will soon arrive. I would like to invite Tobelle and you to stay with me and attend the festival as my guests.'

Seren looked at Marcus. 'That's a kind offer, Marcus, but we couldn't impose on you for that long, we should leave for the citadel as soon as we can to find Tobias.'

'Dear boy, you wouldn't be imposing, and besides, the snows in the north will still be heavy on the ground. Stay for the festival and leave for the citadel afterwards. You'll be well rested and the journey will be easier.'

'What's this about a festival?' Tobelle asked as she came into the open room.

'I was just telling Seren about the festival that will take place on the next full moon, I would like you both to attend as my guests.'

Tobelle looked at Seren, 'Sounds good, we'd love to stay.'

'We'll stay,' Seren said quietly, nodding in agreement.

***

Sitting alone in the middle of her bed, Laurentis pulled her thick blanket tightly around her, not because of the cold. Her cheeks were stained by tears as she continued to sob quietly. She had been like this since she returned from seeing Archimon. Today, he had presented her with the next stage of her training. Upon entering Archimon's suite, he had instructed her to wait just inside the door. A short time later, he had led her to the usual room, and she sat awaiting his instructions. She hadn't waited long before Archimon levitated what would be her next target into the room, but he hadn't revealed it straight away. Having been instructed to destroy a larger hemisphere, she had done on her first try. Archimon had been pleased and decided that she was ready to move on. With a flick of his wand, the heavy linen covering the target flew across the room. Standing before her, Laurentis was shocked to see the same man she had abducted from Shillington, the high wizard. Archimon then revealed his intentions.

'You have three tasks before you, the first to break into and read his mind, the second to control it, and finally to kill him.'

Archimon had handed her two books, one on telepathy and mind control and another that held no title.

'These will assist you. When you feel you are ready to try, seek me out. Now, I have work to do,' he had said abruptly.

Laurentis had quickly taken up the books and left the suite, returning to her room where she had remained. Wiping her eyes, she pulled the blanket up again and groaned. She didn't know what to do. When she joined the brigands, she knew the sort of things she'd be asked to do but wasn't sure if she could actually kill someone. The thought that she could leave had crossed her mind several times, *but where would I go?* She couldn't go back to Shillington. As much as she wanted to leave, Laurentis knew that Archimon would never allow it and she'd be found and punished.

Peering through the glass doors, it was still light and Laurentis could see far over the mountains. Standing, she crossed from her bed and over to the doors. Pausing for a moment, she gripped the handle and took a deep breath. With a click, the door opened, and she stepped out onto the balcony, the stone cold against her bare feet. Reaching the edge of the balcony, she stopped and gripped the stone wall that enclosed it. Oddly, it didn't feel cold but almost warming, she sighed and looked down at the thick blanket of freshly fallen snow on the ground far below. It was crisp, beautiful and perfect, something she knew she would never be. Gripping the stone tighter, she leaned farther out and could just make out the road in the distance. For a time, she just stared out at the white expanse, as a great feeling of sadness came over her. She wondered what things would be like if she had chosen a different path. A solitary tear traced its way down her cheek, mixing with the earlier stains. It was then that the thought first crossed her mind. Laurentis knew she'd never be able to run, wherever she went he would find her, but in death he couldn't control her. As powerful as he was, he couldn't raise the dead. Her grip tightened further on the stone and her breathing quickened. Though scared, she knew it was the only way she would ever be free. Just one simple move was all it would take, one move to her freedom. However, she hoped in the hereafter her recompense wouldn't prove too severe. Whilst she had done bad things, they weren't as bad as some of the deeds committed by others in this world. Laurentis hoped that she would be permitted to reconcile with her parents when they finally crossed over. No matter what repercussions she would face in the next life, she had made her choice. Holding herself steady, she climbed onto the stone. Letting go of the ledge, she stood straight and looked around. The wind whistled about her for a moment before dropping to nothing. It was almost as if nature were giving her its blessing to re-join the earth itself. Smiling, for the first time in ages, Laurentis felt truly happy, no longer scared but strangely at peace. Taking a last look at the world she had known and loathed at times. she took a deep breath and jumped. Silently, she fell, things seeming to pass her in slow motion. Shapes and colours appeared as she had never seen them before. In the distance, she thought she heard a voice but paid it no mind. Closing her eyes for the last time, the world went black, and suddenly, without pain, everything stopped.

***

Archimon had waited for Laurentis to leave. The shocked expression on her face when he revealed her next task was how he expected her to react. After all, she was still young, and in many ways, still an innocent soul. Normally, he wouldn't have chosen someone like her to join the brigands. The others were undoubtedly dark characters who had all committed terrible deeds, but she had been different, a mere child with great powers. Powers that had been suppressed from a young age. Powers that he had unlocked in her. That was why he had chosen her. He smiled to himself, she would make a worthy wife when the time was right, and he felt that time was drawing near. Upon completion of her next task, they would be bound together and overthrow Him in the north. With their combined powers, no one could stand before them. They would be unstoppable.

Deciding to check on her, he took the seeing stone down from the cabinet. Passing his hand over the stone, the image of Laurentis sitting wrapped up on her bed came into view. She walked from her bed to the balcony, and he saw her pause at the door for a moment. Seeing her clamber onto the stone wall, Archimon was horrified. Without hesitation, he leapt from his chair and ran from his suite. Her room wasn't far away, and he burst through the door as she jumped. Without stopping, he rushed out, drawing his wand as he ran. Halting at the edge of the balcony, he saw her falling. Pointing his wand directly at Laurentis, his spell reacted instantly and caught her. Keeping his wand pointed at her, Laurentis slowly rose back to the balcony, where Archimon grabbed hold of her and pulled her inside. Closing the balcony door tightly behind them, he kept the spell on her and levitated Laurentis from the room.

***

Upon waking, Laurentis found herself in a dark, windowless room. For a moment, she wondered if this was the hereafter, until she heard noises. Deep, rasping coughs, painful groans, and the occasional cry for help. She didn't know how, but she had failed in her attempt at taking her life. She wasn't in the hereafter, she was in a cell, a cell that she knew to be in the deepest reaches of the fortress. Had she not already been on the floor, Laurentis would have collapsed. Putting her head in her hands, she cried, knowing she would never be free now. Unsure how long she'd been in the cell, or how long it had been since she leapt from the balcony, her previous feeling of elation was now gone. Now, she was gripped by a deep fear of what would happen to her. If Archimon intended to kill her for what she had tried to do, she knew it would be in the worst way imaginable. Lying on the cold floor, she fell into a sleep filled with terrible dreams.

The sound of the door opening jolted her awake, holding her hands to her eyes as light filled the room. For a moment, the doorway was clear before the unmistakable shape of Archimon stepped into view.

'My, but haven't you been a silly girl,' he said cruelly.

Stepping inside the cell, he raised his wand at her, making her squeeze her eyes tightly shut as she waited for the impact of the spell. She didn't have to wait long. Archimon's spell hit her and she flew across the room into the hard, stone wall, the impact knocking the wind out of her. Unable to move, she found herself pinned to the wall, completely at his mercy. Trying to speak, no words came from her dry mouth.

'I offered you the chance to join me, but this is how you repay me,' he sneered.

She tried to plead with him but still found herself unable to speak.

'I knew I was taking a chance when I brought you here, but foolishly, I thought under my guidance you would become worthy of me and of your powers. How wrong I was.' Archimon turned away from her. 'All that remains is to deal with you suitably and find someone worthy of this great honour you have shunned.' Turning back, he walked over to her until his face was almost touching hers. 'Now, how do you suppose I should do that?'

Giving her a wicked smile, he turned and left the room, the door slamming shut behind him. As it closed, the spell was broken and Laurentis fell to the floor, landing clumsily on her hands and knees.

Coughing painfully, she called after him, 'Archimon, please wait, I'm sorry, Archimon. ARCHIMON!'

Her pleas went unanswered. As he was walking away from the cell, Archimon heard her crying out, laughing wickedly as he continued without so much as a backward glance. *I am going to enjoy this*, he thought to himself.

Chapter 23

The next morning, Seren sat up in bed, yawning and stretching. He had rested for a few days but today, he would ask Marcus again about teaching him to defend himself. Since discovering the journal, it had been the first opportunity he'd had to relax. As Tobelle practiced her conjuring, he had laughed with her when the things she tried occasionally went wrong. Her accusing him of abducting her father was all but forgotten by both. When she was young her mother had died, and now all she had was her father, making Seren feel sad for her. Behind her smile, he knew she was desperately worried about her father and must be wondering if she'd ever see him again. Seren's thoughts turned to his parents, who must be fretting about him too, especially after the way he left. But he knew he could never have explained it to them face to face. If he made it back home, he promised himself that he would make it up to them, even if it meant harvesting the tugweed for the rest of his life. With a sigh, he threw back the blanket and got out of bed. After washing and dressing, he made his way downstairs where Marcus was already up and tending to their breakfast.

'Good morning.' Seren said as he sat at the table.

Marcus smiled and returned the greeting as he bustled about the kitchen. Although wary at first, Seren had warmed to him. He had done a lot to help them both since they arrived and would accept no offer of assistance with the household chores or any coin. Seren had contemplated asking Marcus to accompany them when they left, but he wasn't sure what his reaction would be. He was settled there, and no doubt could have gone with Tobias if he'd wanted to. His thoughts were interrupted as Marcus set breakfast on the table just as Tobelle appeared from upstairs and joined them.

'Morning,' she said cheerfully, they both returned her greeting.

Not wanting to embarrass Marcus, Seren decided to wait and speak to him later in the day, and so tucked into breakfast. Marcus broke the silence.

'Tobelle, I wonder if I might ask you to run an errand for me today? I don't require much, just need some things for the festival. While you're out, why not treat yourself to something as well.'

Tobelle looked at him, 'Certainly, Marcus, but I must confess I have no coin.'

'Oh, pardon me, my dear, I didn't mean for you to pay for anything,' he said, taking a purse from his belt and placing it on the table. 'Here's a list of the things I want.' Holding his hand out, a small piece of parchment flashed into it, which he then placed alongside the purse, 'And don't forget, please treat yourself to something, anything you like.'

Tobelle nodded, looking a little embarrassed, 'Thank you, Marcus.'

Having finished breakfast, Tobelle left the table, picked up the list and purse and went to retrieve her cloak. Seren was about to get up to help her when Marcus placed his hand on his shoulder, gesturing for him to wait. Helping

Tobelle put on her heavy, travelling cloak, Marcus held the door open, telling her to take as long as she wanted. After she had left, Marcus returned to the table and sat down.

'I didn't think you'd want her to know about your lessons.'

Seren nodded and flushed a little. 'She was a student at the academy before we came here, and knows much more than I do. I didn't get accepted and learning from books just isn't the same as being taught by someone with experience.'

'Don't be embarrassed, my boy, I know many a wizard who wasn't able to attend an academy and turned out just as well as any other. I'll teach you what I can, Tobelle needn't know if you don't wish her to.'

'Thank you,' is all Seren could bring himself to say. The familiar feeling of rejection returned for a moment.

'Well, now,' Marcus said, 'Let's begin.'

***

After an uncomfortable night's rest, Laurentis was cold and ached all over. Archimon hadn't returned and that worried her as she didn't know what his intentions were. She wouldn't put it past him to just leave her in the cell to slowly starve. Being in a cell so deep within the fortress, she had no concept of time and wondered how long it had been since Archimon had been to see her. She pushed herself up, wincing as her muscles cramped with the sudden exertion. In the gloom, Laurentis slowly felt her way around the cell. After a few steps, she found the wall and a small, protruding ledge. It wouldn't be comfortable, but there should be just enough room for her to curl up. Continuing around the room, she trod on something soft. Reaching down, she ran her hands over it. Picking up the heavy fabric, she examined it as best she could without any light. It felt familiar. Pulling it closer, she noted the weight and something metallic attached to it. In the darkness, she smiled when she realised it was her travelling cloak. Wrapping it around her shoulders, she fastened it and drew it tightly about her. Only Archimon could have placed it in the cell. A glint of hope flickered in her mind. If he had left it for her, then surely, she would be released soon, he was just trying to teach her a lesson. Holding the cloak tightly, she made her way over to the corner of the cell and sat down, her back against the wall. She pulled the hood up and tucked her hands into the sleeves. It was the first time she had felt remotely warm since she had been put in there. Closing her eyes, she quickly fell asleep.

***

Seated at his desk, Archimon studied the stone, his eyes narrowing when he saw Laurentis put on the cloak. He had placed it in the cell to give her a false sense of security. It appeared that it had done just that. He knew if he let her out, she would be obedient. But if she were to be any use to him now, he would have to darken her soul, and to do that, he would have to break her. He watched her sleeping for a few moments, and then, with a wave of his hand, the image on the stone disappeared. Getting up from his chair, he replaced the stone. Making his way from the suite, he descended the levels of the fortress until he came to the first subterranean level. Taking his wand from his robe, he inserted it into the lock, which opened with a click. No one else could enter the room that spanned the entire level. Crossing the threshold, he closed the heavy door tightly behind him and began walking through the room. It was dimly lit with torches regularly spaced along the wall. This room had one purpose—to house Archimon's menagerie of creatures—some of which he had caught, others he had created through experimentation. Slowly, he perused the lines of cages that filled the room. He stopped at several of them but moved on until he came to one particular set of cages. A wicked smile crossed his lips. These creatures had been one of his first creations, but he was still proud of his scorpiods. They were strange looking creatures about the size of a large cat, with a large left pincer and a bone hook in place of the right pincer, as well as a potent stinger on the tail. Two-inch-long, jet-black fangs protruded from their small jaws. Their mottled brown carapace reflected the dim torchlight. When they saw Archimon approaching, they retreated, cowering into the corners.

'Fear not, my creatures, today I have a task for you.'

Taking his wand out again, Archimon tapped each of the three cages and they disappeared. With a final look to make sure he had picked the right creatures, he swept around and walked from the room. Locking the door behind him, he descended a further three flights of stairs until he reached the cells. Navigating the narrow corridors in the dim light of the torches, he finally arrived outside Laurentis' cell. The cages were stacked outside the door. He stood for a moment and listened, the cell was silent, she must still be asleep. Quietly, he opened the door and looked in, seeing she was indeed still asleep. Stepping back, he held out his hands. Raising them gently, the cages lifted from the ground. He directed them inside and placed them around the cell. When all three were placed, Archimon waved his hand over the cages. At the same time, he held his other hand over the sleeping Laurentis. Closing his eyes, he focused on her mind, which although she was sleeping was as active as ever. Once he had a hold over her, he focused on the scorpiods. In turn, he attuned each of them to her so they too fell asleep. Once they were all sleeping, he drew his wand, pointing it at the cages. Each of the locks clicked open and the doors fell ajar. Archimon smiled to himself, when Laurentis awoke, the scorpiods would too, and then her torture would begin. He liked the girl in his own way but would make her sorry for what she had done. One way or another, she would break.

As he walked back along the corridor towards the staircase, the torches flickered and went out, plunging the cells back into darkness. Hurriedly ascending the stairs, he returned directly to his suite. He was about to retrieve the seeing stone when he felt His presence. Archimon stopped and waited, clearing his mind so that He would not discover his plans.

'Have you eliminated the threat?' He asked coldly.

'My lord, forgive me, I have identified it and intend to despatch my captain when he returns from his current assignment.'

'This is not good enough, Archimon. I chose you as I thought you could complete the task, I am beginning to wonder if I was wrong. I do not like being wrong, Archimon. This is your last chance. Deal with this threat and go on with your work, or I will be forced to deal with you.'

'Yes, my lord, I will not fail you,' Archimon said, bowing his head slightly.

'See that you don't, you have only until I contact you again.'

Archimon kept his head bowed until he felt the presence disappear. Sitting back on the couch, he thought, *this situation is not ideal.* The brigands were still away recruiting, and he was busy with Laurentis, something that he had to keep hidden from Him if his own plan was to succeed. He looked towards the fire, where the cauldron sat in its usual place in the hearth. Without a second thought, he stood and went to his personal ingredients store. Taking various jars and vials from the shelves, he set them down on a low table close to the hearth. Taking a mortar and pestle down from the mantel, he added spider eyes, foxglove, stargraze, mistletoe and mandrake root and began to grind them. When they were suitably crushed, he added vilanza and elmany and mixed them until they formed a thick, green paste. Taking the mixture, he dropped it into the bubbling cauldron and stirred it gently. After a short while, the potion turned a deeper shade of green, Archimon took up a vial containing the last ingredient to be added to the potion—dragon's blood. Holding it up to the light, he admired the deep red colour. This vial of blood was extremely potent. Normally, the blood was extracted from dragons kept for just that purpose, but this vial and most of the others he possessed had been taken from wild dragons, which gave it its extra potency. Archimon smiled, it had been his test for those who had joined him first. Those who had brought him a vial had been admitted to the brigands, the others had fallen prey to the dragons. He looked at the vial again, it was the one that Laurentis had brought him. This vial had a special purpose, so he took it back to the store and selected another from the shelf. Returning to the hearth, he uncorked the vial and tipped half into the cauldron. Stirring the mixture again, he watched as the colour gradually changed to a very pale blue.

Taking the cauldron from the hearth, he set it down to let the potion cool. He had to think. He needed more brigands if his plan was to succeed, but the newcomers to Hallsrock had to be dealt with, and soon. Crossing the room, he entered his study and retrieved the seeing stone, returning with it to the main room. Placing it on the table, he passed his hand over the stone, it flashed, and a scene appeared. As Laurentis was still asleep, he still had time. Leaving the scene on the stone, he walked over to the cauldron and checked the potion, finding it was still hot. It would have to do, he couldn't linger. Scooping some of the potion into a chalice, he set it on the table and sat in front of it. For a short while, he sat still, eyes shut and breathing calmly. He had to clear his mind in order to establish a strong link. Opening his eyes, he exhaled slowly, now he was ready. Taking a deep breath, he dipped two fingers into the hot potion. Fighting the urge to recoil from the heat, he dabbed the potion onto his temples. With another deep breath, he repeated the process, finally drawing a line with the potion across his brow, joining the dabs on his temples. Closing his eyes, he felt the potion searing his skin. Pushing the pain from his mind, he focused. After a few moments, he felt the jolt that indicated the connection had been made.

'Captain, do you hear me?' he said firmly. After a few moments, the reply entered his mind.

'I hear you, my lord.'

'Report.'

'We have found more willing bodies than we anticipated, our ranks will double if not triple in number.'

'Good. I have another task for you. You are to send a small group to Hallsrock. There is a trio still searching for the wizard. Deal with them, and...' Archimon paused, 'Captain, do not fail me.'

'Yes, my lord, it will be done, how will I know the marks?'

'You are looking for a young male, a female, and a seer.'

'Yes, my lord.'

Archimon opened his eyes, breaking the link. Immediately, he went to the washbowl and washed the potion from his forehead. Taking a cloth, he soaked it in the cold water and held it to his head for a short while. Even he wasn't immune to pain. Replacing the cloth, he went back to the stone. Laurentis was still asleep but appeared to be stirring slightly. Still rubbing his temples, he sat back and continued to watch. After a few minutes, Laurentis awoke. Placing his hand on the stone, he enhanced the scene, the darkness of the cell making the image murky.

Stirring once more, Laurentis opened her eyes, sat up stiffly and yawned, it hadn't been a restful sleep. In the silence of the gloomy cell, she thought she heard something clicking. Initially, she paid it no mind and stood, trying to stretch her aching muscles, but the clicking grew louder and more frequent. Stopping, she stood still. It was coming from inside the cell. Slowly, she walked forward, trying to work out what the noise was. Her leg bumped into something solid, something that hadn't been there earlier. Feeling about blindly in the dark, she leant down and touched the object. It was cold to the touch. When a loud hiss emitted from it, she recoiled quickly, realising that it was a cage, and not an empty one. Another hiss came from her left, followed by another off to her right. Gasping, she took a step back, half stumbling. Laurentis stood perfectly still, not daring to breathe. A sharp squeak pierced the silence, followed by a dull thud. She realised that the sound was that of a rusty hinge, meaning that whatever was in the cage had just let itself out and was loose in the cell. There were another two thuds as more doors opened.

The clicking and hissing started again and began to draw nearer. Stepping back until reaching the wall, she could go no farther. Edging around the wall, she tried to find the ledge. But the creatures seemed to follow her. Creeping slowly, trying not to provoke them, she finally found the ledge. Gradually, she turned to face it, and placing her hands firmly on the stone, jumped, forcing herself up onto the ledge. For a second, she thought she was safe, then she felt it. She hadn't pulled her leg up quickly enough, and one of the creatures stung her in the calf. She cried out as the wave of pain hit her. In a vain attempt to halt the course of the venom, she clutched her left leg. Tears streamed down her cheeks and she was having trouble catching her breath, wanting the pain to stop. All the while, the creatures had gathered beneath the ledge, waiting for her to come down. Laurentis was scared, about as scared as she had ever been. Leaning back against the wall, she tried to block out the pain, thinking of happier times, times when she had been free from both worry and responsibility. Eventually, the pain took its toll and she fell unconscious, still on the ledge. Moments after Laurentis passed out, the scorpiods went silent, lay down, and slept, being still attuned to her.

Archimon sat back and smiled, this was but the first stage, he would make Laurentis regret her actions. Leaving his suite, he made his way down to the cell and quietly entered. Placing the scorpiods back into their cages, he waved his wand and they disappeared. Carefully, he lifted Laurentis' leg, checking the wound. The sting had penetrated deeply into the muscle, it would be painful for a great many days but wouldn't prove fatal, the scar, however, would be everlasting. Leaving the cell, he made his way back up to his suite, where he would rest a little before he started with her again. It had been a trying day in many ways, and suddenly, he found himself exhausted.

Chapter 24

Despite the previous day's events, Archimon had slept peacefully and risen early to make ready for the next stage of Laurentis' punishment. After being stung by the scorpiod, he knew she would be on edge and had decided to play on this with illusions. Initially, he would use the high wizard and her parents, if needed, he would introduce other characters from her past as well as himself. It would be easy enough to create visions as she was within his grasp, and he could simply use the smoke of illusion. Making his way into his store, he returned to the hearth with an armful of ingredients. He filled a medium-sized cauldron with elmany, the deep red blood from the elmany beetle and menza, a green liquid distilled from the leaves of the plant. Placing the cauldron into the hearth, he lit a fire and left the liquid to boil. Whilst waiting, he ate a light breakfast, which he conjured with a simple wave of his hand. Having finished his food, he returned to the cauldron. The pungent smell of the liquid indicated it was boiling. Standing over the cauldron, he added dried mistletoe, zareeba, mandrake root, spider eyes, and stirred the contents vigorously. Gradually, the liquid thickened and turned a muddy, grey colour. When it was thick enough, he added the final two ingredients—foxglove and harpentia. A puff of grey smoke rose from the cauldron announcing the brew was ready. Taking the cauldron from the fire, he set it down alongside his desk. Now, he had to embed the brew with the illusions he wanted to create. Using his wand, he conjured images of the high wizard and Laurentis' parents, directing them into the cauldron where they were swallowed by the thick liquid. Closing his eyes, he levitated the cauldron and clapped his hands, making it disappear.

The cauldron reappeared outside the cell where it began to smoke lightly. The smoke crept under the door and began to accumulate, resembling a light mist, unnoticeable in the darkness. When Laurentis regained consciousness, following the previous day's ordeal, the illusions would be waiting for her. This time, Archimon decided not to watch, he wouldn't be able to see the illusions, as only the person who they were intended for could see them.

Laurentis opened her eyes, wondering if it had all been a terrible dream. The creatures, the unending darkness and the pain. She remembered the pain the most, it had been the worst she had ever felt. Rubbing her eyes, she sat up, still on the ledge. She pushed herself off and landed on her feet, collapsing to the floor as searing pain shot through her left leg. She screamed. Reaching down her leg, she felt her calf until she came to the large puncture wound. It hadn't been a dream. Laurentis was shaking, the wound was large, felt hot, and it hurt to touch it. She leant back against the wall and began to cry. She couldn't understand why Archimon would do this to her. She understood his anger at her attempt to take her life, but why put her through this, she was sorry. As she leant against the wall, she didn't notice the thin layer of smoke creeping under the door, nor did she notice the faint mist that was beginning to cover the floor. If Laurentis had seen the mist, she would have witnessed it beginning to take the shape of the high wizard. The mist gathered and rose, undulating and swirling until the fully formed figure of the high wizard loomed tall in the cell. Laurentis still hadn't noticed. The figure moved forward, the mist cloaking the region where the legs would have been, making him appear to float.

'Laurentis, why did you bring me here?' the figure said calmly.

Looking up, at first, Laurentis saw nothing. 'Who's there?' she said, her voice shaky.

The figure moved closer, now she could see him.

'You. It's not possible, Archimon has you captive.'

'Why did you bring me here?' the figure asked again.

Laurentis didn't know what to say, she just looked at the high wizard, aghast. Had he escaped, if so, how could he have overpowered Archimon in his weakened state?

'Laurentis, why did you bring me here? Answer me girl,' the figure said sharply.

'I, I had no choice, I had to bring you here, I was ordered to.'

'You knew what he would do and yet you still brought me here.'

'I didn't know. He ordered me to bring you here. If I had known...'

'If you had known you would still have done it.'

'No.'

'Yes, there's no way out for you now.'

'No, please no,' Laurentis said quietly, crying.

'You're an evil child, Laurentis, rotten to the core, you deserve this.'

Laurentis didn't reply.

'One way or another, everyone will know what you've done. The penalty will be the highest we can lay against you.'

'Please, it's not too late.'

'It was already too late when you took me from my home.'

Laurentis couldn't look at the high wizard, she knew he was right and now there was nothing she could do.

The figure stepped back, 'You know what you are, Laurentis,' he said before disappearing.

Laurentis didn't see him go. The mist circulated for a moment, and then began to form again. This time, it took the form of two figures. They were a middle-aged couple but looked much older. Now, Laurentis would have to face her parents. They stepped forward. Laurentis was still crying, and so, once again, didn't see them approach.

'Why did you leave us, Laurentis?' one of the figures asked.

Glancing up, Laurentis saw her parents standing over her.

'You just left without a word, we thought you were dead.'

'I had to leave.'

'We searched for months, we sacrificed everything to find you, and now we find that this is what you have become.'

'What do you mean?' Laurentis asked tearfully.

'We tried to bring you up well, give you a good education, all the chances we didn't have, and you turned your back on us and everything we gave you.'

Laurentis looked at them. 'Why are you here? Why did you come? To torture me like the high wizard?'

'You don't deserve your family, Laurentis, you're evil. The teachers warned us, but we thought you could be saved. We were wrong.'

Her parents' words hurt her.

'Hence forth, Laurentis, you're not our daughter. You've done nothing but hurt or disappoint us. Don't return to Shillington. You aren't welcome in our home any longer.'

Laurentis watched as her parents turned and walked into the mist, slowly dissipating. Sinking back against the wall, she put her head in her hands and sobbed loudly. They had all said she was evil, and her parents had disowned her. Now, she was completely alone. Lying down on the cold, stone floor, the mist swirled and then enveloped her. Closing her eyes, she fell asleep and dreamt of all those who had hurt her in her past. The mist caught hold of those dreams and dragged the images back into the cauldron. Those images would create further illusions to break her down, but they wouldn't be used just yet.

In his suite, Archimon clapped his hands and the cauldron appeared once more. Sitting over it, he circled it with his wand, the smoke clearing, revealing the change in colour of the brew that had captured her dreams. He smiled. It hadn't taken as long as he thought it would. He would let her sleep for a short while before continuing.

In the early hours of the morning, Archimon awoke from a light sleep and made his way into his potion store. The shelves were packed full of vials and jars containing a plethora of potions. Many of them were his own concoctions, and it was one of these he wanted now. Tucked away on the top shelf, he found what he was looking for. He took a small vial containing a pearlescent blue liquid and tucked it into his robes. Leaving the suite, he made his way down to the cells. Silently, he opened the door and entered. Laurentis was curled up against the wall still sleeping. Taking the vial from his robes, he removed the stopper and threw the contents onto the floor. Exiting the cell, he closed the door tightly behind him. As soon as it was shut, the potion took effect. A thin sheen of blue liquid began to spread across the floor, filling every corner of the cell before beginning to rise. Eventually, if left for long enough, it would fill the cell. He had used it in this way on many occasions, and now it was time for Laurentis to experience its power. He knew it would take around two hours to fill the cell and so he left. He would return a little before the cell filled to stop the potion. After all, he wanted to break her, not kill her... yet.

Inside the cell, Laurentis slumbered as the liquid steadily began to rise. After a short time, Laurentis roused, shivering and wiping her face, her clothes feeling damp. Standing stiffly, she was surprised to find the floor covered with water.

'It's not enough to keep me locked up in here, now the place is leaking,' she said to herself, angrily.

What she couldn't see, however, was that the "water" was rising. She scrambled up on to the ledge. *It is cold enough in the cell, I don't need to be made colder by leaking water*, she thought. Thankfully, her cloak was on the ledge, so, she wrapped it around her and leant back against the wall, trying to go back to sleep. It didn't take long. Her ordeal the previous night had exhausted her. She lay down on the ledge, trying to make herself more comfortable, her arm slipping and hanging limply over the edge. All the while, the liquid inside the cell continued to rise.

After an hour, the liquid was already just beginning to creep over Laurentis' fingers. She roused but remained asleep. The level of the liquid continued to advance and soon was nearly up to her elbow. With a start, she awoke, pulling her arm from the liquid, gasping as she realised that it had risen. Leaning down, she felt to check just how high it really was. When she found it was just below the ledge, she began to panic.

'ARCHIMON,' she shouted, 'Help me, the cell is filling with water, please help me, Archimon.' Laurentis' voice faltered.

Jumping off the ledge, the icy-cold liquid took her breath away. Forcing her way across the cell, the cloak swirled behind her, hindering her progress. She tried to untie it but it caught under her foot and she slipped under the liquid. The cloak enveloped her, making it difficult to get a purchase on the floor. Fighting with the knot, she desperately tried to free herself from the cloak before she ran out of air. Her lungs were burning, and she was petrified. Just as she thought her lungs would burst, she finally felt the knot give. And with a final tug, the cloak came free. Laurentis burst up through the surface, gasping for air. Her whole body ached, and she was tired. Forcing herself to continue, she reached the door and began pounding on the wood.

'Archimon, please, please help me, the water is rising fast,' she cried.

Unbeknown to Laurentis, Archimon had returned and was standing just on the other side of the door, listening to her anguished cries but doing nothing. He knew the liquid would have reached no higher than chest height by this time. He continued to listen.

Inside the cell, Laurentis felt the last of her strength ebbing away. Pounding on the door had done nothing, she sighed, nobody was coming. Desperately, she turned, deciding to try to get back to the ledge, forcing her way through the liquid. Halfway across the cell, she slipped and once again fell beneath the surface. However, with no cloak to pull her down, this time she soon broke the surface and continued struggling on. With her last ounce of strength, she reached the ledge and managed to pull herself up. The liquid was just lapping at the top of the ledge, it wouldn't be long before it crested. Pulling her knees up to her chest, she hugged them, wondering if this was the end, if Archimon had had enough and would leave her to drown. Her thoughts turned to her parents, the high wizard and the things they had said. She rested her head on her knees, *they were right*, she thought, *I am evil, I have always been evil.* Strangely, she felt calm, as calm as she had felt that day on the balcony, having accepted what she thought was to be her fate. All she could do now was wait for the liquid to claim her, there was no way to fight this.

After a short while, the liquid crested the ledge and lapped at her ankles. It wouldn't be long now. Outside the cell, Archimon was still waiting, not wanting to halt the potion too soon, it could only be used once against a person. It wouldn't have the same effect on the victim as it did the first time.

As the liquid rose above Laurentis' knees, she sat straight against the wall. Still calm, she closed her eyes and waited for it to take her. As she felt it lapping around her shoulders, she thought she heard a noise. Opening her eyes, she watched as the door opened. The light from the corridor blinded her and she raised her hand to her face to shield her eyes. She was amazed to see that the liquid stayed within the cell. Archimon stood just beyond the doorway. Taking the vial from his robes, he reached into the liquid and refilled it. As he stoppered the vial, the liquid inside the cell began to fall. It fell quickly, until moments after Archimon had opened the door nothing remained, the floor and walls weren't even wet. Laurentis stared at Archimon who stared straight back at her. The silence seemed to span the ages. Finally, Laurentis spoke.

'Please, Archimon, I'm truly sorry, please free me from this cell, I have learnt my lesson.'

Archimon regarded her for a moment, 'No, my dear,' he said coldly, 'You have not. I'm not finished with you by a long way, you will see things my way or no way at all.'

He closed the door and the cell fell into darkness once more. The feeling of calm had left her, and once again she felt scared, she knew Archimon was capable of dreadful things and now her mind began to swim as she wondered what he might do next.

***

Following her ordeal with Archimon's potion, Laurentis had tried to sleep to recover her strength but had been unable to do so. She was soaked through, very cold, and had spent several hours shivering on the ledge. When the door opened, she lifted her head slightly. Archimon had returned. Laurentis pushed herself up so that she was sitting, as tired as she was and as much as she ached, she wanted to face him, to look him in the eye. He walked into the cell, leaving the door open. Stopping in the centre of the cell, he drew his wand from inside his robes, making her flinch. He smiled wickedly but didn't turn it on her. Instead, pointing it at the floor, he conjured two chairs and a small table. With a wave of his hand, the table filled with food. Laurentis tried not to show any emotion but she was ravenous and relieved to see he had finally brought her something. It felt like an age since she had eaten. Archimon seated himself in the more luxurious of the two chairs and gestured for her to sit opposite him. She lowered herself from the ledge, wincing as the now all too familiar pain shot through her left leg. Pausing for a moment, she composed herself and ambled to the table and sat awkwardly on the chair opposite Archimon.

'Please eat,' he said softly but in his usual, cold manner.

Hesitant at first, she took a piece of bread but after the first two bites she could contain herself no longer. She wolfed down as much as she could, not knowing how long Archimon would allow her to eat. Archimon sat in silence watching her. Laurentis finished everything on the table, then picking up a jug, poured herself some adaman juice. She drank the thick, red juice down in one and poured another mug full, which again she drank in one. Sitting back in the chair, feeling a little better, she looked at Archimon who up until now had said nothing.

'I'm glad to see you still have your appetite.'

Laurentis nodded and began to relax. She hoped that this signalled the end of her torment. Archimon regarded her for a moment longer, then spoke.

'You are sorry for what you have done?'

'Yes, sir, truly sorry,' she replied.

'And you understand why I have done this?'

'Yes, I deserved to be punished for what I did.'

Archimon smiled, 'Good, then you will understand why I have to do this.'

Archimon raised his wand, Laurentis could only stare, eyes wide, having thought it was over. The spell hit Laurentis with a force she had never known before. She flew back across the cell hitting the wall hard before crumpling to the floor. Then she felt an intense heat that began to envelop her entire body. She felt as if she were being burnt alive, and yet there were no flames. She emitted a bone-chilling scream, Archimon who still sat in the chair, laughed cruelly as he watched her writhing on the floor. The spell was truly terrible, it had been known to turn its victims mad in some cases, which could happen to Laurentis if she wasn't strong enough.

Archimon remained in the cell for a further three hours, never once undoing the spell. Laurentis had screamed herself hoarse and now the only noise was her rasping breath. Archimon stood from the chair and lazily flicked his wand over the still writhing Laurentis. The spell reversed instantly, the pain disappeared, and Laurentis became still. He looked down at her emotionlessly.

'Do not doubt, girl, you will travel to the very depths of despair before I am finished with you. By that time, you will either have turned fully to who you should be, or you will die. There are others in this world who possess your level of power. Don't think that you are irreplaceable.'

With a final sneer, he left the cell, the door slamming behind him. As it closed, the furniture that he had conjured disappeared. Laurentis could only watch. Whilst the pain from the spell had gone, the exertion of the last few hours had left her physically exhausted. Every inch of her body ached. She closed her eyes, her last thought before she fell asleep was that she would live through this.

***

For a further two weeks, Archimon continued to torture Laurentis. Of all the methods he had used in the first few days he used the smoke of illusion most frequently. Every night, the cauldron would appear outside the cell, and Laurentis would be confronted by visions from her past. When she could take no more, she would fall into an exhausted sleep and the mist would capture more of her dreams, ready to torment her the next night. While the various methods that Archimon used against her weakened her physically, inside, her mind grew stronger and darker with each passing hour. On what was to become the final day of her imprisonment, Archimon entered the cell to find her sitting in the centre of the floor. She didn't look up at him. Without a word, he raised his wand at her. Still she didn't look up. The spell hit Laurentis and she flew back against the wall. The now familiar burning began inside her, but she forced herself up onto her knees, and looking straight at Archimon. she cried, 'No.'

Archimon laughed at her vain attempt to break the spell, but then, to his astonishment, she stood and walked towards him. She was different, her eyes had grown dark and her hair had turned jet-black. He felt his spell dissipate—she had thrown it off.

'It's over, Archimon, you will torture me no longer.'

'Then it has worked, you finally see things as I do.'

Laurentis considered him for a moment, 'It would appear so,' she said calmly.

'Then there is no reason to detain you any longer, you are free to return to your quarters. I will send for you when I am ready to resume your training.'

Laurentis inclined her head and left the cell. Falling into her own bed, she fell asleep almost instantly. Things would be very different now.

Chapter 25

The day of the festival had finally arrived. As the sun crept over the town's walls, there was already a buzz of activity in the square, with people setting up stalls and stages and various other attractions. Seren, Tobelle, and Marcus were up early cooking and baking, as were many others throughout town. Everyone contributed to the festival, and so in return for his hospitality, Seren and Tobelle had offered to help Marcus with preparing his contributions. It took most of the morning to cook, but when they had finished, the table was laden with cakes and biscuits, as well as two large pots filled with beef and mutton stew, a game pie, and several large loaves of bread. Packing their supplies into baskets, they left the house fully loaded and headed towards the square. Making their way through the gathering crowd, they arrived at the banqueting table and laid out the food. The table soon began to fill as other people added their own offerings.

The bell in the tower chimed three times signalling the beginning of the festival. The long table set up in the square was overflowing with food. Cold meats and cheese, cakes and biscuits, sweet and savoury suet puddings, pies, and breads of all shapes and sizes, bowls of fruit and vegetables, honeyed nuts and berries, stews, casseroles, and pot roasts were just some of the delights on offer. People began seating themselves along either side of the long table. At the head of the table a man stood, everyone seated fell silent as he began to speak.

'Welcome, friends, today is the day of the new year festival. So, let us celebrate the start of a new year and welcome the warmer climes that are returning to our land. Now, please eat, drink and enjoy the festivities.'

A cheer arose from everyone around the table, and people began to help themselves to the food.

'Marcus, who was the man giving the speech?' Seren asked.

'That, dear boy, was Hector Longthorn, the longest serving wizard of the triumvirate.'

Seren nodded and served himself a large helping of game pie.

After everyone had eaten their fill, some migrated to the outside bar, which one of the taverns had set up, others browsed the stalls, whilst some just chatted with old friends. As dusk fell, people began to gather in anticipation of the bonfire. As it grew a little darker, the appointed torch bearer approached the pyre. A great cheer went up from the crowd as he touched the torch to the pyre and it erupted into flames, more cheers followed as the music began. People gathered around the fire, dancing and singing until the early hours of the morning.

Seren and Tobelle left a little after midnight, as they intended to leave for the citadel in the morning. They said goodnight to Marcus and returned to the house. Climbing into bed, Seren tried to sleep, he tossed and turned but to no avail. He couldn't shake the uneasy feeling that had been with him for the last few days. He lay back staring at the ceiling. It would be easy to stay there and just forget everything, but he knew he couldn't. No one with any authority believed him, and so if he did nothing then no one would. He rolled over again and closed his eyes, thinking of Tobelle and wishing she would stay there or return to Shillington where she would be safe, but she was stubborn. Although, if he were in her position, he'd probably be doing exactly the same thing. Resigning himself to the fact that he wouldn't sleep that night, he got out of bed, dressed, and went downstairs. After making himself a mug of nettle tea, he sat in the armchair by the window and looked outside. The moon was large and bright. He hoped it wouldn't be the last time he saw it like this. He remained by the window for the rest of the night, watching the sunrise in all its glory. He was so engrossed he didn't hear Marcus coming down the stairs.

'Up early this morning, lad?' Marcus enquired.

Seren looked around, 'I couldn't sleep,' he said, turning back to the window.

'Understandable, you have a long journey ahead of you, there's no reason why you shouldn't be nervous about it. It is, after all, a step into the unknown.'

Marcus walked over to the stove and began making breakfast. Seren turned and watched him for a moment, realising he never had asked if he would accompany them. It was now or never. He walked over to Marcus as he busied himself at the stove.

'Marcus.'

Marcus turned. 'Yes, my boy.'

'Would you come with us, to the citadel, I mean?'

'Seren, as much as I would like to accompany you both, I can't. I'm not as young as I once was and fear I would only slow you down. But don't worry, I'm sure our paths will cross again one day.'

Though disappointed, Seren tried not to show it. 'I understand. I hope we will meet again.'

Marcus nodded, 'Now, let's get on with breakfast, shall we?' he said cheerily.

They had just finished cooking and laying the table when Tobelle came downstairs. For the last time, they sat and ate together, making light conversation. When they had finished, Tobelle helped Marcus to clear up while Seren went upstairs to collect his bag. He wondered if he should leave the journal there, it would be safe, of that he was in no doubt, but maybe Tobias could shed more light on both the journal and James himself. He had to take it, and so pushed the thought to the back of his mind. Picking up his satchel, he made his way back downstairs where Tobelle was sitting at the table with Marcus.

'Well, that's just about everything I think,' he said.

Tobelle sighed and stood. They both faced Marcus.

'Thank you for everything, Marcus. I'm just sorry we have to leave,' Seren said.

'It was no trouble, dear boy. You are both welcome in my home anytime. Now, before you go, I want to give you this,' he said, handing a full satchel to Seren. 'There's enough in there to keep you going until you can stop to resupply.'

Seren was about to tell Marcus it was too much, but Marcus put up his hands.

'It's no trouble,' he said with a smile.

Seren smiled back. They walked to the door and picked up their things. Saying goodbye, they mounted their horses, Marcus waving them off as they rode down the street. He knew this would not be the last time he would see them. With a last look down the street, he closed the door, going inside to wait for his vision to play out as he knew it would.

Seren and Tobelle rode through Hallsrock. When they arrived at the north gate, they paused and looked back down the road. They both felt a little sad to be leaving Marcus, as it had been a peaceful couple of weeks. Now, however, the road to the north stretched out before them, it would take at least three weeks to reach the citadel, and that was only if the weather held. If it turned, as it had a habit of doing this time of year, then it would slow them down. With a last look at the town, they nudged the horses on. Riding through the gate, they took the first steps of their journey to Tobias, and hopefully, some answers.

***

Since regaining her freedom, Laurentis had spent her days in her room, waiting for Archimon to summon her. She felt ready for anything he would make her do. Undoubtedly, she had changed, her mind now closed to whatever good had been within her, and she felt a darkness that was familiar to her from long ago. To match her new persona, she had commissioned several new sets of robes in the deepest black available. When they arrived later that day, she changed immediately. Admiring her new robes, her eyes flashed as a wicked smile crossed her lips. A knock at the door interrupted her. Turning, she looked towards the door. Focusing solely on it, she waved her hand and watched as it opened. Archimon almost looked surprised but stepped inside and walked towards her. This was the first time she had seen him since he had released her. Laurentis stood her ground. In her mind, she knew it wouldn't be long until she could match him in both power and knowledge if she studied the books. Archimon stopped a few paces short of her.

'I see you have sufficiently recovered,' he said, slightly less coldly than usual.

Laurentis nodded.

'Good, then you will come to my suite tomorrow and resume your training.'

'Yes, Archimon.'

She looked for his reaction at her use of his name, but he showed nothing. By opting to use his name instead of calling him sir, she was proclaiming herself as his equal. Without another word, Archimon turned and left the room. As if to reply to her proclamation, Archimon waved his hand as he stepped through the door, closing it himself. Laurentis smiled, tomorrow she would have to prove herself to regain his trust. Sitting at her desk, she opened the first book on telepathy and began to read.

Back in his suite, Archimon smiled to himself, she truly had changed and was now beginning to assert herself. The task hadn't changed since before Laurentis had made the attempt on her life. If she could complete it without the emotion that caused her to jump in the first place, then she would be ready. He would then take her as his bride. He suspected her change in persona meant that the barriers that had been put in place to contain her power as a young child had been destroyed and she was now realising its full potency.

Working into the early hours, Laurentis managed to read both books on telepathy and mind control. She slept for a few hours and woke early. Since her release, she had needed very little sleep each night and put it down to her power. It was helping to fuel her very being. After eating a light breakfast, she dressed in one of her new robes and made her way to Archimon's suite. She knocked and waited for the door to open. Entering the suite, she walked into the main chamber to see the high wizard in his frozen stance. Looking at him, she felt nothing.

'Please sit,' Archimon said, entering the room.

Seating herself on the nearest couch, she waited for him to speak.

'Your task remains the same, I want you to concentrate on reading his mind. Whilst his body is paralysed, his mind is active. You are to read it to find out if he or anyone else is aware of what we are doing. It is imperative that we can continue unhindered.'

Laurentis stood and walked towards the high wizard, observing him closely. Although his eyes were slightly dulled, she could see that there was still life within them. Laurentis circled him once and came back to face him. She had read that the most effective way to read a person's mind was to be in contact with them, but she knew that wouldn't always be possible. She was sure that Archimon was testing her, and this was her chance to prove she was his equal. Sitting on the couch, she made herself comfortable. Closing her eyes, she took a deep breath. When she opened them again, she looked directly at the high wizard, blocking out everything else in the room. Her mind had to be completely in tune with his if this was going to succeed. It took some time, but finally, she felt a connection open. She would have to be cautious, if he felt that she was trying to read his mind it might still be possible for him to try to block her. If that happened, it would take far longer to extract the information she needed. Carefully, she probed the edges of his mind. Nothing. She pushed a little more, there was a girl, his daughter who he hoped was safe. She picked up his mental image of her and her name, Tobelle. Slowly and carefully, she began sifting through his thoughts, many of them taken up by his daughter. Then she felt it, she pulled back swiftly, he was searching for her intrusion. Laurentis hoped she had pulled back in time. She stood and walked away, she would wait a few moments before trying again.

Pouring herself a glass of water, she took a book from one of the many bookcases around the suite, unsure if the high wizard could see her, but if he could, she didn't want to arouse his suspicions any further. Sitting back on the couch, she quickly regained the connection but stayed on the edge of his thoughts for a short while. When she was certain he was no longer searching, she began again, moving swiftly through the thoughts of his daughter. After a time, she began finding other fleeting thoughts of no relevance.

Laurentis sighed, she was starting to think there was nothing to be found when she came across a familiar name—Seren Hiptamus. She probed the thought a little more and was taken to the scene in the high wizard's office when Seren had tried to convince him about the journal and what was happening to the magic. He seemed to have come back to this thought again and again. Now, he knew what the boy had said was correct, and more than anything, he was sorry that he hadn't taken the time to investigate further, as he was now powerless to do anything. She pushed even further, moving quickly now, looking for anything that he might have said following his meeting with Seren, but found nothing. Laurentis felt him searching again, but this time didn't pull back, she wanted him to detect her. That way, she'd know if there was anything else he would want to keep hidden. She felt a push. He knew she was there. Laurentis fought to stay in his mind for a little longer. He didn't try to conceal anything, just rid her from his mind. She didn't resist and felt the connection sever. Looking at him, she smiled, if Seren was the only other one who knew, then they could continue without worry.

'Well, what did you find?' Archimon asked curtly on his return to the suite.

'There is only one other who knows, and it was he who told the high wizard. His name is Seren Hiptamus, a boy from Shillington.'

Archimon looked at her, 'A boy you say, then we have no worry. He and his friends will be taken care of soon.'

Laurentis looked puzzled, 'You already knew about him?'

'Yes, shall we say I was warned. There is no need to worry about one so powerless, we shall continue. Now, you have done all I have asked and so you are dismissed. I will expect you again tomorrow and we shall continue.'

Stepping out of the suite, Laurentis watched as he closed the door. A little aghast, she turned and walked back to her room. She slept soundly that night knowing that she had done well, hoping tomorrow would be as successful. The next morning, Laurentis awoke early, as was now usual, and dressed. She recapped the mind control book while taking a light breakfast. Finally, she made her way to Archimon's suite. Knocking on the door, she waited, but it remained firmly closed. Impatiently, she knocked again, finally the door opened and she made her way into the main chamber. She stopped short, shocked to see the high wizard seated on the couch, Archimon sitting opposite him.

'Sit down,' he said firmly.

She took a seat in the armchair across the room from both men.

'You seem shocked.'

'I thought he was the enemy, and yet now you are sitting here like old friends,' Laurentis replied.

Archimon laughed, 'I have unbound him in preparation for your task today, he is in a simple trance for your protection while you learn to control his mind.'

She nodded.

'What you make him do is up to you, but see that he comes to no harm, for the moment, anyway.'

Archimon got up and walked across the room. Turning, he said, 'You're confident that you can accomplish this?'

'Yes.'

'Then you have until the end of the day. When I return, I expect to see results.' Archimon left the suite.

Laurentis remained seated observing the high wizard, who just sat still staring into space. In order to make him do anything, she would have to take complete control of his mind so that he couldn't think for himself. She stood and walked closer to the high wizard, he remained motionless. Standing a few feet away from him, she took a deep breath and cleared her mind, once again focusing on entering his. After a short time, she felt the connection, finding no defences, no meandering thoughts, seemingly a blank canvas. Remaining cautious, she began to envelop his mind with hers. She had almost gained complete control when, without warning, his mind came alive and she was flung back. In that second, Laurentis' focus dipped, and she was pushed from his mind, losing all control she had held. She landed on the floor, her back to the chair where she had been sitting. Looking up, to her amazement and horror, the high wizard was steadily advancing towards her. Archimon's trance had failed. She reached into her robes for her wand, but it wasn't there. Looking around, she saw it lying against the foot of the table across the room.

He was almost on her now, in a last-ditch attempt to save herself, she extended her hand and shouted, 'STOP.'

Her eyes flashed and she felt a surge of power. Staring at the high wizard, he had stopped in his tracks. Standing, she took a step forward, hearing the door of the suite close as Archimon strode into the room, smiling. As he walked towards her, he held out his hand and her wand drifted up to him.

'Congratulations, you have succeeded in your final test,' he said, handing her wand back to her.

Laurentis took the wand and glared at him. 'A test,' she spat angrily, raising her voice. 'He could have killed me.'

Archimon laughed, 'No, my dear girl, he couldn't have, as you well know. Look at him.' He pointed at the wizard. 'Without even thinking about it, you took full control of his mind and stopped his attack. Your powers are limitless. You can do anything you want. You have proved that twice now.' He paused, 'All that remains is to finish him. Now that you truly know who you are, he can be of no further use. I leave it to you to decide how to do it, but, Laurentis, do it today.'

Laurentis turned back to the high wizard. 'Follow me,' she said firmly.

Without another word to Archimon, she walked across the room, and as commanded, the high wizard followed her. Leaving the suite, Laurentis made her way to the ground level of the fortress, stopping outside a locked door.

'Wait here,' she said to the high wizard.

Taking her wand from her robe she unlocked the door and entered the old armoury. Looking around the room, she took in the vast array of weaponry that lined the walls. She could have used a spell to kill him, but the use of a weapon was much more personal. It took courage to look your victim in the eye and inflict the fatal wound. This one act would prove beyond doubt to both Archimon and herself that she had changed and was ready to take what he had promised would be hers. Exiting the armoury, she locked the door and told the wizard to follow her once again, leading him outside the fortress and a little way down the road. Heading off the road and into the deeper snow, she told him to stop. She looked out across the mountains for a moment, it was idyllic. Snow was beginning to fall again. In the mountain range it was always winter. Turning back to the waiting wizard, she forgot about the view. Drawing the sword, she had selected from the armoury, she admired it for a few moments. Raising the ornate sword, it gleamed in the afternoon light. Without so much as a second thought, Laurentis brought the blade down and thrust it into the high wizard's chest. His eyes went wide. In his final moments, he regained control of his mind and realised what Laurentis had done to him. With pity in his eyes, he sank to his knees, giving a final look at Laurentis as he took his last breath and fell back into the snow. Blood flowed from his chest and turned the snow around him red. Wiping the blade on the wizard's robe, she replaced it in the scabbard and walked back towards the fortress. Having watched the execution from his balcony, Archimon smiled—she was ready. With a last look at the lifeless body of the now former high wizard, he turned and went inside. It was time to summon the priestess.

Chapter 26

Since leaving Hallsrock, Seren and Tobelle had made good progress. The snow wasn't as heavy on the ground with the onset of the milder weather. They arrived in Halingshire after only three days of gentle riding and had spent just the one night in the village, wanting to be on their way quickly. Now, once again, they were moving steadily north. The next stop on their journey would be Sandown, a small town a little over six leagues south of Shillington. On the fifth day following their departure from Halingshire, they came in sight of the town on the horizon. Still some distance away, they halted the horses and found a spot to have lunch. Although both were burdened with their own thoughts, they were jovial in their conversation, trying to make the best of their situation. After resting for an hour or so after lunch, they mounted once again and set off for Sandown.

It took a little over two hours to cover the distance to the town, which sat atop a great hill and was enclosed by ancient walls. As they crested the hill, they took in the spectacular view. Gently undulating meadows stretched for leagues, dotted with the occasional clump of trees. In summer, they would be filled with flowers, but for now, they were a patchwork of verdant green and white as new grass sprouted between pockets of stubborn snow that was slow to melt. They understood why the ancient people would have chosen to build there so long ago, although Seren was sure that it would have been more for defensive purposes than the perfect views. They entered the town by the south gate. Evening was approaching and the streets were busy with people doing the last of their shopping and heading home after a day's work. They halted their horses a little way down the road, in need of finding a place to stay for the night. As more people took to the streets, they dismounted and led the horses. So far, they hadn't passed an inn and dusk was fast approaching. Turning off the main road, they headed west until they finally reached an inn called 'The Spring'. They hadn't realised it. but they had walked so far down the road that they were almost at the wall. They stopped and admired it for a few moments, although it was old it was well maintained, intricate reliefs covered it from top to bottom. The colour had faded but the carvings themselves looked as if they had been carved only yesterday. With a final admiring glance, they led the horses to the inn's stable block where they were greeted by a stable boy.

'Do you have any stabling for the night?' Seren asked.

'Aye, don't get many travellers this time of year, plenty of stalls to be had.'

Seren handed his reins to the boy and held Tobelle's horse as she dismounted, passing the second set to the boy before making their way to the entrance of the inn. Walking inside, they were greeted by the warmth of a crackling fire in a large, stone fireplace and the smell of suckling pig cooking slowly on a spit. Crossing the room, they waited at the bar. After a few moments. the keep approached them.

'Welcome to The Spring, my young friends, what can I do for you?'

'We'd like two rooms please.'

The keep took out a quill, 'How long will you be staying?'

Seren looked at Tobelle who shrugged. 'Three nights,' he said finally.

The keep entered the details into his logbook and handed them both a key.

'Make your way up the stairs to your right. The rooms are opposite one another at the end of the hall.'

Thanking the keep, they headed towards the stairs. After finding their rooms, they stowed their few possessions and made their way back downstairs. The inn was beginning to fill. but they soon found themselves a table. Not long after they sat down, a maid arrived to take their order.

When she had left, Tobelle looked at Seren and asked, 'Why did you book for three nights? We should be getting along to the citadel.'

'We agreed that we wouldn't stop in Shillington, the horses need to rest and we'll have to buy provisions. When we leave here, it'll be more than sixteen leagues before we can stop again, and that won't be until we are well north of Shillington. Let alone how long it will take to reach the citadel.'

Tobelle nodded as the maid returned with their drinks. 'Do you think that Tobias will be able to help us?' she said quietly.

'Honestly, I don't know. But he did serve with James in the mages. If there is anyone who can help us, it has to be him.'

For a time, they sat in silence. It was often like this, jovial whilst travelling, but subdued and almost sombre when they stopped and had time to think about what they were doing. They were both secretly hoping that Tobias would take on the task, relieving them of their burden. A few minutes later, the maid returned with their meals, which they ate in silence. Finished with their food, Tobelle quickly downed her drink, said goodnight to Seren, and retired to her room. Finding himself alone at the table, Seren took his drink and went to stand at the bar. He had never visited Sandown, but the people he found at the bar were friendly towards him, and after a short time, he began to enjoy the evening, his sombre mood all but forgotten.

Eventually, the inn began to empty as people made their way home. Finishing his drink, he settled the evening's bill. Thanking the keep, he made his way up the stairs and to his room. He thought about looking in on Tobelle, but after her abruptness in leaving the table, he decided she was better left until morning. He closed his door quietly, locking it behind him. Even in a place like this, he wasn't taking any chances. Before climbing into bed, he tended to the small fire that was glowing in the hearth. Seren slept well that night, and unusually didn't wake until late into the morning. Climbing out of bed, he washed with the cold water in the basin and quickly dressed. Making his way downstairs, he found Tobelle already eating breakfast at the same table they had occupied the previous night. She looked up as Seren approached.

'Morning, Seren, you slept well I see,' she said cheerfully, evidently in a better mood than she had been last night.

No sooner had he sat down than the maid came to take his order. He asked for some eggs and a glass of adaman juice, the maid nodded and walked away.

'I thought we could just take it easy today, maybe explore the town a little, take in the sights,' he said.

Tobelle smiled in agreement, it would be nice to not be on the road for a day or two. Once Seren had finished his breakfast, they left the inn and made their way into the centre of town. During his conversations with the townspeople the previous evening, he discovered that the town had been built in that location because of the spring that rose in the centre of the hill. It had later been found that the water was medicinal, which caused the town to grow and prompted people to build the walls all those years ago. He also found out that the carvings on the wall told the story of the town's history. By starting at the north gate and following the wall around, the complete story was revealed. From the town square, it didn't take them long to find the building that now housed the spring.

As they entered the building, they were greeted by a kindly, older woman, 'Good morning, dears,' she said cheerily. 'Now, what can I offer you? A tour, or perhaps you would like to sample our wonderful waters?'

Tobelle sighed, 'It would be nice to bathe. We're travelling a long way and our arrival here marks less than the halfway point,' she said quite formally, surprising Seren.

She smiled and looked at them both, 'Our water is just what the weary traveller requires to reinvigorate body and mind, please follow me.'

The woman turned and led them down a hallway, stopping between two doors on opposite sides. 'These are the changing rooms. Inside, you will find boxed shelves containing white robes, please change into those. You can leave your clothes on the shelves. They will be quite safe.'

She gestured to the left for Seren and the right for Tobelle. Entering as indicated, they found themselves in large, airy rooms, tiled in the finest blue glass. They found the shelves along the back walls and changed. Shortly, they emerged from the changing rooms, Seren first and Tobelle a few moments later. The woman smiled and gestured for them to follow her once again. A short distance down the hall, they came to a large door. The woman walked forward, pushing it open as she went. They were greeted by the sight of a large, open chamber with no roof. The chamber was open to the elements.

'This is the open-air chamber,' the woman began. 'The water is fresh, crisp and cold, it opens the body to be cleansed.'

She walked to the edge of the pool, which was long and narrow and featured the same blue glass tiles that had been in the changing rooms.

'To begin the cleansing ritual, step into the pool, immerse yourself once and walk to the other end.'

Seren and Tobelle looked nervously at one another and then at the woman.

'It's all right, you can keep the robes on,' she laughed.

They both breathed a sigh of relief and laughed themselves. Tobelle made the first move, stepping down into the water, gasping at its icy coldness. Doing as the woman instructed, she ducked under the water, quickly surfacing. After one or two deep breaths she began walking forward towards the other end of the pool. Seren followed suit, stepping into the pool, and letting himself slip under the water. He was shocked to find out just how cold it was as he began the walk towards the end of the pool. When they climbed out at the far end, they were met by the woman.

'Shocking at first, I know, but you get used to it after the first few times,' she said. 'Now, let's move on.'

She opened and walked through another large door. The next room was roofed and felt a lot warmer. In contrast with the last room, the glass tiles in the chamber were red.

'This is the hot room. All you do in here is walk through the pool to the other side.'

This time, Seren was the first into the water. He noticed that the pool was shorter than the last by maybe a third. Entering the pool, he found the water hot but not unbearably so, and understood why it wasn't necessary to immerse yourself and why it was shorter. He began walking to the other end with Tobelle soon following him. As before, the woman met them at the end.

'Now, let's move into the final chamber.'

She walked through an open archway into the last room. It was the largest of the three and featured the same decor as the hot room. The pool in there was the largest they had encountered.

'This, the final chamber, is the warm room. This time you don't have to walk through the pool, you can spend as long as you wish in here. When you have finished, you can go back through the preceding rooms or make your way through the doors on either side of the chamber, which will take you back to the changing rooms,' she said pointing to the doors. 'Enjoy your time in the pool, I'll leave you now.'

With a final smile, she turned and walked from the room. Tobelle was first into the pool. It was lovely and warm, the perfect temperature. Seren soon joined her. They spent an hour soaking in the warm water, they could have stayed there all day but wanted to explore more of the town. Reluctantly, they clambered out of the pool and made their way through the doors that led to their respective changing rooms. Seren changed quickly and headed out into the main entrance hall. Tobelle took a little longer, but finally she too appeared in the hall. When they were ready to leave, they walked over to the woman who was seated close to the entrance. As they approached, she looked up.

'All finished, well I hope you have enjoyed your time here and feel more rested.'

They nodded, Seren took out his coin purse and offered some coins to the woman.

Politely, she shook her head, 'No, my dear boy, keep your coins. Our water is for all to enjoy, we never accept any coin for the service.'

Seren, looking slightly embarrassed, put the coins away.

'Thank you for your hospitality, I hope that one day we will be able to return.' Tobelle said with a smile.

The woman grinned, 'I'm sure we will see you again, goodbye, my friends.'

They said goodbye and left the building, feeling rested. Maybe what they said about the water was true.

'What shall we do now?' Seren asked.

'We could go and look at the carvings.'

Seren nodded in agreement and they made their way towards the north gate. The rest of the day they spent walking around the wall, looking at the detailed carvings. In some areas, the colours were a little better preserved, but much of the wall was down to bare stone. The carvings were exquisite. Many of the friezes featured the spring at the centre, depicting the town from its roots when there were just two or three dwellings, up until the construction of the wall as the town reached its peak atop the hill. It took several hours, but eventually, they had walked the entire circumference of the wall.

It was mid-afternoon as they walked back towards the centre of town. Tobelle spotted a small bakery and taking Seren by the arm she led him over to the shop. It was a small place with some tables and chairs outside. Tobelle went inside and bought some pastries and two malts whilst Seren sat down outside. When Tobelle returned with her purchases, they tucked in, not realising how hungry they were, having not eaten since breakfast.

'I like it here, Seren,' Tobelle said suddenly. 'I mean, I know that Shillington is my home, but this place feels like home, too.'

'It's a nice place,' Seren agreed.

'Maybe, one day I might consider moving here,' Tobelle said thoughtfully.

Seren smiled but said nothing, he didn't want to say anything to spoil her mood, but he wondered if either of them would have a future to plan. They were stepping into the unknown and he knew they might not come back. They took their time over their pastries, as it was a pleasant afternoon and they had nothing pressing to attend to. When they finally finished, they slowly made their way back to the inn where they spent the rest of the evening in the bar.

The next morning, they both slept in, it was to be another easy day, but they would have to buy provisions before they left the next day. After a leisurely breakfast, they made their way through the streets to the east to find the shops and market. It didn't take them long. For the size of the town, the shopping district was substantial and crammed with numerous shops and market stalls selling anything and everything. After buying their provisions, they stopped for some lunch at one of the stalls that sold hot bun cakes. The vendor handed over the cakes and some loganberry preserve. They sat on the edge of the fountain in the centre of the marketplace and ate quietly, watching people going about their day.

Once lunch was over, they browsed the shops and stalls, and could have spent so much coin. The town seemed to have everything they could ever want and more. Admiring some jewellery at one of the stalls, Tobelle picked up a silver amulet and chain. Holding it up, the purple amethyst in its centre glinted in the afternoon sunlight.

When she smiled, Seren could tell that she liked it and approached the owner of the stall.

'Excuse me,' he said politely, the owner looked his way. 'How much for the amulet that my friend is looking at?' he indicated Tobelle.

'Ten silver for you, my boy,' he said with a wink.

Seren smiled and took out the silver coins, handing them to the man.

'Thank you, I hope your friend appreciates it.'

Seren thanked the man and strode over to Tobelle.

'It's lovely isn't it, Seren,' Tobelle said, showing him the amulet.

'Yes, indeed. Good thing that it's yours now then.'

Tobelle looked at him quizzically, 'Mine?'

'I just bought it, It's yours.'

Tobelle looked taken aback, then without warning, she threw he arms around him, hugging him tightly. 'Thank you, Seren, it's the nicest thing anyone has ever bought me.'

Seren's face flushed scarlet. 'You're welcome,' he said quietly.

Deciding that they had spent enough time in the shopping district, they made their leisurely way back to the inn for their last night in Sandown. The inn was quiet that night. After a light meal, they spent a little more time talking with the barkeep and a few of the patrons but retired shortly after dark. They planned to get an early start the next morning. It took Seren little time to get comfortable and finally fall asleep. It was a restless night's sleep, filled with strange and disturbing dreams. A little before dawn, he woke, glad to finally be away from the dreams. Yawning, he sat up in bed, lingering for a few minutes, not wanting to leave the warmth of the blankets he had wrapped himself in. With a sigh, he heaved himself out of bed and quickly dressed. Picking up his satchel, he reluctantly left the room, pausing outside Tobelle's door before knocking.

'Tobelle, are you up?'

He heard her sigh and call back, 'I'm not quite ready, I'll meet you downstairs in a minute.'

Seren continued downstairs to wait where he was greeted by the barkeep and his wife, who were just sitting down to breakfast before beginning their day.

'Morning, my lad,' the keep said cheerfully, 'Up early this fine morn.'

Seren nodded, 'I'm just waiting for my friend and then we'll be on our way. We're heading for the citadel to visit a friend.'

Seren regretted the words the moment he uttered them. It was foolish to tell people where they were going. The keep opened his mouth to speak but was interrupted by his wife.

'Without a good breakfast in you, no, dear boy, I won't hear of it. You and your friend will join us for breakfast, then you can be on your way. Now, come and sit down and I'll fetch some more platters,' she said with an authority that was difficult to resist.

Seren smiled and went to sit down. The keep looked at him and laughed.

'She's like that with all our young guests. Not happy till you're all fed and watered. Thinks youngsters these days don't have enough meat on their bones,' he said cheerily.

Finally, ready, Tobelle came into the room. 'Ready to go?' she asked.

'We've been invited to stay and have breakfast,' Seren replied, gesturing for her to come and sit.

Just as she seated herself opposite Seren. the keep's wife returned carrying some extra platters and a carefully wrapped bundle, which she handed to Tobelle as she set the platters down in front of them.

'Just a few little things to keep you going,' she said, smiling. 'Now, dig in, let's not let it get cold.'

They tucked into a grand breakfast of sausages, black pudding, bacon, and eggs with plenty of bread, butter and a variety of jams and marmalades for after. When they had finished eating, the keep's wife began clearing everything away. Gathering their things, Seren and Tobelle thanked the keep for his hospitality. Seren offered him some coins for the food but he refused.

'I'd never hear the end of it from the wife,' he said merrily. 'Now, have a safe journey, and if you're ever down this way again there'll be a warm meal and bed waiting for you.'

Seren smiled and shook his hand, but inside he knew that the likelihood of them even surviving to return was questionable. As they left the inn, Seren and Tobelle looked at one another but said nothing, both remaining deep within their own thoughts. If everything went well, this would be the final leg of their journey to the citadel. Their horses were waiting for them in the stables, the stable boy had already saddled them and handed over the reins. They mounted and rode out into the crisp morning, the sky over the horizon a deep, blood red. Seren watched it for a while and hoped it wasn't an omen of things to come. Nothing good ever happened on a day when the sky was this red in the morning.

Chapter 27

Up and about early that morning, Marcus set about finalising things. Today was the day and he didn't want any loose ends left. He ate his favourite breakfast of thick, honey cured ham and eggs, and then simply sat in his much-loved chair to wait. He hadn't been waiting long when the door burst open and several red-robed wizards entered the seer's house. Two of them ran upstairs, and he could hear them going from room to room, searching.

'You won't find them here, they left days ago. You're too late,' he said calmly.

The bigger of the three men who had remained downstairs approached Marcus.

'Well... that is very unfortunate for you,' he said, drawing his wand and pointing it at Marcus' chest. 'Now, tell me where they are, Seer.'

Marcus looked at him for a moment and then spoke softly, 'Do as you will to me, I have made my peace. I will tell you nothing except that you won't win, you and your wicked master will be destroyed and all will return to how it should be.'

Marcus fell silent and watched the man with the wand.

He didn't act immediately, but spoke once again, 'We'll see how long you can hold out then, shall we?' As he spoke, a blast of white light flew from his wand and struck Marcus forcefully, sending both him and the chair toppling backwards.

Hitting the floor hard, Marcus winced as the air was knocked out of him, but despite this, he laughed mockingly. 'It'll take more than knocking me off a chair to break me.'

The red-robed wizard towered above him.

'You might as well kill me now. As I said before, I won't tell you anything.'

The wizard sneered, 'Well, you see, old man. I am very good at what I do. I have many methods to persuade people to talk, each dreadfully painful in different ways, and all designed to keep you just on the edge of death for as long as it takes to get what I need. So, shall we begin again?'

He pointed his wand at Marcus and was about to cast his spell when the front door opened and a short, sprightly woman entered.

'Good morning, Marcus, sorry I haven't been able to get to you before today, did the children get off all right?'

She hadn't looked at Marcus, and so hadn't seen the red wizards.

'Elmira, get out of here, go now!' Marcus cried.

Elmira looked up, 'Oh, my,' she gasped, and turned to run, but two of the brigands blocked her path.

'Well, now, things may just have been made a little easier for us all,' the captain said with a cruel smile. 'Bring her in.'

The two brigands who blocked Elmira's path took her by the arms and forced her into the large room, pushing her roughly into a chair opposite Marcus who looked sadly at Elmira. He had forgotten that she was due, and silently cursed himself that she was now a captive, having not seen her in his vision of this day. Marcus bowed his head, worried that these wizards would now learn where Seren and Tobelle were bound. Elmira had met them and knew where they were going, and he doubted she would be able to withstand what these wizards would do. Marcus looked straight at Elmira who stared back at him with terrified eyes. Trying to reassure her, he smiled weakly, but as she looked away from his gaze, he knew she felt anything but reassured. The captain, who had toppled Marcus from the chair, watched him for a reaction and had seen what he needed to see. One way or another, he knew he would have the information he needed that day, *and two more bodies to add to my total,* he thought to himself.

'Well, Elmira is it?' he began. 'Before you arrived, your friend, Marcus, and I were having a conversation about the two young people who were staying with him until recently, he was, however, a little reluctant to tell me where they were going.' He looked down at Marcus, 'So, Marcus, I will give you one last chance to tell me what I want to know or I shall be forced to ask your friend here.'

Marcus was torn, on the one hand if he gave away the location there was every chance that Seren and Tobelle would be caught and killed, but if he said nothing, Elmira, one of his oldest and dearest friends, would be tortured and killed in front of him. He looked at Elmira, who after a moment, looked back at him, a deep sadness in her eyes, but he saw something else there also. In that moment, a silent agreement passed between them, and with a nod, Marcus looked up at the captain.

'My answer remains the same as before, I won't tell you anything.'

The captain nodded and smiled. 'I must say there are days when I wish you people would make it easy for me. Today is obviously not one of those days,' he paused and turned away for a moment. Then, turning back, he said with a wicked sneer, 'I must confess, however, I was hoping that you'd hold out, it has been a while since anyone resisted. So, now let me demonstrate my craft to you both.'

He turned and looked at Elmira, 'I shall give you a chance to save yourself many hours of torment, tell me where they are going and I shall give you a quick passing, which I do not offer lightly, but you are a mere civilian in all this. So, tell me, where are they going?'

Elmira looked at the captain, 'Did you not mean to say a mere *mortal*,' she spat.

He smirked.

'No, this mere mortal will not tell you what you want to know. I will not betray Marcus or the children.' She fell silent.

'Loyal. Loyal and stupid,' the captain said fiercely. 'So be it.'

He held his outstretched hand towards Elmira and said, 'I think, first your blood will boil.'

The pain was not immediate, the spell began slowly by heating the blood so that the victim became warm and then began to overheat. Finally, the victim's blood would almost boil, causing intense pain and in some cases result in death. The captain watched as the spell took effect, speaking, not to anyone in particular, almost chatting as if to friends.

'I'm very proud of this spell, I created it myself. The one I serve uses a similar spell, but I wanted to make this one my own, so I took his idea and refined it a little so that it only affects the blood. Clever, don't you think?'

No one answered.

Elmira began to scream as the burning pain began to set in. Marcus looked away, unable to watch what he had brought upon her. He felt sick and prayed to no one in particular that the spell would take her so she would suffer no more. His prayers went unanswered. After a time, he wasn't sure how long, Elmira stopped screaming but continued to writhe in pain. The pain became so intense that she began scratching at her skin, her nails digging in so much that she drew blood on her face and arms, but the pain didn't stop. When Marcus thought she could take no more, he watched as she threw herself off the chair, her breathing ragged, he wanted to cry out, to make her pain stop and just tell them what they wanted to know. But he knew if he did her suffering would be in vain. He turned away from the scene, unable to watch any longer.

The captain observed and enjoyed the entire episode, he knew that if he didn't reverse the spell soon, she would die and she was his best chance of getting the information. With a sigh, he waved his hand over the woman. The spell ceased and the pain that had all but consumed Elmira disappeared. She lay still for a moment and opened her eyes, looking from the captain to Marcus and back to the captain.

'Still with us, well... that's a good sign.'

He turned to face the other brigands who had all gathered in the room to watch their captain work.

'Get her back in the chair.'

The two brigands who had led her into the room dashed forward and grabbed Elmira, hauling her back up. She sighed as she was sat in the chair and slumped forward a little. She didn't know how long the spell had been upon her, but she was exhausted. In reality, the spell had only been at work for around twenty minutes, but the pain it caused could make any amount of time feel like an eternity. The captain turned back to his captives and studied them for a moment. Elmira remained slumped forward while Marcus gazed at her with sorrow in his eyes.

'You know that someone will have heard her screams and will come to our aid. You won't get away with this,' Marcus said confidently.

The captain turned towards Marcus. 'That would normally be the case, but we've taken every precaution to ensure that we won't be interrupted,' he gestured at Elmira. 'Except for the fortunate intrusion of the housekeeper, I don't expect that we'll be bothered again. We have placed veils of deafness and non-sight over this house. From outside, no noise or spell bursts will be seen or heard, all will appear normal. So, no, no one will be coming to your aid today.'

Marcus stared at the captain, he hadn't sensed any veils being placed upon the house, but his mind had been on other things, and maybe his own power had begun to diminish, which would make it harder to sense spells such as these. He felt dismayed, they had thought of everything. Marcus bowed his head. The captain laughed and turned back to Elmira.

'Now that you have had time to think, have you reconsidered your answer?'

Slowly, Elmira lifted her head and looked at him. She was quiet for a time but then she began to speak. 'You're a cruel man, and I'm sure that is but a taste of the evil you could do, but no, I haven't changed my mind.' Elmira fell silent, she knew that her words had condemned her to death, but she didn't want to betray Marcus. It was important to him that the children's whereabouts were kept hidden from these men. No matter what they did, she wouldn't speak a word they wanted to hear, she hoped.

'I admire your loyalty, but I guarantee it will cause you unspeakable suffering, this is your last chance, tell me what you know.'

'No,' uttered Elmira.

The captain drew his wand and pointed it at her, narrowing his eyes. As the spell hit Elmira, she flinched but nothing seemed to happen. For a moment Marcus felt a sense of relief, then with horror, he watched the spell beginning to take effect. Slowly, patches of red began to develop on Elmira's skin. She didn't seem to notice at first, but then one began to develop on the back of her right hand. The redness gave way to a small area of swelling. which soon began to grow. Both Marcus and Elmira stared as more swellings developed. Elmira rubbed the one on her hand as she looked at Marcus.

'What's happening?'

Marcus shook his head, having never seen a spell such as this before. The swellings continued to grow and multiply until they were all over her, looking red and angry. They were beginning to itch, and Elmira began rubbing them more frantically. Finally, they seemed to stop growing. Marcus looked again, they were boils, the type victims of the pestilence were afflicted with many years ago when it had ravaged the land.

'Elmira, don't scratch them, if they burst, their foulness will enter your blood.'

She looked at him, 'They hurt, Marcus. It feels as if my skin is stretched to bursting.'

'I know, but you mustn't scratch them,' he said pleading with her.

'Sound advice, my wizened friend, but it will make no difference.' The captain interjected.

There was a sickly popping sound, and Marcus watched in horror as one by one the boils burst, releasing a foul mix of watery blood and pus. The sight was terrible to behold and the smell unbearable, but he forced himself to watch.

'You know of this disease, Seer,' the captain said. 'You know what will happen next, but unlike the pestilence, the spell can be reversed, if it's not too advanced. Save her from this fate and tell me what I want.'

Marcus kept his eyes on Elmira. She was crying silently and wouldn't meet his gaze, he felt she was beginning to lose her will. As the disease advanced, she would become delirious and could say anything. He could do nothing.

'Reverse the spell and I will tell you where they have gone.' Marcus' voice cracked.

The captain looked at Marcus, 'Tell me, and if I'm satisfied, then I will reverse the spell. Think carefully now, Seer, there is little time left to her in which the spell can be reversed.'

Marcus sighed, 'They've gone south towards the hills, heading for the vale. I don't know where they intend to go after that.' He bowed his head.

The captain looked at Marcus, regarding him for a moment, 'You're lying, there's nothing for them in the south.' The captain came closer to Marcus until their faces were inches apart. 'Don't toy with me, old man, where have they gone?'

Marcus looked at him and said nothing, knowing he wouldn't believe him if he changed his story, but he also knew the wizard was right, there was nothing in the south. He looked at Elmira, her hands were clenched, and her jaw set into a painful grimace. He knew how this disease progressed. First, the foulness from the boils affected the muscles, eating into them, making them clench in painful cramps. The victim would go rigid as every muscle tensed, then relax for a moment until the next wave overtook them. Following this, the muscle would give up its fight to repair itself and the victim would begin to waste. When there was no muscle left for the disease to feed on, it would move onto the organs and bones, causing a slow and painful death. Even using magic, there was no sure way to cure the pestilence. The majority of those who were afflicted died. Those who survived were left with what could be considered a half-life. They were alive but were unable to care for themselves properly and could never again work in any capacity. Under normal circumstances, the disease worked its way through the body over a period of approximately two weeks. However, the spell had sped up the process, but by how much Marcus was unsure. He watched helplessly as Elmira continued to clench and unclench. He could only imagine what pain she was going through. The captain laughed and stepped back from Marcus.

'It hurts you to see this woman in pain. I can see it in your eyes. Shall we sit a while and watch her?'

The captain sat opposite Marcus, looking first at Elmira and then to Marcus. She lay silently on the floor, having once again fallen from the chair, continuing to clench, her eyes tightly shut, her tears had stopped.

'What do you hope to achieve holding out like this, Marcus, make it easy on yourself and your friend, end her suffering.'

'So, you can cause further suffering, not only to the children but to all else in the land. No, I don't wish to be responsible for that.'

He looked at Elmira who had stopped clenching but was now visibly beginning to waste, not at terrific speed, but faster than the natural disease would have done. It was horrifying to watch but his resolve held.

'Well,' the captain said calmly, 'We shall sit here and watch your friend slowly waste away. It makes no difference to me whether we are here for hours or days, I will get what I want.' He motioned to one of his companions. 'It appears we shall be here for a time yet, find me something to eat.'

The brigand moved off towards the kitchen and began rifling through Marcus' stores in search of something. A short time later, he returned carrying a roasted fowl and handed it to the captain, who began to eat. He motioned to Marcus with a leg of the fowl.

'This is awfully good. Would you care for some?'

Marcus watched him eating. 'I wouldn't eat with you if it were to be the last meal of this world.'

The captain laughed. 'For you, my friend, it may just be that, but no matter, I am quite enjoying it all to myself.'

Marcus shook his head and looked back to Elmira. Her face had become gaunt and pale. Her cheekbones were prominent in her face now, and dark circles were taking shape around her eyes. The captain said nothing more. Marcus knew there was no point trying to talk his way out of this. They sat in silence for a time, watching one another before Elmira began to quietly ramble to herself. Marcus caught the occasional word as she spoke softly, but much of what she said was incomprehensible. He thought back to his vision, and this wasn't the way he had seen it happen. Elmira hadn't been part of the vision. She wasn't supposed to have been caught up in this. He had seen himself being tortured, not her. Marcus knew that visions weren't always accurate portrayals of coming events, but this one had felt real enough. He wasn't sure what it could mean, but maybe there would be a chance of coming out of this. He was snapped from his thoughts by the sound of Elmira's voice. She was still rambling, but the words were clearer now. She looked up at him with tears in her eyes and shook her head.

'I'm sorry, Marcus.'

He could see the pain in her eyes but also sorrow. The captain looked at her.

'I want this to stop, this terrible pestilence.' Elmira took a deep breath, 'They have gone to the citadel to find a man named Tobias. That's all I know.'

The captain regarded her for a moment and then smiled.

'Please, I have told you what you want to know, please end this spell.'

'Yes, you have. Thank you for the information, we shall take our leave.' He turned and began walking towards the door, but then stopped and turned to address his companions. 'Put the house to the flame and see that they don't leave.'

The brigands nodded their ascent, and the captain turned and exited the house. Three of the remaining brigands went outside to cast the flames. Another began a low chant to remove the veils that still hung over the house. The remaining two approached Marcus as he knelt next to Elmira, trying to help her up.

'She won't budge, look at her. Just take care of him and let's go.'

The brigand who had spoken turned and walked towards the front door. The remaining one stepped up to Marcus and hit him hard on the side of the head, knocking him to the floor next to Elmira. The brigand watched for a moment to make sure he was unconscious before turning and leaving the house. The door slammed, and Marcus looked up, to see if they had gone. He checked Elmira, only to find she had stopped breathing. He bowed his head. He hadn't meant for her to die. However, it did confirm his thoughts on his vision. Someone had died in his place, he had to make sure that it wasn't in vain. He stood shakily, feeling a trickle of blood flow down his cheek from the head wound. As quietly as he could, he moved to a cupboard in the corner of the room and took out his seeing stone and wand. Tapping the stone with the wand, a bird's eye view of the outside of the house appeared. Marcus watched as the brigands surrounded the house and pointed their wands toward the walls. Multiple jets of flame shot out and individual pockets of fire sprang up around the walls. Before the fire took hold, he had to get out, as he knew he couldn't extinguish it. Glancing back at the stone, to his surprise he didn't see any of the red-robed wizards still gathered around the house. Taking up a small, cloth bag, he placed the stone inside. From the kitchen, he took his coin purse and a loaf of bread, there was no time for anything else. Marcus ran to the front door but hesitated. If he was to flee and remain undetected, people had to believe him dead. If even a rumour of his survival went around, he would undoubtedly be pursued. Taking down a dark travelling cloak from the hook behind the door, he left his normal, multi-coloured cloak behind. The fire was growing louder as it took a firm hold. He had to leave. Hesitating for a moment, he glanced at Elmira, a tear rolling down his cheek. Shaking his head sadly, he made his way to the back of the house through the kitchen. A small door was set into the far wall, little used and blocked by an end table.

Scattering the items from the table, he began to pull it an inch at a time until finally, there was a gap big enough for him to squeeze through. Marcus pulled open the door, which jammed against the table, eventually pushing his way out into the early evening. He didn't linger and hastily made his way to the overgrown bushes at the rear of the garden. Turning to look back, he was just in time to see the fire engulf the doorway he had just exited. It wouldn't be long until the entire house was in flames. Shouts were drawing near, as the fire had been spotted and people were making their way over to try to fight it. Forcing his way through the bushes, he made it into a back lane. He had to get out of town. As the light began to fade, Marcus moved away from the devastation of his home and into the gathering darkness.

The fire burned all night, and the efforts of the townspeople were in vain. Try as they might, they couldn't extinguish it. By the next morning, it finally burnt itself out, having consumed everything it could. It was only after the remains of the building had cooled for a day it was discovered that Elmira had died in the fire. Of Marcus, there was no sign either dead or alive. He had simply vanished. The town went into mourning. It wasn't discovered that the fire had been deliberately set and was put down as a tragic accident.

Chapter 28

As the day dawned bright over the mountains, Laurentis was already awake. Archimon had chosen today as the day they would be bound. Nervous, Laurentis wanted the power but not Archimon. Not being the type of girl who dreamt of being bound to another, Laurentis hadn't made any special preparations. Wearing her new robe would be good enough for her. The previous night, she had met with the priestess who had cut Laurentis' finger and collected a small vial of her blood. The priestess had said it was for the ceremony. Laurentis wasn't sure for what purpose, but it wouldn't be long before she found out. Although she wasn't hungry, she summoned a light breakfast, knowing it would be better to eat. Still, it took her a long while to finish it. Eventually, she dressed in her freshly pressed robe, smoothing it out a couple of times, trying to waste time. When she could preen the robe no further, she sat in an armchair by the fire to wait. There were still several hours before the ritual would take place. Letting out a deep sigh, Laurentis looked around for something to occupy the time, but finding nothing she left the room and found herself descending the stairs on the way to the stables. Upon entering, the stable master nodded as she went over to her horse's stall and stroked her head. She stayed with her for a short time but knew she couldn't hide in the stables all day. Patting the mare, she turned and made her way back up into the fortress to her room. Opening the door, she stepped inside, stopping dead in her tracks. The room was bare. Except for a few larger items of furniture, all her belongings had gone.

'I took the liberty of moving your things to our suite.'

Laurentis jumped, she hadn't heard anyone coming up behind her. Turning, she faced Archimon. 'Our suite?'

'Indeed, you didn't expect to remain in this room once we were bound, did you?'

'I suppose not, I hadn't given it much thought,' she said quietly.

'Shall we go then?'

'The ritual isn't until tonight.'

'No, but I wish to show you something, to help you understand just what you will have.'

She nodded, and Archimon gestured for her to follow. They went past the suite and up a small flight of stairs that she had never seen before. As they climbed up and up, Laurentis was confused, Archimon's suite, *our suite now*, she thought, was at the top of the fortress. *We must be in the mountain.* Finally, they came to the top of the stairs. Set into the wall a short way along the passage was a small wooden door, which Archimon touched with his wand, making it vanish.

'A security measure, only my wand can open the entrance. After tonight, you'll also be able to gain access.'

Stepping inside, Laurentis followed. The room was dark, there were no windows and no other doors. Looking up, there was a small, circular hole in the ceiling, but it didn't let any light in. Standing in the centre of the room, Archimon gestured for her to join him.

'You're the only other person who knows of this room and it must remain that way.'

Laurentis nodded. Archimon lifted a black veil from a stand that stood in the middle of the room. Above the stand, the air shimmered, then slowly a dark orb took shape, criss-crossed with what looked like lightning bolts that smoothly flowed across the surface.

'The power I have been taking from Soastan is supposed to be sent on to Him.' Pausing, he closed his eyes for a moment, reaching out with his mind to check He wasn't present. When Archimon was satisfied there was no presence, he continued. 'I have been siphoning much of the power and storing it in this orb. Just enough is sent on to satisfy. Tonight, after the ritual, as my gift to you all of this power will be yours.'

Feeling the power emanating from the orb, Laurentis wanted it. 'I'm honoured that you consider me worthy to share this with you.'

After Archimon covered the orb, they left the room, making their way down the stairs and back into the fortress proper. Gesturing for her to enter the suite, he followed her inside. They made their way into the main room and sat down. Looking around, Laurentis could see some of her things placed about the room.

Discovering that Archimon had been siphoning some of the power shocked her. When he had spoken of his plan those many weeks ago, Archimon hadn't revealed that to her, but Laurentis was pleased that she would be taking that power for herself. Though powerful now, she had the opportunity to gain even more. If she played this just right, she could potentially become more powerful than Archimon. Turning to face Archimon, Laurentis smiled inwardly, determined that she would ensure things went her way.

'You didn't tell me that you were siphoning the power,' she said firmly.

Archimon looked a little taken aback. 'When we spoke of my plans, I did not feel that you were ready, you seemed worried about the idea as a whole, so I thought it best to keep it from you. But from today, I will not keep anything from you.'

Laurentis smiled, it was already working. Spending the afternoon talking together, Laurentis took time to re-arrange her things.

Finally, the time came, and the priestess entered the suite and announced, 'The ritual will be performed out on the terrace.'

The priestess turned and began ascending the stairs that led to the topmost terrace at the rear of the suite with Laurentis and Archimon following. Standing near the low wall that surrounded the terrace, the priestess took in the view of the mountains in the fading dusk before gesturing for them to approach her. Tall and slim with white hair, and dark, almost red tinted eyes, Laurentis thought her to be only a few years older than she was. But in truth, knew she was much older and must have wrought powerful magic to preserve her youthful appearance.

'Face one another and join hands.'

Taking Laurentis' hands, Archimon noticed their clamminess, even in the cold of the evening. From a bag, the priestess took a small bowl and two vials containing the blood she had taken from them the night before, and a third that Laurentis recognised as her vial of captured dragon's blood.

Opening one of the vials, the priestess poured it into the bowl, saying as she did, 'Dragon's blood to power the ritual and allow you to share one another's power.'

The two other vials she poured into the bowl simultaneously. 'Your blood combined to tie you together.'

Before taking a long strip of linen and immersing it in the bowl, she let the blood mingle. When the linen was soaked through, she lifted it from the bowl and began wrapping it around their hands and arms, binding them together. Tying it off, the priestess placed her hand over the knot and closed her eyes. A dark glow emanated from her hand and coursed through the linen, making it gleam for a second. Opening her eyes, she took her hand away and reached into the bag once again. Removing a small dagger, she cut the palm of her hand, placing it back onto the knot.

'This final offering of blood seals the ritual, you are now bound to one another. This bond can only be broken by death, whereupon the survivor will take into them the power of the other.' Using the dagger, she began to cut the linen at the knot, then into two equal lengths. Taking first Archimon's and then Laurentis' arm, she fastened one strip around each of their arms. 'You must keep these strips bound about your arms until the night of the new moon, this ritual only begins the binding. It will take time until you are fully bound. After the new moon, you may remove the linen if you wish, but it should never be discarded, or the bond will be weakened.' She stepped back. 'It is done.'

With that, she began packing her things away, 'I will take my leave.'

The priestess bowed and walked away, leaving the pair on the terrace. As Laurentis was looking out over the mountains, Archimon came and stood beside her.

'We do not share affection for one another, and I will not ask you to share my bed, yet we are now bound in every other way. Your rank in this fortress has risen dramatically, but I still retain ultimate power here, I trust you will remember that.'

Laurentis nodded once.

'Good, now let us go inside and you shall receive your gift.'

After a short time, they arrived back at the small door.

'Go ahead and open the door,' Archimon prompted.

Stepping forward, she drew her wand, touched it to the door and smiled as it disappeared. Moving inside with her, Archimon once again removed the veil from the orb.

'Place your hand into the orb and you will absorb the power it contains.'

Doing as he instructed, nothing happened for a moment, then little bolts of energy started crackling around her wrist, like little pinpricks, more annoying than painful. After a minute or so, the sensation began to die down until finally, it stopped. Laurentis withdrew her hand, already sensing her newly acquired power coursing through her body. Enjoying the feeling, she wanted more.

'You can take power from the orb whenever you wish, however, a word of caution, you must give yourself time to adjust to the new power. If you take too much in too short a time, the worst-case scenario would be death.'

Savouring the feeling of new power, Laurentis barely heard his words,

That night, as Laurentis lay in bed, she felt relieved that Archimon didn't expect her to sleep with him. In truth, he was only eight or nine years her senior and to some would be thought of as quite handsome, but she had never felt that way about him and knew she never would. She fell into an easy sleep. Things were looking up.

Chapter 29

Poking at the fire with a stick, Seren placed the last piece of fowl on the makeshift spit, turning it slowly. Their food had run out four days ago, and Seren had quickly learnt to hunt. Having only stopped two hours ago, Tobelle had curled up in her cloak and fallen asleep almost immediately. He decided to leave her for a while longer, but they'd have to be on the move before dawn, as they still had ground to cover before reaching the citadel. The journey had taken longer than expected. To avoid Shillington, their route had taken them far from the usual roads and they'd become lost on several occasions. Thinking about the events of the last few months, Seren wondered what would happen when they finally reached the citadel. His thoughts were interrupted by the smell of burning, the fowl on the spit was rapidly blackening. Cursing under his breath, he quickly took the spit down and placed it on a platter leaf he had found. Resigned to a burnt dinner, he went over to Tobelle and shook her lightly. Stirring, she opened her eyes.

'Time to get up, we need to get going soon,' he said and walked back to the fire.

Stretching, she untangled herself from her cloak and came to sit down next to Seren, yawning.

'Why do we have to leave so soon? We've not long stopped.'

'If we leave now and don't stop, we might just be able to reach the citadel by nightfall.'

'Another day of non-stop riding.'

There was a tone in her voice that Seren had heard before.

'If you can't take it go home, this isn't down to you.'

'It's not down to you either, you just found the book.'

'Yes, the book that your father didn't want to know about.'

Glaring at him, Tobelle didn't reply. She had been acting like this for over a week and Seren had had enough. He thought that she'd gotten over her past feelings but now it seemed they were surfacing again. Standing, he picked up his things and walked over to his horse. Mounting, he turned to Tobelle. 'I'm leaving, go home, Tobelle. Go home and forget about everything.' He turned his horse and rode away without looking back.

***

The campfire was visible in the distance.

'Do ya think it's them?'

'Who else would be this far out here, course it's them.'

'Shut up, you two, do you want them to hear you coming?' a harsh voice snapped.

The two brigands fell silent.

'Right, quick and quiet, hear me, let's end this ridiculous pursuit now, shall we.'

Silently, the brigands crept forwards, taking up positions to surround the makeshift camp. Close enough to observe, they stopped. There was no movement, the camp was quiet. The captain signalled for four of them to move forwards, the four closest to him drew their wands and closed in. As they approached the fire, they saw only one person. Glancing back at the others, the captain signalled for them to get on with it. Looking at one another, they shrugged and swiftly moved towards the person on the ground. Two of them grabbed the sleeping form and hauled them up while the other two kept their wands trained on them. Pulling the cloak back, they found it was Tobelle.

'Where's the other one?'

Tobelle remained silent. At that moment, the captain came up.

'There's supposed to be two of them, go and find the other one,' he said to the two who still had their wands trained on Tobelle. 'Are you going to tell me where your friend is?'

Tobelle remained silent, scared since Seren left her on her own. Bowing her head, she began to cry. Staring at her, the captain debated trying to make her talk, but given the state she was in, he doubted she would for a while.

'Put her on the horse and get the other two back, he can't be that far ahead. We'll pick him up on the way back to the fortress.'

Tobelle was led away and roughly shoved up onto her horse. It wasn't long before they were on the move. She kept her head down, wishing Seren hadn't left her alone. All she wanted was to be at home. If she hadn't been so stubborn in the first place, then she'd still have been in Shillington, and her father might have even returned. Silently, she cursed herself for her stupidity and settled low into her saddle.

***

Although Seren felt bad about leaving Tobelle, she had become unbearable in recent days. It had been two days since he left her and he hadn't seen any sign of her trying to catch up, so assumed she had returned home. *If I ever get home,* he thought, *she will be another one to add to the growing list of people to make it up to*. His initial estimate of reaching the citadel by the end of the first day had been wrong as they hadn't travelled as far as he thought but hoped that tonight he would finally arrive. Feeling tired, a loud burst of thunder echoed in the sky and large drops of rain began to fall.

'Oh, wonderful,' he muttered and pulled the hood of his cloak up.

The road he had been travelling for the last two days had steadily become more heavily enclosed by the ancient woodland. Little did he know that this was the same route that Laurentis had taken after abducting the high wizard. After another hour of riding in the rain, he came upon a small stream and decided to stop and refresh his water skin. As he crouched on the bank of the stream, letting the water slowly fill the skin, something shining in the wet grass of the bank caught his eye. Stoppering the skin, he stood and approached the object to examine it closer. He gasped when he saw a silver ring. Picking it up, Seren turned it over and realised he had seen it before. With two stones set into the silver band, a large emerald and an equally large onyx, there could be no mistaking it. It was the high wizard's ring. He remembered seeing it the day he spoke to him in his office. He couldn't believe it, this wasn't the sort of ring a person would suffer losing lightly. *The high wizard and his abductor must have passed this way.* Tucking the ring into a pocket in his robes, Seren mounted his horse and galloped from the stream. To his relief, half a league farther down the road, he came to the edge of the forest and joined the main road that led south to Shillington and north to the citadel and mountain pass.

After another league, he could finally see the citadel in the distance. The rain was falling in sheets and thunder and lightning ripped through the sky. *This isn't a day to be out*, he thought, *with any luck Tobias will be at home, all I have to do is find his home.* As he drew closer to the citadel, he was struck by the size of it. Having read about it, pictures and words in a book didn't do it justice. Outside the grey, stone walls, small farmsteads dotted the landscape. Finally, Seren arrived at the gate and looked intently at the large archway. For a few moments, there was nothing, and then he saw a shimmer, faint but it was there. It was a magical barrier, the only one still active in Soastan.

'Excuse me, lad, but if you're not going through the gate, could you move aside so I can get the wagon in,' a voice said behind him.

Turning in his saddle, he saw who had spoken. 'Sorry, sir,' he apologised, moving his horse to the side of the road.

When the man drove his wagon through the gate, nothing happened. It seemed simple enough, so he rode towards the arch and through the gate. Once again, nothing happened. Breathing a sigh of relief, he suddenly remembered the ring. What would have happened to him if it had set off the barrier? Quickly pushing the thought aside, he looked around, having no idea where to find Tobias. The streets were empty, the rain keeping people inside. The Fennbane Citadel was made up of three levels, with a keep enclosed by a substantial curtain wall occupying most of the top level. It was vast and not simply one curving street to each level as Seren had thought it would be. There were back alleys and main roads running back from the gate to the central rock column that the entire structure was built around. Sighing, he set about finding somewhere to stay for the night, as he couldn't sit out in the rain. Nudging his horse on, Seren started down the wide, cobbled street. with shops and stalls lining both sides. There were no lights in any of the windows and he didn't see a soul as he rode. Almost a quarter of the way around the first level, he finally came upon a place that had a little life to it. Dismounting, he found a makeshift hitching post for his horse and went inside what he supposed was the inn. There were few customers that night and so he easily found a spot at the counter. After a few moments, a man wearing plain black robes approached him.

'Can I get you anything?'

'Do you have any rooms available?'

The man looked at Seren, 'I'm sorry, lad, but we're not an inn, just a tavern and the only one in Fennbane at that.'

'Is there nowhere I can stay?'

'Go up to the keep on the top level, they always have rooms for wizards,' he paused, 'You are a wizard, aren't you? Those without magic don't tend to come here.'

'Yes, I'm a wizard, does that matter?'

The man looked at Seren, 'This is a magical community, son, all those living and working here are witches, wizards, seers... you get the idea?'

Seren looked puzzled, 'Why?'

'It's always been this way. Some things never change.'

Thanking the man, Seren left quickly. He hadn't heard that the citadel was exclusively for those who possessed the ability to practice magic. In Shillington, he had friends in both communities, magic and non-magic alike, and they all lived side by side. He didn't understand why it wasn't the same there. Unhitching his horse, he led him round the main street until he came to the path leading up to the higher levels. Thankfully, it was covered. *Finally, a little shelter from the rain*, he thought to himself.

It took a few minutes to ascend to the uppermost level, and when Seren finally emerged from the sheltered path he was a little out of breath. The keep loomed up beyond the wall. He paused as a bolt of lightning illuminated it just for a moment, making it stand out from the dark sky, looking ancient and foreboding. Leading his horse towards a gate in the curtain wall, he was relieved to find it open. Walking through, he entered a large, open courtyard with the keep set back towards the northern section of the wall. When he noticed a man waving frantically to him from an outbuilding set against the wall, Seren walked over to him.

'Bleak night to be out, lad, are you looking for a place to stay?'

'Yes, I was told to come here by the man in the tavern.'

The man ushered Seren just inside the doorway. 'Before I can admit you to the keep, I must ask to see a wand. I trust Samuel also told you that we only cater to the magical community.'

Seren retrieved his wand from inside his robes and passed it to the man who examined it for a moment before drawing his own. He tapped Seren's wand once with his own and it lit up for a few short moments before handing it back to Seren.

'Sorry about that. We've had to start checking of late. You can leave your horse with me and I'll see he is stabled, now just go on over to the keep and they'll find you a room. You might even be in time for a bit of supper, I doubt the kitchen will be closed just yet.'

Nodding, Seren pulled his hood up went back out in the night, crossing the courtyard hastily. Finding the door to the keep closed tightly, Seren knocked and waited. The door creaked open, and a kindly looking woman gestured for him to come inside.

'Welcome to the keep, we have plenty of rooms, but I expect you're hungry, travelling in this weather. Come with me and I'll show you to the dining room, there's still plenty of food.'

Seren followed the woman who continued talking at him the whole time. He smiled and wondered if all the guests evoked this reaction. On his way to the dining room, he noted the interior of the keep. It was in stark contrast to the outside and felt quite warm and inviting. Torches hung along the walls at regular intervals, interspersed with bright, wall paintings and aged tapestries. Finally, they arrived at the dining room. It was a long, wide room with a high ceiling and many more paintings adorning the walls.

The woman led him towards a long, oak table and indicated for him to sit.

'I'll have some food brought out to you. It'll be along shortly.'

She turned and walked towards what he assumed was the kitchen. After a short wait, two girls brought out some plates of food and a jug of ale. He ate hungrily, it was nice to have hot food, and even better that he hadn't had to catch it himself. Once he had finished eating, he poured himself a cup of ale and sat back with a satisfied sigh. Although he had made it to the citadel, he had lost Tobelle along the way and had no idea where to find Tobias. Finishing the ale, he stood, and without warning the woman reappeared.

'All done I see. My, you were hungry. Well, if you're ready I'll show you to your room, please follow me.'

Seren chuckled to himself and once again did as he was told. His room was on the highest level of the keep in one of the towers. As soon as the woman had left, he locked the door, threw his things into a pile on the floor and fell into bed. Feeling like an age since he had slept in a bed, it took just a few minutes to fall into a deep sleep.

Chapter 30

Noon the next day, Seren finally awoke but didn't recognise his surroundings. It took him a moment before he remembered where he was and relaxed back on his pillow as light streamed through the window across the room. With a gasp of realisation at how late it was, he jumped out of bed and dressed hurriedly, foregoing his robes, which were beginning to look a little worn in places. Instead, he pulled on dark riding trousers and a loose tunic since it was finally getting warmer. Picking up his wand and cloak, he hurried out of the room and down the corridor. After four flights of stairs, he reached the ground floor of the keep. Turning down the wide corridor he made his way towards the door, almost reaching it as the woman from the previous night came around the corner and spotted him.

'Good afternoon, dear boy, I trust you slept well. Have you eaten yet?'

Seren opened his mouth to speak but the woman got there first.

'No, I didn't think so, come with me, lunch will be ready by now.'

'No, thank you, I'll eat down in the citadel.'

'Don't talk nonsense, please follow me.'

She turned and began walking towards the dining room, Seren followed, casting a longing glance back at the door. Almost an hour later, the woman relented and Seren left the keep beginning his search for Tobias. Before leaving the grounds, he checked on his horse, he seemed happy enough so Seren decided to let him rest. With a pat on the neck, he left the stables and began the descent into the heart of the citadel. Reaching the second tier, he paused on the path, not knowing where to begin. Perhaps naïvely, Seren had thought it would be easy. As Marcus had found them before, Seren supposed he expected something similar to happen here. With a sigh, he made his decision to start from the bottom and work his way back up.

When he reached ground level, he found it awash with people and stood at the end of the path, just watching. There were so many people, he hoped Tobias was amongst them. Not wanting to draw attention to himself, he reasoned that the only way to locate Tobias would be to ask around. The mingled cries of the market traders in the distance drew his attention, he would begin there. Leaving the path, he followed the street north until he came upon the market. Picking his way through the crowd, he made for the nearest stall and waited for the trader to finish dealing with a customer. The stall had all sorts of little trinkets, mostly superstition wards. Seren stifled a laugh, he couldn't believe people still used those things.

'Can I help you?' The trader asked expectantly.

'Do you know where I can find Tobias Helmand?'

'Sorry, lad, never heard of him, don't live here, just passing through. 'Appen you should ask one of the other traders. Now, can I interest you in anything off me stall?'

'No, thank you,' Seren said politely and turned to leave. Looking at the other stalls, he picked out the meat seller and walked over.

The woman serving behind the stall looked his way as he approached.

'Sorry to trouble you, do you know Tobias Helmand?'

'No, sorry, name's not familiar.'

Seren thanked the woman and walked away with a sigh.

It continued like that for the rest of the afternoon until the sun began to set and the traders started packing up. As the crowds dispersed, Seren bowed his head and rubbed his face. Feeling drops of rain, he turned back towards the path, not wanting to be caught in another cloudburst. Making his way hurriedly up the path, he entered the keep just as the rain began to pour.

Seren made his way straight to the dining hall, realising how hungry he was. In the hall, he found a few other people seated around the table. No sooner had he sat down than one of the girls from the kitchen brought a plate of game pie and vegetables and set it before him. Thanking her, he poured himself a small mug of ale from the pitcher in the middle of the table. As Seren began to eat, the three men and four women sat at the table chatting amongst themselves, but he paid them little attention. Disappointment set in, he had spoken to almost every trader at the market that afternoon and not one of them knew Tobias. Huffing, having forgotten the other people in the room, he looked up to see that they were all staring at him.

'Sorry.'

'Not to worry, dear boy. Bad day?'

'Just long,' he hesitated, 'I'm supposed to be staying with a friend, but it seems he's gone away, and no one appears to know when he is due back.' Cringing at the lie, but not knowing the people, it was the best he could come up with.

'That's bad luck. What will you do now?'

'I'm not sure. I might stay for a few more days. Hopefully, he'll return.'

Smiling, the man turned back to his group, while Seren carried on eating his pie, grateful that the conversation had been short. Pushing his plate away a short time later, he sat back, ale in hand. There wasn't much left, so draining the mug, he rose from the table and left the room.

Wearily, he climbed the stairs, relieved when he finally reached the topmost level and his room. As he closed the door behind him, he was grateful that he hadn't run into the woman, she meant well but was too overbearing. Sitting at the desk in the corner of his room, he took a book from the shelf, turned a few pages, skimming but not really paying much attention. His thoughts turned to Tobelle and he looked out into the night. Seeing it was still raining, he hoped that she wasn't out in it and had gone home. But she was just as stubborn as he was, and so he doubted she had. If she came to the citadel, she would have to stay in the keep anyway so their paths would cross. Seren thought about home and what his parents were doing. By now, the novatice would be ripe and need liquefying before being jarred, so they were probably busy with that. However, he hoped they weren't worrying about him. Closing the book, he got ready for bed. It wasn't particularly late, but he wanted to be up early the next day to continue his search. Extinguishing the candle on the desk, he climbed into bed and closed his eyes.

***

A knock at the door roused the dozing man, and he wondered who would be calling at this hour in this weather. Crossing the room, he opened the door to find a young woman waiting.

'Maya, please come in out of the rain, what can I do for you?'

'Tobias, I just thought I ought to let you know there is someone looking for you. A stranger asked every trader at the market if they knew where to find you, including me.'

Tobias thought for a moment, 'Did they leave a name or reason why they are seeking me?'

'No, nothing. All I can tell you is that he's a little younger than I, with dark, blond hair and wearing well-worn riding clothes. I've never seen him in the citadel before.'

Tobias nodded.

'Well that's all I came to tell you, so I'll be on my way before this rain gets any worse.'

'Thank you for coming to me, Maya, now hurry home.'

The girl left the house and Tobias went back to his chair, *who could possibly be looking for me*, he wondered. *Presumably, whoever it is will be staying at the keep. I must find out more*. Entering his bedroom, he took some old travelling clothes from a chest at the foot of the bed and changed. Standing in front of a large mirror, he took out his wand and pointed it at himself, picturing a guise he used in the past. He watched as his appearance changed. Although he looked younger, unfortunately, he didn't feel it. Tucking his wand into his clothes, he retrieved his cloak and set out into the night. Making his way towards the path, he moved slowly. If his deception was to work, then it had to look as though he had been on the road for some time. When he arrived at the path, he stopped and remained there for a few minutes. When he was sufficiently soaked through by the rain, he continued on his way. Upon arrival at the keep, he presented himself to the night watchman who proceeded to check his wand. Moments later, he made his way to the door and was met by the same woman who had greeted Seren. She looked at him pitifully.

'My dear boy, come in, you're soaked to the bone. Now, follow me and we'll find you something to eat. The girls have already gone home for the night, but there is always something left over, and the fire is still warm.'

Tobias nodded and she began walking in the direction of the dining hall. Once there, he was promptly seated by the fire and told to wait while the woman went to get him some food. He sat alone warming his hands, although he hadn't been outside long, the rain was heavier than he had expected, and the cold had soon set in. A few minutes later, the woman appeared from the kitchen carrying a tray laden with food and a glass of warmed wine.

Setting it down, she said, 'This is the best I can do at the moment, now eat up and I'll be back soon to show you to your room.'

Tobias thanked her before looking at the plate of food in dismay. He had already eaten earlier in the evening and now here he was faced with one of the largest portions of "the best I can do" he had ever seen. He would have to try to eat, having the feeling this was a woman who didn't like to hear the word 'no'. Taking a knife from the tray, he cut a thin slice of bread and buttered it. Managing two slices of bread, some cold meat and a little cheese, even that small amount was difficult. When he felt he couldn't take another bite, he sat back with the glass of wine. *I should have waited until morning,* he scolded himself silently as the door opened and the woman returned.

'All done, now, I'll show you,' she paused looking at the tray, 'You've not eaten nearly enough, my boy. Come now, tuck in.'

Tobias looked at the tray, which was still full of food, and then at the woman. 'I'm sorry, it was delicious, but I really can't manage anymore, I'm quite tired,' he said trying to sound apologetic.

The woman considered him for a moment. 'Not much of an appetite? Well, for now, I'll let you retire, but tomorrow, you will have a good breakfast. Now, please follow me.'

Embarrassed that he hadn't managed to clear his plate, his cheeks flushed, making him feel like a small child again. He followed the woman up the four flights of stairs that led to the top level, his room was at the end of the south corridor. When the woman had left, he locked his door and reversed the glamour spell. He had to keep his strength up. Maintaining his guise would be taxing, so he would only use the spell in and around the keep. The rain was getting heavier, and in the distance, thunder rumbled across the sky. It was late, so Tobias decided to turn in, he would find this stranger tomorrow. Still full from his second supper, he fell into an uncomfortable sleep.

As the sun crept over the horizon the next morning, Tobias awoke and begrudgingly got out of the warm bed. He thought about his duty to the academy, *I should be teaching today but that will have to wait. I must find out who is looking for me and why.* Taking out his wand, he cast the glamour once again, changing his appearance. Leaving the room, Tobias made his way downstairs, keeping an eye out for other people on the way. He was the first to arrive in the dining hall, the table hadn't even been set. The door to the kitchen opened and one of the girls entered carrying a large breadbasket. Tobias recognised her from the academy but couldn't recall her name. When she saw him seated at the table, the girl stopped, visibly startled.

'I'm sorry, breakfast won't be ready for a little while yet, we've not long arrived.'

'Not to worry, I can wait,' he paused. 'You don't live here, then?'

'No, I live near the academy down on the second level, I just come up here to work mornings and evenings to make a little coin. I'm still attending the academy.'

Tobias nodded, 'Sounds like hard work to me.'

'Sometimes, especially when the weather is cold and we must be here early in the morning, but it will be worth it. I'm going to be a healer when I finish my studies.'

'An admirable profession.' Hearing the door open, Tobias turned, standing in the doorway was the woman who greeted him last night.

'Arabella, please don't bother our guests, go and attend to your duties.'

The girl flushed red, 'Yes, Cimelle, I'm sorry,' the girl replied and went about setting out the bread.

'I'm sorry, Cimelle, is it? It was my fault. I distracted the girl,' Tobias interjected.

Cimelle approached, 'Well, not to worry, I must be getting on, so much to be done before our other guests arrive expecting their breakfast.' Cimelle hurried off towards the kitchen, quickly followed by Arabella.

Alone at the long table, Tobias waited for the other guests to arrive, hoping the boy would be among them. Although, Maya hadn't exactly been detailed in her description of him. After a short while, Tobias discreetly watched as people began filing in. None appeared to be of the right age, some looked older than him. As they seated themselves, the first food appeared from the kitchen. Tobias helped himself to a small bowl of porridge and a sweet bread roll.

No other guests arrived before the first plates were cleared away and the second course was brought out. More rolls, savoury this time, renewed the breadbasket. Plates of thick bacon, boiled, poached, and fried eggs, tomatoes, boiled potatoes and mushrooms were placed down the middle of the table. Tobias was about to serve himself when the girls returned with yet more plates of sausages and black and white pudding. He sighed, he'd be putting on weight if he was here for too long but helped himself to a conservative plate of food and began to eat. It wasn't long before Tobias heard the door open but paid it no mind, now engrossed in his food. A boy approached the table, seating himself opposite Tobias, he began helping himself to breakfast. The boy was young, not too young but young, nonetheless. One of the other men at the table had noted his arrival and greeted him.

'Going out to look for your friend again today, lad?' the man enquired.

The boy looked at him, 'Yes, might as well now I'm here.'

The man nodded and turned back to his food.

As nobody else entered the room, he decided, for now at least, to keep an eye on the boy. If he did turn out to be the one, he didn't want to lose him. When Cimelle approached, Tobias immediately turned his attention back to his food, not wanting to be engaged by her again, but thankfully, she went to the boy.

'Now young sir, you've missed the first course and there's only a little left of the second. Finish up that plate, and I'll have some more brought out to you.'

The boy swallowed and looked at her. 'There's no need, I have plenty here, please don't trouble yourself.'

Cimelle looked at him with dismay, 'If you're sure?'

'Yes, I'll be leaving promptly after breakfast, please don't worry.'

Cimelle nodded and walked away, seeming a little put out. Tobias seized the moment to start a conversation with the boy.

'Pardon me, I couldn't help overhearing, she's on at you as well?'

The boy looked up at Tobias. 'Yes, I think she's trying to fatten me up,' he said between mouthfuls.

Tobias smiled, 'Me too. I'm Geta,' he offered his hand.

'Seren,' the boy replied, shaking his hand.

'Will you be leaving today?'

'No, not leaving, just going out to find someone, yourself?'

'No set plans, thought I might explore a little, only arrived last night. I lost most of my things on the road, so I'll need to buy a few items. Do you know where the market is?'

'It's down at ground level, I was there yesterday. I hope you like crowds, it was very busy.'

Tobias nodded, 'Would you mind if I walked down with you?'

'Not at all,' Seren replied, 'If you're ready, we could go now.'

Tobias pushed his plate away. They both stood and made their way out of the room before Cimelle could give them any more food.

Considering the amount of rain that had fallen the previous night, it was a surprisingly dry and pleasant morning. As they left the grounds and ambled down the path, they chatted like old friends. By the time they reached ground level, Tobias had discovered that Seren had recently travelled from Hallsrock in search of someone, although, he didn't say who. Tobias felt certain this was the boy who was looking for him. He seemed to be a good person, and there was no malice about him, but he wanted to find out more before he revealed himself. They stopped at the end of the path.

'Well, Geta, this is where I leave you, the market is to the north. I'll see you back at the keep.'

They shook hands once again and Seren left Tobias standing at the foot of the path. He wanted to follow him but Seren was moving south and "Geta" was supposed to be going north so he couldn't trail him in his current guise. Reversing the spell to reveal his true self could lead to someone pointing him out. That left only one option, he would have to cast on himself again, deepening the glamour. He was reluctant but felt he had no choice. Checking the immediate area, he spotted a small alley running between the main street and the lesser streets deeper within the citadel. Quickly, he ducked into the alley and found a sheltered spot. Taking out his wand, he pointed it at himself, picturing another guise he had once used. The spell took immediate effect and he was changed from Geta to a slightly younger man around Seren's age. After the spell took effect, Tobias waited in the alley for a few moments, hoping he wouldn't have to maintain the double guise for long as he could already feel it draining his strength. Walking back out onto the street, he looked about trying to catch a glimpse of Seren. Slowly, he made his way down the street paying attention to the shops and other establishments that he passed, until he finally glimpsed Seren in the robe shop. Entering the shop, he positioned himself close enough to Seren to hear what he was saying and pretended to look at some of the displayed robes.

After waiting patiently to speak to the man serving behind the counter, when he was finally free, Seren approached him. 'Excuse me, sir, do you know Tobias Helmand?'

The man looked at Seren and thought for a moment. 'Tobias,' he muttered quietly, 'Ah yes, the old mage. He teaches at the academy. Not seen him around for a time, though.'

'Is there anybody else I could ask? It's important that I find him.'

'You could go up to the academy and speak to the head wizard, Eramiah Sinton, aside from him, I don't think there's anyone else who would know.'

'Where's the academy?'

'Up on the next level, the biggest building up there, you can't miss it.'

Thanking the man, Seren and left the shop. Waiting until he left, Tobias began to follow, once again, keeping a respectful distance between them. Tobias wanted to be in the head wizard's office when Seren spoke to him, then he could find out what his intentions were. Ducking back into the same alley as before, he reversed the second glamour and once again took on the guise of Geta. Hurrying back into the crowded street, he ran to catch up with Seren who was already on the path heading to the second level. Finally, a little out of breath, he drew level with Seren and slowed to match his pace.

'Seren, did you find the person you're looking for?'

'Oh, Geta, not yet, but hopefully soon. Did you find anything at the market?'

'No, it's far too crowded. Mind if I come along with you?'

Seren hesitated but couldn't think of a convincing reason to say no, 'Sure, it would be good to have some company.'

They chatted until they reached the gates of the academy, where the gatekeeper stopped them.

'State your business,' he said firmly.

'We've come to see Eramiah Sinton,' Seren replied.

The gatekeeper looked at them, 'He's here, but he may not see you. He has had to step in to cover old Tobias' classes.'

Tobias looked at him, *why is everyone calling me old today,* he thought, *and besides, the gatekeeper is much older than I am.* The gatekeeper beckoned them to follow and led them into the academy. Soon, they arrived outside the head wizard's office, the gatekeeper opened the door and told them to wait inside, adding not to touch anything as he pulled the door to. The office was small and dark, the walls lined with dusty old tomes, which looked as if they hadn't been touched in years. They sat waiting for ages, until finally, the door opened, and the head wizard entered.

'I'm sorry to have kept you waiting and can spare only a minute or two.' The head wizard made his way to his desk and sat down. 'Now, what can I do for you?'

'I'm trying to find Tobias Helmand, I was told you might be able to help me.'

'Alas, dear boy, I wish I could, but I don't know where he is. He was supposed to be teaching today but never arrived this morning. I have had to take all of his classes.'

Seren groaned, *another dead end.*

'I'm sorry to disappoint you, son. Now, I really must get back for the next class.'

The head wizard got up and hurried from the room. Seren watched him go, having lost heart. It seemed all he had was the journal and that couldn't help him. He needed to find Tobias.

'Well, there's no point staying here,' Tobias said quietly, breaking the silence, 'Why don't we go back up to the keep. We've missed lunch, but at least we'll be in time for supper.'

Seren nodded and they left the office. They walked back to the keep in silence. Seren was lost. He had hoped that once he arrived at the citadel, he would find Tobias who would know what to do. Entering the keep, they made their way to the dining hall and found it empty. After going off to the kitchen, Tobias returned with a jug of mead and two tankards. Setting them down on the table, he poured the drinks and offered one to Seren who was lounging in a chair.

'What's so important about this Tobias that it's got you traipsing high and low trying to find him?'

'I was hoping he could help me with something. I found something out by accident, something serious. I've exhausted every path, he's my last hope.'

Tobias looked at him, 'Sounds dramatic.'

'If you're going to joke...' Seren began.

'I'm not making fun, it's just a little hard to believe without understanding the whole story.'

'You wouldn't believe me if I told you,' Seren said glumly, taking a sip of his drink.

For a time, Tobias fell silent, not wanting to push Seren too far. He felt a little awkward, but was saved by the girls bringing the first dishes for supper from the kitchen. Eating in silence, they listened to the others gathered around the table, laughing and talking amongst themselves. Seren ate very little that night and retired early. Watching him leave, Tobias felt sorry for Seren even though he didn't yet know his plight. Tonight, he would find out. He remained in the hall for an hour or so after Seren left and then returned to his own room. When he was safely inside, he removed the glamour. He would have to wait until everyone was asleep then find Seren's room.

The night grew darker, the moon waning and giving off little light, and when it passed into the grasp of the clouds, it was time. Quietly, Tobias left his room, not bothering to use the glamour. He didn't expect to run into anyone at this time of night.

The keep was large with rooms for guests on three of the four levels, and he decided to make his way around the top first. It would take time, but that way he hoped to discover, once and for all, why Seren was seeking him. Moving down the north corridor, he came to the first room, standing quietly he listened but heard nothing. Placing his right hand flat on the door, he closed his eyes, and in his mind's eye he could see the interior of the room, finding it empty. Opening his eyes, he moved to the next door, but once again it was empty. Moving systematically around the upper level, he repeated his actions, finding many of the rooms unoccupied.

The light in the corridor began to diminish as the torches slowly flickered and began to burn out. It wouldn't be long before dawn began to creep towards the citadel, so he had to find Seren's room quickly. Pausing at the south-east tower, he had searched half the upper level and so far, there was nothing. Pressing his palm to the door of the tower room, there was someone inside. He focused on the occupant, then opened his eyes, pleased to have located Seren. Checking that no one was around, he tried the door, but it was locked. He suspected that, as with the rest of the citadel, there would be protective wards that would prevent him using any unlocking spells. With only one option in mind, he knew he wouldn't be entering Seren's room that night as he'd need to make preparation. Though he would need to get home, leaving now might raise suspicion if he were seen, so he returned to his room. He would leave in the morning.

Tobias didn't sleep for the rest of the night, trying to recall everything he would need to make the potion. It had been a long time since he had had to use it and it wasn't the sort of formula you wrote down as it could do a lot of damage in the wrong hands.

Eventually, the morning light crept over the horizon, looking as if it were going to be another gloomy day. Tobias hoped this would keep people inside, as he didn't want anyone seeing him coming and going from the house as Geta. He would have to be careful. It wasn't long before he heard people moving about, going down for breakfast. Taking out his wand, he cast the glamour and left the room. Moving quickly down the stairs, he kept an eye out not only for

Seren but also Cimelle. He couldn't afford to be waylaid this morning. When he was sure that neither was around, he crossed the corridor, slipped through the door, and out into the grounds.

It didn't take long to descend to the second level and soon he was standing just across from his house. When he was certain no one was watching, he dashed over and let himself in. Leaning against the door for a moment, he breathed a sigh of relief. He was tired, keeping the glamour in place was taking its toll, so once again he reversed it. Making his way into the kitchen, he opened the cabinet that held his potion ingredients and equipment, pondering what he would need. Taking two small cauldrons, he set them over the hearth and went to fetch water from the well in his small garden. Returning with a bucketful, he half-filled the two cauldrons and lit a fire beneath them. It would take some time before they were hot enough, so he decided to use the time to make some of Marcus' mud brew.

He hadn't taken the recipe from his friend but had found it among his belongings on his arrival home. While the taste hadn't improved, he had to admit that it had good restorative properties. Taking a small brewing kettle from the cabinet, he filled it with the remaining water. To the water, he added the gold liquid vilanza, and whole carpocha leaves and left them to steep. Checking the fruit bowl, he found it empty, but needed purple quinces for the brew. Searching through the cabinet, he came across a small jar, which upon closer examination he found to hold the pulp of the fruit. It would have to do. He didn't want to go to the market to buy any. Setting the jar aside, he took a black container and a small mortar and pestle. Opening the container, he took out a dansis seed.

Sighing, he began to grind it, he hated crushing dansis, the outer shell always took so long to powder, and the smell was foul, *at least the brew only needs one of them*, he thought thankfully. His arm began to ache long before the dansis was crushed, but finally, all that remained of the once plump seed was a fine, orange powder. Satisfied, he added the quince pulp and mixed them together until they resembled a brown, coagulated lump. Checking the kettle, he dipped a small spoon into the liquid and tasted it, the revolting flavour signalling its readiness. Adding the brown lump, he stirred it a little and placed it on the stove, waiting until the kettle began to steam gently. While waiting for his mud brew, he checked the heating cauldrons in the hearth, which were still not hot enough to proceed.

Sitting at the small table in his kitchen, he wondered how Marcus was, he hadn't had the chance to write to him since his return to the citadel. Tobias hoped he would have some news for him, but until the current situation was resolved, he wouldn't have time to find out. Roused from his thoughts by the whistle of the brewing kettle, the mud brew was ready. Removing it from the stove, he poured the contents into a wooden mug. It always struck him how the thick liquid was of a darker, more unappealing colour than the wood. He hesitated to drink, instead swirling it around for a moment or two. Raising the mug, he closed his eyes as he drank, shivering slightly at the taste as he swallowed. *Repulsive!* But he knew it would do him some good.

Placing the mug back on the table he sat letting the taste subside, knowing it was a flavour he would never get used to. Returning to the cabinet, he gathered everything for the separate void potions. Placing the armful of ingredients on the table, he returned for those he couldn't carry. The void opener potion would take the longest to make, it was one thing to cast an illusion of an object, but to make a solid door disappear was something else entirely. Beginning with the base ingredients for the opener potion—dragon's blood and gillink—he was a little unsure about this batch of dragon's blood, the last time he made the potion he had still been an active mage with access to blood from the mages' dragons, second only in potency to wild dragons. This particular batch was from the "domesticated" dragons, but he hoped it would be fit for the purpose. Mixing the gillink into the blood in a small bowl until it formed a loose paste, he added it to the first cauldron. The water turned cloudy and began to boil. It would be ineffective if the first stage of the potion wasn't boiled for just the right amount of time, so he upturned a sand timer and set to work on the twin potion, adding all the ingredients at once. The second potion wasn't as demanding, and a perfectly acceptable batch could be made by putting everything in together, providing it was brewed for long enough. Gazing out the window, the rain had started again, it seemed to be getting heavier every day. Returning his attention to the sand timer, the last few grains of sand fell from the top chamber. Checking the first cauldron, he noted the colour and began to add the other ingredients, stirring each into the mix as he went. It took some time, but finally, he added the last ingredient and gave one last stir to the mixture. Now, all that remained was to let them brew for a further two hours and they would be ready. Settling down in a chair with an old book, he waited.

Chapter 31

As her horse came to a stop, Tobelle jerked awake. It had taken four days to reach the edge of the forest, the unending rain turning the track to sludge, hampering their progress. Cautiously, she looked round, trying to ascertain why they had stopped. Her captives had dismounted and were talking quietly. Straining to hear what they were saying, she didn't manage to catch anything. Slumped down in her saddle, she waited, wanting to cry but not even having the energy to do that. She had thought about trying to get away but didn't fancy her chances against a dozen wizards who didn't care at all for her wellbeing. Hearing footsteps approaching, she raised her head, seeing one of the wizards coming towards her, stopping alongside her horse. Roughly, she was pulled from her saddle, stumbling slightly as she hit the floor. The wizard dragged her towards the others, holding her robe tightly. The wizard in charge looked at her and gestured for her to come forward, and with a sharp shove from behind Tobelle followed him, walking towards the tree line.

'Beautiful, isn't it,' the wizard said, gesturing towards the citadel that could be seen on the horizon. 'Tell me, is that where your friend has gone?'

Looking towards the citadel, she bowed her head, knowing that Seren would be there and nothing she could say would change his mind, so she said nothing. The wizard nodded, not expecting an answer but he didn't need one.

There was nowhere else that the boy could go except into the mountains. Turning, he walked back towards the other brigands, leaving Tobelle fixed to the spot, wishing she could get a message to Seren, to warn him somehow, but she didn't have that type of power. Besides, she had never mastered telepathy, the skill just hadn't materialised. Tears began to well in her tired eyes, but she had no time to dwell, as once again, she was pulled back beyond the tree line.

***

With his potions safely tucked away, Tobias had returned to the keep in the guise of Geta. He had no idea where Seren was, however, and he would have to wait until after dark before attempting to enter his room.

Safely back in his room, Tobias reversed the glamour and collapsed onto the bed. Maintaining the guise of Geta was beginning to take its toll. It didn't take long before Tobias' head started to loll to the side, dozing off in his wearied state. When Tobias finally opened his eyes, the rain had stopped and the moon was high.

'You old fool, Tobias, how could you fall asleep,' he berated himself.

Quickly, he set about gathering his wand and potions. Pressing his ear to the door, he listened before venturing out of his room. Once in the corridor, he quickly made his way to the southeast tower. When he was sure no one was around, he placed his palm on the door and focused, sensing Seren's presence in the room. He would have to take the chance that he was asleep, it was not something he could sense. Withdrawing the potions from his cloak, he opened the vial containing the void cover and applied it to the door and the surrounding stone. When he was satisfied that he had coated enough of the door for the illusion to take hold, he carefully placed the open vial in the left corner of the doorframe. Taking the void opener, he splashed some of the potion on the top of the door, and again, placed the vial on the floor, this time in the right corner. He watched as the potion ran down the wood, mixing with the first as it made its way towards the floor. It seemed to take an eternity, but finally, it reached the floor, spreading both left and right, pooling around the vials and completing the connection between the two potions. Hearing footsteps on the stairs, just in time Tobias stepped through the door and out of view. Had the witch coming up the stairs been a second earlier, it would have appeared that Tobias had just walked through a solid, wooden door. In fact, what had happened was a void had opened in the space where the door stood to allow Tobias to pass through, while the cover potion gave the illusion of the door still being firmly in place.

Hastily scanning the small room, Tobias had to find Seren's reason for seeking him out. The room was not unlike his own, maybe a little bigger, but furnished in the same way. Quietly, he made his way around, searching the dresser and bureau as he went. Checking the bookcase, the fine layer of dust on all the books told him that none of them were new additions to the shelf. Stealthily, he moved towards the bed and the sleeping form of Seren. A small table stood next to the bed but all that sat on it was a jug of water and a wooden beaker. He moved to turn away when something under the bed caught his eye. Crouching, he found a satchel, but hesitated as the contents were Seren's personal belongings. If someone did the same to him, he knew how he'd feel, but he didn't have a choice. As silently as possible, Tobias began rifling through the satchel, finding an old journal buried at the bottom. Removing it, he turned the first couple of pages and almost dropped the book in surprise, the hasty scrawl across the pages was unmistakable. Seren had a journal written by James. With the journal in his hand, he replaced the satchel and hurriedly left the room. Taking a third vial from his cloak, he opened it and poured it over the door. The vial only contained well water, but it had the appropriate nullifying effect. Collecting the two vials from the doorway, he returned to his room.

Safely inside, he sat down and began to read. Some of the information he already knew, but there was plenty that he didn't. As he turned the pages, he faintly sensed his friend's power still imbued in the journal. He wondered whether Seren had been able to read the entries or whether the journal had protected itself. Recalling Seren saying that he had found something out, implied that he had been able to read it. *I will have to speak with him in the morning and no longer with the glamour,* he thought to himself. Turning the last page, he closed the journal, still no closer to finding his friend, and after reading the last entry, even more concerned. For the remaining hours of the night, he would try to get some sleep, as tomorrow was going to be a long day.

As dawn broke, Tobias awoke from a fitful sleep, doubting that Seren would be up just yet, he decided to wait in the dining hall in order not to miss him. He was first to arrive that morning, even the kitchen girls were nowhere to be seen. Seating himself at the table, Tobias settled in for another long wait.

That morning, Seren woke later than usual, the previous day having been yet another disappointment. With a sigh, he rolled out of bed and dressed, hoping the dining hall would be quiet, as he didn't feel like company today. When he finally entered the hall, he found a few people still seated around the table, one of whom he didn't recognise. Seating himself away from the others, he helped himself to a small breakfast, not noticing the man approaching until he seated himself opposite. Still Seren didn't pay him much attention.

'Seren,' he looked up, the man was offering a book to him. 'I think it's time we talked properly.'

Realising the man was holding the journal, Seren was confused. 'What are you doing with that? Who are you, and how do you know my name?'

'My name is Tobias Helmand. You know me as Geta.'

Seren looked at the journal and back at Tobias. 'You were here all the time. Why are you only telling me this now?' He was angry, nearly all the time he had been searching for Tobias he had been by his side. Glaring at him, he snatched the journal back. 'How did you get this?'

'An old mages trick, but we shouldn't talk of such things openly. Please, if you'll come with me I'll explain all.'

Pushing his plate aside, without a word, Seren stood and walked away. He needed to talk to this man, but he was far too angry. He had been deceived and didn't like it. Tobias remained at the table for a second, unsurprised by Seren's reaction but had hoped that he would at least stay and talk. With a sigh, he rose and began to follow.

***

The brigands had used the darkness of night to move closer to the citadel. After finding a suitable spot, they had made camp and cast a veil of non-sight to hide them from anyone who might pass too close. Tobelle had been put into a makeshift shelter and all but forgotten, lucky to receive scant rations on the road. But since they had stopped, she hadn't been given a thing. Tired, aching, and cold, all thoughts of escape had left her and now she just lay curled up on the floor, pitying herself.

Outside, there had been little activity, the time had not yet come for them to make a move. The brigands knew that the citadel still had its magical barriers in place. They would be unable to pass until the barriers had been brought down, but a direct assault would never work. They were designed to withstand that sort of attack. The brigands needed some way to bring them down from the inside. The captain had been watching the road intently all morning, trying to work out some way to breach the defences. A few people had passed through the gates, which had given him an idea, and he just had to wait for the opportune time. Taking a large hemisphere from one of the bags, he set it down in the damp grass. It would take an immense amount of power to level the barriers, but that was what had to be done. The hemisphere would need to be charged by all the brigands, but that might not be enough. Then he thought of the girl, he could drain her power. Picking up the hemisphere, the captain walked towards the shelter where Tobelle had been left. Finding her curled up on the floor, he shook her roughly. She looked up at him through half closed eyes.

'Get up.'

Staggering slightly, Tobelle got to her feet, the captain proffering the hemisphere.

'Take it in both hands and don't let go.'

Tobelle looked at the hemisphere and back at the captain.

'Do it or I'll make you.'

Frightened and not wanting to anger him further, Tobelle did as instructed. Nothing happened at first, but then she felt a sudden rush. It was like being caught in a strong wind, but at the same time felt an intense tingling sensation in her hands. She tried to let go but couldn't. It didn't take long before Tobelle began to feel weak, the realisation dawned on her then that she was being drained. She remembered reading about the possibility of such things but didn't think that it could actually happen. Still grasping the hemisphere, Tobelle sank to her knees as she felt her power leaving her. Struck by a sudden dizziness, she blinked, trying to clear her head but it was no use. As her breathing became shallow and rapid, she felt she was nearing the end, her final thought before blacking out was of Seren. A single tear welled in her eye and she fell to the floor, the hemisphere rolling from her hands and stopping at the feet of the captain who smiled and bent to retrieve it. He didn't bother to check if she was still alive, he didn't care. She was a burden that he no longer had to bear. With not so much as a backward glance, he left the shelter and returned to the spot he had occupied all morning. With the other brigands milling about with no sense of discipline, he beckoned to his second in command.

'Get everyone over here.'

His second walked away towards the others and began rounding them up. When they were all gathered, the captain brought the hemisphere forward and set it down.

'The hemisphere holds the girl's power, but it isn't enough. Each of you must contribute power of your own. Eight of you will cast a destruction spell into the hemisphere.'

Inspecting the group, he selected the eight who would cast. Pointing at each in turn, those selected moved forward and surrounded the hemisphere. The first brigand stepped up and placed the tip of his wand into the hemisphere. Taking a breath, he focused his mind and cast his spell. His wand flashed, the spell bouncing around inside for a moment before coming to a dead stop in the centre, where it emitted a faint glow. Bending on one knee, he grasped the cage surrounding the hemisphere and sent forth a small amount of power. When he felt it trying to latch on to this newfound source, he released his grip. He knew how "thirsty" these objects were for power and didn't want to end up the same as the girl. Satisfied that he had given enough, he stood and backed away. The remaining seven then took it in turns to make their contributions. As the last one stood and backed away, the captain took a step forward.

Pointing at the remaining three, he said, 'To bring down the barriers we only need to strike at the gate, it is the strongest point, but when it fails the citadel will be defenceless. Cast the targeting spell and contribute your power.'

The three brigands looked at one another before the first stepped forward, repeating the actions of those who had gone before. Moving closer to the hemisphere, he visualised the gate and cast his spell. Once again, the hemisphere caught the spell. Hesitantly, the brigand gripped a bar and contributed to the growing power. With a sigh of relief, he let go and moved away. When all had taken their turn, the captain picked up the hemisphere and contributed some of his power, his spell, however, very different from the others. To cast his spell, he tapped the top and bottom of the hemisphere, a faint shimmer briefly encompassing it before disappearing. His would be the spell that destroyed the hemisphere when it had done its job.

'How are we going to get it into the citadel, we can't just walk in with it?'

The captain looked up at the interruption, glaring at the one who had spoken. 'The opportunity will present itself.'

The brigand who had spoken nodded and looked away.

Knowing exactly how to get the hemisphere into the citadel, the captain scanned the surrounding area, waiting for the right person to come along. He didn't have to wait long. A small girl no more than five or six years old came into view. Following closely behind were a young couple.

The captain smiled, 'Perfect.'

The girl skipped ahead, getting closer. They would have to make their move soon or the opportunity would pass. The captain took but a moment to act. Picking up the hemisphere, he walked a little way from the group towards the child. Still covered by the veil, his approach was unseen. Stopping at the limit of the veil, close to the road that led to the citadel, he waited to see which way the child would go. To his delight, she turned north, and without a moment's hesitation, he stooped and rolled the hemisphere forcefully along the ground. For a moment, he didn't think she would see it, but breathed a sigh of relief when she stopped and watched it rolling towards her.

At first, the girl was hesitant, gazing about to see where the strange object had come from. When she was sure no one was looking, she ventured forward and looked closely at it. She wanted it but didn't want to take it if it belonged to someone else. Slowly, she bent down and touched it, finally picking it up. Turning it around in her hands, it sparkled as it caught the sun's rays. It wasn't heavy, so she threw it up and caught it, liking her new toy.

'What have you got there, dear?'

Her parents had come up behind her.

'A new toy,' she said, holding it out for them to see.

'That's nice,' her father said, lifting her into his arms.

He carried her down the road as they came closer to the citadel, the girl's mother a short way behind, enjoying the walk. All the while, the captain was watching the scene unfold. Father and daughter approached the gate, stopping just short and turning to look back at the mother who was still a little way behind. The girl smiled and waved at her.

'Come on, Papa, I want to show Nana my toy,' the girl said impatiently.

Her father turned and began walking again. The gate loomed above them as they crossed the threshold. Passing under the old portcullis in the centre of the gate, the hemisphere came to life. The immense explosion ripped through the gate, bringing part of the arch crashing down, sending fragments of stone flying in all directions. The mother who had just arrived at the gate was thrown back by the force of the explosion. Gradually sitting up, she looked around. The gate was destroyed, reluctantly she stood and walked towards the carnage. As the dust settled, she approached shakily, amid the rubble about a yard apart lay her husband and child. Sinking to her knees, she began to sob uncontrollably. In her grief, she touched her child's arm. The two most important people in her life had just been ripped away from her. All was silent, she hadn't noticed the gathering crowd. Nor did she notice the twelve red-robed wizards who stormed past her, wands drawn, attacking those who had gathered. As soon as they had seen the explosion, the veil was struck, and all the brigands rushed forward as one. Picking people off from the crowd inside the gate was easy, no one knew what was going on. So, when they rushed in, everyone stayed where they were. When the crowd finally realised they were being attacked, they scattered in every direction and the brigands regrouped.

'The boy is here somewhere, leave no one alive, burn the place to the ground.'

The twelve of them separated off in different directions. It didn't take long before the first fires were set, and parts of the ground level were ablaze.

***

In the keep, everyone stopped when they heard the noise of the explosion. People looked around in bewilderment. A small crowd began to gather in the entrance hall, talking quietly amongst themselves. The talk was abruptly halted as a young wizard crashed through the door, almost falling as he entered.

'The citadel is being attacked,' almost completely out of breath, he struggled to get his words out, 'The barriers have been destroyed, red wizards are attacking people.'

Tobias, who had been walking along the corridor in search of Seren, stopped to listen to the boy. He couldn't believe what he was hearing and wondered if these were the same wizards that Marcus had seen. It was now even more vital that he find Seren, and fast. Hurrying, he made his way towards the staircase, *where else would a boy go to sulk in a new town if not in his room?* As he reached the third of four staircases, he was met with a small crowd of people hurrying downwards. Standing back, he let them pass, scanning each face for Seren. As the final few passed, he continued on his way. Yet more guests were converging on the stairs as he reached the fourth-floor landing, and he wondered if they would all make it out. Pushing the thought aside, he made his way to the southeast tower. Coming to the door, he knocked loudly. No reply came. He knocked again, more urgently this time.

'Seren, if you're inside you must open the door, we have to leave.'

There was a short pause, then finally, a reply, 'Why do you need me to open the door, you managed it perfectly well when you stole my journal.'

'We can discuss this later, please, get the journal and come with me, we have precious little time.'

The door remained firmly shut and Tobias was beginning to get angry. Glancing out the small window set into the thick wall, he saw smoke rising from ground level. It wouldn't be long before the fires spread upwards. Turning back to the door, he clenched his fist and hammered against the wood.

'Seren, open the door, we have to go.'

At last, the door opened, and Tobias stepped inside. Seren began gathering his things.

'Leave those things, they're not important. Just bring the journal,' Tobias said impatiently. Taking his shoulder, Tobias led Seren to the window.

'Look at what's happening, we have to leave now.'

Seren was silent but nodded. Crossing the room, Seren took the journal from his satchel.

'Good, let's go.'

It took them less than a minute to descend to the ground floor. It was deserted except for the young wizard who had announced the attack and was now cowering in the corner. Tobias went over to him.

'Come with us, lad, I'll get you to safety.'

The boy looked up at him, 'This is a keep, we are safe here.'

'No, we have to leave.'

As Tobias took the boy's arm, Seren grabbed the other. Between them, they got him to his feet and led him from the keep. It seemed like an age before they reached the path. The sight that greeted them was horrific. Fires had begun to spring up on the second level now, and from their vantage point they could see several bodies lying in the streets. A lot of people had died already today, many more would meet their end before the day was out. Seren and Tobias looked at each other, helping the boy would slow them down.

'Now, lad, you can come with us, but we can't carry you.'

The boy just nodded. With Tobias leading the way, Seren and the boy followed. Reaching the bottom of the path, they stopped once again.

'We can get out, but it won't be easy, do exactly as I say and follow me.'

The street they turned down was so far free of fire, but the smell of smoke was strong. Hearing hurried footsteps approaching, Tobias suddenly stopped and listened. Looking around, he turned and ran towards a narrow alley. It wasn't ideal, but it would have to do. Ducking inside, they waited silently, pressing themselves against the wall. The footsteps were getting closer. A small group of people ran past, clearly running from something. Moments later, two wizards in red robes followed with their wands drawn. A second later, a scream rang out, then all was silent. Tobias peered out, seeing no sign of anyone, except a person lying motionless on the ground. Checking one last time, they exited the alley, turning left and hurried to the end of the street. Once again, Tobias turned left, the boys hesitating when they saw the thick plumes of smoke coming from the buildings that lined the street.

'Don't tarry, boys, come on,' Tobias shouted sharply.

Reluctantly, they followed him. The road was strewn with debris and bodies. Picking their way through became difficult as they moved farther down the road. As they passed the burning buildings, Seren felt guilty. If it had been down to him, he would have stopped and checked that people weren't trapped, but Tobias wouldn't stop. Seren knew he was right, they had to get out, but it still didn't make him feel any better. Eventually, Tobias halted outside one of the buildings, and taking a key from his robe, quickly unlocked the door and pushed the boys inside, slamming. the door behind him.

'Wait here and be quiet.'

Taking the stairs two at a time, Tobias raced into his bedroom. He pulled a drawer from his cabinet and tipped the contents onto the floor. Dropping to his knees, he rummaged through the pile until he found his old mages wand. When leaving the mages, wands were supposed to be handed in to stop them being used by the inexperienced or ill-intentioned, but Tobias had managed to keep hold of his. The wand would allow him to cast certain spells reserved only for mages. Taking a last, fleeting glance at the portrait of his late wife hanging on the wall, he turned and left the room. The boys were waiting for him in the hallway.

'Right,' he paused, a note of sadness in his voice, 'Time to go.'

Without a sound, Seren opened the door and checked in both directions, finding the road quiet for the moment. Tobias locked the door behind him as he left the house, it was a futile gesture as a lock wouldn't keep the fire out. Turning, he led the boys back up the street. Making their way back to the crossroads was increasingly difficult as more debris from the burning buildings fell into the street. With the fire spreading farther, Tobias sighed as he accepted the realisation that he had probably just left his house for the last time. They didn't stop at the crossroads but carried on straight over to where it was a little clearer, but with fewer places to hide. Feeling exposed, Tobias picked up speed as the street began to wind around the inside of the second level's wall. As they rounded a corner to take them back into the midst of the level, they saw another crowd of people running straight towards them. Only just managing to get out of the way, they found themselves separated. Seren pressed his back against a building, as Tobias and the boy dived left into the relative shelter of an alley. Tobias waved at Seren to get across the road and into the alley, then saw why the people had been running. Three red-robed wizards were tearing down the street towards him, panicked, Seren ran. The alley seemed a lot closer than it was, but before Seren knew it the three figures had closed the gap and now had their wands trained on him. As they flew towards him, the flashes from their wands found their mark. The last thing Seren felt before he hit the ground was a searing pain shooting through his ribs, then the world went dark.

Chapter 32

Watching in horror as Seren fell to the ground, Tobias stood pressed flat against the wall as the robed figures passed. Not stopping to check Seren, they moved on quickly and rounded the next corner. Tobias raced onto the street to where Seren lay face down, gently turning him over. A small pool of blood had gathered beneath him and his breathing was shallow. Tobias was thankful that Seren was alive and selfishly relieved that the journal remained undiscovered. When he gestured for the boy to come and help him, he reluctantly left the relative safety of the narrow passage and came to kneel by Tobias' side.

'We have to get to the academy, it's our best chance of escaping, but you'll have to help me carry him.'

The boy nodded. They had helped him earlier in the keep and it was time to repay their kindness. As gently as possible, they lifted Seren and moved him to the alley. Propping him against the wall, they sat either side of him to keep him from falling. More footsteps echoed somewhere to the south, but no one came their way. It wasn't safe to try to move him while people, friend or foe, were still around. They would have to take their chances and wait until nightfall. If the rogue wizards or the flames didn't find them, it would give them their best chance to reach the academy. Knowing that Seren needed to get to a healer, Tobias hoped he could hang on until they got him out of the citadel, but he wasn't optimistic. He was clinging to life by his fingertips.

The day passed slowly, but finally night fell. Carrying Seren between them, they left the alley. Fires were burning all over the citadel, making the sky unusually bright. Although the glow would make them easy to spot, it did make avoiding the debris a little easier than traversing it in the pitch dark. The most direct path to the academy had been blocked, so they were forced to backtrack and take the longer route around the outer street of the level. After twenty minutes, they had to rest. Normally, it wouldn't have taken so long, but ordinarily, they wouldn't have been carrying another person. Taking shelter in a long porch, they crouched behind the low wall that enclosed it. Seren was hanging on, but they still had quite a way to go until they reached safety. So far, they had managed to avoid running into anyone else since Seren was attacked, but the sound of conflict was still all around them. After a few minutes rest, Tobias stood and looked around. When he was sure it was clear, he gestured to the boy, and once again they lifted Seren and began moving slowly towards the academy, covering the remaining distance in ten minutes. At the academy, they found the gate blasted open and hanging by one hinge. It was a sorry sight.

'Stay alert inside, it's a small academy, but there are plenty of places someone could hide,' Tobias whispered.

Slowly, they moved forward to the main entrance, which too had been blasted open. The grand, oak door that had once dominated the ornate archway now lay in a thousand pieces, strewn across the floor. Carefully, they picked their way through the splinters and across the entrance hall. Tobias navigated the corridors and staircases as quickly as he could, cursing that his office was in such an out of the way area of the academy, but it had been his choice. After ascending the fifth staircase, they finally made it to the office. Once inside, they sat Seren in a chair and Tobias locked the door.

'We'll be safe in here, at least, for the moment.'

The boy looked at Tobias, 'How is this our escape route? This is the top floor of the academy.'

Slumping back into his chair, Tobias closed his eyes for a moment. 'This academy was built five centuries ago, just as the Asimian War began.'

The boy looked at Tobias, 'Asimian?'

Tobias sighed, 'What have they been teaching down at that school? The Asimians were an ancient civilisation, but unlike us, their culture was devoid of magic. For years, an uneasy peace ensued, but the Asimians grew to hate and distrust any who had the craft. Eventually, they took up arms against the magical community. It was their intention to rid the world of magic, but they failed and in turn were themselves wiped from the world.' He paused, forgetting for the moment the situation they were in. 'By the time the war began, the citadel was already old, it was built by the Asimians as a show of might and engineering skill. It was the first of their strongholds to be captured. A small group of mages had secretly been living among the Asimians of the citadel. When the war began, they threw open the gates and let the army in. The citadel fell in one night and the construction of the academy was already underway.'

'Why did they start building an academy if magic was frowned upon?'

'The mages used their magic to disguise what they were building. As the war intensified, it was decided that the academy would be one of the more prominent targets should they try to retake the citadel, and so a safe escape route was created. To my knowledge, we will be the first to use it.'

The boy looked at Tobias, 'I've never heard of that war. Our teacher only taught us the lore of magic, not the events surrounding it.'

'Unfortunately, much of the early lore of our world is overlooked in teaching. It's a shame, but alas, this is not the time for a history lesson. Maybe, one day, I will tell you more.' Tobias paused and looked towards one of the many bookcases that had been crammed into the office. 'What's your name?'

'Warren.'

'My name is Tobias, this is Seren.' Tobias gestured to the unconscious Seren.

'If we get out of the citadel, where are we going to go?'

'There's an old mages camp to the southwest. It's hidden away, but we should find help there.'

Warren nodded. Tobias stood and went to the window that faced east. An eerie, orange glow filled the sky. He knew that much of the citadel, except for the walls themselves, would be reduced to ashes before the fire burnt itself out. The thought upset him as the citadel had been his home for many years. After today, even if it were rebuilt, it would never be the same. Shouts came from nearby, and although the window didn't offer the greatest view, he could clearly make out wand flashes. The attackers were still in the area and there was nothing stopping them from coming back to the academy. If they were to escape, they had to go now, they couldn't wait any longer.

'Warren, it's time to go.'

Crossing to the bookcase he had been looking at earlier, he removed a single book from each of the six shelves. Concealed in the bookcase were small, almost undetectable levers. Working from the top shelf down, he flipped each one. As the last one clicked into place, a deep rumbling came from the wall. Warren watched in amazement as the wall and bookcase slid back, disappearing from view. He was still staring as Tobias came around the desk and gripped Seren's arm.

'Warren, come on, we have to go.'

Moving around the chair, Warren grasped Seren's other arm. As they lifted him, Tobias noted that he was growing colder as time went on. His time was running out, and they still had a way to go. Doubtful that Seren would last the night, he was gravely concerned. As they entered the passage, Tobias pushed on a stone that jutted out from the wall, and the door began to slide back into place.

With no time to find a torch, the passage was dark, so Tobias had to feel his way with his free hand. In places, the floor was slippery, hindering their already slow progress, and it wasn't long before they had to rest. Too tired to think let alone talk, they sat in silence. After a short time, Tobias got up and tapped Warren on the shoulder, indicating that it was time to set off again. They hadn't gone far when Warren slipped and fell, it took all Tobias' strength to hold Seren upright. Warren landed hard, crying out in pain. Setting Seren down, Tobias went over to Warren who was still on the floor, doubled up, gripping his left ankle. Although he couldn't see very much, Tobias knew the boy was obviously in pain.

'Let me look,' he said softly.

Letting go of his ankle, Warren sat back, and Tobias ran his hand over it, feeling the swelling and heat from the freshly injured ankle.

'Do you think you can stand?'

'I'll try.'

Leaning on Tobias' arm, Warren shifted his weight onto his right leg and tried to push up. As he stood, he cried out in pain once again, barely managing to stand. Tentatively, he placed his left foot on the floor, drawing in a sharp breath as pain shot up his leg. Trying to take a step, he stumbled, nearly falling, but thankfully, Tobias had a firm grip on him.

Warren sighed, 'I don't think I can walk.'

There was a note of fear in his voice, he was becoming upset again. Holding him upright, Tobias thought for a moment, *things have just become far more difficult*. There was still some distance to go before they reached the end of the passage, then several leagues between the citadel and the camp. The solution wasn't ideal, but there was no choice, he would have to take Warren to the end and then return and bring Seren down. Having no idea how he would get them both to the camp, for now, he pushed the thought aside, deciding to deal with it when the time came.

Still holding Warren up, he carefully shifted sides to give support to his injured leg.

'Lean on me and use your good leg. I won't rush you, but we must get to the end of the passage as soon as we can.'

'What about Seren?' Warren sounded apologetic.

'I'll take you down and come back for him, you can't carry him anymore.'

Letting Tobias take the lead, Warren lowered his head and quietly sobbed to himself, *these people have helped me and now I've become a burden*. Until they finally made it to the end nearly an hour later, he remained silent.

'How do we get out?'

'The wall will retract and lead out through a series of doors that take us back up to ground level just beyond the citadel's walls. From there, we will move to the camp.'

Gently, Tobias sat him down. Taking off his cloak, he rolled it up and placed it under the boy's injured ankle, hoping elevating it would alleviate some of the pain.

'I will return as soon as I can, for now, just stay put. Try to remain calm and quiet.'

Warren nodded in the dark, 'I don't think I'll be going anywhere in a hurry,' he paused, 'I'm sorry, Tobias.'

'These things happen, dear boy. It might well have been me, now get some rest.'

Peering into the gloom, Warren settled back against the wall, then closed his eyes. Turning back, Tobias made his way up the long passage as fast as he safely could. By the time he reached Seren, he was exhausted and out of breath. Checking Seren, he found that his breathing hadn't improved, but his temperature seemed to be holding. If he got much colder, his body would start to shut down, and whatever small force was keeping him alive would be extinguished. Carrying him alone was going to be an arduous task as Seren was a dead weight. Slowly, half shuffling, Tobias began moving down the passage for the second time in as many hours. Several times, he had to stop and rest before he finally came to the end once again.

With a final effort, he laid Seren down next to Warren who appeared to be asleep. Sitting next to Seren, Tobias leant back, *it would be all too easy to fall asleep*. He was exhausted but sleep wasn't an option, *we have to get out, but how? The horses will have fled. If any are still in the area I doubt they would allow themselves to be caught let alone ridden. I will have to leave the boys and go and find something or someone to help.* With a sigh, he stood and made his way to the wall. Feeling his way along, Tobias found the stone and pushed it in, making the wall slide back, revealing another passageway. Slowly moving forward, he carefully placed his feet trying not to make a sound. Reaching the first door, he stood and pressed his ear to the wood. Everything was silent, so he tried the door, catching his breath as it opened with a creak. Quickly, Tobias moved through the door to the next passage, which sloped sharply upwards. After ten yards, it levelled out and ended at another door. Again, he stopped and listened. This time, the door opened without a sound. Creeping forward, he neared the exit, not wishing to draw attention to himself. The exit was disguised to look like a drainage grate. Stepping closer, he shielded his eyes from the thin shafts of dim light filtering through, indicating that it was almost dawn. He had hoped to still have the darkness to cover their escape, but it wasn't to be. The limited view that the grate afforded him showed a barren plain. No people, no animals, nothing, just emptiness. Gripping the thin bars, Tobias pushed against the grate, but it didn't move. Trying again, he applied more force this time, and it gave a tiny amount. Putting his shoulder against the corner, he threw all his weight into his third push. With a groan, the grate gave and fell outwards to the ground, Tobias tumbling with it. Landing heavily on his arm, he shook it off and got to his feet. The passage had brought him out on the western side of the citadel. The foothills of the mountains were visible in the dim light to the north, it would take them longer to go through the woods that covered the hills, but in daylight it was the safest option. Now, he just had to find some way to move the boys. Picking up the grate, he pushed it back in place, doubting anyone would notice, but not taking any chances.

Moving quickly, he followed the wall to the south, looking for anything he could use. As he suspected, there were no horses to be seen. Nearing the gate, he slowed down and approached it cautiously. Stepping just inside the gate, the sight that greeted him was horrific. A pile of bodies lay just beyond the gate on the road, the carrion birds already gathering, picking at their leisure. He bowed his head as he passed, so many had died in recent hours. As he looked up, he saw the answer to his prayers. A small trap stood next to the wall, completely untouched amid all the carnage. It was small enough that he should be able to pull it himself, although it would still be difficult getting it through the woods. Taking up the short shafts, he pulled, and the trap moved. It was light and the wheels seemed in good condition, so it wasn't such an arduous task. Skirting the pile of bodies, he began to pull the trap through the gate. Reaching the midpoint of the ruined entrance, he was faced with a pile of rubble. It would be difficult, but he would have to try to lift it, as the road was just too clogged with rubble.

Stepping up onto a large piece of stone, he gripped the shafts and pulled, the front wheels of the trap coming up relatively easily. But getting it fully up onto the rubble took a little more manhandling. Tobias was halfway across the rubble when he stood on something soft and stumbled back. Regaining his balance, he looked down and saw one, then two, then three bodies, one of which was that of a small girl. *They must have been some of the first to fall,* he thought. Thinking he saw one of them move, he blinked and looked again, *no, just my mind playing tricks.* Taking up the shafts once more, he began pulling the trap, taking care to avoid the bodies, *these people have suffered enough.* When he was almost clear of the bodies, the back wheel slipped from the rubble and pulled the cart sideways, landing on top of the dead. Cursing himself, he tugged it free and righted it. Then he saw it again. One of the bodies definitely moved. Making sure the trap was secure, he stepped down next to the body. Placing his hand on their shoulder, he gently shook them.

For a moment, nothing happened, then, 'Kill me.'

Tobias jumped, not expecting a reply.

'You have taken my child and husband, why spare me? Just do it.'

Taken aback, Tobias replied. 'I'm not going to hurt you, please let me help you. You can't stay here.'

'I won't leave them,' she said defiantly.

'There is nothing you can do for them now. Surely they wouldn't want you to linger here in this place.'

Without replying, she started to sob loudly.

Tobias held out his hand, 'Take my hand, I'll take you somewhere safe.'

For the first time, she turned her head to look at him. Her eyes were red and swollen, tracks of dirt lined her cheeks where her tears had fallen. Her dark hair was caked with dust, her clothes much the same. She gazed up at him for a few short moments before silently reaching up and taking his hand. Gently, he lifted her onto the rubble. Not having moved since her family had died, she walked stiffly. When she was safely across the rubble, Tobias went back to the trap and pulled it the final few yards to the entrance of the gate, finally free of the rubble. Expecting her to climb into the trap, he waited, but instead, she grabbed the other shaft. Without a word, she nodded, and Tobias led the way. Five minutes later, they arrived back at the grate and found it still in place. Without hesitating, Tobias removed it and hurried inside, relieved to find both boys where he had left them. Seren had grown paler, his skin clammy, and his breathing now coming in shallow rasps. Looking up, he found the woman standing next to Warren who was just beginning to stir. As Tobias started to pick Seren up, the woman rushed over to help him.

When Tobias had a good grip, he said, 'I need you to help Warren,' he gestured to the boy still sat on the floor.

'He's injured his ankle and will need some help to walk. We have to get them on the trap and away from here.'

Nodding, the woman went back to Warren. Tobias started the walk toward the entrance to the passage, taking Seren with him as best he could. Soon, the woman was following with Warren limping beside her. As they emerged, they heard voices from just out of sight around the wall. Gesturing to the woman, Tobias indicated for Warren to be helped up first. When he was safely in the trap, Tobias and the woman lifted Seren up. Taking hold of his arms, Warren tried his best to help by pulling him in. With Seren in the trap, Tobias and the woman quickly took up the shafts and began pulling. The voices were growing louder but they couldn't move any faster with the weight of the boys in the trap. Turning to look back, the woman saw two red-robed wizards standing, staring at them. Glancing at one another for a moment, the two wizards drew their wands and advanced towards them. The woman's reaction was instantaneous. Dropping the shaft, she ran around the trap and stood firm.

'You have killed my family and many others, you won't take any more,' she shouted.

Laughing, the brigands continued their advance. Spreading her arms wide to her sides, wand in one hand, palm outstretched, she cast her first spell just as the two brigands released their spells at her. Striking the small, shimmering shield she had cast, the spells dissipated as she cast her next spell. The flashes re-appeared and flew back towards their casters. The brigands didn't have time to react and the spells hit home, killing them instantly. Tobias was dumbstruck as she returned to the shaft.

'Let's go,' she said almost calmly.

Taking the strain, they resumed pulling the trap. A short time later, they made it to the woods and the relative safety they offered without further incident.

Chapter 33

As dusk fell, they finally reached the camp, but many had arrived before them. Finding a spot to stop, with Seren still just hanging on, Tobias hurried off in search of a healer. After a short while, he returned with a stout woman.

She took one look at Seren and cried, 'Samson, Artilius, bring a stretcher immediately.'

Moments later, two men appeared through the throng of people.

'No stretchers left, ma'am,' one of them said.

'For goodness sake, well carry him to the pavilion, he must be treated at once.'

The two men lifted Seren from the trap and carried him away, the healer turning to look at Warren. 'You're hurt?'

'Just my ankle, nothing serious.'

Scanning the area, she called out, 'Apia, yes, dear, over here.'

A girl came hurrying over, she didn't look much older than Warren.

'See to the boy,' the healer said firmly, 'One of my best students, you'll be in good hands with her.'

Without another word, she hurried off in the direction that Seren had been taken, Although Tobias wanted to go, he felt guilty about leaving Warren. The woman who had helped him walked over and gently put her hand to his arm.

'Go to your son, I'll wait here with Warren.'

Tobias nodded. He would correct her later. Unsure where Seren had been taken, he hurried off after the healer. As he neared the pavilions, he lost sight of her. Looking at the long line of tents, he sighed, not relishing the thought of having to search for Seren. About to enter the first tent, he heard that same firm voice.

'Ah, there you are, now, I need to ask you some questions about the boy, please follow me.'

Tobias obliged and was led into the pavilion where Seren was being treated.

'What happened to him?'

'He was hit by a spell, but I couldn't tell you the exact workings of it.'

'How long has he been unconscious?'

'Ever since he was hit,' Tobias sighed, 'It must be almost twenty-four hours by now.'

'Unresponsive throughout?'

'Yes.'

She nodded again. 'We'll do all we can for him, but I can't make you any promises.'

Tobias bowed his head slightly, 'Do you mind if I stay with him?'

'Not at all, but don't get in the way.'

She walked away and took over Seren's treatment. Finding an unoccupied chair. he sat down heavily, remembering the pavilions from his days in the mages. He hadn't liked them back then, as many of his friends had spent their final moments within these canvas walls. Now, however, he felt strangely at peace, safe even. More and more people filtered into the ever-decreasing space of the pavilion, some walking, some being carried in. He heard a shriek, and someone started to cry. Another person had just died, the body being carried out to make room for the next casualty. There would be no time for grief for a good while yet. Suddenly, a man burst in and looked around.

'Asperilla, come quickly.'

The woman treating Seren looked up, 'I'm a little busy right now.'

The man went over to her, 'A girl has just been brought in from the plains.'

'And?' Asperilla asked impatiently.

'She appears to have been drained.'

Asperilla looked at him, 'That's nigh on impossible, are you absolutely sure?'

The man nodded.

'Bring her in then, a bed has just become available,' she said with a sigh, gesturing towards the bed opposite Seren's.

The man left briefly, returning with two others who were carrying the girl. Tobias felt helpless but there was nothing he could do, having never trained as a healer. The girl was as unmoving as Seren. With a sigh, Tobias sat back, knowing there would be many more yet to come.

***

Sat in front of the seeing stone, Archimon surveyed the devastated citadel, which was still ablaze. He smiled, 'Captain, your report.' In his mind he waited for the reply.

'My lord, the citadel is destroyed, all who were found within the walls are dead. We sustained only minimal casualties.' He paused, Archimon waited for him to continue. 'The boy and girl you sent us looking for are dead, we set ablaze the seer's house in Hallsrock with him still inside.'

The captain neglected to mention that they hadn't identified the boy Archimon wanted dead, but as far as he was concerned, they had done their job.

'Very well, you are to return to the fortress with haste. Contact your lieutenants, have them do the same. Our time is drawing near.'

'Yes, my lord.'

Archimon severed the link, feeling the familiar presence gathering in the room.

'Is it done?' The voice seemed to resonate around him.

'The citadel and all its inhabitants are dead.'

'I care not for the citadel, only those I spoke of before.'

'They died in the citadel. The way is clear. All who knew are dead.'

'About time, finish your task, Archimon.'

'Yes, my lord.'

The voice didn't reply, and Archimon waited as the presence faded from the room. *I will indeed finish his task,* he thought to himself. The sound of the door opening caught his attention, but it was only Laurentis entering. He didn't need to ask where she had been. She'd gone to draw more power from the orb. Hungry for power, her trips upstairs had become increasingly frequent since their binding. If she continued drawing power at this rate, she would soon surpass him, and he wouldn't allow that. Archimon decided to move the orb that night. Turning back to his desk, he unrolled an old chart and began to study it carefully. There was much to prepare if he was going to succeed in his takeover.

Going straight to her rooms in the suite, Laurentis felt fresh after visiting the orb to take more power, and it felt good. Over the last few days, she had distanced herself from Archimon. As her power had grown an idea had taken shape, *why should I be subordinate to him?* Now her power was great, she didn't need him. She had thought about going away, but they were bound and their powers were intertwined. If she killed him, she would take his power, but had to come up with a way to do it. Since the binding, Laurentis had spent much of her time studying. At school, she hadn't been the most attentive student but she more than made up for it now. But she did have an idea. As a witch or wizard your power was part of your very being. Health and magic were intertwined, you couldn't wield magic without your health, but it would take serious injury or illness before power became unusable. Her problem was that she had never known Archimon to be even slightly unwell, so she would have to make him ill. Lying back on her bed, Laurentis closed her eyes and tried to think. She had to come up with a plan. *Access to him isn't a problem, but how could I actually do it? Poison would be the simplest solution, but over a prolonged period he would surely become suspicious. Then there is the question of delivery. He always conjures his meals directly from the kitchen, so lacing it would be difficult.* Having thought about stabbing him in his sleep, she knew that wouldn't work as he had protected himself from "mortal" weaponry a long time ago. If she tried the blade would turn on her, *things are never simple,* she thought.

Archimon waited until well after dark before checking whether Laurentis was asleep. Leaving the suite, he made his way up to the room that housed the orb. Once inside, he flicked his seldom used wand and the stand that held the orb slowly lifted from the floor, levitating towards the open door. This level of the fortress had many concealed rooms, some he used whilst some remained empty. As Laurentis only knew about the room that held the orb, he doubted she'd find it again. Halfway down the hall, he stopped and turned to face what appeared to be a blank stone wall, but he could see the door. As master of the fortress, only he could see the door. Placing his hand on the stone, the outline glowed for a second before slowly opening. The room was vast but empty, the orb would be safe there. Bringing the stand to rest on the dusty floor, Archimon exited quietly, the door closing silently behind him. Without a second thought, he returned to the suite, finding the thought of Laurentis searching for the orb mildly amusing. She would be angry when she discovered that it was gone.

Awaking the next morning, Laurentis once again found she was levitating. But this time she didn't panic, simply relaxing and gently floating back down onto the bed. She'd become used to it as it often happened when she fell asleep with a question playing on her mind. Laurentis was annoyed with herself for falling asleep, she had hoped to finalise a plan the previous night. She needed somewhere quiet to think, somewhere she wouldn't be interrupted. Thankfully, she knew just the place. Without making a sound, Laurentis left the suite, glad that Archimon was nowhere to be seen. She knew she would have to keep him on her side but that would take effort, effort she didn't wish to waste right now. Making her way through the fortress, she came to a narrow staircase and began climbing. She had found it quite by accident, but it led to the perfect thinking place. The stairs went up to the very top of the fortress, bypassing the last few levels. Finally, she reached the top, where a dimly lit passage ended at a stout, wooden door. Opening the door, she emerged onto a covered terrace. Unlike the others, this terrace faced north over the mountains to the land beyond. Now Laurentis found herself looking out over those lands again. She had been there many times since discovering it, as no one else seemed to use it and she enjoyed the solitude. There was no equal to her within the fortress now and their company bored her. The time since the brigands left had been peaceful, and she knew they would soon return, but she thought they would return to her rule.

'Ha, my rule indeed, but not if you don't have a plan,' she said quietly to herself.

She knew exactly what she would do once he was dead. Take those brigands who bowed to her and go north. That was where true magic and immense power lay. She had been there once, to find a dragon to obtain a vial of blood and had felt truly at home, more so than in the south where they just played at magic. Her power would be revered by those in the north. It wouldn't take long to dispose of Him once she moved north, with the power she knew she could obtain, He wouldn't be able to stand before her. Yet, the problem of how she would rid herself of Archimon still plagued her. Laurentis drew her cloak around her as the wind moved in, throwing up little flurries of snow. She watched as one flurry danced upwards, staying together for a moment, almost resembling a perfect sphere. Suddenly, it came to her, the orb. It was the one thing she could guarantee he would use and the one thing that wouldn't arouse suspicion. It would have to be some sort of potion, something that his body would absorb as he took power, but she knew of no such potion. She would have to create one. A smile crept across her lips. It was the perfect plan. Shivering slightly against the wind, she turned and went back into the fortress, the terrace having done the job once again.

Returning to the suite, Laurentis went directly to her rooms. Still Archimon was nowhere to be seen. Checking her small ingredients store, she found nothing that would make a particularly life-threatening potion. She knew she could take what she needed from Archimon's store, but if he noticed certain items missing then he might guess what she was doing, and all would be lost. She knew the trader would be due to pay a visit soon. Hopefully, he would have what she needed. Her next problem was slightly greater, having never created her own potion before. She would have to ask Archimon to teach her. She had managed to avoid being in his presence for some time but now she had no choice, so went in search of him.

Halfway down the stairs, Laurentis thought of the orb. Knowing Archimon hadn't drawn any power from it for the last week, she thought he might have gone there. With a sigh, she turned on the step and began the walk back up. As she approached the stairway that led to the orb, Archimon appeared, having just descended.

'Archimon, can I ask you something?' She said as politely as she could.

He nodded curtly.

'You've created many potions, could you show me how to do it?'

Archimon remained silent for a moment, then smiled his slightly creepy smile, 'Come with me, I'll teach you. We shall start simply. You will make a fortifying potion for body and mind. It can be used to regain strength when required. It should be easy enough.' He sat down on one of the couches. 'Potion ingredients must be put together for a purpose. Therefore, all potions must be imbued with their creator's will, without this they are merely a mixture, an inedible soup if you will.'

Laurentis nodded, as much as she didn't like him, he was a good teacher, and surprisingly patient at times considering his usual manner. Standing, Archimon moved to his ingredients store, returning with four different containers, which he set down on a small table.

'These are all you will need to make the potion. To begin, fill a small cauldron with water and using your wand give the base—the water—its purpose. Then you simply prepare the ingredients and heat them until it is ready.'

'How will I know if I've prepared it correctly?'

'It's your potion, you know the ingredients and the different ways in which they can be prepared. Take control and it will work.'

Laurentis nodded, 'Must I imbue it each time I wish to make it?'

'No, once made, it becomes part of the craft. Magic threads itself through the ingredients and the will of the creator, binding them to the potion.'

Laurentis understood now, she would make the fortifying potion in case he asked to see it, she would also start work on her intended potion, but she would have to acquire some new ingredients first.

'May I test potions on the prisoners?'

Archimon smirked, 'Do not test this one on them, but those with more damaging properties you may. The cells are a little crowded.'

Laurentis nodded and stood, picking up the ingredients as she made her way to her rooms to prepare the potion. Archimon was pleased that Laurentis was taking an interest in learning once more, he had thought her naïve to stop her training. She still had a lot to learn.

As the day wore on, Laurentis grew increasingly impatient, the sooner she started the potion the sooner she would be rid of him, but how, she had nothing in her store of any potency. Her thoughts were interrupted by a knock at the door.

'Yes,' she said firmly.

When the door opened, a young woman not much older than Laurentis entered the room, she was one of the few servants who Archimon permitted in the fortress. Not that she or her fellow domestics had really been given a choice in coming there.

'Begging your pardon, miss, the trader has just arrived, would you like me to purchase anything for you?' There was a slight nervousness in her voice.

Laurentis smiled, maybe things would go her way after all. 'No, I'll come down and meet with him.'

The woman nodded and left the room.

'You are venturing into dangerous territory, Laurentis.'

Jumping at the voice, she drew her wand and looked around. When she was sure no one was there, she let out a breath.

'And now I'm hearing things,' she said to herself.

Putting her wand away, she left the room and went to meet the trader. As she closed the door, the priestess who had performed the binding appeared in the corner of the room.

Entering the great hall, Laurentis saw Archimon talking with the trader and realised she would have to be careful while he was there. Putting on a smile, she greeted them both as she approached.

'That concludes our business, until next time.'

Gathering up his purchases, Archimon turned and left the hall leaving Laurentis alone with the trader. Casually, she looked over his latest offerings with feigned interest. There was one item that caught her eye, a small vial of yellowish, white powder, picking it up, she examined it closely.

'Careful with that, lass,' the trader said. She looked inquisitively at him. 'That there is deathcap, quite potent an' all, picked and powdered on Midsummer's Eve.'

'Interesting,' she set it aside.

Another vial tucked away behind some more generic ingredients caught her eye. Picking up the bottle of clear liquid she asked, 'And this?'

'Ah that, well that is helixium, the venom from the helix spider. It's very rare and very expensive.'

Nodding, she placed it down with the deathcap. There was little else that piqued her interest, but she couldn't just appear to buy poisons, so she selected a few other items and placed them all together.

'That will be all,' she indicated the small pile of jars and vials.

The trader looked nervous. 'Thirty-five sovereigns,' he stuttered, mopping his brow.

Laurentis smiled and took out her coin purse, counting out the coins and handing them to the trader, who quickly put them away.

'Mind how you go with some of those.'

Gathering her ingredients, Laurentis turned to leave.

'Oh, trader,' the man looked at her, 'The less Archimon knows about my purchases the better for all of us.' She turned to look at him, he was staring, mouth slightly agape. Dropping something on the table, she nodded. The trader looked down to see five more sovereigns.

'Yes, lass,' he said quietly as he took the coins.

Pleased with herself, she left the hall glad he had accepted the bribe. As her only alternative would have been to silence him, she would have needed a good explanation to get out of that one. Making her way quickly through the suite, she arrived at her rooms, carefully locking the door behind her and placing her ingredients on the bed. Taking those of lesser importance, she placed them on the shelf in her store.

'Deathcap, my girl, you want to make him sick. That will hardly touch a sorcerer such as Archimon.'

Laurentis froze, this time she wasn't hearing things, someone else was in the room. Worst of all, they knew about her plan. Turning, she drew her wand, shocked to see the priestess standing in the middle of the room.

'Why are you here? How do you know what I'm planning?'

'You admit it then?'

Stupid girl she thought, her silence telling the priestess all she needed to know.

'He'll know you're here.'

'No, he won't. I am veiled to all but you. My power comes from the north and is far more potent than that of the south,' she paused, 'Except maybe for yours.'

The priestess studied the other vials on the bed. 'Helixium, better, but only if mixed in the right way.'

'Why are you here?'

'When first we met, I saw something in you, something more than being confined to this place in servitude to him.'

'Servitude,' Laurentis snorted, 'I'm his equal.'

'No, you might think you are, he might even say you are, but you're not. He wants your power and nothing else.'

Bowing her head, in her heart Laurentis knew it was true that he would never share what he hoped to obtain.

'I kept some of your blood from the ceremony and have been using it to watch over you ever since. I know what you want, and I can help you if you'll let me.'

Laurentis nodded but remained silent.

'Hide those well,' the priestess pointed at the vials, 'I'll return tomorrow, you'll have your potion and your power.'

When the priestess disappeared without warning, Laurentis wondered what she meant about seeing something in her but couldn't think about that now as she had to hide the poisons. Looking around, her eyes fell on the water jug standing in the wash basin. *If they leak, I'll poison myself. The bookcase.* She went over and moved some of the books. Placing the vials at the back of the shelf, she replaced the books. *It will do for now,* she thought to herself.

Chapter 34

Opening her eyes early the next morning, Laurentis found the priestess standing at the foot of her bed. Still tired, she wearily climbed out of bed and readied herself for the day. The priestess watched her in silence, almost as if she were in a trance.

'Shall we begin?' Laurentis asked quietly.

Nodding, the priestess moved towards the bookcase, finding the hidden helixium with ease and taking it from the shelf.

'Helixium used in the right way will give you the results you desire. However, you don't have the time for him to sicken slowly.'

Laurentis looked at the priestess, unsure what she meant.

'Elsewhere, events are conspiring that will soon bring an end to this place. I know this to be true, so you mustn't question it. Go on with your plan, and when the time comes you must be the one to kill him.'

Laurentis agreed but wondered who else would stand against Archimon.

'I know what you're thinking, but I won't speak of this anymore. Now, bring me a cauldron.'

Retrieving the cauldron from her small store, Laurentis set it alongside the hearth and began lighting the fire. The priestess took a pouch from inside her cloak and offered it to Laurentis who took it without question.

'This is everything you will need to mix with the helixium, it's all prepared. All that remains is for you to give the potion its purpose and we can begin the brew.'

With the cauldron suspended over the growing fire, Laurentis half-filled it with water. Withdrawing her wand, she stepped forward and placed the tip in the water.

'What are you doing?'

Puzzled, Laurentis frowned at her.

'You must wait until it boils before you do that, then add the helixium and do it once more.'

Archimon didn't tell me that, she thought.

'He didn't tell you because he wanted you to fail, in that way, you would rely more upon his knowledge rather than trusting your own.'

Laurentis scowled, *Archimon deserves this*. It didn't take long before the water was boiling, so once again, Laurentis stepped up with her wand and placed the tip so it was just submerged. In her mind, she gathered her thoughts, focusing on sickness and a growing weakness, her anger fuelling her thoughts. With her eyes closed, she didn't see what was happening, but the priestess saw her wand beginning to emit a faint glow. The water began to boil more rapidly and slowly started to turn cloudy. As her wand began to heat up, Laurentis held it tightly until it was almost too hot to hold, then it immediately cooled again. She opened her eyes and saw that the water had turned a murky grey. Taking her wand, she wiped it on her robe and took up the vial of helixium, glancing at the priestess who signalled for her to continue. Uncorking the vial she poured all of it into the cloudy boiling water and the venom slowly combined with it. She let it boil for a short while before repeating the process with her wand. Once she had imbued it for the second time, the priestess stepped forward with the pouch.

'To make the potion as potent as it can be will take three days. The two roots must boil for one day before anything else can be added.'

Taking the roots from the pouch, Laurentis examined them, identifying them as mandrake and tilers root. Placing them into the cauldron, she stepped back as it began to boil violently then turned a deep violet.

'At this time tomorrow, add the remaining ingredients, except for the arrowroot. At midnight, tomorrow crush the arrowroot and add it. Stir the mixture exactly five times and leave it to boil. Ensure that the fire doesn't go out, it must boil for three days to combine or it won't work.'

Laurentis nodded.

'I will return in three days when it's ready. Keep to yourself and let him think you're working.'

As before, the priestess disappeared from the room leaving Laurentis alone. Over the next three days, she did as instructed. By the third day the potion had turned a deep crimson and began to smell like she imagined a grievous, lingering sickness would. As she sat eating lunch that day, the priestess returned. Without a word, she went to the cauldron and inspected the contents.

'You've done well,' taking up a small bucket she doused the flames, 'When it cools it will be ready.'

It took the rest of the afternoon before it cooled, but finally, Laurentis divided it into three vials. 'This is all it made,' the disappointment was clear in her voice.

'This is all you will need, and all that time will allow. There are two more things you must do now. Find the orb that was moved six days ago.'

'He moved it?'

'Yes, but you will find it, when you do, use a whole vial. Use the second vial a week later and the final one a week after that. When all three have been absorbed, he will be weak enough for you to dispatch him easily.'

'And the other thing?'

The priestess looked into her eyes, 'You must kill me,' she said calmly.

Laurentis stared at the priestess. 'Kill you, why?'

'My time is ending. If I die naturally, my power returns to the world, if you kill me you can take it.'

Laurentis was confused, she had killed the high wizard but didn't receive his power.

'You will take my power as I have chosen to let you end my life. As a priestess, in death I have the choice to pass my power to one deemed worthy. You are worthy, Laurentis, and where you will be going you will need all the power you can get.'

'I can use the orb,' she said quietly.

'No, once you use that potion you must never touch it again,' the priestesses' voice was firm.

'When must I do it?'

'Tonight. It would be better to wait for the full moon, but tonight will be close enough.'

Laurentis gave a slight nod and remained silent.

***

As the moon appeared, Laurentis led the priestess up to the northern terrace. Taking her through the fortress had been risky, but as the priestess explained, it was the best place to carry out the ritual. The sky was unusually clear, and the crisp air bit at their faces as they stood in silence. When the priestess held out her hand, Laurentis handed her a dagger. With one smooth motion, the priestess cut her left hand and let the blood pool in her palm. As the priestess proceeded to draw the intricate symbol on her forehead with the blood that would assure the transfer of power, Laurentis remained still. Once she was finished, the priestess gave the dagger back to Laurentis. Taking a deep breath, Laurentis moved forward and with a last look into the dark eyes of the priestess, plunged the dagger into her chest. Gasping as the dagger thrust into her heart, the priestess smiled at Laurentis for the final time and crumpled to the floor. *It is done,* Laurentis thought and turned to leave.

Just as dawn was breaking over the mountains, Laurentis awoke on the cold stone of the terrace. Dizzy, she sat upright, unsure of what had happened. It took a few moments, but the memories of the previous night returned. Glancing around the terrace, she saw the body had disappeared leaving only the bloodstained dagger in its place. Rubbing her hand across her face, she felt the traces of blood still on her forehead. Grabbing a handful of snow, she wiped the blood away. Slowly, Laurentis clambered to her feet, the force of the priestess' power must have made her black out. She'd been warned that it could happen but hadn't worried about it. If she couldn't have handled the power, she wouldn't have woken up. Shivering, she carefully made her way back down into the fortress. As she descended the stairs, she remembered what the priestess had said about the orb being moved. Despite her tiredness, she made directly for the room where it had been housed.

Entering the room, she found it empty as expected. A thought struck her, *Archimon descended the staircase less than six days ago when I asked him about making potions. Why would he have been up here if he had already moved the orb?* As far as she knew, there were no other rooms, although she'd never really looked, so she couldn't be sure. Cold and weary, she wanted her bed but decided to look around. Exiting the room, she took the corridor to her left. As she made her way around, all she saw was blank, cold stone. The only door she had seen was the one that led into the room, which had housed the orb. *Something isn't right.* Not wanting to miss anything, she ran her hand over the wall as she went, it felt strange, cold like stone, but there was an energy about it. Then she felt something else... concentrated energy. She stopped and looked at the wall. Placing her hands against the stone, she pushed gently, nothing happened. She pushed harder, but still nothing happened. With a groan, she gave up but would come back.

Thankfully, Archimon was still asleep when she entered the suite, quietly making her way to her rooms and quickly getting into bed. It didn't take long for her to fall into a deep sleep. Dreams came to her almost as soon as her eyes closed. Most made no sense, but one was so vivid it could have been real. In her dream, she saw Archimon with the orb, levitating it along the corridor before putting it down. Then, placing a hand flat on the wall, a doorway appeared. She couldn't see inside. but she did see him place the orb in the room. Snapping awake, Laurentis ended the dream. *Was it real or was my mind playing tricks on me*? She had definitely felt something in the corridor, *I have to find out.* Tired but determined, having only slept for a short while, Laurentis took one of the vials, tucked it into her robes and left the suite. Hastily, she made her way back up to the corridor, running her hand along the wall until she felt the energy. Once again, she pushed but nothing happened. Thinking back to the dream, she focused on what Archimon had done. Placing her palm flat on the wall, she waited, but nothing happened. Angrily, she kicked the stone. Trying once again, this time she focused on a door. A smile spread across her lips as a faint outline appeared and the door began to open. Moving forward, she suddenly stopped as a sharp pain shot through her foot. Kicking the wall had been a bad idea. Limping inside, she found the orb in the centre of the room. The temptation to draw power was great, but if she did Archimon would know she had found it. Without a second thought, she took out the vial and poured the contents into the orb. For a moment, the power it contained was still. then small bolts of energy resembling lightning danced across the surface.

'No, don't do that,' she hissed.

Finally, the orb settled down. Inspecting the orb, it didn't look altered in any way, *this just might work.* Hobbling, she made her way out of the room and watched as the door began to close. Starting back along the corridor, she halted, thinking she heard something. Listening, barely daring to breathe, she realised that the sound was footsteps and they were approaching fast. She panicked. *It can only be Archimon.* Turning, she started limping back the way she had come, the footsteps growing louder. With the agonising pain in her foot and it beginning to swell, Laurentis could go no faster. Her attempts to run turned into more of a fast hop, but finally, she rounded the corner, just getting out of sight as he came into view. Not daring to breathe, she peered around the corner to see him entering the room. A short time later, he reappeared in the corridor and walked away. Breathing a sigh of relief, she stayed put for a while longer. Staggering back down the corridor, she eventually made it to the stairs. Using the wall to lean against, she gingerly made her way down, stopping at the bottom to rest. Finally, she reached the suite, limped inside and headed for her rooms just as Archimon came out of his study.

'What have you done to yourself?' He sounded almost genuinely concerned.

Laurentis looked at him, 'I fell going down to the stables.'

'Let me have a look.' Helping her to one of the couches, he carefully examined her foot, 'You've broken it,' he announced at last.

Laurentis moaned, *now I will be confined to the suite with him.* 'Can you fix it?'

'I'm not a healer, I'm afraid you'll have to rest and let it heal naturally.'

At least I accomplished what I set out to do, Laurentis sighed, annoyed with herself.

Chapter 35

For the last few days, Seren had been drifting in and out of consciousness. He didn't remember much about the attack but preferred it that way. Though still unable to get out of bed, he was beginning to feel better. He'd become used to waking and finding Tobias sat next to the bed, but so far today he hadn't appeared. As no new patients had been brought in in recent days and some had been released the pavilion was a little emptier now. Others hadn't been so lucky. Drifting off again, he awoke later that evening to the sound of raised voices just outside the tent.

'We have to act now before this happens again.'

'Tobias, you're no longer a mage, you are a schoolteacher, keep out of this.'

'Like it or not, Captain, there are certain things I know that you don't, so I am involved.'

'Back down, Tobias, or I'll have you placed under guard. I'm in charge here, you and your charges will leave with the wagons and be transported to Shillington. My decision is final, don't challenge me.'

Seren sat up, he couldn't go back to Shillington. He hadn't come this far just to be sent home but knew if he tried to leave. he would be stopped before he got out of the camp. He wasn't strong enough and knew it. A moment later, Tobias entered the pavilion and rushed towards him.

'I'm not going back to Shillington.' Seren's voice was firm.

'Good, I have no intention of going there either.'

For a moment, Tobias sat and thought silently.

'The wagons will begin to leave tomorrow. We'll be unable to slip away before then. so we'll have to make it look like we're complying. Get some rest, I must find Warren. We might need his help if we are to make our escape.' Taking a small flask from his cloak, he placed it on the table next to the bed. 'Each time you wake, drink some of this, it's no vintage but it will help you regain some of your strength.'

Tobias left, making his way across the camp to a small cluster of tents. Entering one of them, he found Warren sat on his makeshift bed, the woman, Vela, nowhere to be seen.

'How's Seren?'

'Getting stronger every day, should be up and about soon I hope.'

Pouring himself a mug of nettle tea from the kettle on the small stove, Tobias sat on his bed, took a sip and sighed.

'Do you know where Vela is? There's something we need to discuss.'

'Haven't seen her since this morning, she didn't say where she was going.'

'Warren, where do you intend to go when we leave this place?'

Warren looked at him. 'I hadn't thought much about it, the citadel has been my home for most of my years.'

Considering what he said, Tobias thought the boy could start over again in Shillington, but perhaps not, he could be useful on the road.

'Well, I can give you a choice, you can return with the wagons to Shillington, or you can come with us.'

'You're not going to Shillington?'

'No, Seren and I must go into the mountains, those responsible for the attack lie to the north.'

Warren's eyes flashed with anger. 'I'll come north.'

'You're sure?'

'Yes. That attack cost me my family and a great many friends. I want to help.'

'Very well, we leave soon.'

Giving a slight nod, Warren said nothing more.

The evening passed slowly, and it was well past dusk before Vela returned.

'Good evening, Tobias,' she said as she entered the tent, 'How's Seren?'

'Much better, eager to be up and about.'

Vela smiled, there had been little good news in the last few days and still the loss of her husband and child weighed heavy upon her.

'I've decided to stay in Shillington, there will be a great many people who still need help when we arrive. I'm not a healer, but I want to try to help.'

Tobias nodded, 'Shillington is a nice place, you'll like it there.'

'Will you be staying?'

'No, I have a friend farther south in Hallsrock, I shall visit him. Who knows, I might even settle there.'

It was a lie, of course, and it wasn't that he didn't trust Vela, but if she didn't know where they were going then she couldn't be forced to tell. He knew she'd probably go with them if he asked, but she had suffered so much already. *Let her find some peace in Shillington.* Tobias noticed Warren staring at him, looking puzzled. Indicating Vela, Tobias shook his head. Seeming to understand, Warren looked away. Tobias thought he would have to ensure that Vela went on ahead. She could then persuade the healers to allow Seren one more day to rest so they could leave on the second wagon train. Sitting on his bed, he waited for the others to fall asleep. Persuasion worked best when the subject was asleep.

Finally, an hour or so later, the tent had fallen silent. Quietly, he made his way towards the front of the tent where Vela slept. He wouldn't need to do much, just sow the seed in her mind that she had to get to Shillington. When she woke the next morning, her mind would do the rest, not letting go of the idea until she was safely inside the walls. Kneeling beside Vela, he made sure she was sleeping soundly. It wouldn't take long to do what he needed to, but he didn't want her waking up before he was finished. Holding out his hand, he began to conjure an image of Shillington. Slowly, the image took shape until it was an almost perfect match for the town.

'I must get to Shillington,' he whispered over the image.

It flickered for a moment, seeming to absorb his words. The conjured image lifted from his hand and drifted slowly towards Vela, stopping just above her forehead. It dissipated above her and slowly soaked into her skin. It was done. As she slept the idea would form in her mind like a dream. Upon waking, it would settle itself as her own idea. The fact that she had already decided to go would make it all the more urgent that she get there. Silently, he stood and made his way back to bed.

The next morning, the sound of someone rushing around roused Tobias. Raising himself on his elbows, he was pleased to see that his persuasion had worked. Vela was hurriedly moving about the tent packing a small bag with purpose. He watched her for a while longer until she noticed he was awake.

'Oh, Tobias, I'm sorry for waking you. I should have been quieter, I'm just in such a hurry to leave. I have to get to Shillington.'

'Is there anything I can do to help?' Tobias asked, feeling a little guilty.

Vela stopped for a moment, 'No, I don't have much here. I'm almost ready to go.'

Climbing out of bed, Tobias smiled at her. By the time he had made himself ready for the day, Vela had finished packing and seated herself on her bed.

'Will Warren and you be travelling today?' She asked suddenly.

Tobias looked at her, 'It depends how Seren is. Ideally, he wouldn't be out of bed for at least another week if I had my way. I think I'll speak to Asperilla, see if I can't buy him one more day. Her word seems to be law around here.'

Vela nodded, 'You had better find her soon, she'll be leaving on the first of the wagon trains as will I.'

Tobias looked at her, 'Then allow me to escort you to the wagons. Hopefully, we will run into her on the way.'

'Oh, I'm sure we'll hear her long before we see her,' Vela laughed.

Tobias picked up the small bag and together they left the tent. The wagons had been hauled to the centre of the camp. As each wagon was filled, it was hitched to a team of four draught horses and pulled into the line of the growing train. The camp would be moving in three such trains. The first would be leaving today, taking most of the healers, their supplies and the sickest of patients. Tomorrow, the less urgent patients would be moved. The following day, the remaining survivors who weren't in need of healers, and the few supplies and pavilions that had been left behind would join the train. It was the second of these trains that Tobias hoped to be on. In truth, neither he nor Warren should be travelling until the third day, but he wouldn't allow Seren to go on ahead.

Vela had been right when she said they would hear Asperilla before they found her. Her voice carried along the wagons as she tried to organise everyone, wanting to be away by noon. It would take two weeks for the wagons to make the trip and she was eager to be underway. Having finally located the source of her voice, Tobias approached.

'Asperilla, a word if you please.'

The healer stopped and turned to face him. 'Tobias? Yes, are your wards ready to travel?'

Tobias looked at her, 'Not quite. That's what I'm here about.'

Asperilla looked at him.

'I would appreciate it if you would let Seren have one more day abed and put him on the wagons tomorrow.'

'I saw the boy this morning.'

'Then you will know that he is no longer in immediate danger, but barely strong enough to be on the road,' Tobias interrupted.

Giving him a fierce look for interrupting, Asperilla sighed, 'If we were in any other situation, then I would be inclined to argue with you. But the extra space in the healer's wagons would be welcome. It will be enough dealing with those we have already loaded' She walked over to the nearest wagon, took out a cloth bag and handed it to Tobias. 'Most of the healers will be leaving today. If he should worsen, you will know enough to use what's in the bag. It will keep him until the healer assigned to the train can get to you.'

Taking the bag, Tobias thanked her. *That was easier than I thought it would be.*

'Vela, come with me. I'll show you to your wagon.' Asperilla began walking away even before she had finished speaking.

'Thank you for everything, Tobias, I hope to see you in Shillington soon.'

'Have a good journey, Vela, I'm sure we'll meet again. Don't let her boss you around too much.'

Chuckling, she turned away to follow Asperilla to her assigned wagon.

Tobias made his way back to the tent where Warren was just beginning to stir.

'Good, you're awake,' he said as Warren sat up groggily. 'I've spoken to the healer in charge, we'll be leaving tomorrow. I need you to do something for me.'

Pulling his boots on, Warren stood, and Tobias handed him a bag.

'I need you to gather supplies, enough food and water for...' he paused, not having thought about how long the journey might take them. '...for a week or so. Only take what will keep and nothing too bulky, we must be able to carry it.'

Warren nodded sleepily and left the tent, as Tobias began packing up their few acquired possessions. They wouldn't need them where they were going, but he did it anyway. Hearing raised voices, he stopped packing and went outside to investigate. Following the sound, he found himself back at the wagons. The voices were coming from the lead wagon where the mage captain he had argued with the previous day was standing in front of Asperilla. In the stillness of the morning, their voices had easily carried across the camp, and they were beginning to draw a crowd.

'You're not taking any of my healers, the mages have their own.'

'Be that as it may, Asperilla, they're not here now. Shillington has plenty of healers to assist you.'

'Alas, Captain, we are two weeks away from Shillington with these wagons. How can you expect me to care for three trains of people with a handful of healers and apprentices? I can't be in three places at once, and we are carrying some gravely injured souls. Your regiment is at full strength.'

Ready to intervene before things became any more heated, Tobias stepped forward.

'Asperilla, my orders are to march north, I can't do that without healers. Our healers are spread across the land dealing with...' he stopped himself, not wanting to tell her more than she needed to know, 'Other matters. I'm authorised to conscript who I need. I don't wish to use this right, but I will if I have to. Now please, select a cohort of healers to accompany my force and say no more on the matter.'

It was clear from the tone of his voice that the argument was over, and it was one she wouldn't win. *Twice in one day*, Tobias thought, *she won't be happy*. He was glad they wouldn't be travelling with Asperilla and pitied Vela. As the captain walked away, the crowd began to disperse. Tobias shook his head. He had known some hard-faced captains during his time as a mage but none as bad as this man. His last few words intrigued Tobias. A regiment never normally moved without healers, what "other matters" could be so urgent that they would take them away from their duty to the mages? Walking back to the tent, he was troubled, there was something going on. Whether connected to recent events or not, it was obviously a serious matter. Tobias sighed, though he still had some connections within the mages, at this point it would be difficult if not impossible to get in touch with them. Even if he managed it, they would be moving north tomorrow, so receiving a reply was just as unlikely as making contact in the first place. After all, he wasn't a telepath.

With little to do to prepare for their departure, he decided to rest. As of yet, he hadn't visited Seren today, but it would do the boy good to rest without disturbance. The journey through the mountains wasn't especially long, but the snow would be thick on the ground and the going difficult. Even the fittest would struggle, let alone an ageing man and two boys who were both injured. Entering the tent, Tobias lay on the bed and thought of happier times. He remembered the first time he had met James and all the experiences they had shared whilst in the mages. He wondered where his friend was, daring to hope that he was still alive. It didn't take long before Tobias began to doze. His resting mind brought strange dreams, chaotic and fragmented. Interspersed with the images was a voice that would periodically call out his name before a hushed muttering could be heard, but not loud enough to be understood. The voice continued calling out until Tobias snapped awake. Rubbing his eyes, he looked around the tent, seeing that Warren hadn't returned. Then he heard the same voice from his dream calling his name. He shook his head, putting it down to the stress of recent days. Tobias got up and splashed his face from the small wash basin set between the beds. Hearing it again, the voice called his name, but this time it was followed by other voices, not calling out for him but trying to quieten the first voice. Rushing out of the tent, he searched for the source of the voice.

'Tobias. Tobias, I must find him, please tell me where he is. I must find Tobias.'

'Sir, please, quiet yourself. You're not well. Let us put you on one of the wagons where you will be tended to while you travel to Shillington. You'll be safe there.'

'Tobias,' he called, 'Unhand me, boy, I'm perfectly well. I must find Tobias.'

'You, girl, go and find Asperilla, she will have a tonic that will calm him, hurry now. Please, sir, take my arm and I'll take you to a place of comfort.'

'Are you deaf, man, I told you I'm in perfect health, I simply must find my friend. He was a resident of the citadel. I must find him.'

'If your friend survived,' the man paused, he was supposed to be trying to calm the man not incite him further, 'Which I'm sure he did, he will be on his way to Shillington by now. Let us find you a place in the healer's wagons, they will take you to the town where you will find your friend.'

'Please, I must find Tobias, I must know if he and the young ones are safe.'

At the same moment that Tobias arrived at the back of the crowd, Asperilla pushed her way into the centre of the throng.

'What is the meaning of this, why was I called away just as the most severely ill of patients are being moved onto the wagons?'

'Asperilla, I'm sorry, but we had no choice. This man is clearly in a great deal of shock and requires treatment. I thought it best for you to deal with him.'

She turned to the man, 'Sir, if you will just follow me to the wagons we'll have you loaded and treated in a short while.'

'Madam, as I have told this man repeatedly, I have come here to find my friend, Tobias, who until recently resided in the citadel. I am fine and need no treatment, just tell me where I can find him.'

Opening her mouth to speak, Asperilla was interrupted by a shout from somewhere in the crowd.

'Marcus, is that you?'

'Tobias, where are you.'

Managing to push his way through the crowd, Tobias joined the small band of people in the centre.

'Finally, Tobias, you don't understand how happy I am to see you. What about Seren and Tobelle, are they safe?'

Tobias looked puzzled, 'Seren is in the healer's pavilion he was injured in the attack but is recovering well.' He paused, 'Who is Tobelle?'

Marcus looked at him not quite seeming to comprehend what he said.

'Tobias, this is a conversation best saved for another time,' Asperilla interjected, 'You will see one another soon in Shillington, please let me get him onto a wagon.'

'Asperilla, if you please, I'll take care of him. Looking at him, I would say he's just in need of a good night's rest.'

'I have too much to organise to argue all day. If he requires a healer bring him to the wagon.' She shook her head and walked away, the crowd parting to allow her to pass.

Taking Marcus' arm, Tobias led him away from the staring crowd, back towards the tent. Upon entering, Tobias was relieved that Warren hadn't returned yet. Marcus appeared to be in quite a state, and he wanted to speak to him alone. Sitting Marcus down, he went over to the small stove and put the kettle on to boil. Studying Marcus, he could tell that he hadn't slept properly for days and certainly looked thinner. *Obviously, he hasn't eaten much either.*

'Tobias, what do you mean, who is Tobelle? She came to you with Seren. They were bringing James' journal to you. Surely, she must be here.'

'Seren arrived at the citadel alone and hasn't mentioned anyone by the name of Tobelle. I've never met the girl.'

Marcus sighed. It didn't make any sense to him. Adding some leaves to the boiling kettle, Tobias left them to steep.

'Later, when you are rested, we'll visit Seren. Hopefully, he'll be able to explain to both of us. Tell me, Marcus, what happened to you?'

Exhausted, Marcus lay back. 'Do you remember when we spoke of the red-robed wizards that I saw in one of my visions?'

Tobias nodded.

'I had a further vision in which I died at their hands. I accepted my fate, but another died in my place.' He paused, the events of that day still weighing heavily on his mind. 'They put my house to the flame while we were still inside. I escaped just as it was engulfed and have been on the move ever since. Eight, nine days, maybe more. I forget.'

'You said we, who was in the house with you?'

'My housekeeper, Elmira, she was killed by those abominations.' Marcus' voice was almost a whisper.

It was clear that Marcus didn't wish to discuss her part any further, so Tobias let it rest. He was sad for his friend. It seemed like such a long time ago now, but when he left Marcus' house, he had expected that to be the end of his involvement in all of this. One thing had become clear, however, none of them were safe. He wondered whether they would make it through the mountains at all. Tobias was curious as to what Marcus intended to do now. After what he had endured, it might be best if he were transported back to Shillington. Pouring two cups of tea from the kettle, he went to sit by Marcus as he lay on the bed. Taking the proffered cup, Marcus sat up.

'Was Seren badly injured?'

'It was quite serious, yes. We were worried that he wouldn't pull through for a time, but thankfully, he's on the mend now. When you consider how many people didn't survive, I suppose you could say that he was one of the luckier souls to come through this.'

'What is the world coming to, Tobias?'

'I can't answer that, Marcus, we must hope that we can put an end to it soon.'

'I assume Seren is to be sent back to Shillington? He must be pleased.'

'On the contrary, my friend, he doesn't want to go back.' Tobias paused, 'He wishes to go on. We are planning to go north tomorrow.'

'I'll accompany you.'

Tobias looked at him, 'My friend, the journey will be hard, and you look as though you could do with a rest.'

'From the sound of things, Seren isn't fit to travel and yet he's going. I won't argue with you, Tobias, I'll accompany you. I can help with Seren.'

Chapter 36

As the candle sputtered and went out, the mage furrowed his brow. With a sigh, he got up from the desk and took another candle from a box on the shelf in the corner of the small room. Because of the amount of time he had spent moving from village to village, his accommodation of late had been sparse and hastily organised. Stoking the dying fire until a small flame took hold of the glowing wood, he took a taper to light the candle from the fire. Returning to the desk, he set the glowing candle on the desk and resumed studying the charts he had been perusing for the last hour. He had circled several villages with a charcoal stylus and had begun making notes on a stack of parchment. The notes weren't extensive, but they said enough, detailing the cases of a new plague that had taken hold in the southern reaches of Soastan. It had struck suddenly, and despite all their efforts was rapidly moving throughout the southern villages. The strange thing about it was that it seemed confined to the magical communities. There had been no reported cases among those who didn't possess the craft. To make it worse, nothing the mage healers tried had cured it. It hadn't even seemed to slow its progress. When the door opened, the man looked up from the parchment as another mage entered the room, seating himself opposite without being invited.

'The riders have returned, Captain.'

'All of them?'

'All but one. Syrem was dispatched to Myanhall but we've heard nothing from him.'

The captain nodded, 'What do the others have to report?'

'The villages of Cronmar, Elusid, and Ivory Cliff have all reported their first cases. So far, the southern islands of Turney and Inshire are free of the plague.' Reluctantly, the mage added, 'There is some more alarming news, however.'

The captain indicated for him to continue.

'The town of Thwain closed their gates with the last waning moon. No one has entered or exited, and yet they are now seeing their first cases. This plague isn't like those of old, Captain, it seems to move of its own accord, even with quarantines in place.'

'Plagues don't just move around by themselves, Lucius. Somewhere it has slipped through the gaps. We must tighten the lines and halt all movement, not just that of magical folk but all people. Send the riders out again, absolutely no movement in or out of any of the afflicted towns or villages.'

Reluctantly, Lucius nodded his assent and stood, leaving the room. The captain turned back to the chart and drew four new circles around the affected areas. He was dismayed to see that these new reports had shown the plague to have moved slightly farther inland, and even worse, to be moving among larger populations. He hoped that stricter quarantines would halt the spread but couldn't rely on it. They had to discover the cause before it was able to move north. All plagues had a beginning and ultimately an end, he just hoped it would be they who put an end to it and not the plague that put an end to them.

Lucius left the small house that the captain was currently occupying and made his way down the main street towards the contingent of mage healers and riders who had taken up residency.

'How did the captain take the news?' One of the riders called out as Lucius approached.

'He's convinced that all we need do is tighten the quarantine, stop all from moving and we will beat this.'

'You don't sound so convinced, Lucius.'

'I'm not. Doesn't it seem strange to you that only we who possess the craft have been affected by this? My knowledge of plagues tells me that they are indiscriminate about who they take, affecting us all regardless of whether we can work magic or not. This is something new, something that seems able to seek out a specific group and appears to be avoiding our quarantines.' He paused with a sigh, 'Gather your riders in the hall, I'll deliver the captain's orders to them all.'

As the rider nodded and walked away, Lucius made his way across the open courtyard to the council hall. Just a week ago, it had been a bustling place but now it stood almost empty. Many who had worked within the walls had been afflicted by the plague and were either sick in their beds or had already died. It was interesting the way in which the disease seemed to affect each person in different ways. In some cases, the strong had been taken in a day, while others lingered. There seemed to be no set pattern to how it progressed, which had made treating it almost impossible. Those who had lingered had given the mage healers the chance to try out potions they had concocted, but to date, nothing had worked. He stopped his musing as the riders began to filter into the hall. A hush descended as the last of the riders entered, and Lucius stepped to the front of the gathering.

'As you might have noticed, our efforts to contain this plague have thus far been unsuccessful. To this end, we must now enforce stronger quarantines. All people in affected towns and villages are to be quarantined whether they possess magical abilities or not. So far, non-magical folk seem to have avoided contracting it, but that doesn't mean they don't have the potential to be carriers. So, it is necessary for all movement to be restricted. No one is to enter or leave, any supplies required will be provided by us. Traders mustn't move freely between the areas. These new measures are to be put into force at once. You are to ride to your assigned destinations to repeat the orders. Should extra help be necessary, you're to stay and assist. Any resistance from any still functioning councils must be put down. It is imperative that we contain this before it can spread north.' Lucius looked over as the door at the back of the hall opened and one of his healers rushed in. 'See your commander for your designated town or village and ride with haste.'

Stepping away from the front of the crowd, he moved to the side of the hall where the healer was waiting.

'Lucius, we have a problem. You must come with me.'

Not waiting for him to answer, the healer rushed back through the door. With Lucius following, the healer led him to the second hall had been set up to house the sick. Leading him to the back of the room, he stopped between two low beds and signalled for Lucius to look. They were his own healers.

'Our own are now starting to fall to the disease. What troubles me is that they haven't been in contact with the sick. They were assigned to potion making in separate quarters from everyone. They tell me they haven't left those quarters, so I can't explain how they have contracted it.'

Lucius was disheartened, if his own people were getting sick, what hope did they have of beating this plague?

'Do we have anyone to replace them?'

'We have two others already working in their place. They aren't as experienced but are doing what they can. Thankfully, these two left extensive notes.'

'Do what you can for them and keep them comfortable.'

Leaving the hall, Lucius walked back through the village. It was quiet, people were staying in their houses out of fear, but also because of the smell. They were taking every precaution with this outbreak and had burnt the bodies of those already taken by the disease. Hot fires were kept burning every day, ready to take the dead. It was an unpleasant business but something that had to be done. It was just another method to try to stop the spread of the disease.

Entering the small inn, Lucius sat himself at a table by the fire, the weather was unusually cold, the new year had come and gone and the milder weather had yet to arrive. Shivering, he pulled off his damp gloves and hung them on the mantel. The inn had remained open even after the plague had taken hold in the village, although most of their recent custom had come from the mages. Ever the astute hostess, the barkeep's wife had noted his entrance and was already carrying a jug of mulled wine over to his table. It wasn't his normal drink, but many of the locals had taken to it, as if it were some kind of preventative tonic and he didn't wish to offend. Besides, it was a pleasant enough drink for a cold day.

'There's boiled beef and carrots on the stove, or a fresh joint of crackling pork,' The keep's wife said, placing the jug of wine down.

'Thank you, the wine will be sufficient, I really haven't much time to rest.'

'Nonsense, you can't be expected to toil all these hours on nothing. Stay there and I'll bring you something.'

As the woman walked away, he realised she was right. He had been working almost unceasingly of late, but then so had the other mages. In the face of this plague, it seemed all they could do. His thoughts were interrupted as a large, meat filled trencher was placed before him.

'There's a bit of both joints in there and plenty of stock. When you've finished, there's a fresh pear tart warm from the oven. Maybe even enough for a cheeseboard in the pantry.'

When she walked away, Lucius smiled and picked up the trencher. The smell of the meat made his stomach rumble. Not having eaten all day, he bit into the trencher with enthusiasm. It didn't take him long to finish it and he found himself asking the keep's wife for another round of meat and wine. After polishing off his second trencher, he sat back with a satisfied groan, a full stomach was the simplest contentment in these times, and he was grateful that he could still enjoy such things.

Sipping his wine, his thoughts drifted back to the task at hand. There had been many theories about the plague, where it had come from, how it had started, the transmission and incubation times. But each time they thought they were making progress something new would arise and dispel all previous theories. One idea that he hadn't voiced and kept coming back to him, concerned the people in the lands far to the south, across the sea in Erium. A millennium ago, they had strong trade links with the people of Erium, but relations had soured when they turned away from religion in favour of magic. This new practice, which had originated in the far north over the mountains, had come south with migrants seeking new areas of land to settle. Through marriage and mingling of bloodlines, the craft began to flourish in Soastan. The people of Erium didn't share the same gods as those from Soastan and were enraged when they pushed aside the gods they worshipped in favour of this new power. Severing all links, the Erians raised their first ever army, roused their gods and sailed north. Their intention had been to invade Soastan and restore the gods and their own religion. Their gods were vengeful when roused, and for a time the Erians moved farther north with each passing lunar cycle, until the small, remaining force of mages were caught between the Erians to the south and the still neutral Asimians in the mountain hinterland. The Asimians, although somewhat distrustful of this new power took no part in the fighting. At this time, they had no real cause to fear the mages and so stayed behind their walls, a tactic that, in future centuries, would come to be their undoing. With their gods on their side the Erians fought savagely, but vengeful gods can also be petty, they grew tired of the conflict and deserted the Erians.

Their ever-pious priests sacrificed captives and their own people alike in an effort to appease the gods and bring them back to the war but to no avail. Soon after the desertion, the mages began to win back ground against the Erians. Less than six months later, they had pushed them back to the coast. The main host of the Erians had been smashed, the few who survived retreated to their own lands across the sea, and so ended the first war of the Erians. That had been a millennium ago, and since then they had twice ventured north across the sea to invade. But as the centuries had advanced, the craft had grown stronger and each time the mages pushed them back into the sea. Lucius pondered all this for a moment. The last attempted invasion by the Erians had been a little over two centuries ago, it was possible that they were once again preparing to cross the sea and this plague was to act as the vanguard. He thought about going to the captain, but in his current state of mind, Lucius didn't think he would listen. He raised his hand to beckon the keep's wife who came over to him.

'Good lady, may I trouble you for another cup of wine and a scrap of parchment, quill and ink?'

'I'll see what I can find,' bobbing her head, she walked away towards one of the back rooms.

A short while later, she emerged from the back carrying a small tray, which she set before him. Lucius looked at the tray to find that as well as the wine and writing materials she had included a generous slice of pear tart with a small jug of fresh cream. He chuckled, if they didn't move on to the next town soon, he would be asking the fitters to let out his robes. Taking the parchment, he wrote a quick note and folded it several times, concealing the writing within. Leaving his table, he strode to the door, where a young boy was waiting in the porch.

'Take this to Errol, he is quartered with the other mages in the hall, see that only he reads it.' He said, pressing a copper halfpenny and the parchment into the boy's hand.

The boy looked at the coin and smiled before dashing out the door into the early evening. Lucius returned to his table and began writing another note between mouthfuls of tart.

***

As the evening drew on, a few more patrons arrived, some of the village folk having ventured out. So, when Errol entered the inn, no one paid him any mind as people had become used to the mages' comings and goings by now. Without waiting to be invited, Errol crossed to Lucius' table and seated himself opposite the mage. Beckoning a passing serving girl, he instructed her to bring a tankard of ale. As she headed towards the line of casks at the back of the room, he turned to Lucius.

'A little late to send a boy to fetch me don't you think.'

'Perhaps,' Lucius looked thoughtful, 'But a little less conspicuous than me hurrying to find you. I'm glad you waited a while before attending.'

'Not out of choice I grant you. It's not often one receives a summons from the captain's second.' There was a hint of jest in Errol's voice.

Lucius nodded but remained silent as the serving girl returned with Errol's tankard. Taking a swig, he waited until she was out of earshot.

'I wouldn't have called you away from your duties if I hadn't needed you, old friend.'

There was an almost awkward silence between them for a few moments. Errol had also been in line for the place as second, and it had been a close vote. Officers were elected in the mages, even in times of dire need. It was the way it had always been and the way it would continue.

Lucius took another sip of wine, 'The matter I asked you here to discuss must be met with the utmost discretion, the captain knows nothing about it, and it must stay that way.'

Errol looked at him, raising an eyebrow. 'Going against the captain?'

'No, not going against him, but I know he wouldn't sanction my plan if I were to bring it to him.'

Errol nodded, 'He has seemed somewhat absorbed in his own musings recently.'

'Which is why he can't find out about this.'

'Go on.'

'I require two shades. They are to travel to Erium, but I will say no more.' He pushed two small, sealed scrolls towards Errol. 'Everything they need to know can be found in these.'

Errol took the scrolls and placed them in a pocket in the sleeve of his robe. 'Only two? What if they are discovered?'

'Two separately can blend in where more would draw attention. You know that as well as I, Errol.'

'Yes, but two sent and two caught means nothing for you. Are you willing to take that risk?'

Lucius looked at him silently for a moment. 'Only two, Errol. That's all I require.'

Errol nodded in agreement, knowing better than to try to argue his case against Lucius.

'How quickly can they be dispatched?'

'There's a small detachment of shades in the southern hills. It should take no more than three days unhindered to ride from here. I will go myself, later tonight. If anyone questions me, I shall tell them that you are sending me to assist in Selyse.'

Lucius smiled, 'Always ready with a cover story.'

'Naturally,' Errol paused, 'I shall take up residence in Selyse until such time as I have any news to report. I think it would be better if I'm the contact. It covers us both then.'

Lucius nodded, Errol was a good healer, but he had always been better suited to his role in the shades, the double life he led didn't seem to tax him in the least.

They passed the rest of the evening in reminiscent conversation, sharing ale and wine and old stories until the keep's wife announced that the inn was closing. Walking

Errol to the door, Lucius lightly clapped him on the shoulder.

'Good travels, my friend, I shall await your news.'

Errol smiled, tilted his head and stepped out into the night.

Chapter 37

Certain he had only just closed his eyes, Warren found himself being shaken awake. Disoriented, he waited for his eyes to adjust to the dimness in the tent.

'Where's Tobias?' he asked, rubbing the sleep from his eyes.

'He has gone to rouse Seren and make sure we are placed on the end wagon, come now, it's high time you were out of bed. We have a long day ahead of us.' Marcus said as he stood over him proffering a mug, 'Drink that up, it'll give you what you need to get you through the day.'

Warren took the warm mug, raised it to his lips and took a large gulp, almost gagging as the taste of the viscous, mud like liquid began to develop in his mouth. He looked at Marcus, swallowing with difficulty.

'Good isn't it,' Marcus said smiling, as he disappeared outside the tent.

Warren stared into the mug with dismay, seeing it still more than three quarters full.

By the time Warren had washed in a bowl of cold water and dressed, Marcus had reappeared carrying two small bowls. He passed one to Warren, taking the other and sitting on his bed. Warren inspected the bowl, relieved to find it was only porridge. Ignoring the mug, he hoped Marcus wouldn't notice he hadn't finished the contents. Eating the porridge a little too quickly, he winced when he burnt his tongue. On the other side of the tent, Marcus was reflecting silently, but Warren found the silence stifling.

'How are we to get away from the other wagons?'

Marcus looked at him with a glint in his eye, 'Dear boy, it would be better if you didn't know.'

It seems just lately there are too many things it would be better not to have known about, Warren thought, as Marcus handed him his bowl.

'If you would be so kind as to return these to the cooks, then it will be time to be on our way.'

Exiting the tent, he walked across the camp, noting how much quieter it was than in recent days. People were beginning to pack up to make the journey to Shillington. Those who were lucky enough to have family in other places had already left of their own accord, making for other towns and villages across Soastan. A small queue of people were gathered at the cooks' station waiting to wash up, so he joined the back of the line. The queue moved slowly, and Warren grew impatient, seeing the cooks preparing food for the wagons. An idea came to him, he had already laid by a small amount of provisions for the journey, but now he thought to add to them. He was still watching the cooks as his turn at the wash water came.

'Boy, are you going to stand there daydreaming all day?'

Warren turned to look at who had spoken, 'Sorry,' he started, 'My mind was elsewhere.'

Stepping up to the squat barrel, he hastily washed the bowls, placing them on the table when he had finished. As he walked away from the washing area, he looked back towards the cooks. Only one remained and he had his back turned. Taking advantage of the situation, Warren hurried towards the makeshift barrel and plank stand that was beginning to sag under the weight of the food. A large pile of skillet bread had been prepared and stacked at one end of the stand. With no ovens or other such amenities in the camp, it was the best the cooks could do. Next to the bread, two small wheels of cheese had been stacked, the topmost of the wheels partially sliced into wedges. Among the other items were varying amounts of salted beef and other preserved meats, some small pitchers of milk and cream, and a small sack of nuts. The fare on the wagons would be sparse. Edging closer to the stand, a loud blast of horns suddenly sounded somewhere to the east of the camp. He stopped and turned, other people were looking too, *are we under attack again,* he wondered. A sound like the beating of a drum drifted in the breeze, but it couldn't be a drum, it was softer and somehow deeper. Unsure what was happening, momentarily he feared he had escaped the citadel only to be attacked in the camp. A passing man saw the look on his face.

'There's nought to worry about, lad, tis only the mages moving off.'

'They're leaving us?'

'There's nought for them to stay for now the threat of attack has gone and the camp grows smaller every day. Soon enough, we'll all have moved on and this place will be just a field again.'

'I suppose,' Warren said quietly.

He watched the man walk away, *how can he be so sure we won't be attacked again?* he thought. *Maybe those red robes have just been waiting for them to move off before coming back.* Warren shook his head, thinking he was being irrational, but still the thought lingered at the back of his mind. Turning back to the stand, he saw that the cook had moved away and was helping his fellows with some crates. *This is my chance.* Sidling up to the stand, he took up an empty sack from the ground. Moving deftly, he stuffed several small wedges of cheese, five rounds of skillet bread and a small haunch of salted beef into the sack. When he came to the nuts, he hesitated as the cook had started back. Warren's eyes went wide as the cook came towards him. Turning, he slung the sack over his shoulder and began to run, the cook shouting after him and people starting to stare. One man made a grab for him, his fingers just brushing his arm as Warren dodged around him. Not stopping until he was well clear of the camp, he spied a small copse and pushed his way through the undergrowth, slumping beneath a tree. He was relieved when no one followed him, but his guilt began to gnaw at him... he was a thief.

***

Tobias had left early to attend to Seren, but on entering the pavilion he found that he was still asleep. In his bed, Seren still looked weak, so Tobias left him to sleep a while longer. The journey ahead would be arduous, and he would need every last bit of strength. Seren didn't rouse until the horns were sounded. Knowing that it meant the mages were on the move, Tobias' sense of urgency increased. They had to get there first.

'Is it time?' Seren asked as he sat up in bed.

'Yes, we must hurry. The mages are leaving.'

The clothes he had been wearing during the attack had been thrown away, but Tobias had found Seren a fine woollen tunic and breeches, which he helped him put on. He had also managed to acquire a heavy, grey cloak with a deep hood, which he wrapped about the boy's shoulders. Finally, he helped him with his boots and gently stood Seren up as he tightly held onto his arm. This was the first time he had been out of bed since he had arrived, his legs weak and heavy, but still he tried taking a step. Tobias assisted Seren as he cautiously began to walk. They were almost past his bed and into the aisle when Seren stopped. On the table next to the bed that had been opposite his, something caught his eye.

'Tobias, what is that?' He asked between deep breaths.

Something small and silver had been left behind. 'Somebody's necklace, nothing more.' Tobias shrugged.

'No, it's not just somebody's necklace.'

Letting go of Tobias' arm, Seren supported himself with the aid of the bed and gradually made his way towards the table. It was only a few feet, but it left him exhausted. Sitting heavily on the bed, he picked up the necklace, turning it over in his hands.

'Seren?'

'Who was in this bed? A girl?'

'Yes.'

'What happened to her?'

'She was sent to Shillington, they took her on the first train of wagons.'

'No, I mean why was she here, what was wrong with her?'

Tobias sighed, 'She was brought in shortly after you. Someone found her on the plain to the south of the citadel. When they brought her in, they said she had been drained.'

'Drained?'

'Her powers, the very essence of her magic had been taken from her. The powers that we possess are entwined with our life force. When they took her powers, her life ebbed away with them.'

'She's dead?' Seren interrupted.

'No,' Tobias paused, 'She was among the first taken back to Shillington. Seren, forgive me but I must ask, why does her story so concern you?'

He held up the amulet, 'I bought her this.'

Tobias saw that Seren's breathing had become shallow and rapid and he was visibly distressed.

'We travelled many leagues together.' He took a breath and hung his head, 'We parted ways on the forest road before reaching the citadel, on somewhat less than amicable terms.' He faced Tobias, 'Her name is Tobelle.'

Tobias stood stock still for a moment, having thought Marcus confused by his flight when he asked about her. Obviously, he had been wrong.

'Seren, I think it would be best that you go back to Shillington on the wagon.'

'No, I have to go on, as much for Tobelle now as for myself.'

'Seren.'

'No, Tobias, this started with me and it'll end with me. You can't make me go back.'

Tobias knew that he could, a simple spell would render Seren unconscious, it would only have to last a day and they would be away. But in his heart, he knew it would be wrong. Seren was right, he had found James' journal and acted on it, Tobias had no right to deny him.

'Very well. We shouldn't linger here. The wagons await us.'

Moving to Seren's side, he helped him to stand once again, as Seren lifted the amulet and pulled the silver chain down over his head. *I hope I'll be able to give it back to Tobelle when this is all over.* Bit by bit, they made their way from the pavilion and crossed the short distance to the last wagon in line where Marcus was waiting for them. He clasped his hands to his mouth when he saw Seren.

'My dear boy,' he said, taking Seren's arm as they came to the wagon, 'I was greatly saddened to hear you had been hurt.'

Seren was shocked to see Marcus, as he had been insistent that he couldn't accompany them when they left Hallsrock, and yet, here he was.

'Marcus, you're here, but why?'

'There will be time enough to explain later, come now, let's get you settled in the wagon.'

Together, Tobias and Marcus helped Seren up the two high steps into the back of the wagon and settled him under a rough spun woollen blanket and a fur. When the two men climbed down from the wagon to await Warren, Seren put his head back against the padded wood and closed his eyes. He thought about Tobelle and the way they had parted, ashamed that he had left her and blaming himself for her attack.

Walking a short way from the wagon, Marcus and Tobias stood out of earshot of Seren.

'He should be going back to Shillington, Tobias,' Marcus began, 'He's too weak to make the journey. The mountains take their toll on the most robust of us.'

'He is weak, but I fear that if we send him back, he will only defy us and try to make his own way. At least, if he accompanies us, we can attend to him if need be.'

Marcus rubbed a hand over his forehead and sighed, 'He is wilful, I'll admit, but still I don't like this, Tobias. It is a great risk, not only to Seren, but to us as well. My visions can only tell us so much, I can't say with any certainty what awaits us.'

'Good sirs,'

Marcus and Tobias turned to see a young, grey robed wizard striding towards them.

'Are you travelling on the wagons?'

'We are,' Tobias replied.

'I would ask that you make your way to your assigned wagon, we shall be leaving forthwith.'

'We still await one of our wards.'

'I cannot delay the wagons for one ward, we must be on our way promptly. We have many leagues to travel,' the young wizard paused, 'Sir.'

'You can't mean for us to leave him behind. He lost his entire family in the attack. We are all he has now.'

'Many people lost their families in the attack, sir, some are still suffering the wounds taken in their defence.'

'We have two wards. One is aboard the wagon already. He suffered grievous wounds in the attack. Without Warren, I wouldn't have been able to get him out alive. I won't leave him behind.'

'What would you have me do?' The wizard asked, a tone of insolence in his voice.

'Take the wagon train, we will follow on behind when we have both of our wards safely on board. We shan't be far behind.'

'Asperilla placed me in charge of this train. It is a great honour to bestow upon an apprentice, even for one as skilled as I am, but I think no, I can't permit the wagons to separate.'

'I don't look for your permission, boy. I too am a mage emeritus and a senior wizard at the academy. Asperilla placed the care of my wards in my hands, and I won't let this wagon leave until I have both boys with me. Stay or go, it makes no difference to me, but I will suffer your insolence no longer.' Tobias' voice was calm but exuded a quiet forcefulness.

'Very well, but Asperilla will hear of this.'

The young wizard turned on his heel, his robes swirling about his legs and stalked away.

'It seems Warren might have bought us our escape.' Marcus said quietly, even though the young wizard was well out of earshot.

'It would seem so, but I would like to know where he is.'

Chapter 38

With dark clouds gathering, came the promise of yet another fresh layer of snow and a bleak day. Of late, Laurentis' mood had turned sour, not helped by her foot still bothering her when she put her weight on it. Making trips to the orb with the second and third vials had only made it worse, although she had tried to rest it as best she could. The potion was already beginning to take effect and Archimon called for her assistance more frequently. For a time, she lay in bed staring at the cold stone ceiling. Late last night, Archimon had left the suite. When he returned coughing sometime later, she knew he had been back to the orb. Of late, his symptoms had become more noticeable, which meant he must still be drawing power. For all his self-proclaimed greatness, it seemed that her little potion had gone undetected. Hoping he would sicken more swiftly, Laurentis smiled to herself. Although she would be made to run around after him more often, it wouldn't be long before she could deal with him permanently. The priestess' words still played on her mind, but the urgency that she had pressed upon her, now seemed unnecessary. Nothing had befallen them at the fortress unless you counted being snowed in with the undesirables Archimon attracted.

Sighing, she pulled herself from the bed and slipped on yesterday's robe. The thick wool was rough and heavy against her skin, but it was the warmest thing she had short of donning a cloak. She thought about eating. Lately, she had been taking her meals in her rooms instead of the great hall, disliking the company she was forced to keep on the rare occasions she dined with the newer brigands. Olivia and the others had been dispatched to the field some time ago, and only a small number had returned thus far. *It won't be like this forever,* she mused, *soon I'll be free of this rabble.* A sharp knock on the door interrupted her thoughts. With a flick of her hand, she opened it. Having subdued the power the priestess had bestowed upon her, it pleased Laurentis that this little display always set those beneath her on edge. They knew she was powerful and could do things they had no notion of, though she exercised a modicum of restraint when they were around. Should word get back to Archimon, he would know something was amiss.

The young brigand at the door glanced fleetingly at her but cast his eyes downward when she looked upon him. Archimon had garbed the new brigands in robes of deep red trimmed in blue. There was a division between the old and the new even if only subtly displayed.

'My lady,' he kept his eyes to the floor, 'Lord Archimon requests your presence. If you would follow me...'

'Wait a moment,' she said firmly.

Sitting on the bed, she pulled on a pair of soft leather boots lined with wool and ran her hands through her hair. Glancing at the brigand, his eyes remained fixed on the floor as he shuffled his feet nervously, and a smile played on her lips. Glad that he was always uncomfortable in her presence, she intended to keep it that way. Making her way to the door, she waved her hand at him and he turned and walked away. Casually, she followed, in no hurry to see Archimon.

Stopping at the door to Archimon's private chambers within the suite, he turned to her. 'Please wait here, I shall announce you.' He disappeared into the chambers.

She rolled her eyes, of all the people in the fortress she didn't need announcing. The daily escort and announcing her before being allowed to enter his chambers was laughable, but she went along with it. It was easier for now just to play along as her time would come soon enough. The door opened and the brigand stepped outside.

'Lord Archimon will see you.'

'He wouldn't have sent you to fetch me if he didn't wish to see me. You may leave us now.'

His eyes darted to her face before quickly finding the floor once more. 'My lady, I must insist.'

She held up her hand, 'Must we go through this every day? I know you attend him personally and think that makes you better than the rest of us within this fortress, but I am bound to him. I'm one with him and so it is also me you serve. You will leave us now. Archimon,' she placed the emphasis on his name without his lordly title, 'will summon you when he next needs you.'

As he glanced at her before taking his leave, she noted a hint of anger in his eyes. She held his gaze for a moment before he turned and hurried from the suite. Licking her lips, she enjoyed the fact that he wasn't just uncomfortable around her, he was afraid of her. She liked that a lot and would make use of him when the time came.

Entering the darkened chambers, she held her hand to her nose. The sweet, cloying smell of incense hung thick in the air. Archimon had been burning it for days but it hadn't been as strong the last time she had visited him. Making her way carefully through the room, she took care to avoid colliding with the clutter of furniture. The last thing she needed to do was to make her foot worse again. She found Archimon abed, wrapped in a robe and layers of fur. With a fire roaring in the hearth, his chambers were in stark contrast to her own chilly rooms. Finding Archimon's suite too warm, she walked to the heavy drapes, drew them back and flung open the shuttered window. As a gust of cool, clean air drifted in, Laurentis took a deep breath.

'What do you think you're doing?' Archimon coughed deeply, holding his chest, 'Close the shutters.'

'Lying in this dark, stuffy room will only make you worse.'

'You're a healer now as well, Laurentis?'

'No, but I have been sick before. You need fresh air, something good to eat and you'll be right as rain.'

'What I need is this.' He brandished a small piece of parchment at her.

Taking it from his shaking hand, she saw Archimon's small scrawl covered the parchment.

'It's a health tonic, the strongest I have come across. I want you to make it.'

She looked at the parchment again. 'It looks simple enough.'

Coughing again, Archimon spat into a small bowl on the table next to his bed.

'Make sure you follow the instructions to the letter. You would do well...' he paused to take a breath, 'you would do well to get this right.'

Giving him a cold look, she turned to leave, the parchment screwed into a ball in her fist.

'Laurentis.' groaning, she turned back.

'You will need this.' Archimon declared, holding out the bowl that he had spat into.

Grimacing as she took the bowl, Archimon snorted a short laugh followed by another bout of coughing. Holding the bowl at arm's length she exited the chambers, making her way back to her own rooms. Closing the door, she set the bowl down on a side table and sat down heavily in her armchair. Increasingly, her days seemed to be spent as a nursemaid and she was growing tired of it. Unscrewing the parchment, she read it properly. For the potion to work it had to "sample" the sickness. Now she understood why Archimon had given her the bowl. The ingredients had to be tailored to the individual sickness, and a list of substitute ingredients were marked next to the potion list. Archimon had scribbled a note below the substitutes saying that they should only be used in the event of an extremely adverse reaction. It seemed that he wanted the strongest potion possible and was determined to cure himself. At a glance, she knew she didn't have everything on the list and Archimon had depleted his personal supplies as his sickness grew. With a sigh, she rose from the chair and left the suite. As her foot had begun to ache, the walk down to the lower levels was a slow one. It was still early and some of the newer brigands were seated in the great hall at breakfast. As she walked the length of the hall, their eyes followed her, but she didn't acknowledge them. When Archimon was gone, she intended to get rid of them all as well. All she would need were the few she knew she could trust.

Set back into the thick wall at the far end of the great hall was a small but stout oak door, carved with vines. Lifting the latch, she gave it a shove and walked inside closing it behind her. The small corridor led to a single door, not as ornate as the one from the hall but just as sturdy. Taking up the entire level of the circular tower it occupied, the potion room could only be accessed from the great hall. Since Archimon had taken up residence in the fortress, the upper levels of the tower had seen little use but could still be reached from the higher landings. As the new crop of brigands had little interest in furthering their knowledge or creating their own brews, she found herself alone. The shelves that lined the walls were fully stocked and she easily found the few items she needed. Spending a few moments longer perusing the various shelves, she saw nothing of interest. She was ready to leave when the door opened, and a young brigand entered. Seeing Laurentis, she gasped.

'My, my lady,' she stammered, 'I'm sorry, I didn't know you were working here. I shall leave you.'

'No, please, I was only gathering supplies. The room is yours.'

Blushing, the girl hurried to the table, dropping a parchment on the way. Laurentis stooped and picked it up. Passing the parchment back to the girl, she noted the ingredients for a sleep draught, impressed that it was a complicated potion. Younger than Laurentis by at least two years, she suspected her to be a runaway just as she had been when she came to the brigands.

'A sleeping draught and a complicated one. May I make a suggestion?'

The girl looked at her for a moment and nodded meekly.

'Substitute the hellebore for mistletoe. Hellebore can be volatile if not prepared correctly. In a draught like this, it could cause an eternal sleep. Mistletoe is gentler and easier to prepare but will be just as effective.' She paused, 'Unless you don't want the person to wake that is.'

The girl blushed again, 'No, of course not, I mean, it's just for me.'

'Why would a girl as young as you need a sleeping draught?'

Wringing her hands, the girl responded, 'I... I'm having trouble sleeping. I work so hard during the day, but no matter how tired I am most nights I just lay awake.'

'Is something troubling you? Or someone?'

'No, nothing like that, my lady.'

'Are you unhappy here?'

The girl bit her lip.

'You can tell me, it's all right.' Laurentis lay a hand on the girl's arm.

'I just thought it would be different here. And that this was somewhere I could belong.'

'You feel as though you don't belong?'

'All I want is the chance to prove myself and show you all what I can do. Some of the others have been sent out on tasks and returned after proving their worth. Yet I linger here day after day with only a list of chores.'

Laurentis remembered her early days at the fortress. Having been sent to take a vial of blood from a dragon and succeeding, she knew that others hadn't been so lucky, and some had never returned. 'I didn't receive my task until I had been at the fortress for six moonturns. Yours will come in time.'

The girl hung her head.

'What is your name?'

'Adisine, my lady.'

'Adisine, come to my suite after dusk, I might have something you could do for me.'

'Yes, my lady.'

Smiling, Laurentis turned and left the room.

By the time she returned to the suite, her foot was throbbing. Closing the door to her chambers, she slumped into her chair and kicked off her boots. Her foot was still bruised a pallid purple, and the exertion of the stairs had made it swell again. Groaning, she knew that one day she would have the time to rest, but not today. Gradually, she made her way to the hearth and lit a fire. Archimon's potion was simple to make, comprising three lots of three different ingredients, none of which reacted violently when introduced to Archimon's spittle.

By early afternoon, the potion had turned a deep mossy green and was cool enough to bottle. Sneering, Laurentis knew exactly what she could switch it with. Having made enough for ten vials, most of it would be discarded. Taking a ladle, she poured a small amount of the potion into each of the waiting vials, just enough to fill the bottom. Putting the rest of the concoction aside, she stood, grimacing, her foot still aching. Making her way to her ingredient store, Laurentis took three stoppered flasks, each containing a different green liquid. The first being simply moss steeped in lake water, the second, pulverised tugweed, and the final flask held distilled nightshade. The potion Archimon was expecting would be little more than a mixture of inactive and poisonous ingredients. Returning to her small work-table, she emptied the flasks into a bowl and stirred it together. As the ingredients mixed, vapour rose from the bowl, inactive as the moss and tugweed were, the nightshade could still be dangerous if she inhaled too much of it. Wrinkling her nose in disgust, she took up the bowl of Archimon's sputum once more and tipped it in to the green mixture. Walking to the window, she opened the shutters and tossed the small bowl outside, not wanting to use it again. Returning to her mixture, she gave it a final stir and decanted it between the vials, giving each a little shake to mix the potion into the liquid. The colour of the new mixture was a near perfect match to the potion, even smelling similar. As for the flavour, well she didn't intend to taste either of them so she would never know. Stoppering each vial, she left them on the worktable and tidied everything away before summoning a small mid-afternoon meal.

***

An hour after dusk fell, there was a sharp knock on the door. Archimon's personal brigand stood, glaring in the doorway.

'There is a girl outside the suite asking to see you.' He announced, dispensing with the formalities of title.

'Oh, yes, Adisine. Send her through if you would.'

Facing away from the boy with a grin, Laurentis strode off, hearing him turn and stamp back through the suite. Although the boy had left the door open, Adisine approached Laurentis' rooms and knocked all the same.

'Adisine, please come in.'

Laurentis welcomed the girl and ushered her in, closing the door softly behind her. 'Please be seated.'

Sat on the corner of the couch, Adisine smoothed her robe out, looking uncomfortable. Taking the chair opposite, Laurentis picked up a vial from the end table and offered it to Adisine.

'This is a sleeping draught of my own making. It's gentler than most but can bring a disturbed sleep pattern back in line with the more natural rhythms of the body. Use it for five days or so and it should get you back to normal. Just a sip, mind you, no more.'

Adisine took the vial. 'Thank you, my lady.' She paused, 'My attempt at the potion didn't turn out so well, even with your suggestion.'

'I'm sorry to hear that, but these things take practice. Perhaps when you have some free time, I could give you a lesson or two?'

Adisine blushed, 'That would be most kind, my lady, thank you.'

Laurentis smiled.

'You said there was something I could do for you, my lady. If I can be of assistance, I will.'

For a moment, Laurentis looked thoughtful. 'The boy who admitted you to the suite, do you know him?'

'Yes, my lady, his name is Jeremiah.'

'Ah, yes, I remember Archimon telling me his name now,' she swept a loose strand of hair behind her ear looking pensive. 'What do you know of him?'

Adisine bit her lip, 'Very little, my lady, he keeps to himself when he's around us. Most of the others think him haughty, but I think he's just shy.'

'He comes across as very brash and has never treated me with any kindness.' Laurentis turned her head away. 'I feel as though he's trying to keep me away from Archimon. There are days when he won't admit me to his chambers.'

Adisine remained silent.

'That is where you come in.'

'Me, what can I do?'

'Tomorrow night will be the third full moon since Archimon and I were bound,' Laurentis hesitated, taking a deep breath. 'I would like to spend some time alone with him, I have something special planned. If you could distract Jeremiah, take him away from the suite for the evening, I would be most grateful.'

Adisine looked at her uncertainly before quickly averting her eyes.

'You can speak freely to me, Adisine.'

'I fear that I can't achieve what you ask of me. Unlike the others, I've tried to befriend him but he rarely acknowledges me. As I said, I think he's shy.'

Or plain pig-headed, Laurentis thought. She looked at the naïve young girl for a moment before producing a tiny, clear vial from the sleeve of her robe and held it out towards Adisine. 'This is a little creation of mine. Use this and he'll do what you ask of him.'

Adisine looked puzzled.

'It bends a person to your will. All you need to do is apply a small amount to each of you and he'll be under your control for a time. Just a dab for you each will suffice.'

Taking the vial, Adisine still looked uncertain but nodded her assent.

Chapter 39

Errol hadn't ridden to the camp of the shades as he told Lucius he would. Instead, he had gone directly to Selyse and installed himself in the small town. Keeping to himself since arriving, he chose to take up residence in the coaching inn rather than the rooms in the common hall set aside for the other healers. The other mages hadn't objected and as Errol had always kept to himself, he saw no reason to change his character now. He had made sure to visit the hall each day to keep abreast of any new cases but mostly he kept to his small room at the inn. Upon his arrival, he took a day for himself to recuperate from the ride and gather his thoughts. Though Lucius was his friend, he was also his rival, and while he meant him no malice, he thought his own plan had a better chance of succeeding. Although the two scrolls remained on the small writing desk where he left them when he unpacked, he hadn't been idle. He had already dispatched four pairs of shades, the fifth and final pair would leave later that day after he had briefed them. Each pair had left two nights apart with instructions to travel from a designated port.

Since trading had decreased between the countries, only three ports in the south sailed to Erium, but it was still possible to find the odd ship making its way across the sea. Once more, Errol looked at the scrolls on the table, wondering what to do with them. Even though he hadn't detected any spells upon them, he was still wary of using magic to destroy them as some spells couldn't be detected until it was too late. Taking his cloak from the hook behind the door, he scooped up the two scrolls and concealed them in the sleeve of his robe. Voices drifted up to him as he made his way down the main stairs of the inn. As it was breakfast time, the common room was beginning to fill up with patrons, many of them travellers either coming from or going to the ports in the south. So far, the captain's sanctions on travelling hadn't reached this far south. Errol wondered how long it would take before the roads and inns fell quiet as more and more people were quarantined. Stepping out into the crisp morning air, he took a deep breath. The weather remained stubbornly cold this year. Spring was late but Errol was grateful, he suspected the plague would have spread much farther and faster had the normal spring heat manifested itself.

The common hall where the mages had taken up residence was across the town square, set slightly back on the main north-south street. It was a long, but relatively narrow stone and timber building. The newly thatched roof shone in the early morning light, the solid oak doors of the hall standing open to the morning. Errol entered, noting a further two people taken in during the night. The healer in charge was a wizened old mage, who Errol found sitting behind his small desk half-hidden behind a stack of dusty old tomes and yellowing scrolls.

'Hiding yourself away, Oelin?' Errol asked the old mage. Picking up a book, he read the faded words on the spine. 'Ancestral Plagues of Soastan. What were you hoping to find in this?'

Oelin looked up from his current tome, having not noticed Errol's approach. 'Probably nothing, but one can hope,' he paused, 'We lost another during the night.'

'Who?'

'Our apprentice, Harel. He was struck down only yesterday afternoon. His symptoms developed extremely rapidly, although in one of his more lucid moments he admitted that he hadn't felt right for days. He passed early this morning.'

Errol stared at him, 'How can it have taken him so quickly? The swiftest case I have known has been four days. How could a healthy young man be taken in less than a day? Are you sure it was the plague and not some other affliction?'

'There's no question, but please don't ask me to explain why he went so quickly. I've been pondering that since it happened and can give you no answer.'

Slumping in the chair opposite Oelin, Errol groaned. 'Have you made any advances?' He asked glumly.

'Not since you asked me two days ago, no. If Harel's case becomes the precedent, I don't see what any of us can do.'

'Let's hope his was an isolated case. We need the time to test our remedies if we're to find one that works.'

Oelin nodded but remained silent at the sound of hurried footsteps.

'Excuse me, sir,' a young mage in light grey robes interrupted as he approached the desk.

Oelin looked his way.

'May I speak with healer Errol?'

Errol stood and followed the boy a little way down the hall.

'Sir, two mages have just arrived. They are asking for you, please follow me.'

The boy led Errol back across the square towards the gatehouse, where the gates stood open wide, a steady flow of traffic making its way towards the market square. The traders were later than usual setting up their stalls. *If the cold weather continues,* Errol thought as they walked, *they'll be lucky if there's any market at all.* Gesturing for him to enter the gatehouse, the boy returned to his duties. The two mages were seated on a bench along the far wall but got up as Errol entered.

'Mages, thank you for coming so swiftly. If you would care to follow me.'

Heading back out of the gatehouse, Errol thought his room at the inn would be quieter and a safer place to talk. The mages followed. Once safely ensconced in Errol's room, he began to brief the mages.

'I'll get straight to the point. I'm sending you both to Erium.'

The two mages looked surprised as Errol then took out a large map and beckoned them to look at it.

'There are many temples to be found throughout this land, but this one,' he placed his finger on a point marked on the map, 'is believed to be their most sacred site. This is your destination. You're no doubt aware of the plague that has descended upon us. A few of us believe that it might be connected to Erium. If they are beginning to mass, or there's any hint that they're once again looking to invade

Soastan, it's your job to uncover it. This plague has weakened us, not terribly, but nonetheless, we have lost powerful witches, wizards, and mages. If the Erians are coming, the sooner we know the better.'

The two mages glanced at one another before one stepped forward and spoke.

'Are we the only ones being sent?'

'For the moment, yes. It wouldn't do to send too many over. Two are more easily concealed than twenty, after all.'

In unison, the two mages nodded.

'I'll leave it to you to decide how you wish to proceed, but I'd recommend some kind of glamour, whether it be a spell or potion. I'll expect your reports periodically, but don't compromise yourselves. Are there any other questions?'

'How long are we to be away.'

'There's no designated time limit. If you're certain that you've uncovered a plot return to me. Otherwise, I'd say no more than five or six moonturns. If you have found nothing by then, I think we can judge ourselves safe and you may return. However, I would ask that you set out immediately. There are few enough ships as it is, and it wouldn't do for you to be delayed. The port of Tantem is due a small contingent of ships over the next few days, I suggest you try there. I will remain here for the duration, but ensure any correspondence is properly sealed and guarded.'

The mages nodded and turned to leave.

'One more thing, gentlemen.'

They spun around to face him.

'If you're caught...'

'We'll escape or go to our graves in silence,' both mages recited together. It was a simple oath but binding, and all those who spoke it could never break it.

Errol smiled and slowly inclined his head. The mages about turned once again and left the room. Sighing, he was glad it was the last time he would have to recite his well-rehearsed speech. Five different pairs had been sent to Erium, each given the same speech, except for being sent to a different temple and one of three ports. In that way, their paths should never cross. Now he had dealt with the issue of the shades, he had nothing to do but focus on his cover for being in the town. Sinking into a low armchair, he sighed. Now, he was only a shade in passing, and only when others couldn't be relied upon to get the job done. He was a healer, and so he must heal.

A loud banging on the door woke Errol with a start , realising he must have dozed off. Heaving himself from the armchair, he made his way to the door and pulled it open roughly. Standing at the door was the same young wizard who had escorted him earlier that morning.

'Please, sir, you must come with me at once. There has been a terrible accident at the quarry. There are horses waiting for us.' Saying no more, he began to hurry back down the corridor.

Taking his wand from the desk, Errol tucked it into his robes and followed the boy, pulling the door closed as he went. Sure enough, two horses stood saddled outside the inn. The boy gestured to the nearest horse as he mounted the other. As soon as Errol was in the saddle, they rode towards the gate where they were forced to halt. Two wagons commandeered by the healers had preceded them, and the lead wagon had thrown a wheel, blocking the gate. Three healers were repairing the wagon, but it was taking time. Dismounting, Errol made his way towards the wagon. As two of the healers lifted the wheel between them, the third shakily held the wagon level with a weak levitation spell.

'Stand aside,' Errol said firmly, his left hand outstretched towards the wagon. Immediately, the healer felt the burden lighten and moved back. Taking his wand from his robes with his free hand, Errol pointed it at the wheel the two mages were still struggling to lift, and it flew from their grasp. Shocked, they hadn't noticed Errol taking charge. The wheel skimmed the ground as it glided towards the wagon and set itself neatly back on the axle. Gently releasing the wagon, Errol watched as the wheel easily took the weight. Stepping up to the wagon, he tapped the axle with his wand, then the wheel and back to the axle once more. Giving the wheel a sharp tug, it stayed firmly in place. Pleased with the result, Errol walked away, the healers staring after him. They were all wizards or mages, but some were handier than others. When Errol remounted, the two wagons began to move off. As soon as they had cleared the gate, Errol and the boy moved forward at a swift trot.

'Tell me what happened at the quarry.'

'The details are sketchy, sir,' the boy said, not taking his eyes from the road, 'All I can tell you is that some have died, and others are in danger of passing.'

'Then let us hurry on our way.' Errol said, urging his horse into a gallop.

The boy followed suit, and they passed the wagons, taking to the road proper.

The sight that awaited Errol was something he had hoped to never see. The normally orderly quarry pit was strewn with rubble. Thick dust hung in the air distorting the mid-morning sun. The pit was deathly silent. Riding down the track into the main pit, Errol and the boy were the first to arrive. It would take the wagons time to make the trip from town with the other healers. Dismounting, they hobbled the horses and went on foot. Freshly cut stone lay strewn across the ground, its intended destination had been Selyse. The town had been steadily expanding for the past three years with most of the raw material coming from the quarry. There hadn't been an accident since the quarry opened, but now it seemed things had changed, and Errol wanted to know why. The boy stopped.

'Did you hear that, sir?'

Halting, Errol strained to hear.

'There it is again.' The boy said as he began to move off down the track.

Though he hadn't heard anything, Errol followed as the boy began to run into a dense area of broken and strewn stone. Stopping, he bent down almost out of sight as Errol came up behind him panting. Lying on the ground was a boy, maybe a little older than his companion. His lower body was pinned beneath a large piece of stone, and Errol could see the deep red stain in the dusty ground slowly seeping farther away from the boy.

'Run back up to the bunkhouse, gather whatever you can, sheets, blankets, anything. Also find some skins and bring fresh water down. Quickly now, I'll attend to him.' Errol said forcefully.

The boy looked at Errol for a moment, then nodded and started back up the track. The bunkhouse had been provided for the men and women who worked in the quarry, so they wouldn't have to make the trip from town every day. It was one of the few buildings to be found at the site, other than the mess hall and duty cabin. There wouldn't be much in the way of resources there to help the wounded, but Errol hoped the boy would bring something back. Kneeling to examine the wounded boy, he placed a hand on his brow, finding his skin fevered and clammy. His eyes flickered open and he looked up at Errol, silently pleading with him for help. With the pool of blood steadily growing and his breathing becoming shallow, in his heart, Errol knew the boy wouldn't survive. *It would be kinder to ease his passing*, he thought, but didn't act. Killing an enemy was one thing. but to take an innocent life simply because he couldn't be saved was quite another. When Errol had chosen to become a healer in his later years, he had made an oath to himself that he wouldn't take another life, not unless he or any of his own were threatened. That was the problem with being a shade, for secrets to be kept, lives had to be forfeited, and Errol had done a lot of "forfeiting" in his time. He sighed and watched as the boy closed his eyes for the final time. His last, rattling breath left him, and it was over.

Bowing his head in silent prayer, he let his mind drift towards the heavens. Like everyone in this land, Errol didn't keep with the gods, but nevertheless, in that moment all was peaceful. Standing, he backed away a little. The boy was dead, but he would remove the stone so he could be covered and marked for burial. Pointing his left hand, he focused on the stone and it slowly began to rise. With his wand in his right hand, he pointed it at the stone and moved it sharply to the right. The stone followed the path of the wand and came to rest in an empty area of ground with an echoing crash. The boy came running back down the track towards him with an armful of blankets. Taking one of the blankets from him, Errol quickly covered the dead boy whose legs had been crushed almost beyond recognition. It wasn't a sight he wanted the boy to dwell on.

'There was nothing to be done for him,' he said resignedly, 'But perhaps there are others we can help, come.' As Errol strode away, the boy took one last look at the blanketed body and followed, his head bowed.

By the time the wagons arrived at the quarry, Errol and the boy had found several others. Two were already dead, four were critically wounded, and one was in such shock that all he could do was clutch his knees shouting, 'LOOK OUT.'

They found a young woman who had a broken arm and a deep laceration to her right cheek but was in relatively good health. She explained with little prompting that the four wizards working at the ramps had suddenly collapsed, almost simultaneously as if struck down. The ramps were the part of the quarry where magic was most readily used, the wizards used their power to move each load of stone to the top of the quarry for collection. When they collapsed, the loads they had been moving simply crashed back down the ramps onto the people below. Miraculously, the four wizards hadn't been killed but none were conscious. Errol had purposely kept them apart from the other survivors who were now laying outside the duty cabin. All the dead and wounded were from the non-magical populace who worked alongside the wizards. Errol felt especially bad about it. If the wizards hadn't been taken ill, none of this would have happened. As he helped the healers tend to the wounded and load them onto the wagons, the thought played on his mind. *If they had been struck by the plague, which looks to be the likely cause, then they had all been taken at once. Up until now, it seemed to have struck at random.*

'Sir, there's no more room on the wagons.'

With his thoughts interrupted, he looked to the ageing healer who had spoken to him. 'Are all the wounded aboard?'

'Yes, and the wizards. We'll have to return for the dead.'

'Very well, go back to Selyse and have a wagon sent out at dawn to collect the bodies. Their families will want them returned as soon as possible.'

'What of the other workers?' He pointed to the small crowd gathered outside the bunkhouse.

'The quarry will cease to operate until further notice. I won't risk another accident happening, too many have died already. Lodgings are to be found for them in the town if they have no family. They will remain there until such time as the quarry reopens or they choose to move on.'

'Should I send another wagon for them?'

'No, I'll see to their return.'

The healer nodded and turned away. Errol watched him go, still troubled by all that had occurred.

Chapter 40

With growing trepidation, Adisine had spent the afternoon watching the sun trace its path. All day, she had been stealing glances at the small vial that sat on the bedside table and her nerves were beginning to get the better of her. The task Laurentis had given her seemed simple enough but taking control of someone's will was wrong. Adisine had only been at the fortress for a short time but there had been many instances when she felt she didn't belong and that what she was doing was wrong. This was one of those instances. When she had been recruited, she hadn't realised what she was getting herself into, and now she was beginning to regret her decision. Taking a deep breath, she looked once more at the vial. It was too late to back out now. If she didn't do as she had asked, Laurentis would be furious with her. *But maybe,* she thought, *if I just do this one task I could slip away afterwards*. She didn't have anywhere to go but had been on the streets before and anything would be better than this.

***

Since dusk fell a little over an hour ago, Laurentis had been hovering around her door. She had expected Adisine to have made her appearance by now and her patience was beginning to wear thin. Taking a flask from the mantel, she poured herself another cup of wine and took a deep draught. She didn't often drink heavily as she liked to keep a clear head, but tonight she had a taste for wine. Cup in hand, she began pacing the room once again. The thought that Adisine had backed out had already crossed her mind. Although it wouldn't mean the end to her plans, it would certainly complicate things. She didn't want to kill Jeremiah just yet as his disappearance would arouse Archimon's suspicions. And weak as he was, she had no desire to reveal her true intentions so soon. Quickly tiring of pacing, she sank into her armchair by the fire and picked up a book that was lying on the table. Absentmindedly, she turned a few pages without taking any of the words in. Letting the book fall into her lap she closed her eyes and sighed heavily.

The dream came upon her quickly, it was the same one she'd had for the past three nights. All around her the brigands were scrambling through the fortress. A great booming sounded above her and several small breaches in the walls were letting through the early evening light. She felt a flash of pain in her leg as she ran up the stone steps, a stray jinx had hit her making the old scar flare up momentarily. With a grimace, she continued up the stairs, the priestess' words ringing in her ears. 'You must be the one to kill him', the voice said repeatedly. Redoubling her efforts, she gained the top of the stairs, turned sharply right, and dashed down the corridor. She wasn't far from the suite when, rounding the corner, she collided with someone coming from the opposite direction. Laurentis landed heavily on the floor, knocking the wind out of her. Staring down the hall, she saw Jeremiah running off in the direction she had just come from and wondered why he had abandoned his beloved Archimon just when he needed him the most. Gripping the rough stone wall, she pulled herself up. Landing heavily on her hip, coupled with the spell that had hit her, her whole left leg was throbbing. Limping along as best she could, she finally reached the suite. Finding the door ajar, she listened for a moment. All was quiet inside, so pushing the door open she entered. All the sconces in the suite had gone out, and as there were no windows in the main room the darkness was all encompassing. Raising her left hand, she conjured a small ball of pure white light and sent it ahead of her. As the light drifted in front of her, she checked each room in turn. The suite was deserted. Archimon was gone.

Laurentis woke abruptly. She had never been past the deserted suite in the dream, but it was something else that had woken her. Getting to her feet, she made her way back to the door and listened attentively. Adisine had finally arrived. Moving close to the wall, Laurentis pressed her ear to the door.

'Can I help you?' Jeremiah sneered.

'Jeremiah, I, I just wanted to,' there was a pause followed by a soft thud and the sound of a vial breaking.

Holding her breath, Laurentis silently prayed that Adisine hadn't dropped the vial. It had taken two weeks to brew the potion and it had used her entire stock of phalanx root. The root was hard enough to come by in well-stocked shops, let alone the occasional trader that passed through the fortress. If the potion was lost, Laurentis knew she wouldn't be able to make any more and there would be consequences for the girl.

'I'm so sorry, Jeremiah, let me help you.'

'Oh, it's of no matter, Adisine. Now, what can I help you with.'

'I,' Adisine paused, 'I would like you to accompany me downstairs. There's something I would like you to do for me.'

'As you will.' Jeremiah obliged.

Laurentis smiled, surmising that Adisine had tripped and smashed the vial directly into Jeremiah. Whether on purpose or by accident she couldn't say, but it had worked. Hearing the door to the suite close, she set to work. Long ago, she had realised that during her imprisonment the visions were nothing more than an illusion potion. Whilst browsing an old grimoire that Archimon had written, Laurentis had discovered the potion. Making a little tweak to the potion to allow it to be bottled, she found it kept for longer without diminishing its effect. She had learned a lot from Archimon but had found that, in many of his potions and spells, she had been able to make improvements of her own. Taking a vial full of her enhanced potion from a small cupboard, she placed it in the sleeve of her robe before conjuring a tray of food for two.

Pausing at the door to Archimon's bedchamber, Laurentis decided against knocking. Knocking would suggest she still felt subservient to him, and that was something she was not. Smiling to herself, she pushed the door open and entered the gloomy room. There was a musty smell to the place, as the shutters were closed, and the heavy drapes had been pulled tight across them. Squinting in the dim light, she placed the tray down on a small table at the foot of the large, four poster bed and made her way to the drapes. Pulling them aside, she unlatched the shutters and pushed them open. The reaction was instant.

'Jeremiah, what are you doing? I,' Archimon coughed violently, 'I told you to keep those shutters closed,' he coughed again, 'I am unwell, close them now, or do you want me to take a chill?'

Laurentis sneered again, he already seemed to be paranoid. 'It's not Jeremiah, Archimon.' Her voice was soft, but the emphasis was on his name.

'Laurentis. Why have you come? Where is Jeremiah? I asked for food and my potion.'

'Jeremiah left the suite some time ago and has yet to return, but I have brought food. I thought we might eat together on this most joyous of days.'

Archimon looked at her, 'What do you mean?'

'Surely you haven't forgotten?' Archimon stared at her intently as she turned her head away, 'Tonight is the third full moon since we were bound, I thought we might dine under her light to celebrate.'

For a moment , Archimon continued to gaze at her, 'I do not wish to leave this room, surely you can see how unwell I am.'

'You don't have to leave,' she indicated the moonlight flooding through the open shutters. 'We can dine here.'

'My potion...' Archimon began.

'I'll get it, but you must eat something before you take it. Will you sit with me by the window?'

'No,' he tried to voice the word sharply, but a cough wracked through him, 'I will consent to eat with you, but I will remain abed. Fetch my potion.'

Laurentis left the room, easily finding the potion. Taking it from the small shelf, she placed it on the sideboard alongside her potion, which she had extracted from her sleeve. Removing the stoppers from both vials, she tipped a small amount of the illusion mixture into Archimon's potion. Purposely, Laurentis had stationed two of the newer brigands in the corridor outside the suite so there would be witnesses for what was to come. Placing the stopper back into Archimon's potion, she took both vials from the sideboard but didn't return immediately. Instead, she walked to the door between Archimon's rooms and the shared rooms. Upturning the illusion vial, she poured the contents onto the floor. With a smile, she placed the empty vial back into her sleeve and made her way back to Archimon's bed chamber where she found him still abed. She had expected nothing less. Ill as he was, he was still stubborn. With a casual wave of her hand, the small table at the end of the bed gently levitated towards her and set itself down so Archimon would be able to eat with her. With a look of contempt, he turned himself in his bed to face the table. With a small smile, she conjured a chair for herself, and sitting down placed the vial next to her plate. As Archimon reached for it, Laurentis pulled it towards her.

'Not until I've seen you eat something. You look awfully thin. I'm inclined to think that Jeremiah hasn't been taking very good care of you. Why won't you permit me to attend you? We are bound after all.' Picking up the small jug of wine, she poured some for Archimon before filling her own glass. 'He could still attend to you, but under my supervision, I want to be involved, Archimon.' Once again, she placed the emphasis on his name.

'The boy tends to me well. If I choose not to eat what he brings me that is my business.' Coughing once more, he took a moment to regain his breath before continuing. 'There are days when I am so weak, I cannot bear even the thought of food. No, I think we will continue with the current arrangement. Although, I am not pleased that he seems to have deserted me tonight.'

Laurentis tried to look abashed, 'I just thought it would be more fitting if I tended to you.'

Archimon didn't reply, the look on his face was almost pitying. Laurentis paid him no mind, although the look on her face told him otherwise. Raising her glass, she took a small sip, still trying to look meek although a smile played on her lips. Grudgingly, Archimon looked at the potion and then at Laurentis, but made no move to take it. Instead, he picked up his cutlery and began to eat, albeit unhurriedly.

The meal passed slowly and in silence, Laurentis watching Archimon closely. Not once did he look at her, instead his eyes remained fixed on his plate as he stoically made his way through the small meal. As he placed the cutlery down on the plate, he coughed and cleared his throat. As he reached for the vial, Laurentis placed her hand on it, but with a glare from Archimon, she gently pushed it towards him. Snatching it away from her, he uncorked it and drank the contents down in one. Clearing his throat loudly once more, he let the vial drop back to the table. Laurentis looked at him and smiled sadly.

'I have missed our meals together. I feel as though we never see one another anymore, even though we share this suite.' She feigned dabbing at her eyes with the sleeve of her robe.

'Spare me your sentimentality, it does not suit you.' He coughed again but stilled himself and slowly turned to look towards the door. 'Did you hear that?'

'Hear what?'

'Hush,' he commanded sharply, 'There is someone in the other room. Listen.'

She was silent, it was his illusion. Even though she had created it, she couldn't see or hear it. It was the perfect way to sow the final seed of doubt among his oh, so devoted followers.

'There it is again, help me get up.' He raised his voice, 'Laurentis, help me to get up.'

Knowing it cost him to ask for her help, she lingered in her seat for a moment before moving to his bedside and taking his arm. The door to the room was closed, but to Archimon it appeared to fly open. To his eyes, in the doorway stood a robed and cowled figure. His face was in darkness, but Archimon heard his malicious laughter.

'Just as I expected,' the figure said with the same malice as he walked towards Archimon.

'No, stay back, stay back I say.' Archimon raised his hand to ward off the unseen foe, his voice rising to an unusually high pitch.

As Archimon collapsed back to the bed, his arms shielding his face, Laurentis heard the brigands enter the suite, their footsteps echoing on the flagstones as they hurried towards the room. As the door to the room flew open, Archimon screamed. Laurentis stepped back as the brigands rushed towards Archimon who spoke to them hoarsely.

'You must find him, search the fortress.'

The two brigands looked at one another, puzzled.

'Well,' Archimon coughed and spat a glob of phlegm into a kerchief, 'Why are you just standing there? He's still in the fortress, and you let him get past you, now go.'

They looked to Laurentis who shook her head and gestured for them to follow her from the room. Closing the door quietly behind them, she took them to one side.

'You must forgive Lord Archimon, he has been most unwell of late. I fear he is having delusions.'

The brigands looked at one another and nodded in apparent assent.

'You may go for the evening. I will tend to Archimon.' She was careful not to use his title again. *Let them doubt him*, she thought, *let them see how little respect I hold for him*. Eventually, they would come over to her or go to their graves still supporting him.

***

Errol turned in the small bed once more and stared into the dying fire. It was mere days since the accident, but he had made the best use of his time. The four wizards had all been returned to town but had since died. Wanting to be sure of the cause of death, Errol had examined each one personally. What he found had left no doubt. The wizards who hadn't had any contact with anyone except those who worked in the quarry had somehow contracted the plague. It was the plague that had caused their collapse and had killed them. To make things worse, three of the four non-magical folk who had been wounded had also succumbed and died since returning to town. After being examined, Errol had ensured that the four wizards had been swiftly cremated. They still weren't sure how the plague passed from one victim to another, so he had managed to convince the families to forego the usual period of mourning before lighting the pyre. He hadn't been so fortunate in his dealings with the non-magical families. Although, to his knowledge, no one outside the magical community had yet contracted the plague, he had still tried to have the bodies cremated alongside the wizards. There had been an uproar among the community, which had come close to becoming a full-scale riot. Reluctantly, Errol had backed down and allowed the families to reclaim the bodies in order that the proper mourning rituals could be conducted, if only to keep the peace. Unfortunately, the whole incident had only served to inflame the population of the town. Afraid that eventually the plague would pass into the general populace, some were openly calling for those who wielded magic to leave the town before it was too late. Others had become violent, with two of his colleagues attacked in the street earlier that day. Tensions within Selyse were at breaking point. If they didn't solve this soon or leave, he feared what the people would do. They were mages and they could use their powers to defend themselves, but as healer's they were bound to help the very people who now threatened them. Errol took this vow seriously, even if he was initially there under false pretences. Sighing, and rolled over once again, but when he closed his eyes all he saw were the faces of those he had failed to save.

Chapter 41

By running off, Warren had cost them precious time. Tobias had wanted them to be on the way before the mages broke camp and to have made their way into the mountains. But Warren hadn't returned for a full day after the theft of the food. Understandably, Tobias had been angry. When they finally began their journey, the atmosphere among the small band of companions was decidedly strained. Although Tobias didn't support what Warren had done, he grudgingly admitted that the extra rations were useful. When he eventually returned to the wagon, Warren handed them over. Tobias had made the decision to retain the wagon until it was unable to take them any farther. Still weak, and since discovering the news of Tobelle, Seren seemed to have withdrawn into himself. With him in no fit state to walk, for the third time the others found themselves pushing the wagon out of the mud. An old cart track ran from the citadel along the foothills, but in recent years it had fallen into disuse, and as they had discovered, in some areas was almost impassable. As they finally freed it from the mud, Warren slumped down against the back wheel.

'Can we stop for a time? We've been travelling since before dawn.'

Tobias turned in the seat of the wagon, 'We can't afford to stop. If you're tired, take a turn in the back if you must.'

Facing forwards, Tobias took the reins and urged the horses on. As Warren wearily moved away from the wheel and climbed to his feet, Marcus was already back on aboard the wagon attending to Seren. Pulling the hood of his cloak up, Warren put his head down and followed. Seriously starting to regret his decision to accompany them, he reminded himself that the current state of affairs was his doing. It didn't take long before he started to fall behind.

As they travelled without lanterns, when the darkness overtook them the wagon soon left Warren's sight. Though he tried to catch up it was to no avail as he was just too tired. Before long, the sound of the wagon slipped away into the darkness. For a time, he tried to follow the shallow ruts left in the track, but as they drew ever closer to the mountains and the track dried out, even the ruts left him. As despair washed over him, Warren sank to the ground and clutched his knees to his chest. *I should have gone to Shillington,* he thought as he wasn't the adventurous type. Having seldom left the citadel when it had been his home, he had always felt comforted by the high walls and familiar streets. But now they were lost to him, just as he himself was lost and alone. Letting out a muffled sob, he pulled his borrowed cloak tighter about himself. *In the morning, I'll be able to find my way back to where the camp was,* he told himself, although he wasn't confident he could even manage that.

Shortly before midnight, Tobias halted the wagon and found himself beginning to doze in the seat. Twice now he had awoken with a start, only to find that the horses had wandered from the track. He was desperate to make up the lost time Warren had cost them. The mages would be well along the road by now, and he feared arriving at the fortress too late. The mages would storm in and cause devastation, but he wanted the chance to try to find James.

'Tobias, you should ride in the back awhile, I can take the reins.'

When Marcus appeared from the back of the wagon, Tobias was grateful for the offer, but in truth, Marcus looked just as tired as he was. As much as he wanted to go on, he knew they had to stop, otherwise, they would never complete the journey.

He smiled at Marcus, 'No, my friend, I think it's time we all stopped for a short while. There's no sense in arriving dead on our feet.'

Jumping down from the driver's seat, Tobias walked with Marcus to the back of the wagon.

'Is Warren already aboard? I'd hoped he would help to water the horses before we turned in.'

Marcus stared at him, 'I've not seen Warren since shortly after we freed the wagon. I thought he might have gone to sit up front with you.'

'No, he didn't.' Tobias peered past Marcus into the darkness, but nothing moved. 'Where can he have got to? Hasn't he caused us enough delay? I should have sent him to Shillington,' Tobias paused, unhitching one of the horses from the wagon, 'I should have sent them both as neither are ready for what lies ahead.'

'Tobias, I'll search for Warren.' Marcus took the reins from Tobias. 'Of all of us, you have had the least rest. Stay with Seren. I will find the boy.'

Tobias opened his mouth to speak, but Marcus held up his hand.

'I won't take no for an answer, Tobias, you got us this far. Let me ease some of the burden.'

With a wave of his hand, Marcus conjured a bridle and saddle and mounted the horse in a swirl of cloak. Nodding to Tobias, he turned the horse and rode off back down the track and into the darkness.

As Marcus retraced their steps along the track, a small ball of light hovered just in front of the horse, illuminating his path. Seldom had he known a night so dark, but then again, he had spent little time out in the open countryside, preferring to spend his time in his little home closeted with his books and experiments. He exhaled, missing his home, although he knew it no longer stood. When all this was over, he would have to start afresh, but wondered if he was a little too old to start again. Focusing his mind on his current task, he realised he'd been riding for almost an hour and hadn't seen any sign of Warren. Twice, he had halted and dismounted to check the track for footprints, but so far, had found nothing and was beginning to worry. If Warren had tried to continue in the dark, he could have simply strayed from the track. Out here, it would be easy to disappear as there were no longer any towns or villages this far north. The citadel was the last settlement before the mountains. None had wished to dwell so far north since the Asimian war, magic and non-magic folk alike. Drawing his cloak tighter about him, he continued.

After a further two hours of riding, Marcus still hadn't found Warren. Arriving back at the stretch of muddy track where the wagon had last become stuck, he halted the horse. Skirting the mud as best he could, Marcus tried to look for any sign as to which direction Warren might have gone in but found nothing. The mud was thick and cloying, but not wet enough to leave any substantial tracks. Rubbing his temples in frustration, Marcus closed his eyes, recalling the scene when the wagon had just been pushed free and he was climbing into the back. Warren hadn't followed, instead he had heard him asking Tobias if they might stop and rest. Tobias had said no and driven on. Keeping the image in his mind for a moment longer, Marcus focused on it before his sight took over. Viewing it from the side of the track as the wagon travelled on, he could see Warren with his head hung, following slowly behind. Next, Marcus observed from where Warren stood as the wagon drew farther away until it finally slipped into the night. He felt a wave of despair wash over him as if he were Warren. The boy stumbled forward, trying desperately to catch up to the wagon before realising he had fallen too far behind.

As the vision disappeared, Marcus opened his eyes, knowing that Warren hadn't gone back but had only tarried. Either the boy had wandered from the track after losing the wagon, or Marcus had ridden past him somewhere farther up the trail. Mounting once more, he turned back the way he had come, casting two further lights, sending them up either side of the track to illuminate the way ahead. Silently, he prayed to himself that he had only missed him because of the darkness.

Though Warren heard the approach of hooves, he hadn't even looked up as they passed him by. Having moved off the track into the cover of some small bushes, he'd curled up and tried to sleep. Resigning himself to not catching up with the wagon, he wasn't even sure that he wanted to anymore. *As I've slowed them down and Tobias hasn't forgiven me for that, it would be better if I just try to make my way back. I never was very good at the practice duels they held at school and wouldn't be any help to them anyway. And now that the citadel is laying in ruins, it's unlikely I'll advance to the academy.* Shifting to try to make himself more comfortable, sleep still evaded him. His mind just wouldn't switch off, and as much as he kept telling himself he didn't want to go back to them, some small, treacherous part of his subconscious was telling him it was the right thing to do. Pushing the thought from his mind, he curled up tighter and screwed his eyes shut, thinking things would be clearer once he had slept.

***

For the fourth time that night, Laurentis climbed out of bed as Archimon was calling for her again. Since the incident with her illusion, he had insisted she be the only one allowed near him and had dismissed Jeremiah cruelly. Had he been in better health, she suspected the boy would have been killed, but Archimon no longer had the strength to perform such magic. That had been the other result of his supposed attack. He had resumed his visits to the orb, now visiting it daily. But the power he drew from it was merely sustaining him. The potion Laurentis had imbued it with was taking its toll. It wouldn't be long before he succumbed, and she would be rid of him. Although these daily visits were helping her cause, Archimon had encouraged her to resume drawing power from it. So far, she had managed to avoid it, on the excuse that Archimon should take all the orb had gathered. She had told him it would help him recover his strength, but lately he was beginning to question why she didn't want the extra power he was offering her. If he suspected her, then he hadn't voiced it, but the way he closeted himself in his room meant he only had her to talk to now. Growing tired of being his nursemaid, she would only have to keep up the pretence for a little longer. Just that day, he had begun coughing up small amounts of blood among his other disgusting products. She had had little time to speak with the priestess about the potion, but felt it was a sign that his time was drawing near. Slipping on her robe and padding barefoot across the cold stone floor, she smiled inwardly. Just a few more days and she would be free. Those brigands who hadn't deserted would either join her or be cast down, and she would begin anew. As she pushed open the door to Archimon's suite, she put her thoughts of her future aside. It wouldn't do to appear too happy when she was supposed to be playing the anxious wife. With a lazy wave of her hand, the few lanterns in the room sprang to life. Archimon screwed up his eyes at the sudden wave of light, weak though it was against the dark confines of the room.

'Are you trying to blind me as well as everything else, woman?'

It wasn't really a question. He was becoming increasingly chiding as the sickness took hold of him. Brushing it aside, Laurentis went to his bedside.

'You called for me?' Whether he knew it or not, he was in her power. She didn't even bother to use his name now.

'Yes, this room is perishing, you have allowed the fire to die. How am I supposed to recover if you do not attend properly to my needs?' He spat the words at her. 'Maybe I was a little hasty in dismissing that boy, he never let me grow cold.'

'You're forgetting that it was I who was here when you were attacked. Where was Jeremiah?'

'Be that as it may, you should attend to me more carefully. Get the fire going and bring me something to warm myself.' Feebly, Archimon waved his hand at her, and she narrowed her eyes but turned to her tasks.

Starting the fire as easily as she had lit the lamps, she stifled a yawn. Conjuring a broth wouldn't tax her, but she wanted to add something extra, something that would allow her to sleep and have some time away from this bore of a man. Swiftly leaving the room, she made her way back to her rooms. Taking a vial from one of the shelves in her cabinet, *just a few drops of my sleeping draught and he will be out for hours,* she thought, *a little peace would be welcome.* With another wave of her hand, a small bowl of steaming broth appeared on the side to which she added three drops of the draught. With the vial safely back in the cabinet, she took the bowl and returned to Archimon, setting it down in front of him without a word, watching as he slowly ate it. The draught took effect almost as soon as he placed the spoon in the bowl. With a weary smile, she stood and left the room, seeking her own bed. She would have peace for the rest of the night and probably all the next morning. When she arose, she would tour the fortress to find out if any others had deserted in the night and curry favour with those who remained. As powerful as she had become, she would need allies for the journey north to find and unseat Him. The thought lingered as she fell back to sleep, *it won't be long now.*

***

On his way back up the track, Marcus had stopped several times, determined to find Warren. But so far, there hadn't been a single sign of him, and he was worried. Unless Warren had strayed far from the track, he couldn't have ridden past him twice. If that had happened, it was unlikely Marcus would find him. As he approached a small clump of bushes just off from the track, his ball of light circled them and began to hover. He thought nothing of it as he rode up to them but noticed a small, dark mound at the base of the foliage. Dismounting, he walked towards it with his wand drawn. The occasional bandit could still be found this far north, and he wasn't taking any chances.

'You there, wake up.'

Marcus took a step back and watched as the shape uncurled to reveal the dishevelled and slightly shivering form of Warren.

'Finally, boy, I've been searching for you for hours. Come now, up you get.'

Warren looked up at him. 'I'm not coming back with you, Marcus, what's the point?'

'What are you talking about? You can't stay out here on your own.'

'I'm of no use to any of you. All I've done is cost you time. Time that Tobias keeps reminding me you can ill afford. I can't fight, nor can I conjure food or anything useful to help us. You would do better to go back to Tobias and tell him you couldn't find me.'

Marcus looked aghast at Warren, 'I'm not leaving you out here. There are plenty of things you can do, and none of us can conjure food unless it is already in our possession. What do they teach you nowadays?'

Marcus held out his hand towards Warren to help him to his feet. Reluctantly, Warren accepted the help, giving up easily, but knew he didn't want to be out there alone even if he was useless to them. In silence, he mounted the horse behind Marcus and allowed himself to be returned to the wagon and probably the waiting scorn of Tobias.

***

The next few days passed slowly as they made their way up through the foothills and finally to the mountain pass. Snow still topped the mountains, making parts of the pass difficult to traverse, but overall, it had been an uneventful journey. At last, Seren had begun to show signs of improvement and had even taken to walking behind the wagon for an hour or two. Colour was starting to return to him, and his appetite had steadily improved, which hadn't helped their meagre rations. He had started joining in with their conversations and was swiftly becoming the jovial young man he had been before the attack, although he still refused to talk about Tobelle. Blaming himself, Seren knew he shouldn't have left her behind, but wondered a little selfishly, had he stayed would he have suffered the same fate. Still, it wasn't a subject he wished to talk about with anyone. It was his burden to bear, and when all of this was done, he would try to set things right. As he walked along behind the wagon, he tried to push the thoughts from his mind, it wouldn't do to dwell when they still had the fortress ahead of them. Nervous that he hadn't used any magic at all since the attack and had never properly fought against anyone, he wondered just how useful he would be. He almost laughed at the thought of the four of them taking on an entire fortress. *Two young, inexperienced wizards who haven't even attended an academy, a retired mage turned teacher, and a seer. A fine bunch of fighters if ever there was one.* He was broken from his musing by the halt of the wagon. As Tobias didn't usually stop during daylight, something must be wrong. Just as the others climbed down from the back of the wagon, he moved forwards, Tobias remaining in the driver's seat.

'I'm afraid we'll be walking from here.'

Looking ahead of them, Seren, Marcus, and Warren saw the pass that they had been following for the last few days had come to an abrupt end. A landslide from higher up the mountain covered the ground ahead of them for some distance.

'What about the horses, we could still use them.' Warren ventured.

Tobias looked at him, 'Horses won't help us over this, Warren.'

'We could clear the pass then.'

'No,' Tobias sighed 'We can't. Do you know how much power it would take to move all this? Let alone the time it would take. No, Warren, I'm afraid we will be going ahead on foot.' Tobias indicated two mountains in the distance. 'The fortress is located at the foot of those two mountains. On foot, it should be no more than ten leagues. We can cover that distance in a few days.'

Warren looked downtrodden, *what is the point in being a wizard if you can't use your power to make life a little easier for yourself?* He was beginning to resent Tobias, it seemed nothing he did was ever good enough, and although he hadn't been too tetchy towards him since his return, there was still an atmosphere between them.

'We'll camp here tonight and go on in the morning. It wouldn't do to try to cross this in the dark.'

Climbing down from the seat, Tobias set about building a fire. They only had a small amount of kindling left in the wagon, but it would have to do as there was no wood to be found this high up in the mountains. As Tobias finished building the ever-dwindling pyre, he shot a small gout of flame from his wand and the wood caught. Soon, the small fire was burning brightly. Though they had nothing to cook over it, the heat it offered was welcome. Marcus passed out a small amount of food between them, having stretched their rations as thinly as they could, but they would be lucky if what they had left lasted until they reached the fortress. As they sat around the fire, Warren stayed a little apart from the group, listening to them talk but not trying to join in. As night fell, he excused himself and went off to find somewhere to sleep. He berated himself for giving up so easily and returning with Marcus. Now he was here in the mountains, he really didn't have a choice in going back. The track would be easy enough to follow, but with no food he doubted he'd last too long, although the alternative Tobias offered didn't seem much better to him. As he closed his eyes that night, he thought of the citadel and how life used to be.

***

Initially, Seren had been worried when Tobias told them they would be walking the rest of the way. Doubting whether he would be able to cope with the journey, even if it were only a few days, he had surprised himself. Although as tired as they all were, instead of not being able to cope, he found his strength was returning to him. By the end of the first day, he was starting to feel like his old self again and wished he hadn't spent so much time huddled in the back of the wagon. As they made camp that evening, spirits were unusually high. Both Marcus and Tobias had noticed the change in Seren and couldn't have been more pleased. On the other hand, Warren wandered into camp a little after they had set up and kept back as he had done since returning with Marcus. They made good progress on the first day, the landslide having covered an extensive area.

But they managed to carefully pick their way through the strewn boulders and debris until they came to a narrow pass. It looked to be more of a goat track than anything, but it was all they had. To the west were sheer cliffs and to the east a deep crevice that formed the valley with the next mountain. From here the path looked as though it hugged the side of the mountain for some distance before descending into the valley.

Marcus had cast along the path as far as he could, but from what he could tell it wouldn't take them all the way to the fortress. Late tomorrow or early the next day they would have to leave it, and the last part of their journey would be through the mountains proper. He decided not to tell the others yet, not wanting to dampen their spirits, although he suspected that Tobias had guessed as much. As they sat near the last fire they would have, Marcus passed around a small flask. By now, they all knew what would be in it, and whilst they still abhorred the taste, they found that the mud brew sustained them, but even that was starting to run low. The next few days would be hard, but what choice did they have?

Chapter 42

Their first night on the path was an uncomfortable one. None of them had been able to stretch out comfortably and had instead spent the night huddled against the rocky cliff face that towered over them. There had been no fire that night, so not only were they uncomfortable but cold as well. The meagre breakfast of stale bread and hard cheese did nothing to lighten the mood. The only one of the four who didn't seem affected was Marcus. As they picked their way down the path that morning, he chatted away in his usual, merry fashion. The others paid little attention to much of what he said, but either Marcus didn't notice or didn't mind. However, when he started talking about how the path had been shaped with magic by the first settlers from the north, Seren started listening intently. Always having an interest in the lands to the north, he looked forward to his history classes and knew they were responsible for bringing magic to the south. Those who had come south had forever cut ties with their kin in the north. There had never been any official relations between north and south, and although they had touched on this in his classes, he had never fully understood why that was. The two lands had never been at war with each other, yet there was no trade and hardly any migration either way now.

'Northern magic is different to ours. Whilst we have the ability to shape stone and wood and raise them into our structures, pure magic like that of the north has the power to reshape nature to a degree. And that is how this path came into being. Don't get me wrong, it can't raise mountains or shape the seas, but work such as we are walking upon will last forever.'

Seren was about to pose a question to Marcus when he continued.

'You wish to know how the path is kept clear, even after all these years. The answer is simple, dear boy, magic, of course.' Marcus turned to see the bemused expression on Seren's face and gave a little chuckle. 'It's simple really, Seren, the path was created by magic and it is that magic that resides within it, which keeps it clear.'

'But how is that possible, it's just bare earth?'

'Bare earth, yes, but as I said, infused with magic. Seren, if this path were through a woodland or field the magic that shaped it would stop things from growing on it to keep the way clear. It would be a waste of power and effort to cut a pathway only to have it swallowed by the earth once you had passed. It works the same with this path, it simply repels what could block it.'

'So, it can't be destroyed?'

'Oh yes, it could be removed with the same type of magic that created it, but neither you nor I could do it. Only a northerner could give it back to the earth, but there is another way. Think back to the beginning of the path when we left the track, do you remember what it was cut into?'

Seren thought about it and realised how little notice he had taken of his surroundings.

'It was an outcrop of rock, jutting from the cliff, really you should pay a little more attention. What you must understand about the magic of this path is that it is dormant. Rocks and other debris are repelled as they land on the path. But with an area such as that outcrop of rock, should a large rock fall smash into it with sufficient force it could destroy that section. After all, if the rock the path is cut into is destroyed there can be no path.'

'Marcus,' Seren paused, 'Can I ask how you know all this?'

Marcus smiled, 'I see the history of the path, Seren. I can sense the magic within it. It is one of my gifts as a seer. If I so choose, I can interact with many things around me and yet the one time I rely on my gift to find a friend it fails me.' Marcus sighed.

Feeling selfish for having almost forgotten about James, Seren wasn't sure what to say. It was his journal that had brought them there, after all. They carried on in silence for a time, Warren at the front of the small line of travellers. As he made his way towards a bend in the path, Marcus called him back.

'Warren, our time on the path is at an end, if you continue you will end up in the far north. This path doesn't take us to our destination. Now we must go through the mountains.'

Warren looked at Marcus, 'Through the mountains, how can we go through the mountains?'

'Well, firstly down that scree and into the valley.' Marcus smiled as he pointed towards the steep slope away to their right.

At once, Seren began the descent, and with a furtive glance at Marcus, Warren followed. As Tobias caught up and made to go after the boys, Marcus put a hand on his shoulder.

'This path will be hard for all of us, but it isn't far now.'

'I fear what we find at the end of the path will be harder still.'

'You're right, but we must get through the end of this journey before we think of that, Tobias.'

'I take it you still haven't been able to sense James?'

Marcus sighed, 'I had hoped I would feel something of him as we neared the fortress, but try as I might, there is nothing.'

Tobias patted his arm, 'Hard as it might be, we must have some hope. It might just be a simple case of wards upon the fortress that impair your sight. Either way, we shall know soon enough.'

Tobias smiled at Marcus as he stepped forward and began his own descent of the scree, Marcus sighed again and followed Tobias.

Moving quickly down the slope, Seren and Warren were almost halfway down before Tobias began his descent. Despite Warren's apprehension, he was enjoying himself. Slipping his way down the loose scree, he overtook Seren. A smile broke across Warren's face, this was the first time since the attack on the citadel that he could put aside his cares, even if it were just for a few minutes. The trials they had faced, the disdain from Tobias, all forgotten for a few short, but blissful moments.

A shout from behind broke his reverie. Twisting in mid-stride, he saw Seren stumble over the loose track that he had left as he overtook him. As if in slow motion, Seren lost his legs from under him and tumbled down the slope. Desperately, he lunged forward to grab Seren and stop his fall, but he had already passed him and was now out of reach. As Tobias and Marcus broke into a half run to get down the slope, Warren surged forward almost leaping down the scree. But ahead of them all, Seren had already reached the bottom, laying prone and unmoving on the rocky valley floor. Warren stumbled the last few steps down the slope before landing heavily next to Seren, just barely keeping his feet. Kneeling, he put a hand to his shoulder and called his name, but Seren didn't respond. Seemingly from nowhere, Tobias reached the valley floor.

'Move aside,' he barked.

Shuffling to the side, Warren watched as Tobias began to tend to Seren, Marcus followed shortly behind and also knelt at Seren's side. For the moment, Warren was forgotten. His earlier feeling of elation descending the slope had fled and he sat morose as the two wizards brought Seren around. Supported by Tobias and Marcus, Seren rubbed his head, his fingers coming away bloody.

'The cut will knit together but try not to touch it.' Marcus said kindly whilst proffering a small flask towards Seren. He knew what was inside it but took it gratefully and drank the viscous liquid.

'Do you think you could stand?'

Looking at Tobias, Seren nodded. Handing the flask back to Marcus, he took Tobias' arm and gently pulled himself up. Testing his weight on each leg, he took first one and then a second tentative step. Thankfully, nothing was broken but he ached everywhere. The fall had knocked the wind out of him, and as well as the cut to his head, his hands and arms were scraped raw. Seeing Warren sat apart from the group, he gave him a weak smile and slowly walked ahead with Marcus. He would have liked to have rested for a time but knew they had to press on. Tobias hung back, his eyes boring into Warren.

'How could you have been so stupid, Warren? Why did you cross Seren's path?'

'It wasn't on purpose. I didn't mean for him to fall.'

'You should never have come, Warren. Against my better judgement I let you accompany us, but now I see that was a mistake. Even before we left the camp you caused us nothing but trouble. We would already be at the fortress had we not had to wait for you. If we get there and the mages have already laid waste to it, all of this will have been for nothing.' Tobias walked away a few steps but turned back. 'I can't send you back as you wouldn't survive on your own. So, you must accompany us to the end of this journey, but have no doubt, at the first opportunity I'll send you home.'

'I have no home.' Warren said darkly.

Ignoring him, Tobias walked away to catch up with Marcus and Seren. For the remainder of the day, Warren lagged behind. When they eventually stopped for the night, he once again kept apart from the rest of the group, preferring to keep his own company. He knew he wasn't wanted there.

***

As dawn broke throughout the valley, Seren stared at the twin peaks of the mountains. Still aching from the fall the day before, *at least, I don't have to climb all the way,* he thought. Marcus' path would lead them between the mountains of the main range and into the smaller rocky peaks that would finally take them to the fortress. Although nearing the end, the mood in their makeshift camp was strained. The atmosphere between Tobias and Warren had reached an all-time low. Neither looked at the other, let alone speak to one another. Seren knew it wasn't Warren's fault he had fallen, any of them could have slipped on that slope, but lately Tobias seemed to find fault with Warren at every turn. He felt sorry for the boy, he had lost everything in the attack, but this was no place for him.

'Are you ready for this, Seren?'

Marcus had come to stand next to him and joined him in gazing at the mountains.

'As ready as we all are, I should think.'

'Well, no time like the present,' Marcus announced before striding off.

With a look back at Warren, Seren, followed.

As the sun reached its zenith, they finally crested the last rise that brought them to the peak between the mountains. Marcus stood atop the ridge and helped the others over the last step of rock. Though Warren lagged behind, Marcus waited, and when he was finally in reach, helped pull him up. Gathered on the top, Tobias silently handed out the last of their rations. He had been brooding since they left camp and now his silence stretched before all of them. In an attempt to lift the mood, Marcus walked to the edge and pointed out across the lesser ranges that spanned the distance.

'We're almost there,' he announced with a smile.

The small group turned to look at him.

'You keep saying that, Marcus,' Warren replied. His voice was small and weary. It was the first time he had spoken since the argument with Tobias the morning before.

'Why don't you see for yourself?'

With a deep sigh, Warren stood and crossed to Marcus, Seren joining them, but mainly because he was interested.

'It's just more mountains, I don't see anything else. No road, no fortress, nothing but mountains.'

'You're not seeing what I see, Warren,'

'No one sees what you see.'

Marcus ignored the slight and continued. 'Can you see the small flat expanse towards the foot on the west of the lower ranges?'

Squinting, Seren shaded his eyes from the noon sun with his hand, as Warren merely cast a disinterested glance in the direction Marcus indicated.

'The lesser range that rises from the expanse borders the road. It is all that separates us from the fortress.'

'I'm not sure. I think I can see it, but it could just be the light.'

'Believe me, Seren, it's there. If we make good time, this time tomorrow we can be at the foot of that range.'

Knowing once they found the road he could leave, Warren said nothing. *I'll be rid of Tobias and this whole mess. If I go back to the citadel, I might be able to salvage something, or at least bed down for a night or two until I figure out what to do next. Anything would be better than this.*

'Well,' Marcus clapped his hands together, 'Shall we go on?'

Without another word, Marcus began the next descent from the ridge, still silent, Tobias close behind him, motioning to Seren as he passed. Seren looked at Warren for a second before following the two older wizards but he appeared to have little inclination to join them. Absent-mindedly eating his now very stale bread and not caring that it was the last of the rations, Warren tossed the end aside. Certain he could find food on the road back to the citadel, he thought he could last a day or two without eating. Being so used to the meagre rations they had been living on lately, it made little difference to him either way. Finally, he stepped over the edge of the ridge and began his descent, keeping his pace slack and not wishing to travel with the others.

The lesser ranges proved to be more difficult to traverse than Marcus had let on. It had taken a full day and a half to reach the expanse that he had spoken of, and they had all suffered during that time. Each had taken numerous slips and falls, Marcus twisting an ankle but insisting on carrying on. Seren had fared worst of all taking another tumble, hitting his head on the way down. Neither Marcus nor Tobias were healers, and all they could do was bring him round and try to stem the flow of blood that seeped from another long gash on the side of his head. It was nearly an hour before it finally stopped bleeding. In the time they had stopped to tend to Seren, Warren had eventually caught up to them.

For a moment, Tobias had caught the worried look in the boy's eyes when he had first seen Seren, but in an instant that look was gone, fading back into the steely expression he had worn since Seren's fall on the scree slope. After Marcus and Tobias had helped Seren to stand they carefully went on their way, but Warren deliberately hung back, feeling conflicted. Having already made up his mind to leave, a sense of guilt now gripped him as he saw Tobias and the limping Marcus assist Seren ever closer to the last of the lesser ranges that bordered the road. The journey had taken its toll on all of them, and if he abandoned them now, what would that make him? Tobias' scorn still burned into him, but the pitiful sight he beheld as the three of them walked off tugged at him. After everything that had happened, if he left them now it would make him no better than the people who had started all this in the first place. And wasn't that why he had agreed to accompany them? His home, everything, and everyone he knew had been destroyed. He owed it to them and himself to see this through to the end. Resigned to go on, he bowed his head and started his walk to catch up with the others, fearing he had left it too long to patch things up with Tobias but he would try to be amicable nonetheless. It didn't take long to catch up. And so, Warren had assisted the injured Marcus while Tobias helped Seren until they finally gained the expanse.

'We'll stop here for the night. I think we could all use the rest.' Tobias croaked.

Hobbling a few paces farther on, Marcus stood transfixed, staring towards the ranges that loomed above them.

'Tobias,' he whispered, 'We can't stop here. The mages are but three leagues away We have no time. We must go now.'

Tobias looked at him, 'You're certain?'

'I can see them, Tobias, it won't be long before we can hear their approach. If we don't leave now, they will gain the fortress before we have even reached the road. If James is alive, I must get to him before they destroy the place.'

'You can sense him?'

'No, I still haven't felt anything of him, but the little hope I have tells me we must get there first. If he is alive, we have to get him out. You were a mage. They'll level the fortress and won't expend the energy looking for captives.'

'We're all tired, and you and Seren are injured,'

'And if we don't get there first, all of this will have been in vain. We may as well turn back now.'

Tobias sighed, 'Then I suppose we must go on.'

Exhausted, they began their final ascent. It was almost midnight before they reached the top, thankfully, with no further accidents. Tobias had conjured two small orbs of light. It wasn't much but was just enough to see by. Resting for a few moments, they all stood in silence, the road just visible below them. The fortress wasn't far away, but with no moon it was hidden in the gloom of the night. As they stood in silence, they heard a soft but deep thrum, slowly getting closer.

'What's that?' Seren asked.

'The mages on the march. We don't have long before they catch up with us.'

Marcus stepped forward into the shadow and began moving downwards. 'Tobias, it would be best to extinguish the orbs. We don't wish to be seen. I can lead the way.'

Against his better judgement, Tobias did as Marcus said and quenched the orbs before taking up the rear of the small group, letting the two boys go ahead of him. Squinting in the darkness he was just able to make out Marcus' form as he moved steadily down the side of the range. Their descent took time in the dark but was still quicker than the climb had been. After two hours of groping and stumbling their way down trying to follow in Marcus' footsteps, they finally reached the road. As Tobias stumbled the last few steps, Warren who was closest to him, reached out and took his arm to steady him. For the first time in days, they looked one another in the eyes, but Tobias who was still angry said nothing, merely nodding to Warren and stepping out onto the road. Having tried, Warren groaned as it seemed that things between them wouldn't be reconciled. Marcus had already started down the road and now motioned for them to follow him. The thrum of the marching mages had become steadily louder as they descended. They had to reach the fortress, and soon. The going was easier on the road, but their weariness and injuries were beginning to catch up with them. Nevertheless, within half an hour of stepping foot on it, Marcus halted and ushered them into the shelter of a small outcrop of rock.

'Why have we stopped?' Tobias asked.

Marcus pointed ahead of them. 'We're here.'

Out of the blackness the fortress appeared, the occasional frame of light picking out the shuttered windows high above them. At ground level, a single lantern burned, but it was difficult to pick out any details. The whinny of a horse belied the stables somewhere in the darkness. It was time to find a way in.

Chapter 43

Cautiously, they crept forward, the night seeming to grow darker the closer they got to the fortress. Tobias had taken the lead of the small band, if there were any guards, he would be the best to dispatch them quickly and quietly. Across the open void of the road was what appeared to be the stables, the only structure not hewn from the rock. Crossing hastily, they crouched in the shadow of the building, leaning against the wooden planking. Waiting several minutes, they saw no one, the fortress eerily quiet. If it weren't for the few lights they had noticed on the approach, it could have been empty. Putting a finger to his lips, Tobias motioned for them to follow. Cautiously, they crept towards the shadows of the fortress, alert for any noise or movement that would betray a guard. Passing under a roughhewn arch, they moved across a covered courtyard, still without any sign of an entrance. They couldn't stay there. Even without the moon, they would be seen if anyone entered the courtyard and the distant beat of the approaching mages would soon be upon them.

'Spread out, search for a way in, but keep quiet.' Tobias whispered.

Fanning out they began making their way around the walls searching for a way in. Straying back towards the archway, Warren ran his hands over the wall, feeling for anything that could be a way in. As he reached the arch, he stopped with a sigh, spun around and looked for somewhere else to search. Moving away from the arch, he thought he heard a noise from inside the stone itself. Turning back, he went to stand under the arch. He hadn't imagined it, there was definitely a rumbling coming from the stone. Looking up at the arch, he squinted in the dim light and thought he could make out holes in the rock above him. The sound echoed from the stone, becoming louder. He called out as he was yanked backwards and fell to the hard, stone floor. Not a second later, a metal portcullis slammed down, embedding itself into the ground where he had just been standing.

'They know we're here.'

Warren looked behind him to find Tobias standing over him. It was he who had spoken and saved him. Marcus came over to them.

'No, they don't.'

'They dropped the portcullis. Why else would they do that if not to trap us?'

'You were right about the wards, Tobias, but we have passed through them. They dropped the portcullis because they know the mages are coming for them. They are preparing as we speak. Come, we have little time remaining. The entrance is this way.'

Warren looked at Tobias who merely shrugged, and with a shake of his head trailed Marcus. Getting to his feet, Warren shadowed them. Marcus stood in front of what looked like bare rock.

'You can't see it, but the grooves are here, this is the door.'

'How do we open it?'

Marcus placed his hands on the stone, feeling the imprints of the countless people who had stood in the exact same position before him. For an instant, he knew them all and saw them whisper the same word that had been used since the fortress was first constructed. The word barely passed his lips when he felt a tremor in the rock. And as he took his hands away, the door began to open. Stepping back, he waited until the gap was wide enough and then passed through into the fortress. Having intended to be the first inside, Tobias rushed in after him. Keeping to the shadows in the dimly lit hall, they moved as swiftly as they could. Marcus led them down a narrow corridor before stopping at a heavy oak door where he stood silently for several moments.

'There are cells below us. If James is here that is where we'll find him.'

Staying in front of the unlocked door, no one seemed to want to take the first step through. In the end, Seren stepped towards it and grasped the handle.

Smiling weakly at Marcus, he said quietly, 'Let's go and find him.'.

Pushing the door open and stepping inside, Seren found himself at the top of a long flight of stairs and began to descend. Sconces with unlit torches lined the walls, but just as he drew level with the first sconce it flared into life. Back in the corridor, the others began to file in after Seren, Tobias being last. As he stepped towards the door, he heard shouting from the hall they had walked along upon entering. A flash of red passed the entrance to the corridor. Reaching into his cloak, Tobias cautiously took out his wand. Raising it at the entrance to the corridor, he lingered by the door for a few moments, but no one approached. Quickly, he stepped through the door and closed it quietly. With the others making their way down the stairs, he hurried to catch up.

'We must move swiftly. They are mustering in the entrance hall. If we find James, we can't go back that way.'

No one answered but their pace increased. Soon, they arrived on a narrow landing, the torches flaming into life as their feet hit the stone floor. The only thing of note was a door set into the stone. As Tobias tried the handle, he was repelled violently, hitting the opposite wall. Slumped against the wall and breathing heavily, Marcus went to him, but Tobias just waved his hand.

'I'm okay, Marcus, just winded. We must go on, whatever is behind that door can stay there.'

The others filed in front of Tobias and began making their way down the corridor as Tobias stood up gradually, pushing against the wall for support. He hadn't been entirely truthful with Marcus and rubbing his chest with a grimace he pursued the others.

***

Many floors above them, Archimon felt a sharp stabbing pain in his chest. He had sent Laurentis to organise the brigands against the mages as soon as the report had come from the top tower. With a moan, he pulled himself out of bed and wrapped his robe tightly around him, even this small effort draining him in his frail condition. After his daily visits to the orb, he always felt better but the feeling never lasted, and he didn't understand why he wasn't recovering. However, the stab he had just felt could only have come from his storeroom in the lower levels. Even in this state, he knew he would have to go down and check up on the room. Only he could enter, but someone had tried the door. Sluggishly, he made his way across the bed chamber, wary of letting anyone see him in his current state, pulling the cowl up over his head. With his wand clutched tight in his withered hand, he left his room unaided for the first time in weeks.

***

The search of the second underground level proved fruitless. The landing had opened out with each side lined with doors, but all they had found were empty rooms, the occasional dusty forgotten crate, and a healthy population of spiders. And so, they had gone down to the third level. Seren went down the stairs first but stopped just short of the landing. He signalled to the others to stop and stood still, listening. He had noted on the higher levels that the torches extinguished themselves when they moved on down the corridor, but here on the third level, he saw the glow of torches towards the far end of the landing. Tobias sidled past Marcus and Warren on the stairs and came to stand with Seren.

'Someone is down here. I heard something, and the torches are lit.'

Tobias nodded, 'Stay here,' he turned, 'All of you.'

Moving forward silently, Tobias had his wand drawn. One of the doors ahead of him was ajar, and as he drew closer, he could hear muffled voices. It sounded as if things were being moved around. Creeping closer to the door, he stopped and listened.

'Why are you trying to dig that out, just take the small stuff. We have to carry it out of here.'

'I'm not after the whole trunk. I just want to see what's inside. There might be something worth selling among all the tat.'

'Well, just hurry it up then, we've got to get out of here. I didn't sign up to be killed by a hoard of mages.'

The room went silent for a time, other than the noise of their rummaging.

'Ha, there you go. Told you there'd be something worthwhile in here.'

'Indeed, you did. I think it's time we were leaving. We can't go out the front though.'

Tobias had to act. Stepping to the other side of the door, he pulled it open sharply, raising his wand at the same time.

'I don't think you'll be going anywhere.'

His spell shot across the room, the two men scattering, narrowly avoiding being hit. Responding quickly with spells of their own, Tobias ducked out of the door, the spells smashing into the wall behind him. With Marcus heading towards him, Tobias flew back into the room, wand raised. For a moment, he couldn't see them, but then a rush of red came at him. As they ran towards him, ferociously throwing spells, try as he might to dodge them, one of the spells caught him in the shoulder and he went down as the men dashed past him. He heard a shout and two soft thuds. Obviously, they had just encountered Marcus, who appeared in the doorway a moment later. Rushing to Tobias, he helped him to sit up against the wall as he clutched his shoulder.

'They were looting.' He said, pointing to the jumbled mass of objects that littered the room.

'Never mind that now, let me see your shoulder.'

Carefully pulling the tattered robe away from Tobias' shoulder, a small trickle of blood oozed from the burned and blackened wound.

'Stay here, I'll take the boys and find James, we'll come back for you once we've got him.'

Tobias opened his eyes wide, 'Where are they, are they safe?'

'Don't worry, I hid them in a room just down the hall when I saw what was happening, they're quite safe.'

'I should come with you.'

'No, Tobias,' Marcus interrupted, 'Stay here, the cells are nearby. I can feel the despair below. Please just stay, guard the corridor if you must, but rest a while.'

Tobias sighed knowing Marcus was right. He nodded his assent and Marcus left the room. A few moments later, he heard them all pass by as they made for the stairs to take them down to the next level.

With Marcus leading, nearing the bottom they saw their way was blocked by a solid wooden door with a small hatch at head height. Warily, Marcus drew his wand and pointed it at the hatch. Banging on the door twice, the hatch remained firmly closed. Taking hold of the handle, Marcus tugged hard and the door opened. They all stepped back as the stench of what could only be the cells washed over them from the open door.

'Both of you stay here and guard the door. If anyone approaches call for me.'

'But we could help you search.' Seren protested.

'Neither of you have ever met James, how will you know if you find him?'

'I hadn't thought of that.'

Marcus smiled, 'Guard the door, I'll be back as soon as I can.'

The boys took out their wands and faced back up the stairs, as Marcus turned and walked into the shadowy darkness of the cells. No torches flared to life as he proceeded down the narrow corridor, so he conjured a small orb of light and let it go before him. Given that there had been no guard at the door, he was unsurprised to find the small guard room empty. The hearth contained old ashes, long cold. Evidently, no one had occupied the room for quite some time. His concern for his friend grew, *would they have let him starve to death?*

Hurrying onwards, he passed through the guard room and into another narrow corridor. In the dim light, he made out the first of the cell doors. They were the same sturdy wooden doors as the entrance, all of them with the hatches shut and bolted. Closing his eyes, Marcus bowed his head and raised both hands, his palm outstretched and his wand pointing directly down the corridor. Taking a deep breath, he focused on the doors, both those he could see and those he saw only with the sight. As he exhaled, he clapped his hands together, his wand emitting a bright screen of light that reached from floor to ceiling. As it swept away from Marcus down the corridor and out of sight, the doors to the cells flung open and he began his search.

The first cells were empty, musty straw lining the floor but nothing else. In some cells he found the old, bleached bones of the long dead, in others he found bodies in various states of decay. The deeper he ventured into the cells the worse the stench became. Holding the collar of his robe to his nose and mouth, it did little to stifle the smell. After a time, he lost count of the number of cells he had searched and was beginning to give up hope, until he came across someone still living. The moment he laid a hand on the poor wretches' shoulder he knew it wasn't James. The man shifted slightly, lifting his head, his eyes opening to narrow slits as he let out a whimper.

'It's okay, my friend, I'm here to help you.'

Marcus stood and walked back to the open door.

'SEREN.'

A few moments later, Seren came into view from around the corner and Marcus motioned for him to enter the cell.

'You've found him,' he exclaimed.

'No, this isn't James but another captive, we must help him. Take him back to Warren. We shan't leave any of these poor people in this place.'

Nodding, Seren crouched down beside the man, as Marcus assisted in lifting him to his feet. Gently, Seren guided him out of the cell and down the corridor. He found one other survivor during the search but still no sign of James. Again, he called for Seren and had the woman escorted out of the cells. As they faded back into the gloom, Marcus began to despair of ever finding James. Emerging from the cell, he followed the corridor for a few more paces but found no more doors, yet the corridor continued. With a heavy heart, he walked down the blank corridor, his orb of light still preceding him. The corridor went on for quite a way, and he was starting to think of turning back when out of the darkness he noticed a door set back into the wall at the end. But this door had remained closed. His spell had not affected it.

Stopping outside the door, he thought about the door that had repelled Tobias. It was possible this one was being held closed by a similar spell. As with the other doors, it had a hatch. Warily, he reached out towards it. As he grasped the small bolt between his fingers, he exhaled, waiting for the same force that had repelled Tobias to throw him back, but it never came. With a screech, the bolt slid back, obviously having not been used in some time. Taking a moment for his eyes to adjust to the dark, he peered through the hatch into the cell and he was able to make out a huddled mass in one corner. Someone was inside, but whether dead or alive he couldn't tell. Reaching for the door handle, he braced himself for the impact of the spell but as his hand wrapped around it nothing happened. As he tried the handle, he found that the door was firmly locked. Placing the tip of his wand in line with the base of the handle, he traced a line up the door to the top of the handle. Listening for the tell-tale click, he heard nothing. It was a rudimentary spell that worked on latch locks, but it seemed this was more than a mere latch. He tried once more, tracing the same line but from top to bottom this time, but still nothing happened.

Lowering the orb slightly, he noticed the large keyhole. This was an old fortress, built before magic had been properly established in the south, and it made sense that the door would use a key. He felt a fool for not thinking of it earlier. Placing the tip of his wand into the keyhole, he gave it a sharp turn to the left until it sparked and gave a satisfying click. Holding his breath, he grasped the handle once more. This time, the door opened. Rushing into the room, he went to kneel at the side of the huddled form. Placing his hand on the shoulder, he gently turned the prone body onto its side. As the face came into view he gasped, he had found him, he had found James.

'James,' his voice was strained, 'James, can you hear me?'

James' eyes opened a crack, 'Please, no more. I can't take anymore.'

'James, it's me, Marcus.'

'Marcus?' James paused, 'Yes, I know a man named Marcus. He lived near me in Hallsrock. He was my good friend.'

'I'm still your good friend, James. I'm here to take you from this place. I've been searching for you for a long time and have finally found you.'

'Found, yes, found.'

A tear rolled down Marcus' face, his friend had obviously suffered in this place, and he wondered if there was much of the old James left for him to save. As pleased as he was to have found James, he was distraught to see his friend in such a state. Remembering the flask, he took it from inside his robes. His brew was all but spent, but there were maybe one or two sips left in the flask. Nevertheless, he removed the stopper and gently lifted James' head until he was able to help him drink. James swallowed before coughing violently and Marcus held him until the fit subsided. Gradually, James rolled over until he was lying on his back, and for the first time, he opened his eyes wide and stared up at Marcus, finally giving a spark of recognition.

'Marcus,' he took a breath. 'You gave me that foul brew of yours, didn't you?'

Marcus smiled down at his friend. *He's still here after all.* 'Come now, James, you've never complained about it before.'

'You've never poured it down my gullet before. I would have preferred some water. There's been precious little of that during my stay.' He croaked.

Marcus stood and went to the door, once more calling for Seren.

'Who's Seren?'

'Seren is the boy who brought me to you.'

James looked at him, puzzled.

'He found your journal, James. In a bookshop in Shillington.'

'He was able to read it,' he paused, 'All of it?'

Marcus nodded.

'Help me to sit up, would you please? I've been on this floor for far too long.'

Marcus went back to his friend and propped him up until he was sitting, leaning against the wall. Seren entered the cell as Marcus rose from helping James.

'James, this is Seren.'

A smile crossed James' face and he clasped his hands to his chest. 'My dear boy, thank you.'

Seren looked at James and then to Marcus who nodded.

'Thank you for what, sir.'

'Please call me James.' He paused to cough, 'Marcus tells me that you were the one who found my journal and you were able to read it.'

Seren nodded.

'You've saved me, my boy, but there is still much to do, I fear we have all come to the wrong place. There will be no resolution here.'

Seren looked towards Marcus once again but said nothing, unsure what James meant. *We found him, and this is the fortress that he spoke of. Surely, it will all end here.*

'Seren, will you help me take James up to the others, it's time we left this place.'

'No, Marcus,' James spoke up, 'We can't leave yet. The sorcerer who claims this fortress must be stopped.'

'You said there was to be no resolution here, James.'

'I know what I said, but he must be dealt with. He is but a small part in something much bigger.'

'The mages are en route and will deal with him, I'm sure.'

'No, we must see it done ourselves, please, Marcus. I have lingered here too long. He must be stopped.'

Marcus nodded more out of politeness than assent. As they helped James out of the cell and down the long corridor, Marcus wondered if James really believed they had to stop him or if he was seeking revenge. Sometime later, they stepped into the room where Marcus had left Tobias who was now tending to the two survivors they had found. He looked up as they entered.

'You found him.' He gasped.

Chapter 44

Between the more able-bodied of the group, they managed to bring the survivors up to the second level and had begun the climb to the first with its isolated door. The landing on the first level was cramped as they all moved along it. Standing in single file, they stopped to rest before tackling the last set of stairs back to ground level. No one mentioned it as they climbed, but all were wondering how they would get out. Tobias walked back down the line to Marcus.

'Can you find us a way out?'

Taking a deep breath, Marcus closed his eyes. Over the years, he had turned his sight to many uses but never to learning the layout of a place. For several minutes, he remained silent, then spoke, his eyes still closed.

'The rear of the fortress backs straight into the mountains.' His voice hushed, he led them through what he was seeing. 'There is one tunnel carved into the living rock. It connects the fortress to a small, winding path that runs to the north before turning back on itself and re-joining the road some miles to the south of us.'

As they all stood watching him, it seemed an age before he spoke again.

'The tunnel is high in the fortress. The door isn't obvious unless you know where to look. Few in the fortress know of its existence, but some outside do. It remains unguarded. If we can reach it, it will become our exit. But before the night is through, it will become an entrance also.'

They looked at one another, a look of puzzlement on their faces.

'Marcus, where is the tunnel?' Tobias murmured.

Marcus' eyes snapped open, 'We have to go up, nearly to the top, but the way is teeming with those in red robes.'

Tobias nodded, 'Then we shall have to find some way past them. A glamour perhaps?'

'Glamours won't work inside the fortress, Tobias. There's an enchantment that prevents them from being cast, and one to strip them on entering the fortress if you try to come in already concealed.'

'Then, what do you suggest?' Tobias' words came out harsher than he meant them to.

'We wait for the battle to commence and then make our way up through the fortress.'

Tobias stared at him. 'And what? Fight our way through?'

'We will have to defend ourselves, but what alternative do we have? Unless you were thinking of just walking out the door when we get to the top of the stairs and passing them while they are gathered in number?'

Their argument was silenced by a great booming from above them.

'What's that?' One of the survivors asked quietly.

'It's beginning. The portcullis won't hold for long. There are mages on the approach to the tunnel, they will breach the secret door to the fortress within the hour. The entrance hall will already be open by that time.' Marcus had his eyes closed again.

'Then we can make for the entrance hall and leave that way.' Tobias' voice was firm.

'No, Tobias, we mustn't go that way.'

Marcus looked at him, knowing Tobias would try to go that way regardless of what he said. He was saddened, having trusted the man implicitly for as long as he had known him, but now it seemed that Tobias didn't return that trust. But Marcus had seen the outcome if they tried to leave through the entrance hall.

***

At last, Archimon had made his way to the top of the stairs. It had taken longer than he had anticipated but he refused to ask for help. He had been about to descend when the noise had started down below him. The brigands had stationed themselves around the fortress, some looking nervously at one another, others staring blankly ahead, refusing to acknowledge what was about to happen. However, Archimon was confident. The fortress had endured worse than a band of mages, even if those he saw now didn't come through this, he knew he would. Still powerful and more than a match for any who might come for him, he sneered. It wouldn't be difficult to find replacements, they were all expendable, even Laurentis. Grasping the stone balustrade, he began his slow descent.

***

With the small band waiting at the bottom of the stairs, Tobias ventured a few paces upwards. The noise from outside had been continuous now for several minutes. It was almost a relief when it halted for a few seconds before a loud crashing reverberated throughout the fortress.

'The portcullis is down.' Marcus drew his wand as he spoke.

Seren did the same, although he didn't know what help he would be. The silence lasted for a short time before a loud explosion made them cower and cover their ears. The mages had broken through, but Marcus didn't need to tell them that. Tobias ran up the stairs as the first sounds of battle came down to them. Warren ran to the bottom of the stairs.

'Warren, no, don't follow him.' There was a pleading tone to Marcus' voice.

'I'll bring him back. We came here together, and we should leave the same way. You shouldn't stay here. I'll get him to the tunnel.'

Marcus sighed. The boy's heart was in the right place despite the differences between the two of them. 'Meet us on the seventh tier. That is where we will find the tunnel.'

Nodding and smiling nervously at him, Warren took out his wand and began moving up the stairs, albeit not as quickly as Tobias had. Moments later, Warren faded from view. Closing his mind to the sight, Marcus tried to block out the last vision, hoping he was wrong.

'When we reach the corridor above, we can follow it for a time and maybe keep out of the throng. We must keep away from it for as long as possible. We only have the two wands between the five of us.' Marcus advised Seren.

Seren nodded, not really knowing what to say.

'You take the rear with James. I'll take the lead.'

Marcus went forward to speak with the other two survivors and placed them in the middle of the line. With Warren and Tobias gone, they would have to support each other as best they could. Standing at the front of the small procession and with a little hesitation, Marcus placed his foot on the bottom step and began to climb. It seemed to take an age to reach the top of the stairs, but eventually, they all stood on the small landing that would take them back out into the corridor. Gesturing for them to wait as he pulled open the door, Marcus taking a step out into the corridor, and seeing it was clear beckoned them to follow. Looking back down the corridor as he helped James through the door, Seren was disappointed to see no sign of either Warren or Tobias.

The corridor followed its straight path for a time before curving sharply to the right, taking them deeper into the fortress. Marcus stopped suddenly at the front, gesturing for them to get back against the wall. The corridor had come to an end and the sounds of battle were all around them, Leaning out a little from the wall, Seren tried to see what was going on and found himself looking out into another hall, grander than the entrance hall. Inside, he saw flashes of red as the enemy wizards fought the onslaught of mages and watched with fascination. It wasn't the first battle he had seen, having come through the attack on the citadel, but that had been very much a one-sided affair.

Some he felt fought with everything they had as if it were something they had been born to do, others cowered away. One had even dragged himself beneath the great table that ran down the middle of the room in an attempt to hide. He watched as the man was found and dragged kicking from his hiding place but even then, he put up little fight against the mage. Marcus carefully made his way back down the line, looking first at James and then at Seren.

'At the end of the hall is another shorter corridor that will take us to the servant's stairs. It would be better to take that way than try to ascend the main staircase.'

'How will we get through all that?' Seren asked anxiously.

'We must pick our moment, but I fear we might still have to fight.'

'The ones in red?'

'Perhaps the mages also, they don't know us. They will see us as more foe even though we aren't dressed in red.'

Gripping his wand a little tighter, Seren tried to swallow his fear, having never fought anyone before. It was true that he had a few lessons when he and Tobelle had stayed with Marcus, but that had just been practice, and he wasn't sure if he could do it for real.

James caught his attention, 'Seren, if you would permit me to take your wand for a short while, I can fight if needs be. It seems that brew of Marcus' works after all, I feel somewhat restored having been made to drink that stuff and being allowed to stretch my legs.' He winked at Seren who passed him his wand.

In truth, James didn't feel much restored at all, but he had seen the fear and doubt that crossed Seren's face and had taken pity on him. The boy bore scars both inside and out, he could tell that just by looking at him. It was because of Seren that he had been found and it was time to start repaying him.

Marcus nodded to them, 'We'll wait a few moments longer, but if there's no lull in the fighting, we'll just have to make a dash for it. The next corridor is only a short way away.'

Returning to the front of the line, he crept a little closer to the entrance to the hall, crouching against the wall. If anything, the fighting seemed to have intensified, with no clear sway to either side. Marcus observed one of the red wizards firing a continuous volley of spells towards two mages, sending the closest mage crumpling to the ground. He didn't get up again. Having dispatched one of his opponents, the red wizard kept up the intensity of his casting against the remaining mage, who Marcus could see was beginning to tire. Being driven back, he stumbled over a body and fell to the floor, his wand slipping from his grasp. The red wizard stood over him sneering and fired his last spell directly at the mage's chest.

Having seen enough, Marcus wanted to get away from there. Taking another creeping step, he gestured to the others who shuffled forwards until they were pressed close together. Raising his wand, Marcus signalled to them, and in one fluid movement, stood and broke into a run. The two survivors followed as best they could as James pushed Seren before him and trailed behind, moving slower than he would have liked. Forging ahead, Marcus raced down the hall, keeping close to the wall. No one opposed them as they made their escape from the corridor, but others were streaming into the hall from an entrance at the opposite end. Slowing, Marcus looked back to check that the others were still following. But the two survivors were struggling, and James looked to be tiring. Marcus stopped and went back to them.

'Come now, we must move.'

A burst of blue light smashed into the wall, passing dangerously close to Marcus' head, small chunks of stone scattering over him. Glancing up just in time to see one of the red wizards rushing towards them, he raised his wand, yellow light bursting forth from the end and countering the spell that was hurtling towards them. Marcus followed up with another spell that caught the man in the shoulder, sending him sprawling.

Marcus' voice grew almost fierce, 'Move, now.'

For a moment, they stared at him but began to move again, still struggling but managing to pick up the pace. Running just behind the two survivors, Seren gently rested his hands on their shoulders, pushing them on. Looking back at James, he saw he was managing to keep up. More spells were coming towards them now, as it seemed that others had noticed their flight. He wondered how many of the spells were coming from the mages, not that it mattered. Pressing on, the next corridor was only feet away. A scream from just in front of him broke him from his reverie, and the man he had been helping crumpled to the ground. Abruptly stopping, bile rising in his throat, the man's severed arm lay at Seren's feet, a pool of blood rapidly enveloping it. He stared at the man on the ground clutching his upper arm's remaining stump, his face ghostly white. Seren felt a firm grip on his shoulder as James came up behind him.

He glanced at the man, 'Leave him, lad, there's nothing we can do.'

But Seren couldn't stop looking at the man on the ground and thinking how, if he had been just a step ahead, it would have been him lying there clutching a bloody stump. James shook him roughly.

'Snap out of it, boy, we have to go.'

As if to reiterate James' point, more spells impacted around them, showering them with pieces of masonry. Swallowing hard, Seren stepped around the body before breaking into a run. The woman he'd been helping had already gone ahead, having the sense not to linger. As they reached the corridor, Marcus pulled Seren inside, another spell narrowly missing him.

'What were you thinking, boy?'

'It could have been me.'

Marcus just looked at him.

***

Warren sat huddled in a dark corner crying, his hands holding Tobias' limp arm tightly. The fighting in the entrance hall was fierce, but he paid it no mind. All he could see now was that terrible scene playing out before him.

He had seen Tobias exit through the door into the narrow corridor while he was still climbing the stairs. Wanting to reach Tobias before he got to the entrance hall, he had hurried. As he emerged from the stairs, he saw Tobias crouched by the wall peering out, watching the battle before him. Warren ran to him and crouched by his side. Tobias had looked back at him quickly then faced back towards the entrance hall.

'What are you doing, Warren?'

'Please, Tobias, you have to come back. Marcus said we can't go that way. We must try to reach the tunnel.'

'You go back to them, Warren, I'll make it through.'

'But how can you just leave us, after everything?'

'I'm not leaving, I can get through and bring the mages back to assist you all in escape. I'm a mage, I'll get through.'

'But...'

Tobias turned back to him, 'But what?'

'You're not a mage anymore.' Warren said quietly.

Tobias glared at him for a moment, the anger flaring in his eyes.

'Go back to them, Warren.' He said coldly.

Drawing his wand, Tobias dashed out into the hall. Warren had to go after him, in the hope that he could still get him back. He ran out into the hall and almost immediately tripped on a body, flying forward but managing to keep his footing, all the while shouting Tobias' name. A little feeling of triumph shot threw him as he saw Tobias turn and start back towards him.

'Warren, look out.'

Throwing himself to the floor, a spell shot over where his head would have been had he still been standing. Tobias fired a spell at someone behind him and another at his side, and then he was next to him, helping him up.

'Come on, boy.' He said not unkindly.

He had hold of Warren by the shoulders as they ran together back towards the corridor, Warren hoping he had changed his mind and was coming back to the group. The corridor was mere feet away when Tobias pushed him roughly aside and to the ground, shouting something incoherent to Warren and raising his wand. Warren watched in horror as dual spells took him high in the chest, Tobias staggering a few more steps towards the wall before crumpling to the ground. Warren crawled towards him, but it was too late. Averting his eyes from the gaping wound in Tobias' chest, instead, staring at his still face. A little blood sat on his chin, his eyes still open, gazing upwards but unseeing.

The battle still raged around him but Warren didn't care. Gently, he placed his palm over Tobias' eyes and closed them before trying to wipe the drying blood from his chin with the sleeve of his robe. Dragging him slowly into the corner where he still sat, he knew he should get away, to try to find the others, or at least somewhere safer than a half-shadowed corner. But he couldn't bring himself to leave Tobias alone amid the carnage. It was his fault, all of it. He shouldn't have tried to bring him back. If he hadn't come back for him, he would still have been alive. If he hadn't pushed him aside, he would still be alive. Bitterly, he thought it would have been better if he had been hit, *what use am I? What use have I ever been? All I've done is bring trouble to them all since Tobias rescued me from the citadel.* Warren put his head down, resting it on his knees, fresh tears welling in his eyes as he began to cry again, still clutching Tobias' arm.

***

As James entered the corridor off the hall, he grabbed both Marcus and Seren and immediately broke into a run again, but his exhaustion was plain to see. Hearing footsteps behind them as they ran, Seren chanced a backwards glance, seeing two of the red wizards pursuing them. Turning a corner, they arrived at the stairs, the woman already beginning her climb. Marcus following, and then Seren, James staying at the bottom of the stairs, wand pointing back at the corner. Seren climbed half-heartedly and kept looking back down. He saw the two red wizards appear round the corner, as James immediately took the shorter of the two down with a spell cast so fast that Seren had barely seen it course through the air. The taller wizard sent his own spell towards James, who dodged out of the way, but his exhaustion overcame him and he stumbled over the corner of the step and fell. Alarmed, Seren called out to him, racing back down the few steps he had climbed. His wand lay at the foot of the stairs where it had slipped from James' grasp as he fell. Snatching it up, Seren pointed it at the red wizard who now stood over James. He hesitated, the wand shaking slightly in his hand, as the wizard spoke.

'James, I seem to recall this is just how you looked the night I captured you. I had orders to bring you back that night Tonight, I have no such orders.'

He laughed a cruel laugh and pointed his wand at James' head. But then his face contorted and he dropped to his knees, the wand falling from his hand. James dragged himself out of the way as the man fell backwards, dead. He looked up to see Seren still holding his wand, having killed the man and once again saving James. With a groan, he got to his feet, taking up the fallen wizard's wand as he did so. Going to Seren, he gently pushed his arm down.

'Thank you, Seren. That's twice you've saved me now.'

Seren looked at him. 'Did you know him?' He pointed to the man on the ground.

'He was the one who captured me along with some of his fellows when I fled my home.'

They stared at him for a few moments more.

'Then he deserved it.' Seren said matter-of-factly.

James gave a small nod and directed Seren back to the stairs. Together, they began to climb, with Marcus still leading the way. James watched Seren as they climbed, as a young wizard, he shouldn't have known any spells capable of killing, let alone, be able to cast them. He had known the boy only a few hours, and yet he felt responsible for everything that had happened to him, and now Seren had killed to protect him. It should never have come to this. He had never meant for things to progress this way.

Marcus had been correct, there was no one on the stairs ahead of them, and they made their way easily up the levels, pausing for a rest after ascending the third flight. There was no sign of the woman, she had fled up the stairs before them and was nowhere in sight. As they rested against the wall, they heard hurried footsteps echoing down the corridor. As Marcus gestured towards the stairs, they began their climb once again. They were almost at the top of the fourth flight when they came across the woman's body.

'Don't go any farther.' James said as he moved past them, stopping on the third stair from the top and staring ahead. 'You should retreat a few steps.' He said without looking back.

Seren and Marcus looked at one another but backed down the stairs a little, still watching James. Taking his wand, James gently extended it before him. A small bolt of green light flew from the tip and rebounded violently, James ducking as it flew over his head. Reflexively, Seren ducked too, although the bolt flew several feet above them before impacting with the sloping rock ceiling. Seren looked back at the top of the stairs and thought he saw a faint shimmering framed in the opening to the next level. Cautiously, he took a step up, but James waved at him to remain where he was.

'We can't continue up these stairs, the mages have placed a barrier. Presumably, they're trying to funnel the red wizards into the more open areas.' He looked at the woman, 'I doubt in her state she would have been able to detect it even if she knew how, but her death would have been quick. She wouldn't have suffered.'

'If they're only trying to funnel people, why does it need to kill?' The strain in Seren's voice was beginning to tell.

'To even the field,' James sighed, 'If barriers like this kill, then there are less for the mages to deal with. I know from personal experience.'

A great booming sound reverberated through the rock.

'We must get out and soon, they have begun spiking the fortress.'

Seren opened his mouth to speak, but James held up a hand.

'There's no time, Seren, it won't be long before they bring this place down on top of us. We have to get moving.'

Marcus began leading them down with Seren between them, James slowly making his way behind them, unsure if he had the strength to go much farther. The serving corridors snaked around the fortress like a warren. Seren wondered if Marcus knew where he was going or if he was just following the corridors. He glanced back nervously. Seeing James starting to lag behind, he slowed his pace a little, hoping he would catch up. Each boom above them made him jump. After all he had seen and been through on this journey, the thought of the fortress collapsing on top of them scared him more than anything. All he wanted now was to get out and go home.

Raising a hand to his chest, he felt the locket he had given Tobelle through the fabric, he would give it back to her when he returned to Shillington. But even thinking of home wasn't enough to block out the ever-increasing noise from both ahead and above him. As James caught up to him, he tightened his grip on his wand and continued. Up ahead, Marcus had stopped, his hand resting on the latch of a door that would take them back into the fortress proper.

Evidently, Marcus didn't intend to return to ground level. Gathered at the door, they hesitated as a loud thud sounded, and the door shook violently on its hinges. Placing himself between the door and his companions, Marcus raised his wand and gently pulled the door open. As the latch lifted, the door flew in. Marcus stumbled back, and all three had their wands raised in an instant. No one stood in the doorway, only a body slumped against it that had been the thud and the cause of the door moving in on them. Trying not to look as they stepped over the body, Seren's eyes betrayed him and flicked to the lifeless man. He lay crumpled on the floor, the hole in his chest still smouldering against his red robe, but Seren was shocked by the lack of blood. The hole was the size of his fist, but only a small spattering of blood darkened the red of the robe. Seren felt James' hand on his shoulder and realised he had lingered too long once again. Tearing his gaze from the body, he hurried after Marcus who had begun firing spells forward in an attempt to clear a path through the mass of fighting bodies.

The main stairs followed much the same layout as those they had taken through the serving corridors. Pressed to the wall, the only difference Seren could make out was their superior width, but they weren't what he would have called grand. As he reached the bottom of the stairs, Seren stumbled and went forward on hands and knees before pushing himself up onto the first step. He was tired. Marcus took him by the arm pulling him up, and with James following, began to climb once again. Reaching the top with no resistance, they doubled back on themselves and ran for the staircase that would take them to the fifth level.

As he ran, Seren kept looking back. They were being pursued by a mage, not by a red wizard. A spell struck just behind Seren's feet, an instant later another bolt smashed into the wall above his head. The combined shockwaves sent Seren reeling, once again showering him in stone. Hitting the ground hard, the wind was knocked out of him. Gasping desperately, he tried to suck in air, but it felt as if his chest were closing in on itself. Time seemed to slow down around him, and he saw James hesitate before raising his wand at the approaching mage and firing back, the spell impacting and throwing him back. Seren could make him out twitching on the floor, but he seemed unable to get up. Almost as if it were coming from many miles away, a great noise came from above them. In his lightheaded state, it felt as if the echoes reverberated within his own head. Seren's hands went to his throat as he felt his airway tighten, his vision beginning to blur, but he could make out James coming towards him. He felt first one, and then a second pressure on his chest, gasping again, as air began filling his lungs. Coughing at the sudden intake of breath, hands grasped his arms, pulling him to his feet. When his vision cleared, he saw both James and Marcus escorting him down the hall, as he coughed once more.

'What was that?' He croaked.

'The spells he fired at you were too close, they combined and began to suffocate you. At a guess, I would say they were meant to disable, not kill. But the combined effects would have resulted in your death.'

'He didn't get back up.' Seren pointed to the mage.

'I didn't kill him, Seren, he'll be paralysed for a time but will recover, just not in time to hinder us any further.'

The next set of stairs were choked with bodies, so reluctantly, the two men let go of Seren as they each picked their way between the entangled corpses. Once again, Seren started to glance back before coming to a dead stop. He stared back to the stairway they had just ascended, he had seen a few women among the red wizards, but this one was different. As she ran down the stairs, she lifted her head just for a moment, but it was all Seren needed. She looked different to the last time he had seen her back in Shillington before all this had begun, but there was no mistaking her face. Laurentis was there. The events back in Shillington came flooding back, and as far as Seren was concerned, her being there proved he had been correct. She was behind the high wizard's disappearance and his arrest, and since they hadn't found him down in the cells with James and the others, he could only assume that he was dead. Still feeling a little lightheaded, he turned and began to pick his way back down the few steps he had ascended before James stopped him.

'We have to go back. She's down there. The one who caused all of this. I saw her on the stairs.'

The noise from above was growing louder.

'We must get out, Seren, can't you hear what's happening above us. The louder it becomes the closer it is to collapsing. We haven't much time.'

Seren shook his head. 'I want to get away from here more than anything but not without her. She has to answer for this.'

Jumping over the body at the bottom of the stairs, he evaded James' grasp and began to run back the way they had come. James shouted to Marcus who had made it halfway up the stairs, and they both began to descend, but Seren had a good start on them. His breath came in ragged gasps, but it wasn't long before Seren reached the top of the next flight. As he swung himself around the stone balustrade and onto the top step, a sharp cracking sound emitted from high above him. Stopping in his tracks, he looked up, dust falling into his eyes as he swallowed hard. Trying to push the thought of imminent destruction from his mind, he started down the stairs but realised he had lost sight of Laurentis. As he reached the bottom of the flight, he caught a glimpse of her descending the stairs that would take her to the ground floor. She moved with a purpose, not seeming to take much notice of what was happening around her, merely stepping over those who had fallen.

Forcing himself to move faster, he ducked to avoid a stray spell, his breathing easier now but his chest ached. His determination to catch her pushed him forwards. As he reached the stairs that would take him down to the second level, another sharp crack, louder than the first, issued forth. Feeling the stone beneath his feet tremble, he needed no more prompting and broke into a full-blown run, almost tripping down the stairs as he went. As his feet touched down on the ground floor, he didn't stop running, crossing the hall towards the door he had seen her enter from the stairs. Bursting in without thinking, she wasn't there, another door lay open at the back of the room. Raising his wand, he moved forward a little more cautiously than he had before.

The door led onto a darkened corridor, but unlike the others, no sconces burst to life as he made his way along it. He could hear footsteps farther ahead, and confident he was going in the right direction he pushed on. A shriek from along the corridor stopped him, he could hear voices but was still too far away to make out the words. As quietly as he could, he crept forward until he came to a corner, the voices coming from just beyond it. Moving just a fraction so he could peer around, he saw Laurentis standing over a cowering man.

From the moment he had entered the fortress, Laurentis had felt his presence, and knew Seren would follow her, which was the only reason she had let him see her on the stairs. She knew she could use him to escape without suspicion or fear of pursuit. It would only take a few well-chosen words and actions and he would believe her story. Even now, she knew he was watching from the corner, and so it was time to be rid of Archimon.

From his hiding place, Seren heard the man on the floor speak to Laurentis.

'It was you all along, you poisoned me, although I could not say how, you have made me into this weak creature.'

'I only did it to escape you, Archimon. You have kept me here against my will, forced me to do unspeakable things. How else was I supposed to escape? I knew that while you lived, I would remain a prisoner here.'

Archimon looked puzzled, 'You are no more a prisoner here than I am, what are you saying, girl?'

'It's just us now, Archimon. You know I have yearned to leave, to return home but you would never allow it. This is the only way.'

Seren saw her draw a dagger from the belt of her robe and kneel next to the man.

'And now, I'll be free. Free to leave this place and you, free to go home.'

'You'll never leave here alive, my brigands...'

'I will, Archimon, it is you who will die here. Your brigands won't help you.'

Archimon tried to struggle as Laurentis brought the dagger to his throat, but the exertion of getting this far down into the fortress had left him with no strength. Sure that the sickness would have nullified the wards against bladed weapons he had placed upon himself, Laurentis merely batted his arms away. Staring into his pitiful eyes one more time, she plunged the dagger into the side of his neck. As she withdrew it, a gout of deep red blood spurted from the wound. Feebly he clutched at his neck, but Laurentis had taken care to ensure that no wound received from this dagger could be staunched.

'I'm finally free of you,' she said quietly.

With his wand raised, Seren stepped out from around the corner.

'Laurentis.'

She turned, her eyes glistening with tears. and upon seeing him her hands went to her face in feigned astonishment.

'Seren? Please, help me get out of this place.'

Chapter 45

Standing a few yards away from Laurentis, Seren's wand pointed at her, he felt torn, sure she was to blame. But after the exchange with the dead man, he had begun to doubt what he thought he knew.

'What are you doing here?' She asked him, 'Are you with the mages?'

Seren hesitated. 'No.'

She looked at him and then at his wand. 'You can lower your wand. I'm not going to hurt you.'

Seren looked at the body on the floor, 'You just killed him.'

'He abducted me Seren, I've been here for a long time.' She paused, 'When you saw me in Shillington, I was there against my will to do his bidding.'

'Did you abduct the high wizard?'

Laurentis looked down and made a point of rubbing her eyes. 'That is what he made me do, yes.'

'Where is he now?'

Laurentis didn't answer.

'Where is he?'

'He's dead. He killed him.' She pointed to Archimon.

'Why didn't you just run away from him? If he let you come all the way to Shillington, why not just carry on going?'

'He bound me to him, Seren, said that he had plans for me. If I had done anything other than what he said, he would have known and brought me back here. This is the only way I can be free of him. With his death the bond is severed.' She looked at Seren who still appeared unsure. Lowering her voice, she said, 'He tortured me, Seren.' She lifted the robe to show him her left leg where her scar was still plainly visible.

'What did he do?'

'A lot that I don't care to recall. Please, Seren, I just want to leave. I know I have things to answer for, but I just want to be free of this place once and for all.'

Relenting, Seren lowered his wand, offering her his hand and helping her to her feet. As she stood, she looked into his eyes and gave him a weak smile before the fortress shook and showered them with ever-increasing chunks of stone. This time, the crashing sound from above them didn't cease, the roof and uppermost levels of the fortress had begun their collapse. Laurentis squeezed Seren's hand.

'We have to get out, Seren.'

With a nod, he spun around and still holding Laurentis' hand, began to run back down the corridor. As they ran, they were followed by a wide crack shooting across the ceiling, stones cascading down around them, but Seren could see the door ahead. Pulling Laurentis down the hall behind him, he wrung every last ounce of speed from his tiring legs. As they neared the door, Seren saw James step forward into the doorway, moving aside to allow them to enter. Seren practically tripped through the door with Laurentis stumbling over him. Stepping back into the doorway, James clapped his hands with enough force to rival the crashing coming from above. In the same instant, he spread his arms wide with palms outstretched, a faint blue, almost translucent shimmer racing around the walls and ceiling of the small room dulling the noise from above. James took a step back from the door, which still held the faint shimmer and collapsed. Seren hadn't noticed Marcus at the other end of the room until he came rushing past him, stopping at James' side. Looking away, Seren noticed Warren huddled in the corner hugging his knees tightly.

'Seren,' He looked at Laurentis, 'You can let go of my hand now.' She gave him a coy smile.

Hastily letting go of her hand, Seren felt his cheeks flush. Laurentis got up and cautiously approached James and Marcus.

'I can help.' She offered.

Marcus turned to look at her, 'We are sealed in this room with no provisions, what aid can you offer?' His usual cheery tone had vanished, his voice taking on an icy edge.

'I have some skill in healing.'

In truth, she had never studied any of the healing arts, but when she absorbed the priestess' power she gained a lot of her knowledge as well. Subjects she knew nothing about before were suddenly as clear as if she had written the tomes of instruction herself. Kneeling next to James, opposite Marcus, she held out her left hand, and an instant later a vial appeared on her palm, which she gripped lightly. Marcus' eyes were wide.

'How did you do that? Nothing should be able to penetrate James' barrier.'

'Although I was as much a captive here as your friend, I learnt a great deal. The power within me is different now. Could you lift his head please?'

Marcus hesitated for a moment.

'It's just a restorative. In his weakened state casting the barrier should have killed him, he survives purely on his last reserves. This will help.'

As if to prove what she was saying, she uncorked the vial and took a small sip. It really was only a restorative. Nodding stiffly after nothing happened to her, Marcus gently lifted James' head. Holding the vial to his lips, she carefully tipped the liquid into his mouth. James gave a small cough but swallowed.

'He needs rest, that's all we can do for him now.'

Marcus nodded and looked down at his friend as Laurentis backed away quietly, leaving Marcus to watch over James.

***

In the hours that followed, James slowly regained full consciousness, although it had taken what they estimated to be a full day and night before the dulled sounds of the collapsing fortress finally ceased. They all listened to Laurentis as she related her version of events at the fortress. For several hours, Marcus and James questioned her unceasingly, testing her story. Even after her assistance with James, they were still suspicious of her. Through all of it, Seren and Warren remained silent, Warren having withdrawn into himself completely. Marcus explained to Seren what had happened to Tobias and how they found Warren huddled over his body in a corner amidst the battle. Seren felt sorry for the boy, but any attempts to comfort him had gone either unnoticed or deliberately ignored. Warren had slept fitfully for an hour or two but no more and now he had huddled himself into the farthest corner from the rest of the group and was just staring ahead, seeing nothing. With a sigh, Seren turned back to the group, Finding James and Marcus still asking questions but not with the same intensity as before.

'Can't you just stop this?'

They all looked at Seren.

'When I saw her, I still thought she was responsible for all this, but you've seen the marks he left on her. Can any of us say that we wouldn't have acted as Laurentis did if under the same torture?'

James and Marcus looked at one another.

'She's told us everything from almost the moment she arrived here. Yes, she killed the sorcerer, but he is the cause of all this.'

'Not the real cause.'

They looked at Laurentis.

'There is one thing I haven't told you.' She paused and took a deep breath. 'The mages haven't really stopped anything here today. They've killed or captured some of those responsible for the attack on the citadel, but a lot of those here are relatively new and had nothing to do with it. Most of the senior brigands, those who took part in the attack, had already deserted Archimon as his health failed him. He was merely a puppet.'

'What do you mean?' Marcus' voice was weak, but his curt tone was unmistakeable.

'You must have noticed that your powers have weakened in the last months?'

Both James and Marcus nodded.

'That is what resulted in my capture.' James added.

Laurentis nodded, 'There is one in the north, someone who believes that magic belongs there and that it was stolen by the south and He is taking it back. He used Archimon to channel it from the south. Archimon thought he was being clever by siphoning some away for himself.' She paused once more, neglecting to tell them that she too had drawn on that power. Having changed or omitted some details entirely, she was pleased with the seemingly helpless girl story she had managed to give them. 'The fortress and its inhabitants may not be a threat any longer, but that doesn't mean that He will stop. He will continue to take power for Himself, until there is nothing left. There is plague far to the south, or what some are calling plague, but it wasn't borne here by ships or rats or any other means. The only people affected are those who possess magic. This sickness is caused by their power being taken from them, and since their power is entwined with their life force, when the last of it is taken, they die.'

'How do you know about this?'

Laurentis hesitated, 'When Archimon bound me to him he took me into his confidence. He talked of taking more power, until he was able to overthrow Him and take all the power for himself.'

'Who is this person in the north?' Marcus asked.

'I don't know, I never had any contact. I'm not even sure how Archimon communicated with Him if he did at all.'

'This is a lot you would have us believe.' Marcus said.

'Marcus, this is what I spoke about to you when you found me' James interjected.

'Unless He is stopped, it will mean the death of thousands, perhaps hundreds of thousands in the south. Are you willing to take that risk?'

'What you're not saying is someone has to go north.' James added.

Laurentis nodded. 'This isn't something that the mages can do. Any number of them going north would be perceived as an invasion.'

'I agree, we have always been at peace with the north, but the mages can't venture past the mountains.' James' voice had softened. With a sigh, he continued, 'I started this, it should be me who goes north.'

'No, James, you nearly died casting the barrier. You don't have the strength.'

James smiled at Marcus, 'Neither do you, old friend.'

'I will go,' Laurentis said quietly, 'I have crossed the mountains once before and know the paths to take.' She hesitated once again. 'I have contacts in the north. If they think I'm still bound to Archimon they might help me find this person.'

James and Marcus looked at one another, 'How do we know that you will stay true to your word and not just disappear? You must still answer for the high wizard.'

'I will go with her, I believe her.'

They all looked at Seren.

'I won't be talked out of this. My friend, Tobelle was drained of her power or so Tobias told me. I won't see it done to others.'

'I'm going as well.' Warren spoke with surprising clarity from the corner, his voice hard.

'That's settled then. We'll leave as soon as we are able.' Seren tried to make his voice sound firm and steady but the thought of venturing north left him feeling anything but brave.

Printed in Great Britain
by Amazon